THE
KITTRIDGE
MANUSCRIPT

BY DON MEYER

———THE KITTRIDGE MANUSCRIPT———

ISBN-13: 978-1-9382715-1-9

Art Direction, Cover Design and Typesetting
Copyright © 2020 Two Peas Publishing

Published by
Two Peas Publishing
Franklin, TN

─────PROLOGUE─────

The heavy laden covered wagon rumbled through the dirt, the horses' heads bobbing with each step and the ever-present dust flying in the air. Leaving behind the open patch of land, the trail led into a clump of trees. As the horses disappeared into the shade, a loud commotion and a huge swirl of dust rose suddenly into the air. The driver pulled hard on the reigns to stop the plodding horses drawing the heavily laden load. As the dust settled, a large force of Union Soldiers surrounded the wagon. The driver waited anxiously as a Union Officer approached on horseback.

"Sir, I am Major Gerald Hornbeck. Might I ask what you are doing in these parts?"

The driver held tightly to the reigns as he looked at the Major and then slowly looked over at the rest of the soldiers that had fully surrounded his wagon. Turning his attention back to the Major he spoke with some hesitation in his voice.

"Sir, with all the soldiers massing around Richmond, I have decided to pack up and move the family further west."

The Major waited for the man to continue, but when he did not, moved his horse closer to the wagon, looking at the rest of the soldiers before speaking softly.

"Might I inquire as to your sympathies sir?"

The driver looked up into the Major's eyes and let a small smile cross his lips as he spoke.

"My sympathies sir, are what is best for my family. I owned a Mercantile, not favoring no man, only what would bring me the most business."

Taking a moment he looked at the Major, whose expression had not changed and quickly continued.

"I beg your pardon sir, I did not mean to sound cavalier. I simply meant that I was operating a business before … well, before the war began and it was in my best interest to remain a businessman."

The Major nodded, keeping his horse in place while he spoke.

"And where might you be heading?"

"We are planning to relocate to Missouri, maybe open a new Mercantile there, away from all of this."

The Major nodded keeping his focus directed as the driver continued.

"My brother and his wife are closing down the store and my father is consigning the small ranch we had. They will be joining us in a few weeks if all goes well. I thought it best to go on ahead for the children's sake."

It was then that the Major noticed the two small heads peeking out of the canvas between the man and the woman. The Major stared at the children for a long moment before turning his gaze back to the man.

"Do you realize sir, that you have entered Union lines? There are Federal troops all about this area. Have you given thought to that?"

The driver nodded in the affirmative. "Yes sir, I have. In fact, I was hoping I might secure a safe conduct letter to continue my journey."

"A safe conduct letter? What makes you think …"?

The driver raised his hand in the air. "I beg your pardon sir, I did not mean to assume. Excuse my forwardness, but I just thought that the first Union officer I came across I would attempt to explain my honorable intentions and inquire as to his willingness to provide me with a document of safe conduct."

The Major kept his gaze on the man, the only sound coming from the horses whining in all the dust stirring about. The Major's horse rose and shook its head in protest, but the Major quickly got the animal back under control. Finally letting a smile form on his face, the Major spoke directly.

"Of course we will have to search your wagon and unfortunately your persons for any contraband. We can't be too careful, as you very well know there are far too many Confederate soldiers and Confederate sympathizers fleeing Virginia these days. Are you carrying anything I should know about?"

The driver looked up at the Major and shook his head yes.

"I have a Spencer repeater rifle for hunting and a shotgun for protection. They are both currently secured in the back of the wagon. I also have a pistol under the seat for protection should the need arise. The rest of the items in back of the wagon are household furnishings, food, clothes and utensils for cooking, things of that nature."

The Major nodded as he pointed to his men.

"Sergeant, have a look in the wagon. Corporal, walk around the wagon, check the sides and the undercarriage, let me know what you see there. Sir, would you present that pistol?"

The two soldiers were off their horses and moving on the wagon as the driver removed the pistol from under the seat, showing the weapon to the Major.

The Major nodded and motioned. "Sir, if you and your wife would be so kind as to step off the wagon, leave the pistol on the seat and bring your two daughters with you, I shall have your persons searched with the utmost delicacy."

The man looked directly at the Major. The Major acknowledged his displeasure, but waved his hand in the air.

"I am sorry sir, I have my orders. Why these woods are full of deserters and … well, we just can't be too careful now can we? I simply cannot let you proceed any further until I do so."

The driver nodded, and jumped down from the wagon. He then took each daughter from the woman, before helping her down. The Major nodded. Turning on his horse and looking at the soldiers mounted around him, he pointed.

"Corporal you search the gentleman and …" Taking a moment to look over the men he smiled and pointed. "Private Jones, you search the woman."

"Sir, I protest having my wife …"

The major waved his hand in the air speaking softly, but with authority.

"I understand and accept your protest, but I have my orders. Private Jones is still wet behind the ears. Probably the first woman he's ever touched. I promise you he will be delicate, certainly more delicate that any of these other men would be."

A soft murmur drifted through the soldiers in response to the Major's words. Looking directly at Private Jones, The Major ignored the inference and pointed his finger.

"Soldier, conduct that search as delicately as possible and if I think you're out of line, I'll shoot you myself. Do you understand Private?"

Private Jones nodded, already turning red as he approached the woman. The man stood glaring as the corporal commenced the search on his person, patting him down straight away.

"All clear, sir."

The Major nodded. All attention now turned to Private Jones as he began his search of the woman.

The Private started on her shoulders by patting the fluffed fabric, then worked his hands down her sides to her waist, bringing them up across her bodice, patting and squeezing the material across her breasts as his face turned a darker shade of red.

The man took a step. "Sir, I implore you?"

But the woman interrupted. "It's okay, I understand this needs to be done. Private Jones, I surely do wish you would get this over with as quickly as possible."

Private Jones removed his hands from her breasts having kept them there while she spoke. He took a moment to wipe his palms across his britches before continuing.

All eyes focused on the woman as Private Jones continued his search down her body. He pulled and squeezed the fabric of her full skirts together, somewhat wrinkling them in the process.

Stepping behind her, he continued the fabric squeeze through the back pleats, finally reaching her backside. She sighed heavily, waiting, but Private Jones hesitated. Finally she blurted out.

"Well, Private, I'd appreciate it if you would just get this over with."

Private Jones put both hands on her butt patting, squeezing and pushing on each cheek, before moving up her back, finally stepping away from the woman, sweat dripping from his forehead, his face even redder, if that was possible. Private Jones nodded in the negative.

"All clear, sir."

The Major looked hard at the private, then the woman and finally at the man, who was obviously quite agitated at the whole ordeal. He spoke with compassion in his voice.

"I humbly beg your pardon ma'am, but I had no choice and your anger will be understood as I proceed. I need Private Jones to search both of your daughters."

The woman reacted sheltering her daughters into her flowing skirts.

"Sir, I do not understand your motives. Having your man violate me is one thing, but to allow his hands to rove over my daughters bodies is just not in keeping with God's good wishes."

The Major sat on his horse, staring at the woman, digesting her words. Finally nodding, he spoke very softly.

"My dear woman, you are absolutely right. I can not in God's good graces order such a thing. However, I do have my orders to follow."

Looking directly at the woman, her daughters tucked tightly into her skirts, Private Jones standing off to the side, afraid to even move, the Major leaned forward and spoke directly to the woman.

"Ma'am, if you would lift their skirts so that I may see nothing is concealed there and give me your word there is nothing hidden upon their persons, I will not have the Private lay hands on them."

At first the woman started to open her mouth in protest, but then thought better of it and, considering the options, removed her daughters from her skirts to stand before her. At four and six years old, the girls were oblivious to the situation around them. She gave a look to the Major who understood.

"Men, please turn your mounts away, my eyes only. Private Jones, about face."

Private Jones snapped to attention and turned completely around, saluting as he did so. The woman nodded. Slowly she lifted the skirts of each of her daughters.

The Major nodded. "And?"

"Yes, I give you my word, they do not have anything concealed on their person."

"Fine, fine."

A moment later the Major motioned the sergeant and the corporal over to his position.

"What did you find in the wagon?"

"Nothing but junk, some furniture, and a rather ugly piece not too well made..."

"I beg your pardon sergeant, but my father made those pieces. It was my dowry and ..."

The sergeant looked at the woman, ready to comment, but after a quick glance at the Major, changed his tone.

"Beg pardon ma'am, I didn't mean no disrespect, I only meant they was basic furniture, no contraband in there."

The Major nodded. "Corporal."

The corporal pointed. "Nothing around the wagon, but the bottom has metal plating."

The Major nodded and turned his gaze to the man, questioning, pointing to the wagon. "And what does that mean?"

The corporal responded first. "Don't know, sir. Doesn't appear to be a false bottom. I checked pretty thoroughly for sure."

The Major nodded, keeping his gaze on the man as he waited. Sensing the Major staring at him, the man looked first at the Major, then at the corporal, both obviously waiting for an answer from him. Waving his hand in the air, he spoke matter-of-factly.

"Hank said ... I'm sorry, our blacksmith said that if I was

going to load up furniture in this tired old wagon I better reinforce the floor. He put a set of fresh wood planks on the bottom and braced them with those metal plates. I didn't think anything of it at the time. Adds to the weight of course, that's why I have the extra team, switch them out every few hours."

The Major nodded, about to speak, but the man interrupted.

"My wife's furniture might not be much to look at, but it sure is heavy. Her father had the right idea, just not the skills of a cabinet maker."

The Major smiled, the corporal nodded and the sergeant stepped forward.

"Again ma'am, I meant no disrespect."

The Major waited for the sergeant to get closer. Keeping his focus on the man he spoke with a smile.

"Sergeant fetch me some writing paper. I'm going to give you that letter of safe conduct. Not sure how effective it will be, but as long as you are passing through Federal lines the letter will show you have been searched and passed through. Hopefully, you shouldn't be affronted again."

"Thank you sir. May I?"

"Yes."

The man helped the woman back into the wagon and then proceeded to lift each daughter into her arms, which she promptly shooed inside the canvas opening. He walked around the horses and climbed up into the seat and set the pistol back underneath.

The company clerk who had been posting details of the event in the logbook tore out a blank sheet of paper from the back of the book and handed the piece of paper and his pencil to the Major. After jotting down a few lines on the paper, the Major rode over, and handed the driver that piece of paper.

"Once again ma'am, I apologize for any indelicacies you may have suffered on our account, but I hope you do understand my position?"

The woman looked at the Major and smiled. "I accept your kind words and will think no further of it."

The Major backed his horse away and tipped the brim of his hat. The wagon started forward as the Union Soldiers still mounted on their horses, moved aside to let it pass. The Major turned as his horse spun around.

"Private Jones, if you dare mention one word of this experience to any of the men, under any circumstance, I will flog you personally. Do you understand me, soldier?"

Private Jones moved his hand down looking at the Major towering above him on his horse.

"Yes sir."

"Good. Let's move out."

The Federal troops reformed back into their line and slowly moved forward, following the Major's lead.

The wagon slowly continued its movements along the trail heading in the opposite direction of the troops, finally clearing their dust and formation. As the horses plodded along setting their own pace, the man turned to the woman, but she kept her gaze forward. Finally she turned to face him a smile forming on her lips.

"I believe that private was far more embarrassed than I was."

The man smiled, and turned his gaze forward. No further words needed to be spoken.

With the letter of safe conduct tucked firmly into his breast pocket and the wagon moving forward with their cargo and future securely tucked into the back, he let himself finally relax. All in all, the ordeal had been tolerable. He certainly had expected much worse. The stories of lawlessness amongst the troops from either side were well documented, anything was possible on the trail.

He reached over and took the women's hand.

She let out a deep sigh. "Do you think the Major believed any of that story you just told him?"

"Enough to let us pass."

ONE

Jeff Morgan woke abruptly and trying to identify the noise, sat upright. As he looked around the living room, he finally realized it was the phone ringing. Reaching for and grabbing the receiver, he put that to his ear.

"Yeah? What? Hello?"

The voice on the other end was soft, a women's voice.

"Mr. Morgan? Mr. Jeffrey Morgan?"

"Yeah. I mean yes, that is me."

"Mr. Morgan, I have a call from Nathan Simon, Attorney-at-Law for you."

Jeff Morgan sat bolt upright on the sofa, wondering what the hell this was all about as he listened to the faint hold music.

"Mr. Morgan?" A man speaking with authority came on the line. "Mr. Morgan, My name is Nathan Simon, I'm the attorney for a gentleman that has recently expired..."

"Expired?" Jeff Morgan interrupted. "You say that as if you're talking about your milk. What is this all about?"

There was a moment of silence before the caller finally spoke.

"Sir, I'm sorry, sometimes we get caught up in the pressures of the day and well ... well you know how it is?"

Morgan didn't answer, but waited for the attorney to continue.

"Anyway, as I was about to say, I represent a gentleman that has recently passed on and he has retained me to find you, to give you a package."

"Me? Who? What package?"

"Mr. Morgan, I would beg your indulgence for just a moment. My client has given me three questions for you to answer to confirm you are the right Jeff Morgan."

"Say what is this, some kind of scam?"

"Mr. Morgan I implore you, just a moment of your time?"

Wanting nothing more than to hang up the phone, Morgan relented.

"Alright, ask your questions."

"Thank you sir, I assure you this will be over quickly."

Jeff Morgan could hear papers being shuffled. Finally the attorney cleared his throat and began.

"The first question sir is: Who was your Lieutenant in Vietnam?"

Jeff Morgan ran his hand across his face as he contemplated the question.

"Say again. Did you just ask who my Lieutenant was in Vietnam?"

"I did, sir. What was the name of your platoon leader?"

"Jesus, that was over forty plus years ago. How do you expect me to remember that? Say, what the hell is this all about anyway?"

"I'm sorry sir, I really can't go into details until you have correctly answered these three questions. Again, I beg your indulgence."

There was silence as both men waited. Finally Jeff Morgan began to answer.

"Well, let me think about that for a minute … I believe it was a Lieutenant Roberts, first name escapes me at the moment, I want to say Henry, Harold, something like that, but I'm pretty sure it was Roberts."

There was silence on the other end as he waited for the attorney to respond.

"That is close enough. It was a Lieutenant Harlan Roberts."

Jeff Morgan smiled, relaxing a bit as he waited, not sure why he cared one way or another, but just happy he got the answer right.

"The second question is: What was the name of your platoon sergeant?"

"Okay, that one I do remember. Yeah, it was Bob Swift. Swifty we called him. He always had a deal of some kind going on. Could get us a case of beer at the drop of a hat. Why he … but you don't care about any of that, do you?"

"Actually, I would have accepted Bob Swift or Swifty, you are correct again. Shall we move on?"

"Huh, yeah sure, it's your dime."

Jeff Morgan heard the attorney clear his throat.

"Right. Okay the last question has two parts."

Jeff Morgan sat back on the sofa, cradling the receiver next to his ear. He suddenly wanted this to be over. Some memories are best left forgotten. He barely heard the attorney, and had to ask him to repeat the question.

"Sorry, I didn't get all that, can you say again?"

Jeff could hear the heavy sigh, suggesting the attorney wanted this over as well.

"Yes, right. The question is: first, there was a man in your unit that had a unique talent that led to his nickname. What was that nickname and what was that talent?"

Jeff Morgan sat upright on the sofa and grabbed the rested receiver with his left hand, before it had a chance to slip down his chest.

"Okay, you may have me there. Let me think about that for a moment."

The line was silent, while Jeff tried to remember back. Suddenly a smile crossed his face and he pointed in the air with his right index finger.

"Yeah, now I got it. There was a guy we called Magic, because the dude was always doing these lame ass magic tricks. Yeah, that had to be him. Hopefully you don't need his real name, because I have no clue what that would be."

Jeff Morgan waited. Once again he could hear papers shuffling in the background.

"Mr. Morgan."

"How about you call me Jeff?"

"Right, okay. Jeff ... you have answered all three questions satisfactorily."

"Four."

"I beg your pardon?"

"Four. I answered four questions."

"Yes, of course."

"Now will you tell me what the hell this is all about?"

There was a long moment of silence before the attorney answered.

"Mr. Morgan, do you know a Robert Kittridge?"

"Not off hand?"

"Perhaps, if I told you he was another one of the men in your unit, back in Vietnam, as well, would that help?"

Jeff Morgan sat back in the sofa, relaxing again, trying to run through the men in his platoon back in the day. "Can't quite say that I do."

"How about Slug?"

"Yeah, we had a guy that could crawl his way into anything and on to everybody's nerves, a real pain in the ass sometimes ... are you saying that Slug was this Kittridge fellow?"

"Mr. Morgan, I regret to inform you that Mr. Kittridge passed on recently and I have been asked..."

"Slug, ah, Kittridge is dead. What happened?"

There was silence as the attorney gathered himself from the interruption.

"Mr. Kittridge died of cancer two weeks ago, and ..."

Jeff Morgan stopped listening. "Died of cancer" kept playing through his thoughts. Having lost his wife to cancer recently, the memory was still fresh, and the pain was still present. Even though he barely remembered who this guy was, the news of his death from cancer rekindled those emotions.

"Mr. Morgan? Mr. Morgan, are you there?"

"Huh? What? Yes, I'm here, just had a moment ... my wife

also died of cancer and … well … when I heard … anyway, yes, I'm here."

"Right. Sorry for your loss. I realize this must be hard now hearing a close friend of yours has passed …" Jeff's thoughts interrupted the attorney's litany, a close friend? I haven't seen or talked to the guy in over forty years and… he cleared his mind and tried to listen to the attorney drone on. "… again, I am very sorry for your loss."

Jeff heard the attorney pause and clear his throat before continuing.

"Mr. Kittridge has entrusted me with a package that I have been instructed to pass along to you. However, it would be best for you to come to my office and pick it up. I understand you are just a couple hundred miles away, so whenever it would be convenient for you to come by, my secretary can set up an appointment for us to meet."

Jeff Morgan realized that the attorney had stopped speaking.

"Come again? You have a package for me. What sort of package? What's in it?"

"I would prefer not to discuss that over the phone. I believe it would be far more appropriate for you to come in and retrieve the package in person."

Jeff Morgan sat in silence once again. The attorney waited. The line hummed. Finally Jeff relented. "Yeah, sure, okay, I can do that."

"Fine, I'll put my secretary on and the two of you can work out the details. She will also give you directions to my office."

Jeff nodded. "One more thing."

"Yes, Mr. Morgan?"

"Why me? Why did he want me to have the package? I haven't seen or talked to the guy in over forty years. I'm not sure I understand?"

There was silence on the line. Once again the sound of shuffling papers could be heard in the background.

"I'd be happy to answer all your questions when you come in, but I can tell you now you weren't the first choice."

"I wasn't? What the hell does that mean?"

"Mr. Morgan, if you let me finish."

Jeff Morgan sat quietly, back up on the edge of the sofa waiting. Finally the attorney continued.

"All right then, as I was saying, you weren't the first choice, you were the fourth."

The attorney waited for Jeff to respond, but when he didn't the attorney continued.

"Mr. Kittridge instructed me to contact five people in order, first on the list was your Lieutenant, but he also has passed away, next I was to contact the platoon sergeant, Swifty as you say, but he is in jail."

"Jail?"

"Yes, as I was saying, he is doing a nickel in a Federal facility. He was convicted of running an investment scam, even burned some of the guys in your platoon. Next, I was instructed to contact Magic, apparently they remained pretty close after Vietnam. However, according to his wife, Elroy Higgins, Magic, to you all has the later stages of dementia. You were simply next on the list. However, since you weren't in contact with Mr. Kittridge since Vietnam, he instructed me to ask you those questions, to confirm you were the Jeff Morgan he remembered. Kittridge said if you knew the answers, you were the one he was thinking of."

Jeff nodded, smiling. "The last one, huh?"

"Actually no. There was one more name, but I believe it would be best to give that name to you in person."

"What would have happened if you couldn't find any of us?"

"Then I was to destroy the package and all its contents."

"Nathan, what are those contents? What is in that package?"

Nathan Simon was a bit put out that he had just been addressed by his first name and made a point of clearing his throat before answering.

"I'm not at liberty to say."

"You're not at liberty, or you don't know?"

"Actually both."

The two men remained silent for a moment. Simon spoke first.

"Mr. Morgan, I'm going to put my secretary on to make the arrangements. I look forward to our meeting, hopefully very soon."

The phone went silent, but in a moment the lady's soft voice returned on the line.

"Mr. Morgan, what would be agreeable to you?"

They discussed various times and finally agreed on the first of next week. She gave him basic directions to the office they both said their pleasant goodbyes and hung up.

Jeff Morgan stared at the phone for quite some time, trying to gather his thoughts. Just what the hell was this all about anyway? Bringing up those old memories of Vietnam, the current fates of those guys he served with … and more importantly, the loss of his wife to cancer, stirring up those emotions, all in one phone call.

He rose from the sofa, walked into the kitchen, reached into the cabinet, pulled out the bottle of Vodka and poured two fingers into a glass. Setting the bottle down on the counter top he marched over to the fridge grabbed some ice cubes and dropped those into the glass, shaking the liquid as he slowly sipped the drink.

An hour ago, he was heavily engrossed in an afternoon nap, now somehow he was in the middle of this … whatever this is … and he was fourth on the list. What's up with that?

What the hell could this be all about anyway?

And what does any of this have to do with Vietnam?

He downed the rest of the liquid, rattling the ice in the glass.

———————— /// ————————

Later that night as he sat in the living room, in the Queen Ann chair his wife had bought him, he couldn't help but remember back to his wife's battle with cancer.

The TV droned on in the back ground with the local news program. The glass in his hand was wet with condensation and the Vodka inside was almost gone. He rattled the glass shaking the ice about, taking another sip of the liquid.

Everything had been fine, then one day … an MRI showed a

mass forming. The biopsy showed it was cancer and it had spread. A massive chemo, radiation session showed some improvement, but beat the hell out of her, leaving her weak and exhausted.

An experimental chemo actually showed some improvement, but too little too late. She continued to deteriorate until finally the decision was made to let her go, no more could be done.

She was moved to an end-of-life facility and made comfortable, diagnosed with a short time to live, she beat the odds and lived a lot longer that expected. Unfortunately the cancer continued to destroy her while her body fought to survive. The end was gruesome, no other way to describe it. No other way could describe it.

Jeff Morgan had done well to get past that and get on with his life. Then that phone call this morning, rekindling those emotions, those memories. The ice rattled in the glass causing him to look at it. Putting the glass to his mouth he drank the last of the liquid inside. The desire to get up and make another was strong, but the feeling to just sit there and be alone with his thoughts was greater. She was gone and there was no changing that. The totally unexpected end to a very vibrant and healthy woman was still very painful. He shook the glass.

So what the hell was this all about? The last thing he needed to hear was "he died of cancer …" That is what he has been saying for a while now, "she died of cancer." She died of cancer. He rattled the glass once more and tried to sip any remaining liquid. The urge to get another drink won out and he made his way to the kitchen, but once there he decided against it and set the glass in the sink. He had an early morning tomorrow. He left the kitchen turning off the light.

TWO

Jeff Morgan woke at 5:30 am planning to be on the road by 6:00 am for the approximately three-hour drive to make his 10:00 am appointment. Showered and dressed, he stood in the kitchen finishing his decaf coffee and a packaged cheese Danish. After taking the last sip, he rinsed the cup in the sink and left it there.

Taking one last look around, he turned off the light and exited the kitchen into the garage. Pressing the button to open the garage door, he climbed into his car. Watching until the door closed behind him, he slowly pulled out of the driveway. It was just after six. He nodded and turned his focus to the road in front of him.

Just over three hours later he pulled into a parking structure. A half-hour early for the appointment, he found a coffee shop and ordered a cup of decaf. Spotting a table by the window, he sat and sipped the hot liquid, watching the people as they walked by.

The woman sitting at the desk as he entered the office was young, pretty and very well built. He recognized the voice immediately. She shook his hand, offered him a seat and asked if he wanted coffee, which he declined. Truth be told, he was wondering if he should hit the restroom before the meeting, but before he could make that decision, the lady looked up and said: "You can go in now." Jeff Morgan nodded as he got up. Looking around the reception room first, he turned and opened the door to the inner office.

The man inside, who he assumed was attorney Nathan Simon was up and moving around the desk to greet him. The two men shook hands and Simon offered the chair in front of his desk. Rather than going back around, he took the other chair next to Jeff Morgan.

"Mr. Morgan, nice of you to come. I'm sure you have lots of questions. Shall we have at it?"

Morgan nodded and smiled, relaxing back into the chair. It was far more comfortable than it looked. Finally gaining his composure he turned to Simon.

"Suppose you start with what you do know and what the hell this is all about."

Simon smiled. "Of course." Nathan Simon stood briefly and retrieved some papers off his desk. "Okay, here is what I know."

Pausing, he looked down at the first sheet of paper in his lap.

"As I understand, Mr. Kittridge was working on a manuscript about his family history, dating back to before the Civil War. I further understood that the manuscript was close to finished, or at least that is what I was led to believe. However, somewhere along the line, Kittridge discovered something in his research that may open other doors and while I'm not specifically sure what that means, nor did I have a chance to discuss that with him, I will tell you he felt further research was needed to be done and then to be decided if any of that new material should be included in the context of the manuscript."

Simon paused and looked at Jeff, but Jeff remained silent. He continued.

"Unfortunately, Mr. Kittridge was nearing the end and he could no longer pursue that additional research. That is, quite frankly the part I do not know anything about. I can tell you though, that he sincerely hoped that the project would not be abandoned upon his death. He felt that it was that important. Certainly to Kittridge it must have been."

Jeff Morgan still sat silent, watching Nathan look through the papers in his lap before looking up and continuing.

"When Mr. Kittridge fell too ill to continue, he packaged all his research, the manuscript and those letters and gave all the materials to me to hold onto, with his instructions to be carried out upon his death."

Simon paused raising his hand in the air in a wait a minute gesture and called out. "Do you have that document?"

The secretary entered the office carrying some papers, handing them to Simon, smiling at Jeff as she did. He noticed the rather short skirt she was wearing and how fine her legs looked and … Simon held the paper in his hand as he spoke.

"This document has been signed by Robert Kittridge assigning all rights to the manuscript and all the research pertaining to that manuscript to whoever accepts the project. You will notice that your name has now been added as the recipient of record of those rights. Do you understand what I have just told you?"

Jeff Morgan nodded, as he took the document from Simon and looked it over briefly, before setting the paper on his lap. Upon watching Jeff do that, Simon continued.

"I also have the original manuscript locked away for safekeeping. Here is a flash drive with a working copy for you to review and work with as requested in my instructions."

Simon paused and looked at Jeff, as he handed him the drive.

"You do know what a flash drive is, don't you?"

Jeff smiled. "You're funny." He took the drive and stuck it in his shirt pocket.

Simon smiled back, returning to the papers in his lap, clearing his throat before starting back up.

"As I was saying, that package has all his research, which he believed may have uncovered something. Unfortunately, as I said, Mr. Kittridge did not elaborate on any of that with me. He was insistent that I track down one of his old army buddies and give the package to that person. He is the one who dictated the order of preference. I have a separate envelope that I was to hand to the person I gave the package to. Mr. Kittridge prepared one for each man on the list, I'm assuming with further instructions inside. I have already destroyed the first three letters and if you accept, I will destroy the last letter as well, also per my instructions."

Nathan paused and Jeff sat forward in his chair, keeping the papers balanced in his lap.

"Well Nathan, what do you think this is all about? What if I don't want the package? Then what?"

Attorney Nathan Simon looked up at Jeff Morgan with the look of—*you used my first name again*—but let it go.

"If you choose not to accept, I still have one more name on the list to contact, which I will do."

"Yeah, who is that last name?"

"I'll get to that in a minute. As to what this is about, I truly don't know. My position in all of this is to carry out Mr. Kittridge's last wishes, which means simply putting that package in someone's hands."

They both looked at the bulging letter size manila envelope sitting on the desk.

"What about family? Did Slug, I mean Kittridge, have a family?"

Simon smiled at the use of the nickname.

"Funny, I never would have thought of Kittridge as Slug, especially at his size."

"Size?"

"Yes, Mr. Kittridge was over six feet and had been pushing two-fifty at the least, until the cancer took over. On his last visit to my office, to give me the package, he was down to half that, one-fifty at the most. Hard to imagine he could slither anywhere."

Jeff Morgan nodded. Patting his tummy, he laughed. "Yeah, I guess you could say that about the rest of us."

"I dare say Mr. Morgan you have done quite well for yourself, still seem to be in shape."

"Hiking, walking, always moving my late wife would have it no other way."

They sat in silence for a moment. Finally Nathan shuffled some more papers before he looked up.

"I believe you asked about family a moment ago. Well, this much I can tell you. Mr. Kittridge went through a very messy divorce some twenty years back ... the wife remarried within two weeks of the divorce being final. Turned the two boys against him. They had been estranged for all of that time, boys must be in their thirties, maybe forties by now. Mr. Kittridge requested that I not contact them under any circumstance, not even on his passing. In fact, he instructed that if they should get wind of the package or manuscript before I had a chance to pass it on I was to destroy everything, before they could take any action."

"Did he ever remarry, girlfriend, anything like that?"

"Not to my knowledge, but he did have a lady visit him at the end-of-life facility during his final days. But again, I don't know anything about her."

Attorney Nathan Simon stood up and retrieved the package off his desk. Sitting back down he handed the bulging manila envelope to Jeff Morgan.

"As I mentioned earlier, I don't know what the contents of that envelope are, and maybe on some level I don't want to know. However, if it is of a legal nature and you feel the need to seek legal advice or representation, I would be more than happy to assist out of respect for my client. That, of course, is up to you."

Jeff Morgan set the bulging envelope on his lap. He set the rights document on top of that and the white envelope with his name typed on it, on top. Subconsciously, he patted the flash drive in his shirt pocket.

"What do you think this is all about?"

Nathan Simon looked up at Jeff. He straightened the papers in his lap and set the pile on top of the desk, before leaning back in his chair.

"Well, as I mentioned earlier, I really don't have any idea what Mr. Kittridge may have found in his research, or why he insisted that one of his army buddies be given the project. My suspicion and it is only that, is that he may have discovered something that only a military person would fully comprehend. And before you say that sounds like vague lawyer speak, just let me say that because he did not entrust that information to me directly, I can only surmise that it may have involved illegal activities, and again that is only my presumption. I could be completely wrong. Suffice it to say, my job was to track down the persons on the list until I found a satisfactorily recipient and hand over what I just have."

Jeff Morgan nodded, resting his hand on top of the items balanced in his lap. "Anything else, I need know?"

Nathan Simon stood up and extended his hand. "No, that is all, other than if you should need legal help, please don't hesitate to seek me out."

Jeff Morgan rose up sliding the envelopes and papers into his left hand, shaking the attorney's hand with his right hand.

Standing for a moment, he nodded again. "I'll let you know if I should thank you or not later."

"Fair enough."

"I just might return the whole thing back to you."

"If that is your wish?"

Jeff Morgan paused, while Simon waited. "What if I did do that?"

"I would simply contact the next person. I will hold that letter until you advise otherwise."

"Right, let me think about it, see what's in here first."

"Completely your choice."

Jeff Morgan turned, and passed through the door back into the reception room. The secretary stood up turning and gave him a big warm smile.

"Everything work out, Mr. Morgan? Do you need a follow up appointment?"

"No, I don't believe so. But if I do, I'll be sure to call." Jeff Morgan shook her hand, locking eyes for a moment. "Boy, if I was twenty years younger, I might …"

She smiled, placing her other hand on top of his.

"If you were twenty years younger, I wouldn't give you the time of day!"

Smiling, he pulled his hand free of hers and nodded. As he reached the door he turned to see her sit back in her chair, the tight skirt she was wearing rose quite a bit up her thighs, before she pulled herself back to her desk.

"Remember you have my number, if you need anything. Good bye, Jeff."

Standing outside the office he took a deep breath. Organizing the materials in his hand, he set the big manila envelope on the bottom, the document containing the rights on top of that and the letter size envelope on top of that, before tucking it all back into his left hand. Patting his shirt pocket, he felt the flash drive still there. Looking up and down the hallway, he finally spotted it. He walked quickly to the men's room.

The materials sat on the front passenger seat on the drive back home. He had resisted the urge to open either envelope, until he got home and had at least the first Vodka in front of him, preferably a second as well, certainly before he tore into either one.

On the drive home, he replayed the conversation with the attorney and tried desperately to remember those days and those guys, so very long ago. He tried to focus in on the guys in his platoon, the Lieutenant, Swifty, Magic and Slug, who he now knew as Robert Kittridge. Was that why he was on the list, because of Vietnam? What did this have to do with any of that? And what is this anyway? So, the Lieutenant is dead, Swifty is in jail and Magic has lost his mind. What the fuck?

Shaking his head, Jeff slipped deeper into thought. What should I be more concerned about, that I was fourth on the list, or that I made the list at all? And what the hell do I know about completing a manuscript? I'm not a writer. And what about this research stuff? What am I supposed to do with that? Am I sup- posed to do the research now? Research what? Some guy's fam- ily, some guy I haven't seen or talked to in over forty years? Why the fuck would I want to do that? What do I care? I certainly don't give a damn about something that may have happened during the Civil War? And for that matter, what do I know about the Civil War? Hell I don't even remember the Vietnam War and I was there. Am I supposed to …?

The sudden realization that his car was drifting into the next lane brought him back to reality. Fortunately this was a four-lane highway and he had only drifted into the passing lane. Directing the car back into his lane, he checked the speed and glanced again over at that stuff sitting in the passenger seat. So what the hell is this really all about?

His thoughts drifted to all sorts of possibilities, but ultimately those thoughts came back to the view he had of those legs, which brought a smile to his face and a momentary distraction from his other thoughts.

Jeff cranked up the music and decided he would concentrate on those legs, rather than the materials on the passenger seat, hopefully the rest of the way home.

THREE

The cell door opened, as the man in the suit standing there walked back to the table.

The prisoner was deposited in the chair across the table already annoyed at being there. "Who the hell are you?"

The man in the suit glared at the prisoner seated across the table before he opened his briefcase and removed a sheet of paper, looking up at the person now seated in front of him, he took a moment before speaking.

"Mr. Swift? Mr. Robert Swift."

"Who wants to know?"

The man in the suit closed his briefcase, keeping the paper in front of him, while he sat on the other side of the table. "My client asked me to follow up with you on your request to see him. As you can imagine, it would not be appropriate for him to … shall we say visit this place under any circumstances. Perhaps you can tell me what you need and I can relay the request, hopefully we can satisfy your needs."

Robert Swift sat back in his chair, the manacles clanking, staring the man in the suit down. "First tell me who you are."

The man in the suit nodded. "My name is Edward Samson. I have been retained by our mutual friend to handle certain matters for him from time to time."

The two men sat in silence for a moment across the table

from each other. Robert Swift leaned forward, placing his man-acled hands on the table, the metal clanking. He smiled as he let out a suppressed laugh.

"You mean matters like me."

"No, I didn't mean …"

"Save it counselor. How about we get down to business?"

The man in the suit nodded.

Robert Swift sat back in his chair and slowly spoke his peace. "A few weeks back a man came to see me, another errand boy, an attorney name of Nathan Simon, said he had a client… that he was instructed to contact me … something about a last request, but since I was in this …" Swift looked around the room. "This country club, I no longer qualified as a recipient, what ever the hell that meant."

Robert Swift sat silently for a moment as the man in the suit waited. Finally Swift leaned forward again, bouncing the mana-cles on the table as his hands rested there and spoke very softly.

"Well, I had my former attorney do some checking around, see what he could find out, you know, sort of a favor for my not going off on him."

Swift looked around the room and leaned further on the table, motioning the man in the suit to do the same, before speaking just above a whisper.

"Well, what he found out is that this client of Simon's is a Bob Kittridge, who apparently wrote a manuscript that he wants somebody to complete for him. I was led to believe the manu-script may have something to do with the war, me and how did you say it … oh yes, our mutual friend were in." Swift paused and looked at the man in suit before continuing. "You may have heard of it, the Vietnam War?" Smiling, Swift continued. "Hell, you're probably too young to know anything about that. Anyway that was as much of the info he could get, but that was more than enough that I wanted to hear, let me tell you."

"And?"

Robert Swift looked at the man in the suit, before sitting back in his chair. The man in the suit did the same. He stared long and hard at the attorney across from him, somewhat pissed that he would send an errand boy to see him.

"What did he say when he got my message?"

"Say? I would have no idea. My instructions were for me to come upstate to request an audience with you on behalf of my client to inquire as to the nature of your request, which by the way, I still don't know what that is."

"My request?"

"Yes, my client simply wants to know how he can help you. Isn't that what you wanted, some assistance with something?"

Robert Swift sat in his chair looking past the man in the suit.

"Help me? He wants to help me? Where the fuck was he when I needed him? You tell him that. Now get the fuck out of here. I don't need him or his errand boys to … "

The man in the suit stood up and opening his briefcase, tossed the sheet of paper back inside. As he closed the case he looked at the prisoner.

"If that is your wish, than I shall be gone."

"Sit down."

The man in the suit looked at the prisoner who motioned with his manacled hands for him to sit. He waited until the attorney sat back down before continuing.

"Look, do tell him I was pissed he sent an errand boy, after all I did for him, but this involves both of us, so I have no choice and he's not getting off so easy this time. Do you hear me? This time he has to take care of it. Remind him, I can't do anything from in here. This time he has to clean up his own mess. Do you understand what I am saying?"

Swift sat silent looking down at the floor. The man in the suit waited. Swift pointed to the table and spoke softer.

"Take out your paper and write this down."

Swift watched as the man in the suit opened the briefcase and removed the sheet of paper. Nodding, Swift spoke softly again.

"Here's what he needs to know, what he needs to understand." Swift paused looking up at the man in the suit, pen in hand, he spoke even softer. "Bob Kittridge was one of the soldiers on the helicopter that day. I don't know what is in that manuscript, but I think it would be in his best interest to find out before any of that story, ever gets out."

"I don't understand."

"You don't have to, just tell him, this Kittridge was one of the soldiers on the helicopter that day. Tell him it might not be too good for business if that story ever gets out for him or me, especially for him. He'll know what it means."

The man in the suit waited, but no more was said. Again, he opened his briefcase and tossed the paper in, closed it and stood ready to leave. Swift leaned against the table, again the manacles clanking.

"Look, I know there's nothing he can do for me in here, but it doesn't mean he can forget about me." Swift paused. "Tell him I'll see him in five years when I get out of here. Tell him, this isn't the first time I saved his ass. I'll expect appreciation for my efforts when I'm released. We'll talk then. But until then don't send any more errand boys without letting me know first. The next time I might not be so understanding. You tell him that. And tell him he needs to take care of this right now before it goes any further."

Robert Swift motioned with his shackled wrists for the man in the suit to leave. The guard nodded, opening the door and removing Swift from the room. Once he was gone the outer door opened for the man in the suit to exit. The sound of slamming bars permeated the air.

———————— /// ————————

Edward Samson walked out of the facility back to his car. Leaning against the car, he pulled out his cell phone and dialed.

"I met with him. Yeah … he said to say this Kittridge fellow, was on the helicopter that day … No, I don't know what it means either, something to do with a manuscript. Something to do with Vietnam, said it needs to be taken care of immediately. That's all I know."

THE KITTRIDGE MANUSCRIPT

Edward Samson disconnected the call and put the cell phone back into his pocket. Setting his briefcase on the hood of the car, he opened it and removed the paper he had been writing on, circling Nathan Simon's name several times before putting the paper back inside. Closing the case, he climbed into his car and drove away from the facility.

———————— /// ————————

Robert Swift walked back to his cell and waited as the guard removed the chains. After the guard closed the cell door, Swift walked up to the bars and spoke barely above a whisper.

"I need to make a call."

"How soon?"

"The sooner the better."

"I'll see what I can do. Jarvis is on later, we might be able to work something out. You'll owe him."

"No problem."

"No promises, but."

"Thanks."

The guard left and Swift sat down on his bed. Smiling he drummed his fingers on the frame.

FOUR

Jeff Morgan sat at his kitchen table early in the morning. The urge to pour a Vodka or two and dive into the package on returning home gave way to fatigue and the overwhelming desire to return the package to the attorney and have nothing more to do with the whole thing. He still wasn't sure if he was upset that he was fourth or that he was on the list at all. Besides, he contemplated, there was one more name on the list. Let Simon give it to that person and let that person deal with all of this.

The cup of decaf was steaming sitting right next to the manila envelope. The small white envelope was right in front of him facing up, his name staring back at him. With a sip of the hot liquid and a deep sigh, he reached for the letter size white envelope. Using a butter knife he slit the top. Turning the envelope he retrieved the contents inside and turned the sheets of paper in his hands. The typewritten or computer printed letter spanned two pages.

```
Dear Jeff,

I suppose you're wondering what this is
all about and probably more importantly,
why your name was on the list. It would be
easy to say yours was one of the few names
```

I remembered, while that is partly true, I should tell you that it just so happens I really do remember you. Patrols together, one jungle shit hole after another and like that, some guys you just do remember, but I digress.

You probably already have been told by now that you were forth on the list, behind the Lieutenant, Swifty and Magic. I picked the Lieutenant first, because I always thought he was a stand up guy and he would seriously consider finishing my project. Swifty, because he was always the deal maker and he would know if this was worth it or not, but either way, I was sure he would take a run at it, anything for a buck, or at least that is what I hoped. Magic was my friend, we stayed close over the years, it was only when my cancer kicked in that we lost contact. Although, I did hear that he finally pulled off his final trick, the old man mind disappear- ing act - at the very least, I was told he was in and out - but by then I was too far gone to pursue it any further. Since you are reading this letter, Magic must really be too far-gone by now. So either you are stewing about being forth or just pissed I picked you at all. Go ahead and get it out of your system, call me whatever you want, take a breath and hopefully we can continue.

With the letter you should also have received a large manila envelope with my research documents inside. You may even have opened that first and wondered what the hell that stuff is. Hopefully I can make some sense of it for you here.

My manuscript (which you should also have a copy) delves into a bit of my family history dating back to before the Civil War. A little over ten years ago (as of the writing of this letter) I had a great aunt that I was helping out, pass away in her late nineties. In her stuff, I found those letters. They were written by a wife to her husband and somehow were passed down to my great aunt. While the letters themselves are not that significant, I thought for lack of something to do, I would research that soldier - her husband, his regiment and see what I could dig up. I won't bore you with those details here other than to say that was the basis for my manuscript, a detailed account of one family of Union soldiers near the end of the Civil War. What I will tell you though is that basically a whole family, all of the men, what I believe to be members of my family were all wiped out in one battle. An older brother, his brother and his two sons - one of which was the lady's husband - another brother and his two sons, seven family members in all, leaving behind four widows, one of which apparently was my great aunts lineage.

Anyway, the other documents are copies or printed documents contained in the package covering the research I did on those soldiers and a particular battle that I used for the basis of my manuscript, pretty straightforward stuff so far.

However, as I continued to put the manuscript together, I realized I was a little thin on how they got to that point in time and started to dig deeper into their lives, or at the very least their time in the regiment, or the Union Army for that matter. That is where it started to get a little fuzzy, but you can see what I mean as you read through that section of the research, a part that is not in the manuscript yet. I was still trying to make sense of it all, when I ran out of steam - and time. Between the chemo and radiation, I had no energy to work, nor did I have the physical capability to sit at my computer for hours on end tracking all that research down.

But enough said about that stuff for now, here is the punch line.

I would be most grateful, if you would agree to complete that remaining section of the research, incorporate anything of value or significance into the manuscript, if appropriate to the story and ultimately complete that manuscript. (I have made arrangements to grant you all rights to the work and research materials.) I would then ask you to work on getting that manuscript published. I believe there is a real story happening here, not just some family history and it appears something else might have been going on. Lastly, if you are not successful, at getting a publishing contract, I have instructed my Attorney, Nathan Simon to allocate monies from my estate to independently publish this work into a book. Call it my last wish, to have my story, this story published.

By the way, the rest of my estate goes to the one who accomplishes that task - and before you go out and spend the money, we are only talking about a few thousand dollars, that I'm sure Nathan Simon will find a way to burn up in legal fees anyway!

Well, I am really tired about now, this shit is kicking my ass and I have one more letter to finish, before I can go off and take some more happy pills, get my beauty sleep and like that.

I will close with a final thought that you can read into anyway you want.

On an incredibly hot day (weren't they all?) in the middle of Vietnam, we got picked to go on a detail to guard a medicine drop near an assumed friendly village. It was you, me, Tony Mags, Swifty, the Pilot and Peter Pilot no door gunners, they said that we didn't want to look menacing, but they did want us for backup. I remember the helicopter landing just out-

side a group of grass huts, sitting idle
while Swifty, Tony Mags and the Pilot
walked into that village, carrying only
their .45s, nothing else, while you and me
stayed in the bird with the Peter Pilot
watching out each side. When they came
back, they were carrying packages, which
I thought at the time was rather strange,
that if we were making a drop, why were
we taking something out. What really made
me wonder, my what the fuck moment if you
will, was when we started to lift off, I
could see from my side of the helicopter,
several NVA soldiers milling about in the
village. You and I discussed this later
that night over a few beers and came to
many, but no actual conclusion, but both
finally agreeing to let it be, none of our
business kind of thing, although quite
certain Swifty made some kind of deal that
day. That is why you made the list. It was
just you and me that day, obviously not in
the know, but also not caring what may or
may not have happened that day. I always
remembered you for that.

Thank you and good luck,

Bob Kittridge

Jeff Morgan set the letter back on the table, swiped his hand across
his face and read the letter again. Still holding the paper in his
hand, he took a sip of the coffee. Once more he gave thought to
returning the whole mess back to the attorney and forgetting he
ever saw any of it. Reading the letter for the third time he focused
on the request to complete paragraph. His thoughts ran rampant.

THE KITTRIDGE MANUSCRIPT

What if he did return the package and that last name didn't want to, or couldn't do it? Since the first three attempts had already failed, and if he did return it, the fourth, how could he be sure the fifth wouldn't either? Could he take that chance? Should he take that chance? And why did he care either way?

Still holding the letter in his hand, he took another sip of the decaf, now rather cold. Standing and walking to the sink he poured the liquid out of the cup, rinsed it out and proceeded to pour another fresh cup from the pot. Sitting back down at the table, he picked up the letter and read parts of it again letting his thoughts wander.

How hard could it be, review the research, maybe do some more research, see what works and what doesn't. The attorney had said the manuscript is basically written all I would really need to do is finalize it. How hard could that be? Besides, what else did I have to do, basically retired and golfing a couple of days a week sometimes to keep from going stir crazy. This certainly would give me something to focus in on, might even be enjoyable.

He tossed the letter on the table and stared at the manila envelope, the assignment of rights document still on top. The flash drive sat there as well. "Okay, that will have to wait," he said out loud and reached for the big envelope, sliding the document off the top.

Using the butter knife to work through the seal, he managed to rip the top open. Gently reaching inside he removed the contents and dropped them into a pile on the table, keeping them in the sequence they were in the envelope.

On the top were the six letters mentioned in the letter, he set those on the side. Next were several sheets of paper containing hand written notes, he would review those in detail later, he turned those over face down. Underneath the hand written papers was what looked like a photocopy of some diary entries, he turned that over as well and placed it on top of the other papers. Following were several packs of printed-paper, clipped or stapled together, what appeared to be the research documents. That was it. He turned everything back to face up and put the letters back on top. Carefully he put everything back in the envelope just as he had found them and pushed the envelope back to the center of the table. He laid the letter and rights document on top of the big envelope, grabbing and crushing the small white envelope the letter came in.

Jeff Morgan sat there and finished his decaf while looking at the pile in the center of the table. For good measure he set the flash drive on top of the letter. Standing, he walked to the sink rinsed out his cup, turned off the coffee maker, rinsed that out and left the kitchen.

Taking the card he was given, he dialed the number and heard that lovely voice again.

"Hello, Mr. Simon's office."

"Yes, it's Jeff Morgan."

"Jeff, how are you?"

"Fine, just fine. Tell Nathan I'm in. I'll do it. The search is over."

——————— /// ———————

After a long hot shower, Jeff Morgan found himself sitting at the kitchen table looking at the pile in front of him. He removed the flash drive from the top and put that to the side. Taking the letter from the top, he held it for a moment and as an after thought, read through it again, before setting that to the side as well. He put the rights document under the letter. Pulling the manila envelope toward him, he stopped and stood up.

From a drawer in the kitchen he retrieved a pad and pen before sitting back down at the table. Removing the contents of the envelope he created a list.

```
The six letters, rubber banded.
The handwritten notes, loose.
Copy of Diary Entries.
```

He got up from the table and retrieved a pencil before sitting back down. He proceeded to label each of the packets of paper with a number: 1,2,3, ... and simply wrote down:

```
Research documents, numbered in order of
stack.
```

Jeff Morgan set the pen next to the pad of paper, nodding. Removing that sheet from the pad, he set that on top of the letter and placed the flash drive on top of that. He felt comfortable having indexed everything before he started going through the documents.

"Okay then." he said out loud. "Where to start?"

FIVE

Nathan Simon stood up behind his desk as the man, dressed in a very nice suit, entered his office. Reaching across the desk he extended his hand as the two men shook. Motioning with his other hand he pointed to the chair in front of his desk. The man sat and placed his briefcase next to the chair.

"Mr. Simon, as I mentioned on the phone, my name is Edward Samson."

Nathan waited as the man retrieved his briefcase, balanced it on his lap, opened it and removed a folder. Closing the case he placed it back on the floor to the side of the chair. Nathan sat back in his chair and waited for the man to continue.

"Once again, I would like to thank you for meeting with me on such short notice."

Nathan nodded, his two fingers to his cheek, elbow resting on the armrest.

"Let me get right down to the purpose of this meeting. My client has recently been informed of the existence of a manuscript that might ... well he has been lead to believe ... how shall I say it, could cause him some embarrassment."

The man paused, then reached into the folder and removed a sheet of paper. "I presume you know of an individual by the name of Robert Swift, currently serving a stretch in one of our Federal country clubs?" The man looked up, but Nathan sat motionless. The man continued. "Very well. According to Mr. Swift, you represent a manuscript …"

Nathan sat forward raising his hand in the air. "Hold on, I don't represent anything of the sort."

"Do you deny the existence of this manuscript?"

"I didn't say that." Nathan started to explain, but was cut off.

"Me dear sir, I have it on good authority that you visited Mr. Swift in his current location with the intent of giving him that very manuscript. Do you deny that, sir?"

Nathan was starting to get irritated and was about ready to ask the man to leave, but took a breath. "What is your point?"

"My point sir, is that you contacted Mr. Swift concerning a manuscript that Mr. Swift feels might be harmful to him and possibly my client and we would like to see a copy of that manuscript, before it becomes public knowledge."

Nathan sat back in his chair. "And who is your client."

Edward Samson sat silent in his chair, eyes locking with Nathan.

"Of course." Nathan leaned forward again, placing his arms on the desk taking a moment before responding.

"Listen Mr. Samson, first off, I don't represent any manuscripts. However, I will tell you that I had a client that recently passed on. He instructed me to turn over a project, a manuscript and some research papers to someone on a short list of names he provided. Mr. Swift just so happened to be one of those names, but as you mentioned, given his current situation, he was not an acceptable candidate. That is all I can say at this time."

Edward Samson sat silent looking across the desk at Nathan, finally nodding. "Would you be so kind as to tell me what is in that manuscript, so that I may pass that information along to my client?"

"No."

"No?"

"No, because I don't know what is in it."

"You don't know? How can that be?"

"It wasn't my job to know, my job was to pass the material on."

"And have you?"

"That is between me and my client."

Edward Samson smiled. "Yes, of course."

The two men sat quietly for a minute. Samson spoke softer. "Do you have any idea what the manuscript pertains to?"

Nathan sat back in his chair, contemplating that question before answering. "Not that I am at liberty to say at this time."

"I see. What if I was to take this to court? Might we be able to reach a settlement in regards to the manuscript's content?"

"Mr. Samson. I don't see how that would change anything, but you go right ahead and do what you think best."

The two men sat in silence again, each with their own thoughts.

"Will there be anything else, Mr. Samson?"

Edward Samson closed the folder on his lap. Retrieving the briefcase from the side of the chair, he opened the case and shoved the folder inside, but did not stand up, looking across the desk at Nathan. Relaxing back into the chair, Samson spoke softly.

"My client served in Vietnam with Mr. Swift and a man named Kittridge, who I understand is the author of that manuscript. While I don't know any other details, Mr. Swift seemed to think that something from that time in Vietnam, which he believes is in that manuscript, might be embarrassing to my client. I thought if we were able to take a look at the work and determine for ourselves if there was anything of an embarrassing nature, perhaps you and I, or your client could come to an understanding. My client has a public face and anything we can do to keep things ... well off the front pages, would be beneficial to his well being."

Nathan leaned forward, nodding, taking a moment before speaking.

"I understand. Quite frankly, I don't know anything about Vietnam. My understanding was that the manuscript focused on an event during the Civil War, family tree kind of thing, nothing more than that."

Samson nodded. "Thank you for that."

Nathan sat back in his chair, waiting for the next question, pretty sure what it would be, but not quite sure how to answer it just yet. Samson asked the question.

"Do you think you could speak with your client and ask him if we … strike that, maybe if I could take a look, privately of course, keeping the confidentially of the work intact? Perhaps that may be all that is needed to inform my client his concerns are unfounded and perhaps remove any misunderstanding Mr. Swift may have?"

Nathan leaned forward. He drummed his fingers on the desk finally clasping his hands together and spoke softer.

"I could certainly ask my client. I don't think that would be a problem, keeping the nature of this work confidential of course."

"I understand, Mr. Simon, I certainly would appreciate that as well as your candor on the subject. For now let us keep this matter between us. I will inform my client as to these developments and look forward to hearing back from you in the very near future with I hope a positive response."

Edward Samson rose up from the chair, grabbing his briefcase. Reaching across the desk, he shook Nathan's hand.

"Good day, sir. Thank you again for taking this meeting on such short notice and certainly for your candor on this matter."

Nathan nodded and watched the man leave his office. He heard the outer door close. Moments later, his secretary walked into his office.

"Here are your messages."

"I think we might have a problem."

She looked up at him. "How so?"

Nathan sat back down in his chair, leaning back. She placed the messages on his desk. He picked up the card from the top of his desk. "See what you can find out about this attorney Edward Samson and what kind of clients he represents. Maybe we can figure out who his client might be."

She nodded taking the business card from Nathan. "Anything particular?"

"I don't know, but said he represents a client that may have a concern about the manuscript we represent. Said he also talked with Robert Swift about it."

"We don't represent any manuscripts."

"Not yet. Better get Jeff Morgan on the phone. '

——————— /// ———————

Edward Samson placed the call just outside the building.

"Is he there? I need to speak with him. Sure, Edward Samson."

"Sir, I just spoke with the attorney ... no, not much ... but he did say that the manuscript concerns the Civil War, doesn't think it has anything to do with Vietnam ... yes, I understand ... yes. Of course sir, one more thing, I asked him to ask his client if we, or at least I, could see a copy of that work. He agreed to do that ... no, I don't know how long that will take ... no ... yes, I understand ... yes sir ... I'll certainly do that ... yes, by the end of the week, if I don't hear sooner ... yes sir ... yes sir ... thank you sir ... soon ... yes I'll keep in touch ... yes ... I."

But the line was already dead. Edward Samson placed the device back into his suit pocket and walked the short distance to his car.

——————— /// ———————

The secretary stuck her head in the door.

"Nathan, no answer, I left a message for Jeff to call us back. Anything you want me to tell him?"

Nathan looked at her and nodded affirmatively, pointing.

"Yes, tell him as of now he is our client, and that I will explain everything later. Just keep trying till you get him. He is to talk to no one unless I am present, or unless he clears it with me first, got that?"

"Yes of course. Where are you going?"

Nathan was standing in front of her, pulling his suit jacket on.

"I have to run an errand."

"Without your phone?" She pointed to the device sitting on top his desk.

"Specifically without that thing."

She nodded. Nathan was past her and stepping through the outer door before she finished turning around.

SIX

Jeff Morgan looked at the pile of papers sitting in front of him on the kitchen table. Deciding to start at the top, he reached for the letters. One by one he read each letter.

They were letters from a wife to her husband, nothing more. No details of anything other than the usual life's events that she had relayed to her husband. The only thing he found interesting was the fact they were written in 1864. Once again he put those to the side.

Next, he picked up the pages of hand written notes.

"Let's see what we have here." he said out loud.

Reading through the top page he saw the following notations:

```
Letters from wife to husband -
Passed down through the family?
Were they ever mailed????
  How did they survive?????
  What is the connection?
  Why were they written?


Diary entries - wagon leaving area to
Missouri.
Was that her?
Another man with her?
```

Remarried?

He set the notes page down, picked up the copy of those diary entries and read through the page.

```
   14 June 1864

Wagon approached our march, stopped and
challenged.

Fleeing the approaching war in Richmond
- Store owner, his wife and two daughters.
- Said they were on their way to Missouri.

Major had us search back of wagon
- Metal plate on bottom to support the
extra weight
- Household items in back
- One ugly bureau!!!

Persons searched - Private Jones about had
a heart attack laying hands on the woman -
green recruit!

Major gave them safe conduct letter - let
them on their way.

Saddled up and continued our March.

Corporal Stevens, company clerk.
```

He reread the diary entries again, not quite understanding their significance. Setting that paper back down and referring back to the notes he saw the next notation.

```
They weren't married!?!? Why?
```

```
What was that all about?
Wife left town with another man - not her
husband.
Husband had been killed at the Wilderness
Campaign
Because they all had been killed!!!
```

He remembered one of the research documents had focused
on the march through the Wilderness Campaign, a particularly
heavy Federal loss of troops. As he read through that document,
he realized that was probably when they all were lost. That last
notation on the page confirmed that fact.

```
All believed lost during the battle at the
Wilderness.
- What happened next?
- Why did she leave town?
```

That ended the first page of notes. Jeff Morgan got up from the
table and fetched a bottle of water from the fridge before sitting
back in the chair. He turned that first page over face down and
proceeded to scan the second page of notes. Most items were
checked off or crossed out, but two notations stood out. The first
was about half way down the page.

```
Herb Miller, Missouri — has the bureau
- Knew the daughters, has information
- Talked to him twice to get some info.
- Can't make it down there.
- Can I get bureau brought here!!!!
```

At first he was confused as to the meaning, but referring back to
the diary entries, he said out loud: "No! No way!" Rereading the
notes and diary entries again, he made a note on his pad to call
Herb Miller himself and confirm. The phone number was listed
under his name.

Almost at the bottom of the page he saw the other notation.

```
Professor Delores Hathaway - "A real
bitch!!!"
- Called several times to ask her help in
organizing -
- Need to get a historical perspective.
- Possibly shed some light on the
information.
- Can't explain a couple of things - need
her help.
- Won't take or return my call.
- Might need to find someone else.
```

"A real bitch" was underlined three times with heavy strokes. He wrote that name and phone number on his pad.

Turning to page three, the notations appeared to be regarding the research, the battle during the Wilderness Campaign, where presumably the men lost their lives, the march to and the aftermath. Page four had a brief history of the lives prior to the war. Page five contained a series of questions that were mostly crossed out. He passed over that page for now.

He picked up the flash drive and turned it over in his hands. He would have to read the manuscript at some point. Most of the items he just looked at had probably been resolved and added to or answered for the manuscript. For now he set the drive back down on top of the index he made that also sat on top the letter on top of the rights document, a nice little pile slowly growing.

Taking a long sip of water, he dialed the second number on his pad, the professor's. A pleasant sounding woman answered on the second ring.

"Professor Hathaway's office."

"Yes, hi, my name is Jeff Morgan, I wonder if I might be able to speak to Professor Hathaway regarding some historical research I am doing?"

"I'm sorry, but Professor Hathaway is quite busy. If I could get your name and number, I'll give her the message and she can get back to you."

Jeff Morgan gave her his name and number.

"When might I expect her call?"

"I'm really sorry Mr. Morgan, but I don't know when she will be able to call back, she really is quite busy, I'm sure you understand."

"Yes, of course, thank you."

He heard the phone hang up on the other end before disconnecting his phone. He dialed the other number and waited. The phone was answered on the third ring.

"Hello."

"Hello, yes I'd like to speak to Mr. Herb Miller. Is he available?"

"Speaking."

"Mr. Miller, my name is Jeff Morgan, I was wondering if you might have a minute to talk with me?"

"Unless you're trying to sell me something, I got the time."

"What? Yes, of course. No, I'm not selling anything."

"Fine, speak your peace."

Jeff took a breath. "Right. An old Army buddy of mine recently passed away and left me a project he was working on regarding family he may have had dating back to the Civil War. In his notes I found your name and number. Something about a bureau?"

"Sounds like you're talking about that Kittridge fellow?"

"Yes. Yes sir, his name was Bob Kittridge. Can you tell me what he meant by the bureau?"

Jeff Morgan heard a chuckle on the other end.

"Oh that. Damndest thing. He was asking about a piece of furniture he thought that I might have."

"And do you have that piece of furniture?"

"The only piece left. It is in the barn. Don't know what shape it is in. Said he wanted to take a ride out and look it over."

"Mr. Miller, would it be okay if I took a ride out and looked it over?"

"You crazy as he is?"

"Maybe. But, since I inherited this project, I thought I should cover all bases, you know do all the research Kittridge thought was important."

"Suit yourself, I'll be here."

"How about next week, Monday. I'll drive down in the morning."

"Fine, you know how to get here?"

"Yes, I have your address in the notes, I'll find it. Say midday?"

"By the grace of God, I'll still be here."

"I'm sorry?"

"Turn ninety-six next month, every day is a plus."

"That so. Alright then, I'll see you on Monday."

"Right, I look forward to it, good bye."

Jeff Morgan hung up the phone smiling and shaking his head. "What a character." he said out loud. Standing and stretching, he left the pile on the table and walked through the house to his front porch. Stepping outside, he sat on the top step breathing in the fresh air. A half hour later he went back inside.

His cell phone still sat on the table, but indicated he had a message. It was the secretary from Nathan's office to call back as soon as possible. Always glad to talk to her, he pressed the key and the phone redialed the last number.

"Nathan Simon's office."

"Hey, it's Jeff Morgan. You were looking for me?"

"Jeff, so good to hear your voice. I have a message for you from Mr. Simon."

"Really, so soon? He miss me already?"

She chuckled. "I'm sure he does."

"So what's he need from me?"

"He said to remind you that you are our client of record and if anybody wants to talk to you to tell them that they have to clear it with him."

"Say what? What the hell does that mean?"

"Sorry Jeff, I really don't know. Right after he told me to call you and tell you that he left the office to run an errand and hasn't been back since. But I believe it has to do with the manuscript."

"The manuscript?"

"Yes, as I'm sure you realize, there are always legal issues with something like that, and of course, the Kittridge estate transfer of rights and all that. Items he probably worked out with Mr. Kittridge and may not have discussed them with you completely. Of course, that is just a guess."

"Legal issues?"

"Jeff, I wish I knew more. He said to also tell you that he will explain it all later as soon as he has a chance, so should anyone contact you to inquire about the manuscript, be sure to mention that you are represented by Nathan Simon, okay?"

"Sure, sure no problem. Why all the cloak and dagger stuff?"

She chuckled again. He could hear her shuffling papers as she spoke softly.

"Well, I can tell you this, a man, another attorney, came by the office today and had a meeting with Nathan, something to do with the manuscript, after that meeting he said to call you, that is really all I know."

"Okay then, I'm at your mercy."

"If only."

"Beg pardon?"

"Nothing Jeff, just having my little fun. Hope to see you soon. Remember, if anyone contacts you about the manuscript, please refer them to Nathan."

"Will do, looking forward to seeing you again as well."

"Bye Jeff."

"Bye."

Jeff Morgan ended the call.

"Now what the hell was that all about?" he said out loud. While he still had the phone in his hand, he scrolled down and redialed another number.

"Professor Hathaway's office."

"May I speak with the professor please?"

"I'm sorry, the professor is quite busy. May I take a message for her?"

"Sure, tell her Jeff Morgan called again."

"Jeff Morgan? Does she have your number?"

Jeff Morgan gave her the number again.

"Thank you Mr. Morgan, I'll give her the message."

"Thank you."

He disconnected the call and placed the phone down on the table, giving the papers spread out there the once over.

"Well that was a good first pass." he said to himself. "Looks like I'm going to Missouri on Monday, that should be interesting."

SEVEN

Standing at the kitchen counter, Jeff Morgan poured a fresh cup of hot decaf, yawning as he did so. The call last night from Nathan had confused him more than rattled him, but none-the-less kept him from getting a full night's sleep.

He took the cup and sat at the kitchen table, looking over the pile of papers spread out in front of him. Reaching for his phone he started to dial, but then realized it was only seven am and set the phone back down. Taking a sip of the hot liquid, he stared at the pile in front of him.

After finishing the cup of coffee, he got up and poured another. Standing and thinking for a minute he went back to the table and reached for his pad and pen. Below the two entries already there he wrote: *Call Hospice Woman*!!! Skipping a couple of lines down the page, he wrote: *Call Magic's Wife*. Skipping another couple of lines he wrote: *Get fifth name and call him*!!

He set the pen back on the pad and put his cup in the sink. As he started to walk out of the kitchen, he stopped and went back to turn the coffee maker off, then decided to rinse it as well as the cup, out. Finally he left the room.

A hot shower later and dressed for the day he went back to the kitchen and picked up his phone, no messages. He dialed Nathan's office and was surprised to have it answered by the secretary.

"Good morning, Nathan Simon's office."

"Yes, hi, it's Jeff Morgan."

"Jeff, so good to hear your voice."

"And yours as well."

"What can I do for you so early in the morning?"

"Actually, I need a couple of things."

"Tell me, I'll see what I can do. By the way did Nathan get a hold of you last night?"

"Yes as a matter of fact, he did. Still don't know what the hell is going on, but I guess I'm a client and any inquiries regarding the manuscript will be funneled through him for now."

"Did he explain how that works? You being a client."

"I guess, but maybe you can clear it up a bit for me."

"Sure Jeff, anything for you."

There was silence on both ends.

"Jeff?"

"Yes, I'm here."

"Well basically since Mr. Kittridge's instructions were to also pass on his estate to the one agreeing to complete the project, we will be monitoring that status before we can make final disposition of the estate, we are now your attorney of record."

"Yeah, Nathan said something like that. Still don't get it."

"Yeah, it may be a bit of a stretch, but we all believe it is in the best interest to have you as a client until this other matter gets resolved."

"What other matter?"

"The inquiry about the manuscript. Jeff, do you have a problem being a client of Nathan Simon?"

"No, not at all, as long as he doesn't start billing me."

"I assure you that is not the plan. In fact all fees are to be paid through the estate."

"Yeah, Kittridge said something along those lines in the letter."

"So I have your permission to move forward?"

"Yes, of course. Whatever you guys think best."

"Good, because I've already opened a new client form and put one dollar in your retainer account, so you are officially a client of Nathan Simon."

"Really?"

"Yes Jeff, welcome aboard."

"Okay then, as a client, I need some information."

"Whatever you need."

"Yes. Right. Anyway. Okay, first, I need that fifth name."

"Sure … it is … let me see … yes here it is: Melvin Anthony Magalito."

Jeff Morgan wrote the name on his pad.

"Do you have a number for him?"

"Of course."

She dictated the number, which he wrote on his pad.

"Don't think I know him?"

"Here is another notation, you may have known him as: Tony Mags."

"Yes, yes of course, Mags. So he was number five and he also was on that helicopter that day."

"What was that, Jeff?"

"Nothing, just making some notes."

"What else do you need?"

"Right, okay. Any chance you have the lady's name that visited Kittridge at the end-of-life facility? Nathan mentioned that there was a lady that visited."

"Let me look."

Jeff Morgan waited as she shuffled through papers, finally coming back on the line.

"No, I don't seen to have her name here, but I can tell you the name of the facility, maybe they have her name and hopefully her number."

"That will work."

Jeff wrote down the information from her.

"Okay, one last question, since as you say, I am a client now."

"Sure, what is it?"

"What is your name?"

Jeff could hear her laugh in the background.

"Don't you think that is rather personal?"

"Huh? What?"

"Just messing with you, it is Donna Millpoint."

"Well Donna, I thank you for all your help. Looks like I need to make some calls, so I better be going."

"Of course. Bye Jeff."

"Bye Donna."

He ended the call and set the phone on the table, but quickly picked it up and scrolling down to a previous number, placed it next. The phone was answered immediately.

"Professor Hathaway's office."

"Professor Hathaway, please."

"Who should I say is calling?"

"Jeff Morgan."

"Will she know what this is in regard to?"

"I need some information of a historical nature."

"I'm sorry, but Professor Hathaway is quite busy, perhaps I can get your number and have her call you back."

"Of course she is. I'll try back later."

He disconnected the call and set the phone on the table. Another urge was taking hold and he left the kitchen for the bathroom. Two cups of coffee required an equal reaction. Lifting the seat, he deposited the morning coffee.

Returning back to the kitchen, he sat down at the table and reached for the phone. He dialed the end-of-life facility number first.

"Hello, yes, my name is Jeff Morgan, I am an old Army buddy of Robert Kittridge. I understand he recently passed away. According to his attorney, he mentioned that there was a woman that visited him. I was wondering if you could give me that woman's name?"

"What's that? Yes, Robert Kittridge. She may have been handling his affairs. Yes, of course."

Jeff waited, listening to the hold music, until finally someone came on the line.

"This is Ms. Olson. I understand you were looking for Robert Kittridge, I'm sorry to inform you that Mr. Kittridge passed away."

"Ms. Olson, yes thank you for that. Yes, I know he passed away, but I was looking for the woman that visited him. Could you give me her name and hopefully her phone number?"

"May I ask who you are, sir?"

"Yes, my name is Jeff Morgan, I am an old Army buddy of Kittridge. Mr. Kittridge's attorney recently informed me of his passing, said there was a woman that visited, I was hoping to get her name to contact her, send my condolences."

"Mr. Morgan, why don't you give me your number and I will pass it along to her and if she wants to contact you, she can directly?"

"Fine, I understand."

Jeff gave the woman his cell number.

"Please, explain to her, I just wish to pass on my condolences."

"I will give her the message, Mr. Morgan."

"Thank you very much for your help."

The line disconnected. He set the phone back on the table, drumming his fingers. Looking at the pad, he picked up the phone again and dialed the next number on the list. A woman answered.

"Hi, yes, I'm trying to reach Anthony Magalito."

"That is my husband, may I ask who is calling?"

"My name is Jeff Morgan, I'm an old Army Buddy of his."

Jeff could hear her talking over the phone. "It's a Jeff Morgan, an old Army Buddy." There was a lot of static, as the phone was passed, finally a man's voice came on the line.

"Jeff Morgan, another Vietnam '69." That was all that came out, interrupted by a viscous coughing fit. "Sorry about that."

"Is this the Tony Mags?"

"One and the same."

"How have you been? It's been what forty years."

"Not good Jeffie boy, not too good. I'm on my last leg here."

"Really? What?"

"Remember that four pack a day habit I had in Vietnam, well I never gave it up. It finally caught up with me."

"Where are you?"

"I'm in a facility … honey, where the hell are we …" Jeff

heard a muffled cough as he covered the phone. "Yes, it's a good bye place, downstate Illinois somewhere, my wife can tell you where." Another violent coughing fit seized Mags, until finally he got back on the phone. Jeff waited for him to speak.

"So, what's up? Why are you contacting me after all these years?"

Jeff took a breath. "Kittridge passed."

"Slug is gone?"

"Yes, long story. Any chance, I can come see you?"

"Sure, but you better hurry. Here's my wife, she'll give you the details."

Jeff Morgan wrote as fast as she spoke.

"Got it, thank you Mrs. Magalito. I should be able to get there in a couple of hours … see you then. Do you need me to bring anything?"

"Just be prepared."

"Yes, of course. Thank you, goodbye."

Jeff set the phone back on the table. He went to his computer, fired it up and waited for the screen to appear. Starting the dial up process, he waited for the search screen to display. He punched out both address, got the directions map and printed it all out. Moments later, he signed off and shut the computer down.

———————— /// ————————

Two hours later, Jeff Morgan pulled into the parking lot of the facility. Within ten minutes he was making his way to Tony Mags' room. A woman was standing out front.

"Are you Jeff Morgan?"

"Yes."

"Hi, I'm Loraine Magalito, Tony's wife."

"Glad to meet you. I wish it were under better circumstances."

He could see tears welling up in her eyes.

"May I go in?"

"Yes, of course."

She followed behind him as he entered the room.

THE KITTRIDGE MANUSCRIPT

Melvin Anthony Magalito was laying in the bed, quite emaciated, graying stubble covering his face, with a breathing line under his nose and IV line in his right arm. He smiled when he saw Jeff.

"Not what you expected, huh?"

"To tell you the truth, I expected the worse. Not bad, old man."

Tony Mags smiled. "So what's so important you have to visit a man on his death bed?"

Jeff Morgan smiled and turned to Loraine.

"Mrs. Magalito, I hate to ask, but may I have a moment in private with Tony?"

"Honey, why don't you go get some coffee, he probably wants to talk war stories, you know how that bores you?"

She smiled. "I'll be back in a half hour, no more."

"Thank you." Jeff said as she was leaving.

Tony Mags raised his left hand waving good-bye as she left the room, closing the door behind her. Jeff pulled the side chair close to the bed, and reached inside his carry case to remove his pad and paper.

"I'd like to ask you a couple of questions, but let me give you a quick update first."

Jeff cleared his throat taking a moment before continuing.

"As I told you already, Bob Kittridge died recently. He hired an attorney to settle his affairs. Well to make a long story short, Kittridge had been working on a manuscript about what he believed to be members of his family that were wiped out in a Civil War battle. Anyway, he created a list of names, including you and me, that he hoped would take over and complete the project for him."

Jeff Morgan paused, as Tony Mags drew heavily on his oxygen.

"The list had five names on it. Starting with the Lieutenant, who also has passed away, Swifty, who is doing a nickel in a Federal Country Club for running an investment scam, Magic, who lost his mind to dementia, me and you."

Tony Mags turned to look at him. "Me?"

"Yes you were fifth, I was fourth."

"Why me?"

"I'm not sure I can answer that, but maybe you can. Hell, I'm still not sure why I was on the list either." Jeff held his hand in the air. "Wait, let me read you this paragraph first."

Jeff removed the letter from the carry case and turned to the second page.

"Here it is let me read it to you … On an incredibly hot day in the middle of Vietnam we got picked to go on a detail to guard a medicine drop near an assumed friendly village. It was you, meaning me, me, meaning Bob Kittridge, Tony Mags, Swifty, the Pilot and Peter Pilot, no door gunners, they said that we didn't want to look menacing, but they did want us for backup. I remember the helicopter landing just outside a group of grass huts, sitting idle, while Swifty, Tony Mags and the Pilot walked into that village, carrying their .45s, nothing else, while you and me, meaning me and Kittridge, stayed in the bird with the Peter Pilot watching out each side. When they came back, they were carrying packages, which I thought at the time was rather strange, that if we were making a drop, why were we taking something out. What really made me wonder, my what the fuck moment if you will, was when we started to lift off, I could see from my side of the helicopter, several NVA soldiers milling about in the village. That's the jest of it. That's the paragraph that has me confused."

Jeff put the letter back into the carry case.

Tony Mags stared straight ahead as he spoke. "And you want me to tell you what that was about."

"I was hoping you might know, maybe help me understand why he included that incident in the letter, or why he picked me, actually us, for the list. Did that day mean something to you, other than we were in that bird together?"

Tony Mags, nodded, suppressing another coughing fit. He took a deep breath before finally speaking.

"What the fuck, why not, I'll be dead in a few days. Got a paper and pencil? You might want to make some notes."

Tony Mags kept his eyes straightforward, while Jeff removed the pad and pen from his carry case and prepared to write. When he thought Jeff was ready, Tony Mags spoke to the ceiling, lying flat on the bed.

"It was nothing more than another one of Swifty's drug runs really. I had been on a few others. Each time we went on one, he put ten one hundreds, American, in my hand and I looked the other way. I mean, what the fuck, I had come straight from college, graduated and got my notice, pretty pissed at the world then for doing that to me. Hell, I was so much older than you guys in so many ways. Swifty came to me one night, asked if I wanted to make a little money. I said what the fuck, why not?"

Tony Mags cleared his throat, reaching for the glass of water on his bed stand. Jeff handed it to him.

"Thanks."

Jeff waited while Tony Mags drank several sips of water trying to clear whatever had come up in his throat. He handed the glass back to Jeff, taking a moment.

"Pilot was a friend of Swifty's, always flew the runs, no doubt in on the deals somehow. I think the Peter Pilot got paid just like me to look the other way."

Tony Mags turned to face him obviously in some pain.

"Here's the thing you gotta know about that day. I'm sure it was the only time you guys went with us. We usually used a couple of other guys, pot heads who didn't care or more likely didn't even know what was going down, but they were too wasted that day to fly, certainly not someone we'd want to handle a gun in that condition. Swifty saw you two sitting on a sand bag having a smoke ... boy, what I'd give to have one now ... anyway he picked you two to fly backup that day. Simple as that ..."

A lesser coughing spasm seized Tony Mags. Jeff waited for it to subside. Taking another deep breath, Mags continued.

"Do you know where we actually were that day? Of course you don't. We crossed into Laos, about five klicks in. I don't remember the conversion from kilometers to miles and frankly I don't give a fuck right now, but let's say a few miles inside the

Laotian border. And that wasn't a village it was a staging area, a camp of some kind that they used. The men Kittridge says he saw could have been NVA, could have been Laotian, hell they could have been VC dressed up, might have even been ARVN, corruption reigned everywhere, even the communists took their share. Did he also mention those men were wearing sunglasses and carried American weapons? How do you like that shit?"

Smiling, Tony Mags reached for the water glass. Jeff stood, refilled the glass and handed it to him. Mags nodded thanks and took a couple of sips before continuing.

"That day we carried out the usual two boxes of heroin, ten pounds in each box. The third box the pilot was carrying was his special delivery, special payment for the use of his bird. You may remember it was a lot bigger and looked heavier and that was because it was filled with Jade."

Jeff stopped writing and looked up. "Jade?"

"Yeah, you know Buddha stuff. During the Tet offensive of '68, Hue was decimated, many of the temples were damaged or destroyed, so somebody … could have even been those guys he saw, looted them, taking statuettes and stuff, priceless stuff, the real thing. It was payment to the Pilot for all his help, something like that. A special payment for sure that time."

Tony Mags began a rather nasty coughing fit, while Jeff waited. As the cough gradually subsided, Mags was only able to speak in a whisper.

"I better finish before I die right here."

Before Tony Mags could say more, he started coughing again, finally gathering himself. Jeff handed him another glass of water. Mags held on to it while he spoke suppressing another cough.

"Here is how the story ends. I don't know how, but I do know the Pilot got that Jade out of the country, Swifty, of course made another killing on his drugs, rumor had it he was shipping the money to some offshore account."

Mags paused, catching a breath, taking a drink of water and another deep breath before continuing.

"As a parting gesture, I'm going to give you a name, a name

that under any other circumstances you wouldn't hear from me, certainly not one I'd ever repeat that I highly recommend you forget as soon as you leave this room. But like I said, I don't give a fuck anymore, I'll be dead soon."

Jeff looked up from his pad, surprised at that last statement. Tony Mags leaned forward as far as he could with all the tubes holding him down pointing with his finger. His speech was labored and his voice cracked.

"And don't write it down, don't even fucking mention it to anybody. Don't ever say the name again outside this room. Do you understand?"

Jeff nodded yes.

"Reginald Harrison, he was the Pilot."

The name didn't register to Jeff Morgan. Tony Mags understood.

"You'll know soon enough who that is, but I urge you to forget I mentioned it right now. Just thought you should know that name, before I die, for future reference maybe. So now you know everything about that day."

Jeff nodded, holding his pen in his hand. Tony Mags sat back in the bed, obviously in some pain for having twisted like that, but smiling.

"Now, my friend, I will leave you with my final thought."

He cleared his throat, taking another sip of water and a deep breath, fighting to hold back a cough.

"James Smith, the Peter Pilot that day had his helicopter shot down on his second flight as Pilot, killed instantly, never left the 'Nam. You just told me Kittridge bought the farm, hell I'll be dead in a matter of days, which means the only persons living from that day are you, Swifty and the Pilot. I don't know why Kittridge brought any of that crap up, but my thought to you is, you better watch your ass, because he did, especially now that you know the actual details of that flight."

Jeff Morgan looked hard at Tony Mags. Mags nodded, pointing his finger.

"Just heed my words, that is all I'm saying. What is this manuscript anyway?"

"Civil War stuff, family thing, I still don't know why he mentioned that day in Vietnam, other than as a basis for the list of names. The manuscript has nothing to do with Vietnam that much I can tell."

Tony Mags looked at him, suppressing a cough, his voice cracking again.

"Really? What the fuck? What's with the Vietnam rant then? Why even bring it up?"

Before Jeff could respond, Tony Mags went into another coughing fit, this time taking quite a bit of time to pull out of it. Finally he gathered himself. Blood and phlegm drooled from the sides of his mouth sweat beading on his forehead.

"Most I've talked in days."

Just then Loraine Magalito walked into the room.

"I think that is enough for one day. You need your rest."

Jeff looked at her and looked over at Tony Mags.

"Yes, of course. Well, I'll be going then, good to see you again Mags, thanks for a most interesting conversation."

Tony Mags just smiled, as Jeff Morgan put the pad and pen back into his carry case. He shook Tony Mags' hand and started to leave, waving goodbye. Tony Mags raised his hand in the air. Loraine followed him into the hall.

"I hope you got what you needed, I don't think he can stand another session."

"I did, thank you for understanding and allowing me the time to meet with him. I am so sorry."

She nodded, reaching out her hand.

"It was nice of you to come. Most of his friends have written him off. He only has me every day. I'm sure he enjoyed having an old Army buddy stop by."

Jeff nodded and then hugged her, she cried into his shoulder, as he patted her back. "I'm so sorry."

Finally she pulled away. "It's life, right?"

Jeff watched her walk back into the room before leaving.

On the drive home, he tried to put these new facts into perspective. Who cared what happened back in Vietnam over forty years ago, what did any of that have to do with the manuscript anyway, why would Kittridge put that in the letter at all?

He turned up the music as he drove, but his thoughts wandered back to what Tony Mags said at the end. It was him, Swifty and the Pilot now. And what the hell did that mean?

He pulled into the garage and exited the car. Watching as the door lowered, he waited until it was down before going in. He set the carry case on the table and pulled the cell phone out of his pocket. Just as he was about to set the phone down, he noticed he had a message.

"That can wait until the morning." He said out loud.

The phone went with him into the bedroom and on to the dresser. Removing his pants and shirt, he laid across the bed. Even with his mind racing, in a moment he was fast asleep.

EIGHT

Just before five in the afternoon, the two men entered the offices. Walking right past the secretary, they barged into Nathan Simon's office, with her right behind them.

"Hey you can't go in there ..." Was all she got out before she was grabbed by the shorter of the two men. Nathan started to come around the desk, but the Glock 9mm, held by the taller man, stopped him in his tracks.

The shorter man holding the secretary used his left hand to grab a hold of her hair as his right hand tore her blouse down the back, the buttons popping off the front. In a singular motion, he wrenched the garment from her arms. She struggled against his grasp, but a blow to her lower back, caused her to stop and catch her breath. A second blow caused her to gasp for air. As she fought to get air into her lungs, he had undone the button and zipper of her skirt and began tugging the garment down past her hips, leaving her panties in disarray from the skirt being violently pulled down. In a moment the skirt fell in a pile at her feet.

The tall man spoke sternly. "That's enough."

The short man holding the secretary nodded, grabbing another handful of hair he forced her forward stepping out of the skirt. A few steps later, he forced her to her knees, keeping one hand in her tangled hair, he now placed the barrel of his gun to the top of her head. The tall man turned his attention back to

Nathan as he spoke.

"Shall we begin?"

Nathan Simon looked at his secretary Donna kneeling on the floor, the barrel of the gun sitting on top of her head. She smiled back at him, taking a deep breath. Nathan sat back down in his chair.

A moment later she planted her right elbow into the groin of the man holding her, causing him to release her hair and move the gun away. A second later she was up and as the man was bent over in agony, she forced his head down smashing his face into her knee. The man dropped to his knees, both hands grabbing his groin, his face a bloody mess. Donna Millpoint stood in her bra, panties and heels in a fighting position ready to deliver the next blow.

"Enough."

She looked at the tall man, still standing in front of the desk he had the Glock pointed directly at her, waving it as he spoke.

"Makes no never mind to me, you can die right now."

Donna straightened up fixing her panties and stood facing the tall man with the Glock still pointed at her. The short man who tussled with her was still down on his knees, blood dripping from his nose onto the hardwood floor.

Keeping the gun pointed at Donna, the tall man glared at the short man on the floor. "Get up, damn it."

Slowly the fallen man rose to his feet, he staggered a moment looking directly at Donna as he spoke. "You'll pay for that bitch." He started to take a step forward, she reclaimed her fighting stance. As the fallen man fought to regain his composure, the tall man motioned using the gun for effect.

"Stop, we don't have time for this shit." The Glock was directed back at Nathan. "We need to get down to business." He looked at the secretary for a moment, then the short man, who was using his handkerchief to dab at the blood dripping from his nose, before turning back. "Simon, where's the manuscript."

Nathan smiled. Donna leaned back against his desk folding her arms over her chest, making no effort to cover herself.

Waving his hand in the air, Nathan spoke loudly.

"I don't have it. Already gave it away."

The tall man doing all the talking stepped forward pointing the Glock directly at Nathan's head. Donna watched the short man take a step toward her. She rose from the desk. The tall man with the Glock waving in the air raised his voice.

"Do you think this is a joke?"

Nathan pounded his desk. "No. No I don't, but your boss just crossed a line that ends all further negotiations. Now get the fuck out of my office before this goes too far. Right now, I'll consider the beating your man took as a fair trade off for breaking into my office."

The tall man smiled. "Listen, I didn't come here to discuss this. I want that manuscript now, or one of you will take a beating until the other one gives it up. Your choice. Makes no never mind to me."

Nathan was out of his chair standing, leaning forward onto the desk. "I told you I don't have it."

"Why don't I believe you?"

"Probably because you're too stupid to understand. Right after the first person asked me for it, I made arrangements to protect it. There's no way I would have kept a copy here after that … along with instructions on what to do with the manuscript should anything happen to me, anything at all."

Nathan sat back down in his chair, while Donna stole a glance at him, but kept her eyes on the short man, appreciating the story Nathan had just made up.

The short man was now directly in front of the desk. Donna actually stepped away from the desk to distance herself, still keeping a watchful eye on the man with the Glock.

The short man, the one she struck, breathing heavy and a fire in his eyes, turned to face her pointing. "You go sit in his lap I need a picture."

"What, fuck you?"

The back of his hand hit squarely on her left cheek forcing her back. Instantly that man was upon her, once again his hand in her hair and his gun butted up against the side of her head. Slowly he pushed her toward Nathan. When she was close enough, he pushed her into him.

She got her balance and lowered herself into Nathan's lap. The tall man kept his Glock on them as the short man came across the desk and using his phone, started taking pictures of her sitting in Nathan's lap in her bra and panties.

"Take the bra off."

Donna started to get up but the tall man reached across the desk and put his Glock in her face.

"Do as the man says or I swear to Christ, I'll blow your fucking head off."

Donna relaxed back into Nathan's lap. She reached around behind her and unclasped the bra, bringing her arms forward she let the material slide off her arms, dropping the under garment to the floor.

The camera on the phone, held by the short man, started clicking again. The tall man waved the Glock at them laughing.

"Look this way. This should put you in good standing with your clients, the boss banging his secretary right here in the office."

Nathan stared the tall man down. Donna gave him a look of contempt. Neither of them saw the short man approach. It was only when she felt the sting in her thigh that she realized she had been injected. Grabbing her arm the short man roughly pulled her off of Nathan's lap pushing her to the floor. Before he could react, a second needle was jabbed into Nathan's leg and quickly pulled out.

"That should keep you two quiet for awhile. We intend to search your office anyway."

Nathan's eyes grew heavy. He tried to look at Donna, but all he could see was a blur on the floor next to his chair. The tall man let the Glock lower to his side. The short man turned off the camera on his phone and slipped it into his suit jacket pocket.

——————— /// ———————

Several hours later, Nathan felt someone tapping him, more like shaking him as he opened his eyes.

"Nathan. Nathan. Are you okay?"

He stirred finally, gathering himself he opened his eyes wide. Donna was standing in front of him. He focused in as best he could. She handed him a glass of water.

"Here, this will help."

Slowly he took a few sips. "What the hell happened?"

"They drugged us and trashed the place."

Nathan could see files and paper scattered around the office. He looked over to Donna, she was still just in her panties and heels.

"Donna?"

"I'm fine. I don't think they did anything to me while I was out. Maybe more pictures."

She walked to the middle of the office and found her skirt, buried under scattered papers, which she put back on. The remnants of her blouse lay on the floor somewhere, but without buttons it would be useless.

"Take off your shirt and give me that or your undershirt. Looks like they took my bra."

Nathan stood up, unbuttoned his shirt and handed the garment to her. She proceeded to put the shirt on and started to button it up. At least she was decent again.

"What do you think the pictures were all about?"

Nathan looked at her as she put his shirt on, buttoning it, but not tucking it in. He put his hands in the air as he answered. "Blackmail. Try to hold it over me, us, some shit like that. Hell, maybe they were just a couple of perverts."

Donna nodded. She grabbed and tied the tails of the shirt together above her skirt.

"That was some shot you gave that guy. Remind me to never get on your bad side."

Donna smiled. "What time is it anyway?"

Nathan looked at the clock on his desk. "Just after midnight."

She nodded and walked over to his desk. He was seated in his chair. She leaned on the desk next to him.

"Anything besides being roughed up bothering you?"

"What do you mean?"

"You're not gonna go all macho on me, couldn't protect your secretary from … you know?"

"Huh? What? No. I know you can handle yourself. Right now, I'm just pissed they trashed the office."

"Hell, I'll clean that up. You know what you need to do?"

Nathan nodded. Slowly he rose from his chair, placing his hand on her shoulder. "See you in the morning?"

"I'll be here."

She watched him as he slipped on his suit jacket and walked out of the office and then took a glance around the room, before saying out loud. "This should be fun."

———————— /// ————————

Nathan left the building, walking briskly to a bar on the corner. At this time of night the crowd was rather thin. Stepping inside, he went to the far end of the bar. The bartender walked over leaning in.

"Nathan, what brings you here at this hour? Late night?"

"Yeah, you could say that. How about a scotch rocks and can I use your phone?"

"Sure, What you don't have your toy with you tonight."

"My toy?"

"That thing you call a phone that you can't ever put down. Hell I don't even hold my dick that much."

Nathan smiled. The bartender reached underneath the bar.

"Here's the phone, I'll get that scotch."

Nathan pulled the phone close to him, picking up the receiver and taking a moment to remember the number. Smiling, he punched in the digits, on his phone all he had to do was select and press dial.

"Yeah."

"Jason, it's Nathan. You good to talk?"

"Yeah."

"Listen two goons just busted into my office, stripped Donna, made us take some pictures that way, drugged us and trashed my office. We better meet."

"Any idea what they were looking for?"

"Yeah, a manuscript."

"A what?"

"Long story. I'll fill you in later. How about tomorrow, my office around eleven-thirty am, you can sweep while we talk."

"What am I looking for?"

"I presume while we were passed out they may have bugged the place, maybe even a camera somewhere. You might want to use a disguise we'll do a divorce meeting."

"Got it, see you then. You know how to reach me. What about Donna?"

"She's back at the office, cleaning up."

"Think that's wise?"

"No, but you know Donna."

"I'll take a ride by."

"I'd appreciate that."

The phone went to dial tone. Nathan placed the receiver back in the cradle. Throwing a ten spot on the bar he walked the distance to the door waving as he did. "Thanks."

The bartender waved back.

———————— /// ————————

Jason wiped his hands across his face and glanced at the clock. He walked from the bed into his bathroom rinsing his face with cold water. Swirling some mouth wash, he spit, ran his fingers through his hair, fluffing it up. He nodded at his appearance and walked to his closet. Selecting a pair of black slacks and a black pullover he quickly dressed. Shoes were his standard "work boots" that he used for times like this. Removing his keys, wallet and money from the dresser top he placed those items in his pockets.

As he was leaving, he grabbed a bag from the hall closet. A minute later he was in his car driving uptown.

——————— /// ———————

As an after thought, Nathan headed back to the office. Donna was on the floor in just the tied shirt and panties. She looked up when he walked in. Nathan stopped in the doorway.

"What the hell?"

"Too hard to do all this bending in the skirt and surely don't need shoes, more comfortable this way. How about you?"

Nathan nodded yes, in case somebody was watching.

"You know you could be putting on a show?"

She understood his drift. Smiling, she said loudly.

"At this point, I could care less. They already had their thrill."

Nathan smiled. He removed his shoes and got on the floor with her.

"Do you have a system or are we just having at it."

"Most of these papers are your work files. I'm not too concerned with the order just yet, mostly focusing on getting them in the right folders, so let's stay on that path."

Nathan nodded, grabbing a pile of papers from the floor, making room in front of him to sort. A short time later he rose.

"Need to hit the restroom, be right back."

"I'll go with you."

Nathan helped her to her feet and together they left the office. She stayed in the tied shirt and panties. Nathan started to ask, but let it pass. Once in the hall, he grabbed her and turned her to face him.

"Be careful, I'm pretty sure the place is bugged, might even have a camera set up."

She smiled. "I saw the camera already, that's why I did the strip act. Thought I'd keep them busy watching me, maybe keep their eyes off the files."

Nathan smiled. "You found it?"

"Yeah, it's in the vent on the back side of your office."

Nathan nodded. "I'll let him know."

"Let me know what?"

They both turned. Jason was standing off in the shadows.

"What? Told you I'd stop by have a look. Nice outfit."

Donna stood up straight and put on a pose. "Why, it's all the latest."

"What are you two up to?"

"Trying to put the pieces back together, but actually, at the moment, we are heading to the restroom. Donna already spotted a camera."

Jason nodded. "Maybe you better call it a night. Let me do some checking after the lights go off."

Nathan looked at Donna. "You ready to give it up?"

"Actually I'm kind of wired. Hell, we just slept for what like six hours."

"Go home. Let me do my job."

Donna motioned. "I still have to go to the bathroom."

"Me too."

Jason watched them walk down the hall. He waited until they came back.

"Wrap it up, get out of here."

They both nodded. Nathan followed her into his office. Standing in the middle of the room, Donna stretched.

"I think I've had enough. I need to go home, take a hot shower get some sleep. This will be here in the morning."

"Sounds like a plan."

Nathan watched her as she gathered her skirt and slipped it back on. Next she stepped into her shoes. Together they walked out of his office. Nathan flicked off the light. They passed through the outer office, once again Nathan turned off the light. Down the hall a ways, he handed a key to Jason and kept on walking.

He walked her to her car and waited until she drove off before getting into his car. As instructed, they both had left their cell phones back at the office on Nathan's desk.

——————— /// ———————

Jason entered the outer office and stood just inside the door. Inside his jacket pocket he pulled out a device. He scanned the outer office first, but came up negative. "Amateurs." He said in a whisper.

Nathan had left his office door open as instructed, so Jason was able to slip in. He went to the camera location first. Standing just below the devise, he pulled a black ski mask over his face. Positioning a side chair, he stood up on it and faced the camera.

"I got your junk, now I'm coming to get you."

He yanked the camera from its mooring and stuck the device into a bag. With the camera gone he went about the office and found the other listening devices. Gathering all the pieces, he placed everything into the bag. Separately, he picked up the two cell phones off the desk and put those in his pocket. He took one more pass around the two offices and coming up negative, he left, locking the door behind him.

——————— /// ———————

The knock on the door was soft. Nathan answered it immediately. Jason entered and put the ski mask back on. He then removed the device from his pocket and proceeded to scan the house. All rooms registered negative. He turned off the device and stuck it back into his pocket. Removing the ski mask, he stuck that in a back pocket.

"You're clean here."

Nathan nodded. Jason pointed back towards the street.

"I've got their junk in the car, shouldn't take me long to find out who they are."

Nathan nodded again. Jason started to leave, but turned back around.

"Cell phones? Want me to check them out or do you want to

get new ones?"

"We'll get new."

"Probably better."

Nathan watched Jason leave and made his way back to the bedroom. Plopping down on the bed, sleep would not come just yet. He got back up and went to the safe hidden in his home office. Spinning the dial, he opened the door. Inside next to some cash and papers was a flash drive, the original manuscript. He had half a mind to plug it into his computer and have a look. Turning the drive in his fingers, he placed the drive back inside the safe and closed the door, spinning the wheel.

Back inside his bedroom, he sat on the edge of the bed thinking this through. He decided it was time to meet with Jeff Morgan again, he would ask Jason to join them and see if they couldn't make some sense of this. Satisfied with his decision he crawled into bed and fell fast asleep.

NINE

Standing at the kitchen counter, Jeff Morgan poured a fresh cup of decaf. Just as he was about to add cream, his phone went off. Walking over to the table he picked up the device and not recognizing the number he simply said hello.

"Jeff, hi, it's Donna."

"Good morning Donna, how are you this fine morning?"

"Just fine, Jeff, just fine."

Looking up at the kitchen clock, he commented.

"Wow, it's only seven-thirty, you're at it early."

"Yes, sorry, hope it wasn't too early."

"No, or course not, I've been up for awhile."

"Good. Listen, Jeff, would you be able to meet with Nathan tomorrow sometime? Some new developments have come up."

"What new developments?"

"I'm sorry, Jeff. I'd rather not get into it over the phone, I'm sure you understand."

"Sure, yeah okay, what time tomorrow?"

"What works best for you?"

"Well it takes me three hours to get there, how about lunch-time, maybe eleven-thirty ish?"

"That would be great, we could take you to lunch for your trouble."

"It's a date then. Anything you can tell me now?"

"Not really. Actually it is Nathan that wants the meet. Oh, by the way, he may have another gentleman join us an operative of ours, if that is okay?"

"Sure, as long as you are there."

"You can bet on it."

"Great, see you then."

"Thanks Jeff, good bye."

The line disconnected. Jeff was about to put the phone down, but then remembered he had a message from last night. Looking at the phone, he walked over and grabbed his coffee, setting it on the table while he dialed the voice mail.

"Hello Mr. Morgan, my name is Sandra Nelson, the facility informed me that you were trying to reach me and they gave me this number. I wanted to let you know I would be okay with that, here is my number."

Jeff Morgan replayed the message, writing the name and number down on his pad under *Call Hospice Woman.* Just to be safe, he saved the message.

Looking at the clock, he decided to dial the number right then and there. The phone answered on the third ring.

"Hello."

"Hello, yes, my name is Jeff Morgan."

"Hello Mr. Morgan."

"Jeff, please."

"Only if you call me Sandy?"

"Deal."

There was silence on the line. Jeff Morgan took a deep breath before speaking.

"Mrs. Nelson ... I'm sorry ... ah Sandy, I am very sorry to here about Bob Kittridge."

"Thank you, Jeff."

"Were you his ..."

"I was his companion."

"Yes, of course. Perhaps I should tell you who I am."

"No need Jeff you were the fourth name on the list. I know who you are, well, sort of."

Jeff sat dumbfounded, not quite sure what to say. Sandy continued.

"Please don't misunderstand Jeff. I helped him put the list together. I'm sure you may have some questions."

"Yes. Yes, of course. Right."

"It's alright really, I was kind of expecting your call."

"Sandy, sorry, you caught me a bit off guard, I don't know what to say."

"How about we take a breath and start over?"

There was silence on the line, Sandy waited, finally Jeff spoke up.

"Then you know that I am the one who got the project?"

"I didn't, but I suspected as much when I got your call."

"Sandy would there be any chance we could get together, I mean meet, there are so many questions I'd like to ask and well … well would that be okay?"

"Sure, that would be fine. Where would you like to meet?"

"I need to meet with the attorney tomorrow, so I'm driving over that way tomorrow for lunch, maybe tomorrow afternoon sometime? I assume you're in that part of town or somewhere nearby?"

"Oh that would work out perfect. Yes, I live about forty minutes from the attorney's office, you could stop by afterwards."

"You know Nathan Simon? He doesn't seem to know you."

Jeff heard a laugh in the background, before she spoke.

"I should say not. Bob wanted it that way. He thought it best to keep me out of the loop on that. But I knew he was meeting with Simon and what his plans were, as you can imagine we did discuss it."

Jeff nodded, making a note not to tell Nathan about her.

"I think I understand, one more thing we can talk about tomorrow. Listen, I don't know how long that meeting will last. What time do you get off work?"

"Not to worry, I'll be home all afternoon. Here is my address."

Jeff wrote down the address on his pad.

"Sandy, I just have one more question for now and I apologize if it is a bit indelicate, but what do you mean by his companion?"

Jeff heard her take a breath.

"We were friends and lovers. We had a good time together until he got sick. I took care of him after that. I never know how to say that so I always say we were companions. A bit old fashioned, maybe?"

"Thanks for being honest. I look forward to our get together, I have so many questions."

"Good bye for now, Jeff."

"Good bye."

The call ended, Jeff made another note and just as he was about to put the phone down, he scrolled down and hit dial on another number.

"Professor Hathaway's office."

"Yes, may I speak with Professor Hathaway please?"

"Who should I say is calling?"

"Jeff Morgan."

"I'm sorry but the Professor is quite busy right now, may I get your name and number and I'll have her call you back."

"You already have it. I'll try back later."

He disconnected the call and set the phone on the table. It was time for a fresh cup of decaf. Sitting back at the table, he scanned his pad. Tomorrow, Friday, he was going to see Nathan, afterwards he would meet with Sandy and Monday he was traveling to Missouri. When did this project become a road trip? He smiled, and sipped his coffee.

——————— /// ———————

Nathan Simon used the office phone on his desk, trying to remember the last time he had actually made a call on that device. Someone answered on the second ring.

"Edward Samson."

"Edward, Nathan Simon."

"Nathan, do I understand by the call that your client has agreed to let me review the manuscript?"

"Edward, after last night's little party, I can assure you that will never happen now. Furthermore ..."

"I'm sorry? I don't understand?"

Nathan paused and took a deep breath, speaking in a harsh tone.

"Sending two goons to my office to harass me and my secretary, not to mention, trashing my office will certainly not convince me to cooperate. In fact it just makes me want to tell you and your client to go fuck yourselves."

"Nathan, I assure you, I have no idea what you're talking about, nor would I, or my client, have anything to do with what you are saying."

"Save it counselor, I'm not buying any of it. You can tell your client any chance he had of seeing that manuscript is dead. Tell him he blew his chances last night."

Nathan hung up the phone. A moment later it rang, obviously a call back.

"Hello."

"Nathan, Edward Samson, please let me speak."

Nathan waited without saying a word.

"Please, I can assure you, my client would have no hand in any such action. My client is purely interested in reaching an agreement, not forcing anyone's hand."

"Well then, your client better find out who is behind that little party last night, because until he does, there will be no deal. Do you hear me?"

Nathan paused and took a breath. "Look Samson, don't you find it strange that the day after you request to see me about that manuscript that two goons try to force me to turn it over?"

"Once again, my client only ..."

"Samson, I just might believe you, but somebody ..."

"Yes. Yes, I understand. Will you give me the weekend to look into this?"

"I look forward to hearing from you on Monday."

Nathan hung up the phone again. This time he smiled. Donna stood on the other side of the desk.

"So, do you think it was his client that did this, or should I say had it done?"

"Absolutely, but in all probability, Samson might not have known anything about it, but then again?"

Donna nodded. "What's next?"

"Let's see if we can clean this mess up before Jason gets here?"

Donna smiled. "That's why I wore pants today, I knew you'd have me crawling around the floor again."

Nathan smiled and sank back into his chair.

——————— /// ———————

Jeff Morgan picked up his phone and dialed the last number on his pad.

"Hello."

"Hello, Mrs. Higgins, my name is Jeff Morgan, I'm an old Army Buddy of Magic, I mean Elroy."

"Yes, hello. What can I do for you?"

"Well Mrs. Higgins, I was recently informed of the death of Bob Kittridge."

"Yes, I received that news as well. Mr. Kittridge's attorney called and said he wanted to talk to Roy or Elroy as he called him, but that is not possible these days."

"Yes, the attorney mentioned that to me as well. I just wanted to call to touch base. It seems like it can't be forty years since we served together. I'm sorry we didn't stay in touch. I'm sure you understand."

"Yes, I do. I only know you boys from stories Roy would tell. Yes, the years do slip by."

"Yes, indeed. The attorney gave me your number, hope that was okay? Like I said, I just wanted to call and touch base. Do give Roy my best. My best to you as well."

"Why thank you Mr. Morgan. I will pas that along. There are good days. I'll wait for one of those. I'm sure he will be happy to hear your name. Good bye Mr. Morgan."

"Good bye."

Jeff set the phone back down on the table and put a check mark on the pad next to *Call Magic's Wife*. Not sure why he had made the call, but he did feel better having done it. He checked the phone, as suspected the battery was low. He plugged the phone in then he went to take a shower and get dressed.

———————— /// ————————

Jason stepped into the office an hour and a half early for the meeting and spotted Nathan and Donna, on the floor in his office sorting through the mess of papers.

"Sorry, I may have stepped on a few of those last night."

Nathan looked up and could barely suppress a laugh. Donna wasn't so delicate.

"What the fuck?"

The person in front of them was wearing a plaid sport jacket, with contrasting pants, thick glasses and a God-awful comb over.

"You said disguise, ask for a divorce. This is one of my favorites."

"Yeah, that was when I thought the place was bugged."

Jason removed the device from his jacket pocket and proceeded to sweep the two offices. "Still clean."

Nathan and Donna got up and walked over to the sofa in Nathan's office, sitting on each end. Jason joined them in the chair across.

"Anything?"

"Not yet, I have some calls out. The equipment will be easy to trace. Should know in a couple of days. Right now it looks like a couple of amateurs did this, not real sophisticated."

"Maybe it was some kind of scare tactic?"

Jason looked at Nathan. "Could be. They sure went about it the wrong way."

"What do you mean?"

Jason looked at Donna and pointed. "Grabbing her up right away was a dumb move."

Donna sat up facing him. He raised his hand.

"You don't want to piss off your quarry in the first moments. Give them time to digest who is in control, talk it out before you get physical. I gotta believe they are new to this. Look at your office. If you are looking for something you don't trash the office, makes it harder to tell if you looked there or not. Did they find anything?"

Nathan shook his head no.

"What were they looking for again?"

"A manuscript."

"Why?"

"I honestly don't know. Had an attorney come by yesterday inquiring about it, said he was led to believe there might be some embarrassing information about his client. Wanted me to give him a copy. I said I would talk it over with my client. We left it at that. Could have been him or his client sent the goons, but maybe not. Attorney sounded like he wanted to work something out, maybe the client didn't want to, or couldn't wait. Maybe some-body else?"

"What's in the manuscript?"

"As far as I know something to do with a man's family being lost in a Civil War battle. He got cancer, wanted me to track down some names to ask if they would be willing to complete the project, which I did. That's as much as I know, really."

Jason nodded. "Have you read it?"

"No."

"But you have a copy?"

"Yes."

"Maybe you better give me one, let me look it over, know what I'm dealing with."

Donna reached into her pants pocked and handed Jason a flash drive.

"It's one of four copies. The original is locked away. A copy is here in this office. I made that copy for you this morning. The third is with our client."

"May I ask who your client is?"

"You'll meet him tomorrow."

Jason nodded, turning the drive in his hand. He stood up.

"I'll be in touch. You need me, you know how to reach me."

Nathan and Donna watched him walk to the door. Before walking out he turned around.

"By the way, I think you're okay for now. I'd say they are still trying to regroup and by the time they do, I'll have them."

He turned and walked through the door. They heard the outer door close.

"You had a copy ready?"

"I knew he would want one."

Nathan smiled. "I knew there was a reason I kept you around."

Donna looked at him and pointed to the floor.

"Yeah, it's so I can clean up this mess."

They both got up and retook their positions on the floor.

TEN

Once sure that the garage door had fully closed, Jeff Morgan pulled out of his driveway to make the trek to the attorney's office. Beyond that though, he was looking forward to the meeting with Sandy Nelson, Robert Kittridge's companion. Another busy day in the life of an information hunter he thought to himself, then smiled. Cautiously he merged his car into the lane, accelerating to meet the flowing traffic.

—————— /// ——————

Nathan Simon walked into the office, stopping at Donna's desk. She was busy at work setting up two new cell phones, punching numbers into the phone contacts from a list she had in front of her.

"Sorry, I'm sure you get tired of doing that."

Donna looked up. "Nope, that is why we keep it simple, basic numbers, nothing more. I should have yours done pretty soon, then I'll work on mine."

Nathan nodded. "You're the best."

Donna smiled back, watching him walk into his office.

"Looks pretty good in here."

"You're damn right it does. Worked on it all last night."

Nathan sat in his chair, spinning toward the door. "Anything I need to take care of before our little get together?"

Donna stood in the doorway, pointing at his desk. "A couple of calls you might want to return, at least pretend things are normal around here."

Nathan nodded, looking at the messages in front of him. "Will do."

——————— /// ———————

Three hours later, Jeff Morgan pulled into the parking structure and made the short walk to the office building. Entering the office, he was happy to see Donna sitting at her desk.

"Jeff, so glad you could make it."

Before she had a chance to tell Nathan that Morgan was here, Nathan stood in the doorway of his office.

"Jeff, thanks for coming on such short notice."

The two men shook hands.

"Shall we go?"

Donna got up from her desk, once again giving Jeff a nice view of her legs and joined Nathan as he escorted everyone out the door. Taking a moment to lock up, he motioned for them to continue on.

Five minutes after they sat down another man joined them at the table.

"Jeff, I'd like you to meet Jason, he's a colleague of mine."

Jeff reached across the table and shook his hand.

"So what's all the mystery?"

Nathan, Donna and Jason all looked at him.

"Well, it all seems very cloak and dagger. I am a little confused and maybe just a bit concerned."

Donna spoke first, looking at the other two for a moment, then back to Jeff.

"Well Jeff, there have been a couple of incidents in the last few days that we felt you should know about. Have you read the manuscript yet?"

"Actually, no I haven't. I've been focusing on the research material, made some calls and tried to follow up on some things, but no, not really."

Jeff quickly reminded himself not to mention Sandra Nelson just yet.

Nathan nodded then asked. "Might we inquire as to what you mean?"

"Sure, but how about you give me something first, you've got me wondering what this is all about … and quite frankly, as I said already, a bit concerned. Am I in some kind of trouble or maybe even some danger here? I mean why all the sudden interest in the manuscript? Seems like that should have been … well, known before it even got to me. Why now? I mean …"

"Of course not." Nathan leaned forward on the table, speaking softly. "Fact is, three days ago, an attorney came into my office inquiring about the manuscript, practically demanding I give him a copy, said he had a client might have some concerns regarding the contents, which of course, I said no, certainly not until I talked with you first."

Nathan paused, looking at Donna then Jason, before continuing.

"Then two nights ago, two goons busted into my office threatening me if I didn't turn over the manuscript to them." Nathan didn't go into the specific details. "Of course, I said no once again, seems someone is suddenly awfully interested in the manuscript."

Nathan stopped, took a drink of water and cleared his throat before continuing.

"Jason here does investigative work for me and I've asked him to look into these incidents. However, we all felt it might be prudent to meet with you since the nature of these incidents involves the manuscript I gave you, well, that Kittridge passed on. We also thought maybe you might have some insight, as to why all the sudden interest in that manuscript."

Jeff nodded, trying to absorb it all, looking at Nathan.

"Did you ever read the manuscript, Nathan?"

Nathan shook his head no. Neither he, nor Donna mentioned that Jason now had a copy as well. Jeff looked around the table before speaking.

"Well to tell you the truth, best I can figure is that the manuscript has basically something to do with the man's family members that were in the Civil War, which appear to be distant relatives of Kittridge. Can't see how that would stir up anybody's feathers, but if that is a problem somehow for somebody, I'm prepared to give you the whole thing back and forget I ever got involved."

Nathan smiled waving his hand in the air.

"No need for that. Anyway, that's what we believe as well. I can't imagine someone would get bent out of shape over a Civil War story? Anything else you can think of, or may have discovered in the research materials that might say otherwise? Anything might be a problem for someone in those documents?"

Jeff looked at the group around the table again.

"Well, there might be one thing."

He bent down to pick up his carry case, opened it and removed the letter, pausing before handing the paper to Nathan.

"You might want to take a look at the last paragraph of Kittridge's letter."

Nathan took the paper, Jeff waited while he finished, then watched as he handed the paper to Jason, asking as he did.

"What do you think that was about?"

Before Jeff could answer, Jason spoke first.

"Sounds like you boys made a drug run that day."

Jeff looked at Jason with a how did you know look, while Jason continued.

"No big deal, I'm sure it happened a lot over there. Why would that be important, other than apparently you and Kittridge got tight, at least in 'Nam?"

Jeff nodded, looking at Jason, before turning to Nathan.

"That's true, we did get tight after that, at least while we were there. And it certainly goes a long way to explain why I made the list. At least, I think it does. I still can't figure out why I would have made the list otherwise."

Jeff stopped and took a drink of water. They all waited for

him to continue.

"And I would have thought no more of it, until I talked with Magalito."

"You spoke with Magalito, the fifth name on the list?"

They all looked at Nathan.

"I gave him the name and number earlier this week."

Now they all looked at Donna, who raised her hands in the air in a "what" attitude. Nodding in the affirmative, Jeff continued.

"Yes, since his name was also mentioned in the letter and of course now that I know he was also the fifth name, I though it might be prudent to get his take on all of this. You know, find out if he had anything to offer on why Kittridge may have picked either one of us for his list of recipients."

"And did you?" Nathan leaned forward.

"Yes." Jeff looked at Nathan.

"And."

Jeff reached into his carry case again.

"I made some notes."

He removed the sheet of paper and set it on the table in front of him.

"Let me read from my notes."

The three others waited for Jeff to start.

"Let me see. Yes, here, let me start here. He said it was nothing more than another one of Swifty's drug runs." Jeff paused and looked at Jason, still amazed at how he figured that out so quick. "There had been others, but this was the only one Kittridge and I was on. Picked at random, the guys they normally used were too wasted that day."

Jeff paused scanning down the paper.

"Said we were in Laos, at a staging area, possibly a camp of some kind, not a village as Kittridge thought. Soldiers could have been anyone, NVA, Laotian, VC, possibly even ARVN. Corruption knew no bounds over there."

Jeff paused, to take a big drink of water.

"Tony Mags ... I mean Magalito said that day they carried out the usual two ten pound boxes of heroin. But this time there was a third box that was filled with priceless Jade, Buddha stuff he said, looted from the temples in Hue during the Tet offensive in '68. He said the Jade was a special payment to the Pilot for the use of his bird, his continuing services … something like that."

Jeff stopped and looked at the others. They had been following his story with great interest. Jason spoke first.

"Jade, huh? That could have been worth some bucks. How did he get it out of the country?"

Jeff looked at Jason, taking a moment before he spoke.

"Magalito said he didn't know how, but he did know that he did get it out. And of course, Swifty made another killing on his drugs. Magalito thought he was sending the money to an offshore account somehow."

Nathan looked at the others before speaking.

"Why would Magalito tell you all this?"

Jeff looked directly at Nathan taking a moment.

"Because he was dying, not much time left. I saw him in one of those good-bye places as he called it. In fact, his wife called me two days later and informed me that he did in fact pass away."

The group sat quietly, until finally Nathan spoke.

"Anything else?"

"Yes."

"Really? What?"

Jeff looked at Nathan, hesitating before speaking.

"He said he was going to give me a name and he highly recommended that I forget that name as soon as I left his room and to never mention it again, but he wanted to give it to me for future reference, thought somebody else should know that name before he died. He also mentioned I might need it later."

Nathan looked at him, even Jason sat forward, while Donna waved her hand in the air and looked at both men before leaning in. Jeff looked at all three bearing down on him.

"I'm not sure I should repeat it, Magalito said."

Nathan leaned forward, speaking softly.

"I'm your attorney, you can tell me, attorney client privilege. That name is safe with me, with us."

Jeff looked at him, than Jason, then Donna, nodding.

"Do you think it's that important?"

"Yes, I believe it is that important. I assure you that name stays with us."

Jeff looked at Nathan, then Donna and finally Jason again. They both nodded yes as well. Jeff took a deep breath.

"He said the Pilot's name was Reginald Harrison."

Jason said it first. "Congressman Reginald Harrison?"

Jeff looked at Jason, pointing.

"Damn, Mags, I mean Magalito said I would know soon enough who that was. When he first told me, I didn't make the connection, but now? So the Pilot that day is now a congressman?"

Nathan shook his head, holding his hands in the air as if he just heard some great revelation, leaving him somewhat anxious as he spoke.

"You mean to tell me the Helicopter Pilot that day you guys made that drug run was Congressman Reginald Harrison, the same guy that got a box of sacred Jade out of the country? That was him? No wonder there is such a panic over the manuscript. No doubt he would have concerns about any of that coming out and probably has been led to believe Kittridge's manuscript might contain information about those Vietnam days or specifically that incident, or that something related to that incident might just be in that manuscript."

The group sat quietly. Jeff spoke first.

"He said one last thing."

They all looked at him as if there couldn't possibly be anything else. Taking the cue, Jeff continued.

"He said he had a final thought for me, sort of paraphrasing the letter."

Jeff cleared his throat and took a sip of water before continuing.

"He said ..." Jeff looked at the paper in his hand and read from there. "James Smith the Peter Pilot that day had his Helicopter shot down on his second flight as Pilot, killed instantly, never left the 'Nam. You, meaning me, just told me, meaning him, Kittridge bought the farm, hell, I'll meaning Magalito, be dead in a matter of days, which means the only persons living from that day is you, Swifty and the Pilot. My, Magalito's, thought to you is, because Kittridge put that in his letter, you better watch your ass."

Jeff set the paper back down on the table and looked at the others. Nathan stayed where he was, while Jason leaned back in his chair. Donna looked at both men, waiting for one of them to respond. Neither of them did. Jeff finally spoke first.

"Do you guys really think the Congressman is mixed up in any of this?"

"That's a real possibility." Jason leaned forward. "Can you say for certain that manuscript is solely about the Civil War?"

Jeff looked at him, then Nathan, before answering.

"No, not for certain, I haven't read it yet, but all the research notes and everything I've reviewed so far focuses solely on the premise some of what appears to be Kittridge's family was involved in a Civil War battle and subsequently were killed. I gotta say it is a family history thing, basically the loss of several members in one skirmish during the Civil War. Look, except for that paragraph in the Kittridge letter, nothing else points to Vietnam. I even asked Magalito what he thought and he thought same as me. That's how the list was created, not sure why Kittridge mentioned the Vietnam stuff either. Otherwise everything I have seen and discovered so far is Civil War related, absolutely nothing to do with Vietnam, certainly not any of that incident, or anything related to that day. Is there more to this that I should know about?"

Jason shook his head no ahead of Nathan.

"Nathan can spell it out for you, but I think it's nothing more than some legal issues regarding that manuscript."

Nathan shook his head yes. Jeff looked at both men.

"How do you mean?"

Nathan smiled. "Well someone in the public eye would be concerned about anything from their past resurfacing, no matter if any of the story is true or not. Either way it certainly would raise some legal issues."

Jason pointed, but Jeff wasn't convinced.

"Really, you think that's it? Not something I should be concerned about? I mean it's a manuscript about the Civil War, how could the Congressman get upset about that?"

Jason nodded and patted Jeff on the shoulder, while they all sat in silence, no one was giving up the fact Jason now had a copy of the manuscript. Nathan sat back speaking normally again.

"Okay, now this is starting to make sense. Harrison is poised to run for Senate next year, the last thing he would want is any ghosts coming out of the closet now and something that may have happened forty years ago would only stir up dust, whether it actually happened or not. Certainly not good for business. At the very least, I gotta believe he's the one sent the attorney to inquire about the manuscript."

Jeff nodded, pointing to the notes in front of him.

"Yeah, but how do we convince him this is nothing more that some Civil War thing, that there is no mention of Vietnam, or him or anything about that day in the manuscript?"

The others looked at Jeff, before Nathan spoke up.

"Let's assume he sent the lawyer first, maybe I can get the attorney to relay that message to the Congressman? You know maybe we can still work out a deal? Maybe even let him take a look at the manuscript?"

Jason leaned in, shaking his head no.

"That didn't work the first time, especially since a day later somebody, maybe even the Congressman himself, sent two goons to try to strong arm you into giving him the manuscript, I don't think he'd be satisfied with anything less than the actual manuscript and even then, he may not believe you gave him everything."

"Then why don't we just give him the original manuscript?"

They all looked at Jeff. Jason pointed as he spoke.

"Because a guy like that would never be satisfied, even with that manuscript. He wouldn't believe it was an actual copy of the actual manuscript, certainly not the whole story. No we need to convince him another way."

"I might have the solution."

They all looked at Donna as she continued.

"My benefactor is rich and powerful enough to get a private meeting with him and if we can convince her of our true intentions of the meeting, I'm sure he'll have no choice but to take the meeting."

Nathan and Jason understood, but Jeff was in the dark. Donna turned to him.

"I'm sorry Jeff, but it is a long story. She rescued me from a very bad time and became my mentor, my lover and most importantly, a very powerful friend. She is one of the few people that can bring the Congressman to his knees, make him listen, nor would she hesitate to do it, given the right reasons, especially if I ask nicely. I think she will do it, for all of us, specifically for you Jeff, so you need not worry."

Jeff sat dumbfounded not quite sure he understood any of it. Nathan put his hand on Jeff's shoulder.

"Politics do make strange bedfellows."

A small laugh went around the table, Jeff bowed his head, still not quite sure he understood, but at least the others seemed to like the idea.

"Shall we eat?"

Nathan motioned for the waitress. In a moment they ordered their lunch. As soon as the waitress left, Donna leaned over to Jeff.

"Listen Jeff, if anybody can help us straighten this mess out, she can. So just relax, enjoy your lunch and let us handle this for now, don't you worry about anything but finishing that manuscript for Kittridge. We'll handle this."

Jeff looked at her, nodding.

"Whatever you say. I don't get any of this anyway."

Donna smiled, placing her hand on his shoulder.

"Tell you what, when the dust settles, we'll go out have a couple of beers and I'll give you the whole story, I promise."

Jeff smiled. "Better make it Vodka, I don't think beer will be strong enough to hear that story."

The laughter around the table was spontaneous and complete.

Nathan reached over and patted Jeff's shoulder. Jason held his water in the air in a mock salute. Donna rubbed Jeff's back and kissed his cheek.

"That's a deal."

Jeff smiled. Whatever else was going on, for the moment there was a sense of relief. The rest of the lunch was filled with normal conversation. As they got up to leave, Nathan picked up the check, Jeff secured his carry case, and Jason moved in beside him.

"Here is a number. You need anything, or think you may be in trouble you call it, day or night, you understand? And do what Magalito recommended, forget that name, forget you ever heard it. Let us worry about that, okay? Trust me, we got this. Besides this whole story might be made up. You know, just a story to piss off somebody. We can't be sure any of this is real. Let us talk to the Congressman and try to straighten this out. You just work on finishing that manuscript. We got this, okay?"

Jeff nodded, sticking the piece of paper in his pocket. Donna stuck her arm in his and walked with him out of the restaurant. In a moment Nathan was beside them, Jason was already gone, as was his way, no good byes for him. Donna turned into Jeff and gave him a rather intimate hug pressing her full body into his. She whispered in his ear.

"Don't you worry Jeff, this will all work out. We'll take care of everything."

She pulled away sliding her hand across his cheek. Jeff watched her and Nathan walk down the street back to their office. She turned and waved.

Shaking his head, Jeff couldn't decide if he should be worried, relieved or turned on. Smiling warmly as he retreated, he walked to the parking structure and climbed into his car.

On the passenger's seat sat the map and directions to Sandra Nelson's condo.

The day wasn't over yet.

ELEVEN

Jeff Morgan parked his car in the visitor's parking area. A minute later he was standing in front of the door. Taking a deep breath, he knocked, waiting as the door opened to a rather attractive forty something lady.

"Mr. Morgan, please come in."

"Jeff."

"Sorry, Jeff."

She closed the door behind him as he entered and stood in the foyer. Walking past him, she directed him to a living room, very neatly kept.

"May I offer you something to drink? I don't have much in the hard liquor area, but I believe there is some cold beer in the fridge and I do have some wine, red or white?"

"No thanks, water will be just fine."

She nodded and went off to the kitchen. He looked around the room, first spotting a picture of her and an older man he assumed was Kittridge. When she reentered handing him the water she motioned for him to have a seat.

"Please."

Jeff nodded and sat on the sofa, while she sat on the other end curling her legs up under her, facing him.

"When you hit the buzzer, I must admit I had butterflies."

Jeff smiled. "As did I when the door buzzed. I kept practicing my first words all the way to your door."

She smiled. "Okay then shall we dance?"

Jeff took a minute then smiled. "Yes, of course." He took a deep breath. "There is so much I want to ask you and yet I think I already know."

"How so, Jeff?"

Jeff put his head down, looked out into the room stopping on the picture and finally looked over at her turning slightly in his seat. Taking a deep breath, he spoke very softly, just above a whisper.

"My wife recently died of cancer."

"Then you know?"

Jeff nodded yes, turning more in his seat to face her, rubbing his hand across his face.

"The chemo, the radiation, the good days, the bad days, the agony, the ever changing news, the finality of it all."

She stood up and sat down next to him, taking him in her arms.

"I know I know … I think the hardest part is knowing they are going to die and still hoping for the best. Watching every day for a sign. Is this it? How much longer, knowing they are suffering something fierce and the damn treatment being worst than the God-damn cancer."

Jeff began to sob. She held him tighter. Through his sobs, he spoke just above a whisper.

"And the pisser is you can't do a fucking thing about it."

Jeff let go, the emotion racking his whole body, the tears were only an outlet. She held him tighter, until finally his sobs subsided. She used her sleeve to wipe his eyes and dry his face.

"How long did she suffer?"

Jeff looked into her eyes, her face was inches from his.

"Not that I'd really know how long. I know it had to be kicking her ass big time, but she hung in there like a trooper, always on her meds, endless trips to the hospital, doctors, nurses, treatments, chemo and radiation, more tests, scans, what have you, always a brave face. She fought it for eighteen months, before the cancer finally put her down."

One more sob escaped him as she held him tighter, rubbing his back, her face buried into his shoulder. They stayed like that for several minutes. Slowly she let go and moved her face within inches of his again. He could feel her breath on his cheek, a bit labored. She used her thumb to wipe off his face this time. Jeff nodded. She pulled back, resting back onto her heels, her breathing still an effort.

Jeff put his hands on her face. "I'm sorry, I didn't mean to ..."

She placed her finger on his lips. "No need for that."

He looked into her eyes, asking with his. She gathered herself, her breathing somewhat back to normal. She was caught up in the emotion as well. Finally taking one last deep breath, she spoke softly.

"Bob went through the same process. Good days and bad. At first, it looked like he was going to beat it, but then out of nowhere, the cancer was everywhere. The doctors gave him days. He lasted six months, but we fought the invasion for two years prior to that. Lot of time to start putting things in order. The end was gruesome."

Jeff put his head down. "So was hers."

She leaned forward again taking him in her arms, holding him tightly before pulling back. She stroked his cheek, again inches from his face. "Sure you don't want something stronger than water? I could pour us some wine? Maybe I have ..."

Jeff shook his head no. Again, they stayed like that for several minutes. She pulled away and got up from the couch. Jeff used his hand to wipe his face. His thumb and index finger squeezing the bridge of his nose. In a moment she was back with a damp cloth, which she used to clean his face.

"I bet you made a hell of a companion to Bob."

"You bet I did."

Jeff smiled as he watched her fold up the wash cloth.

She set the cloth on the coffee table pointing her finger back at him. "We don't have to do this now. Why don't we get a bite to eat, have a drink or two, then we can talk shop."

He put his hand on the side of her face, stroking her cheek with his thumb. "How about we order a pizza and work ourselves into it?"

She nodded yes, holding his hand against her face. Waiting a minute longer, she let go, got up and walked back into the kitchen.

Jeff let his hand rest on his thigh. Taking a very deep breath, he tried to gather himself. He hadn't let go like that in a long time. But this was the first time he had been with someone that knew exactly what he had been through. He heard her talking in the background, and realized she was ordering the pizza.

In a moment she was back and plopped down on the sofa across from him. "What would you like to know first?"

Jeff smiled. "Boy, where to start? How about with you?"

"Me?"

"Yes, you how did you and Bob get together?"

"You really want to know that?"

"Yes, I do."

"Okay, but it is pretty boring."

"It's okay, we got time."

She smiled and tucked her legs under her on the sofa, a smile forming.

"Well, I worked at the library where Bob was doing his research, still do. I would see him come in pretty regularly and we got to talking. I showed him how to use the computer and look things up that way, but he liked digging into books and doing old-fashioned research. I think he did it just to see me."

She put her head down. Jeff smiled and turned into the arm-rest to get more comfortable. She looked back up a wide smile on her face, waving her hand in the air and taking a breath she continued.

"Anyway, one day he asked me out. Now don't misunderstand this, but we wound up sleeping together that first night. I know, pretty scandalous of me right? And yes, I know what you must be thinking, I'll do the math for you, he was almost twenty years older than me. Well, actually he was twenty years older than me."

Sandy paused, waving her hand in the air.

"Anyway, next I know we are going out pretty regular, having a good time. All of a sudden my roommate decides to move out, go live with her boyfriend. Well I can't afford to live there alone, so Bob suggests I move in with him, but he's only got this one room apartment and well you can imagine how that would have worked out."

Jeff watched her talk, noticing she was quite animated. The reliving of the story bringing life back into her face.

"Next thing I know he tells me he's buying a condo, this place, says it has two bedrooms and if it doesn't work out, I could still have my own room."

Jeff watched her chuckle at that last statement waving her hand in the air.

"We had almost three years, before … well before. Somewhere along the line I found out the place was actually in my name and just before he died, he told me where to find enough cash stashed to cover the mortgage for a couple of years. After that, I don't know what I'll do. At present, I wouldn't be able to afford it myself. I've been looking for a full time job, but haven't been very successful, maybe I'm not trying hard enough."

Jeff saw a tear well up in her eye. He half moved to comfort her, but a moment later she was waving her hand and smiling again.

"Listen to me, go on." She used her knuckle to wipe the tear away. "He told me he had it all worked out with the attorney that upon his death the place would be mine. Well, mine and the banks."

"Was that Nathan Simon?"

"Oh heavens, no. He didn't contact Nathan until the very end. This was another attorney here in town did all that paperwork."

Jeff nodded, not quite understanding. She took a breath and continued.

"As sick as Bob was he always took care of me, never thinking about himself. It was only toward the very end that he couldn't do anything anymore."

Jeff nodded. "Same with me. As sick as she was, she continued to take care of me until the end until she couldn't ..." Jeff looked up at Sandy, she nodded she understood waving her hand in the air again.

"There we go again. We're supposed to be conducting business."

Jeff smiled. "Okay then, next question. What do you know about the project?"

She smiled back, perked up a bit and settled back into the sofa.

"Actually not as much as you would think. I only read through the manuscript a couple of times and that was mostly to help keep it somewhat in order. Bob kept finding pieces that he would stick in and usually not where they belonged. You know, I'm not sure I would have called it a manuscript, at least not yet. Just a bunch of stuff put together with very little direction. I'm not sure he even had a direction yet."

Standing and walking away she kept talking.

"As to his research, almost nothing, but I probably should give you this."

She went into one of the bedrooms and returned with a box, which she handed to Jeff.

"Here is more stuff he found or wrote down, or whatever that he said was of little or no value or had already been documented and that it was really all summed up in the papers he put in that envelope. But maybe there is something in there that he missed. Remember, he was pretty done in toward the end and he may not have been completely focused."

Jeff took the lid off the box. It was the size of a boot box. Inside was a jumble of papers, some with handwriting. He put the lid back on.

"Thanks, I'll take a look, maybe you're right, maybe there is something in there that I can use, or might help me to understand some things. Sure can't hurt to have these papers, thank you."

"There were originally ten."

"Beg pardon?"

"The list. There were originally ten names on the list."

Jeff looked at her raising his palms up in a what do you mean fashion. Just then, the door buzzed.

"Pizza's here."

She was up off the sofa, pressing the intercom and buzzing the pizza guy in. Setting the shoe box of papers on the sofa, Jeff joined her at the door and offered to pay, but she pushed him away as she handed the delivery boy a twenty. Jeff stepped back into the room.

"Shall we take this into the kitchen?"

Jeff followed behind her watching as she set the pizza box on the table.

"What are you drinking?"

"Maybe I'll have one of those beers."

"Coming right up. Go ahead, sit down."

She placed plates, a knife and fork and napkins on the table. Next she retrieved two beers out of the fridge.

"Wouldn't want you to drink alone."

They made small talk while they ate the pizza and drank the beer. Jeff watched as she cleaned up.

"Shall we?"

She directed them back into the living room, again each taking their places on the sofa.

Jeff spoke first. "What else can you tell me about the project?"

Sandy took a moment before speaking. "I really wish there was more, but I didn't get involved. I know it began with the letters. When his aunt died, she had some stuff inside a shoebox, actually that box I gave you and that's where he found the letters. That sort of started him on the research. Can you imagine finding six letters dated from 1864? One thing I can tell you is I don't think those letters were ever mailed. I mean take a good look at them. They look like they were written and held maybe waiting for a place to mail them. Bob thought otherwise, but if they were mailed, how come there's no postage on the envelopes? Does make you wonder, doesn't it?"

Jeff nodded and was about to ask another question when he

remembered. He looked up at her and spoke softly. "A while ago you said there were ten?"

She smiled. "Yes, the original list contained ten names."

"Why did he cut it?"

"Money."

"Money?"

"Yes, he said it would cost too much to track down ten people. Besides he had already crossed off two of those names."

"Do you remember any of those names?"

She shook her head no. "I almost didn't see the final list."

"Do you have any ideas about the order?"

Again, she shook her head no. Jeff sat quietly. "I can tell you this though, you were second on the first list."

Jeff looked at her. "Second? There was a first list?"

She nodded yes, a smile forming. "I probably shouldn't tell you this, but the first list didn't include Robert Swift, it had another name fifth, you were second, Magic third, Magalito fourth."

Jeff perked up. "Do you remember who that other name was?"

"Yes, but it doesn't matter, we found out that person had died a few years back."

Jeff put his head down. She reached over putting her hand on his leg.

"I'm sorry, did I say something wrong?"

He put his hand on hers, taking a moment to answer.

"No. No, nothing like that. It's just that I keep hearing guys my age are dead."

"I'm sorry, I didn't mean to upset you."

Jeff looked up at her waving his hand in the air as he spoke softly.

"No, nothing like that. Just knowing guys I served with are dying off is a little disheartening. Did you know the lieutenant, the first name on the list has passed on as well? And the fifth name on the list, Tony Mags, recently died. Jesus."

Jeff paused and took a deep breath, before looking back up at her.

"The list. Do you know how or why he came up with those names?"

She started to answer, but he continued.

"Or more specifically, how I made the list?"

She shook her head no. "All I know is that he wrote names down, would cross some off then redo the list again and cross someone else off. I'm not sure the final list was the final list. It could have been one of the drafts."

Jeff's eyes widened. "Really?"

She nodded yes. "But the list he passed on to Simon was the one he kept coming back to. That one seemed to be the one he wanted to use. Said it was the only one had meaning."

"Meaning?"

She waved her hand in the air. "Something like that. I can tell you he never threw that one away, kept it on his desk even while he made other lists. Seemed like that was the list and no matter what he may have thought, he always would put that list in the center of his desk when he got up. Something about that list meant something to him. Sorry, wish I knew more."

Jeff started to answer, but she slid over keeping her hand on his thigh under his hand, reaching she turned his face toward her.

"You want to know why he put Robert Swift on that list, don't you."

Jeff looked up, her hand holding his chin. She smiled having distracted him. She let go and sat back, but still keeping her hand under his.

"He read an article about Swift's investment firm and thought that Swift would have the know how to market the project, if not for the subject certainly for the money."

Jeff looked at her. "I'm not sure I follow."

"Swift had contacted him asking if he would like to invest, but by then Bob was running low on money and declined. I know they talked for a bit and Bob said later that Swift, actually he called him Swifty, was always looking for a deal and that just maybe Swifty could turn this into something. It was purely about the money. Of course we found out later Swifty went to prison and that he even swindled some of the guys he served with, but by then it was too late. Bob was too sick to deal with any of that stuff anymore. I'm pretty sure he had already turned everything over to that attorney, Nathan Simon by that time as well. I assume when the dust settled he just went with that original list."

Jeff nodded. "And Simon never knew about you?"

"That's the way Bob wanted it."

"Why?"

"I'm not sure. He did say one time, to protect me."

"Protect you?"

"Yeah, I didn't understand it either. But he said that was why he put this place in my name and went over there to find an attorney for this stuff."

Jeff flashed to the meeting he had earlier in the day with Nathan, but didn't say anything about that, he just looked at Sandy and waited for her to continue.

"You know what's funny? Early on he was happy for my help, encouraged it even, but then he just about shut me out. I thought it was the cancer, maybe the meds or something else to do with the illness and let it be."

Sandy paused and looked up at Jeff.

"He seemed to get really paranoid for awhile, but then, as he got worse, he didn't seem to care anymore, so I just focused on taking care of him."

"Simon knew you visited Bob at the end-of-life facility."

She nodded. "Yeah, I thought as much. One time as I was arriving, Simon was leaving. I asked Bob about that, but he said it was just more paper shit."

"Do you know about the letters he wrote to each name on the list?"

She shook her head no. "Not really. I know he wrote them. I saw the five envelopes with each name on the outside."

"Then you probably don't know about the Vietnam stuff?"

"The Vietnam stuff?"

"At the end of the letter he included a paragraph regarding

the time we were in Vietnam. I was wondering if that may have influenced the list at all."

Sandy shrugged her shoulders. "Don't know anything about that. I just know he did several drafts before the final list. I couldn't tell you how or why he created the final list, which I actually believe was the original list, the first draft."

Jeff nodded. They sat silently for a minute before Sandy perked up as if she remembered something.

"I will tell you he spent more time putting the package together toward the end then he did working on the manuscript. As I mentioned, I didn't see it much, probably because he really wasn't working on it. He did say once there was a problem with his research, but we never discussed any of those details again after that."

Involuntarily Jeff yawned. "Well, it has been very fascinating talking with you, but it is getting late and I better get going, I have a long drive back home."

"Like hell you will."

"I beg your pardon?"

"Look, there is an extra bedroom here, why don't you spend the night and leave first thing in the morning. Besides you've been drinking."

"I had one beer."

"Never-the-less, it is a long drive, it's very late. I insist you stay here."

Jeff looked at her for a long time, realizing how late it was and that he had at least a three and a half hour ride home, beginning to accept her logic.

"You're sure that's okay?"

"I would have it no other way. Bob would turn over in his grave if I didn't offer. Besides you're the keeper of the manuscript now. The least we could do is make sure you're safe and sound. Now, no more arguments."

"But I don't have anything."

She disappeared into one of the bedrooms, returning with a bathrobe.

"This should fit you. Are you a PJ guy, undies or in the altogether?"

"I'm sorry?"

"How do you sleep, PJs, in your undies or naked?"

"I don't wear PJs."

"Fine, then I need not get you anything else. Each bedroom has its own bath, so you will have your privacy. Anything else you need? Yes, of course …"

Again, she was gone, retuning with a toothbrush, still in the package and a tube of toothpaste.

"There are fresh towels already in there. The sheets are also fresh."

She stood in front of him, kissed him on the cheek and gave him a strong hug, holding on for an extra moment. "Thanks for coming by, I really appreciated the company, especially someone who understands." She stood facing him about to say something more, but relented and just smiled, patting his shoulder. "Good night Jeff, see you in the morning, I'll make breakfast before you go."

Jeff watched her walk back into her bedroom and heard the door close. Shrugging his shoulders, he made his way to the other bedroom. Turning on the light, he saw the twin bed in the corner, all made up. On the other wall was the bathroom. As he was about to close the door he realized the living room light was still on. He crossed the room and turned that off, following the light from his bedroom back. Closing the door he smiled.

He stood at the sink in the robe and his briefs, brushing his teeth. Finished, he turned off the light and walked over to the bed, pulling the covers down. Placing the robe on the bottom of the bed he crawled in. The emotions of the evening caught up with him, suddenly he felt very tired. A moment later he was asleep.

TWELVE

Donna Millpoint dialed the number from her new cell phone. A woman answered on the second ring.

"Hello."

"Toni, hi it's me, Donna."

"No one's called me Toni in a while."

"Why, what do they call you now?"

"Mrs. Ri-chard."

"Really, no more Richards?"

"Not since my husband started to gain his power base. He hated the fact someone always wanted to put an 'S' on the end of Richard, so he decided we would pronounce it Ri-chard from now on."

"How sweet."

"So my dear Donna, it is so good to hear your voice."

"Yours too, Toni. May I still call you Toni?"

"You can call me anything you like."

Donna smiled, taking a deep breath, before continuing.

"Toni, I need your help with something."

"Really? What is it? I mean what can I do for you?"

"I'd rather not discuss it on the phone. Can we get together sometime soon to talk?"

She heard a chuckle from the other end.

"Well, my dear Donna, you're in luck. I'm home all by myself tonight. He's in New York, putting some new deal together."

"Expanding his power base?"

"You could say that. But remember, at the end of the day, it is my family money and name, no matter how far he thinks he climbs up the ladder."

"Everything okay between you two?"

"Certainly my dear, we have an understanding, as you well know."

"Yes, I do."

"Why don't you come by tonight and we can talk?"

"That would be great. What time would work for you?"

"Anytime is fine."

"I'll be there in an hour."

"That'll be great."

Donna disconnected the call and dropped the phone on her dresser. Her slacks were already half off as she pulled her blouse over her head. Unclasping the bra, she dropped that on the bed. Using her thumbs to slip under the band of her panties, she slid those and her slacks the rest of the way off and deposited those garments on the bed as well.

After a hot shower, dressed in a simple black dress and matching black bra and panties, she slipped into her black strap heels. Only her best for who she was about to see. Fifteen minutes after the call, she walked out the front door of her condo and climbed into her car.

—————— /// ——————

Donna Millpoint took a breath before knocking. A lady, presumably a housekeeper of some sort, answered the door.

"Yes?"

"Hi, I'm Donna Millpoint, Mrs. Ri-chard is expecting me."

The woman stepped back pointing the way.

"Yes, she is in the study, right through those doors there go right in."

Donna looked to where she was pointing. Nodding as she

walked past the woman, she took another breath before entering and walked through the door.

Antoinette "Toni" Ri-chard stood in the middle of the room, dressed in a plain white blouse and mid-length skirt. She smiled broadly when Donna walked in. She waited as Donna walked up to her, shaking hands, but not letting go.

"Donna, so nice to see you."

"You as well."

Donna gave a slight pull on Toni's hand drawing her closer. A moment later, Donna kissed her deeply. She could feel her tremble to the touch. Donna brought her other hand around her back, pulling her in. Toni relaxed and let herself be consumed by Donna's kiss. Breaking the hold, Donna stepped back, looking at her standing still very close, biting her lower lip.

"You sure do know how to make an entrance."

Donna smiled, letting go of Toni's hand. "Thought I'd cut through the preliminaries."

Toni smiled and cleared her throat. "Shall we have a seat?"

They walked over to a sofa, sitting on either side. Donna's dress rose up on her thigh. Toni noticed.

"You look very nice."

"Well, I was coming to see someone very special."

Toni smiled and patted her hand. They sat silent for a moment looking at each other. Toni reached over and touched her hand.

"I have missed you."

Donna put her hand on Toni's. "As have I."

Toni pulled her hand away, setting her hands in her lap look-ing up at Donna.

"So, what is so important that you needed to see me immediately?"

Donna slipped off her shoes, pulling her legs up onto the sofa and in the process of sitting cross-legged on the sofa she lifted the dress up exposing her panties for a brief moment. As Toni watched, Donna smiled slowly raising the dress, giving her full view of her underwear.

Toni reached over slapping her hand. "Enough."

Donna smiled, straightening out her dress over her legs. Placing her elbow on the back of the sofa, Donna sighed.

"It's a rather long story. Do you want the whole thing, or just the highlights?"

"Enough to make me understand."

Donna nodded taking a breath before speaking.

"Well, a while back we took on a client that was dying of cancer. He gave us a project he was working on, a manuscript with a list of five names to contact, old Army Buddies, we believe that he hoped would complete the project for him after he passed on. The first name on the list was his Lieutenant from Vietnam that we discovered had also already passed on. The second and you'll like this name was Robert Swift."

"Swift, that son-of-bitch. He tried to get my husband to invest in his scam, but I reminded my dear husband that it was my family money and … I'm sorry, continue."

"Well, he was this guy's platoon sergeant or something like that, but being in a Federal country club, we had to disqualify him. The next guy on the list has dementia and we had to rule him out as well. The fourth name on the list appears to have worked out okay and he agreed to take on the project. So, we passed the package along to him thinking that was done and went about our business."

Donna paused, shifting slightly on the sofa.

"Anyway, a couple of days later, an attorney marches into our office demanding to know what is contained in that manuscript, says his client has concerns about the contents and like that. Of course, Nathan says no, but agrees to discuss the matter with our client with the possibility of letting this attorney review the manuscript before hand."

Donna stopped and looked over at Toni, smiling. "Do you know you are as beautiful as ever? I do think about you a lot."

Toni smiled, reaching over and patting her hand. "Thank you. Please continue."

Donna took a breath. "So, the next night a couple of goons come into the office, strip me to my panties, make Nathan and I take some pictures like that, demanding we turn over the manuscript. Of course Nathan refuses and in the confusion, with a 9 mil pointed at both of us, they manage to drug both of us and ultimately trash the office, presumably looking for that manuscript."

Donna could see Toni tense up. Raising her hand Donna smiled.

"Not to worry, put one in the short guy's nuts and gave him a good shot to the face, he'll remember me that's for sure."

Toni smiled. Donna continued.

"So now Nathan has had enough. He called in Jason to do some digging. Oh yeah, I almost forgot, they bugged the office, but Jason cleaned it that night."

Donna paused. Toni stood up.

"I'm sorry dear, would you like something to drink? I could fix you something."

Donna raised her hand. "Water would be just fine right now."

Toni nodded, walking over to a small fridge, opening it and removing a bottle of water. "Glass?"

Donna shook her head no. Toni came back to the sofa and handed her the water. She opened the bottle and took a long gulp. "Thanks."

Toni noticed she was staring at her. "What?"

"You have such wonderful legs, and that skirt simply doesn't do them justice."

Toni stood up, pulling the skirt up to her waist, exposing her while lace panties. Climbing back on the sofa, she pulled one leg up under her.

"That better?"

"Much."

Donna took one more drink before continuing.

"Well, just when we thought it couldn't get any weirder, the gentleman we turned the project over to, went ahead and made contact with the fifth name on that list. Get this, two days before the guy died."

Donna paused shaking her head. Toni remained silent. Donna continued.

"We asked him to meet with us to give him an update on what had happened, but he is the one with all the details. Seems this fifth name served with them as well. Wait a minute, let me backup a bit. The list was made up with some of the guys that were on some rogue helicopter flight back in Vietnam. That seemed a little suspicious to them at the time."

Donna paused but before Toni could ask, Donna continued after a quick sip of water.

"Well, long story short if that is possible. Let me get right to the bottom line. On that helicopter mission, or what ever it was, the flight had two characters we both know and love, besides our former and current clients, there was Robert Swift, known to them as Swifty, a deal maker and the Pilot of the Helicopter, the one and only Reginald Harrison!"

"Our Reginald Harrison, Congressman Reginald Harrison?"

"That be him."

They both sat silent for a moment. Toni looked at Donna.

"What was so special about that mission, or whatever it was?"

Donna took another sip of water, her excitement building. Waving her hand holding the bottle, she continued.

"Well, according to this Magalito, that was the fifth name. This Magalito was in on it by the way. Basically that trip was a drug run, specifically two ten pound boxes of heroin that Swift, of course made a killing on, but a larger box was carried out by the Pilot and was full of stolen Jade from some temples that Magalito said he was sure the Pilot got out of the country."

"Jade?"

"Yeah, during some battle some temples got looted and these statuettes or whatever were taken."

"And you're sure that was Reggie?"

"Yes, we believe so now based on the information that was gathered and well it all makes sense. You have a dying man's testimony to that incident and the details that our current client remembered. Plus we saw the letter that our former client wrote to each man on the list detailing that incident. This Magalito only gave our client the name of the Pilot because he was dying, said he didn't care anymore, but he also warned our client never to mention that name again, but to keep it for future reference, should he ever need it. Yeah we're pretty sure it was Harrison."

Toni nodded. "And your client told you because?"

"We convinced him the name would stay with us, attorney client privilege, you know, that the name would be safe with us."

Toni nodded, smiling. "And me?"

"Of course, you had to know."

Toni reached over rubbing Donna's leg "And it will stay with me."

Donna smiled putting her hand on Toni's hand pulling her hand higher up her leg, but Toni pulled her hand away. Donna waved her hand in the air.

"Besides who else would care about a forty year old incident that can't be proven in the best of times."

Toni nodded, pointing. "Do you know what is in that manuscript, could it hurt him?"

Donna shook her head no, taking another sip of water.

"Not specifically. We understand that it covers a battle or something during the Civil War, that our deceased client believes involved the deaths of several members of his family. It's a historical thing, nothing to do with Vietnam or any of that. At present, our current client is unaware of any of this intrigue unfolding around him and this manuscript and we'd like to keep it that way. We're hoping you can help us protect our client."

Donna paused, pointing in the air with the water bottle.

"We told him it is probably some legal issue that we would deal with and that we would take care of everything. He believes it is a Civil War thing and Nathan thinks it best to keep it that way, absolutely nothing to do with Vietnam, the Congressman or that day. That is why we felt it prudent to speak with the Congressman directly to convince him of that. That there is absolutely no threat to him, should he be the one concerned."

Toni nodded. "So what is it you need from me?"

"Need from you? Slide over her and I'll show you what I need."

Toni smiled. "Let me rephrase. What do you need me to do?"

Toni raised her hand in the air. "Tell me what you want?"

Donna smiled fluttering her eyebrows before continuing.

"What I want?"

Toni smiled. "I am pretty sure I know what you want, but let's get back to the Congressman, shall we?"

"We would like you to set up a private meeting with Congressman Harrison and our operative Jason, to explain to the Congressman that there is nothing in the manuscript that concerns him, basically we would like him or his people, or whoever may be involved, to walk away from this. There is no threat to the Congressman what so ever."

"He'll deny any of this of course."

"Of course he will, but we just want to let him know he has nothing to be concerned about, only assuming he might be the one worrying, otherwise we don't think the harassment will stop, because it appears any concerns of his are truly misguided especially any that may be directed toward our client. We just want to assure him there is no threat coming from any of us, regardless of what we think we may or may not know."

Toni nodded, taking a moment.

"I believe I understand. What makes you think this meeting will do any good?"

"Because, if you set up the meeting, he'll have to listen."

"How soon do you want this to happen?"

"The sooner the better would be great."

Toni nodded, smiling again. "I'll call him in the morning, see what I can do. I'll let you know when the meet is set."

"You can do it that fast?"

Toni nodded, taking a deep breath before continuing.

"Reggie is going to run for Senate next year, he needs mine and my husband's endorsement, but more importantly he needs my backing, well my money, he'll do it if I ask him."

Donna smiled. "Thank you."

Toni raised her hand in the air waving it back and forth.

"I thought you were going to tell me Reggie was banging another cocktail waitress and got caught with his pants down again. Keeping Reggie in line is easy, keeping his dick in his pants is a full time job."

Donna laughed. "That bad, huh?"

Toni raised her hand in the air. Donna got up but in an instant was seated next to Toni in between her legs. She leaned in and kissed her gently.

"Anything I can do for you?"

Toni looked into her eyes. "How I wish."

"You know I'll do anything for you, anything."

Toni lightly pushed her away. She took a moment before speaking.

"I know you will, but I have to be careful these days, never know who has a camera. Please understand. Since my husband became so public, we can't go anywhere with out someone snapping a picture, or trying to get something and these damn phones. Everyone thinks they can just take a picture as they please."

"Even in your own house?"

"We have bodyguards now. There are two of them on the property at all times. Can't be sure someone won't walk in here for some reason or another. Privacy is quite a luxury these days."

Toni sighed heavily. "My husband and I always had an understanding, but we've both agreed to be ... well to curtail our extra curricular activities more so now than ever."

"Do you two still?"

"Believe it or not, yes."

"That's ..."

"Strange?"

"No, I was gonna say great."

Toni looked into her eyes, leaning forward. Donna leaned in kissing her deeply. She let her hand slide down to Toni's breast squeezing it gently through the fabric. Donna felt a hand slide up under her dress to the bottom of her panties. Just as quickly the hand was gone and Toni was pushing her away gently.

"As bad as I want to, I can't. Not here, not now."

"You can always come to my place."

Toni leaned in and kissed her. "If only?"

"Why not, two old friends getting together?"

Toni stayed close, her hand on Donna's cheek, the other on Donna's thigh.

"I travel with a driver now, actually one of the bodyguards. How would I explain that … how would?"

Toni was silent, letting her hand slide down to Donna's breast, fondling through the dress, leaning in for another deep passionate kiss, her other hand dabbling at the bottom of Donna's panties, Donna's hand rubbing across Toni's panties stopping just short. Toni broke the kiss and gently pushed Donna away.

"We can't, not here but soon I promise you, please understand?"

Donna nodded, she understood. She let Toni get up from the sofa and watched her as she straightened her skirt back down on her legs. She continued to watch, as Toni went to the desk in the room. She pulled something out of the drawer and picked up a pen. A moment later she was back on the couch next to Donna.

"Here's a check for twenty five thousand dollars made out to Nathan Simon Law Offices. Have Nathan set up a retainer account. I may need his services from time to time." Toni smiled, putting her hand on Donna's leg, sliding her hand up her thigh rubbing gently. "More likely, I may need your services from time to time. That should help explain our getting together on occasion."

Toni's hand reached the edge of Donna's panties and she slipped a finger under the band. Donna spread her legs to give her better access. Toni's lips were on hers.

"I've missed you so much, Lisa."

Donna returned the kiss sliding her hand up under Toni's skirt, resting her hand on Toni's panty clad butt. She hadn't heard that name in a long time. Toni got her the new name and identity, as well as an education. She arranged the interview with Nathan Simon. She gave her a life again. They broke the kiss and removed their hands from each other, taking a breath. Toni got up and sat across from Donna in the chair. She straightened the helm of her skirt. Donna did not move, her dress still hiked up in the front, exposing her panties and sighed.

"Lisa is a name I haven't heard in awhile."

"I'm sorry, slip of the tongue. For a moment ..."

"That's okay, I liked it."

Toni smiled. They sat silent looking at each other. "Anyone in your life these days?"

Donna nodded no. "Not really. Don't have the time."

"Some guy hasn't come along and swept you off your feet?"

"Some guy? Hell no."

"All right some girl then?"

"No, nothing like that."

"Then?"

"I manage."

"You and Nathan ever?"

"No, that would spoil all the fun. Besides he has a steady girl-friend who he really cares a lot about. We've become close, making sure Nathan stays in line, professionally and personally."

Toni let out a little chuckle. "I bet. Hey, I heard the story about the end of the interview you two had."

Donna laughed raising her hand and waving it in the air. Toni pointed.

"So tell me your side of the story. I've heard Nathan's."

Donna looked over at Toni. "Not unless you come sit by me."

She patted the sofa. Toni got up from the chair and sat next to her. Donna began.

"So we went through all the detail stuff, I showed him that I was qualified to do the job and we talked for a bit. He said 'oh hell, I'm tired of interviewing, you come highly recommended and I'm impressed with your skills, you got it if you want it,' which I said of course."

Donna turned, facing Toni full on.

"I stood up and started to strip. He immediately freaked out, yelling to stop he wasn't going to be set up and to get the fuck out of his office right now. You should have seen the look on his face."

Donna paused to laugh, Toni chuckled right with her.

"Okay so now I'm standing butt naked in front of him. He

doesn't know what to do. I stand there in front of his desk and calmly say. Here now you've seen me naked so you won't be wondering every day what I would look like naked. I do a little turn so he can see my butt. This way you won't be hanging over my desk, trying to get a look down my blouse, or watching me bend over, hoping to get a glimpse. My tits are right here for you to see in all their glory as is the rest of me, no more wondering what's underneath, you get to see it all."

Donna let out another laugh taking a moment.

"By this time I know he's thinking about it and no doubt wondering what to do next, so I offer it up. I tell him, if he felt the need to fuck me right now, that would be okay as well, you know get that out of the way, so he won't be wondering about that every day."

Donna paused laughing some more.

"I thought he was going to have a heart attack right then and there. But I tell him this would be a one-time offer, if he said no, there wouldn't be a second chance. Much to my surprise, he did say no."

Donna paused, taking a moment before continuing.

"You know, I really appreciated that. What man would refuse a free fuck from a woman standing naked … right in front of him?"

Donna waved her hand in the air.

"Anyway, I proceeded to sit back in the chair, naked of course and told him the rest—basically that I do prefer woman as a rule, but I am not opposed to the right man. He just sat there nodding. I think he was so dumbfounded, he didn't know what to say or do."

"And then?"

Donna looked at Toni, taking her hand.

"I calmly got dressed, sat back in the chair and said that famous line."

Toni smiled—she had heard the line before, but wanted to hear it from Donna. Donna raised her hand in the air.

"I said. Okay, now that we got all that sexual tension out of the air we can get to work."

Toni smiled squeezing Donna's hand. "That's priceless."

"It's all about the chase. Most men like the chase better than the conquest, you told me that. So if he sees me naked right out of the gate, there is nothing left to pursue, nothing to try to see, no more wondering what I would look like naked, so we can get down to business."

Toni shook her head. The clock in the room chimed, they both looked at the hands standing straight up showing midnight.

"Wow, it's late. My first thought is to ask you to stay over, but ... would you like one of my men to escort you home?"

"No, that is not necessary ... yes, I do?"

Toni looked at Donna, her eyes questioning.

"Yes, let your man bring me home then he'll have to come get me in the morning to bring me back to get my car, or better yet, you drive my car back to my place and we can ..."

"You're priceless. I opt for the former. I let him escort you home tonight bring you back here in the morning and we can have breakfast together."

"Done."

Donna watched her walk to the phone on the desk.

"He'll have the car around front in ten minutes."

"Then we better not waste any time."

Donna planted another deep passionate kiss on her, pulling her close. Toni's hands gripped Donna's buttocks, holding the kiss, finally pushing her away.

"You're incorrigible."

"Yes I am, but as I remember you liked it that way."

Toni smacked her on the butt.

Donna wiggled it. "Ewww, are we gonna get rough now?"

"Out."

Toni pointed to the door. Together they walked into the foyer. Opening the front door they discovered the town car was already parked in front.

"Tell Mr. Simon, I'll speak with him on Monday to work out the details. Thank you for coming by tonight. I'm sorry we ran so late. My driver will see you home. Somebody will be by in the morning to bring you back to get your car. Tell Mr. Simon thanks again."

Toni waved. Donna waved back, smiling as she slid into the back seat. She knew that whole conversation was for the driver's benefit. Still she did have a twenty five thousand dollar check in her clutch. The man closed her door, climbed into the driver's seat and said softly.

"Where to, miss?"

Donna told him where and gave him directions. Upon arriving, he was out of the car, opening the door for her. He walked her to her door and waited until she was inside. She closed the door and leaned back against it, a tingling crossing her body.

"Breakfast should be fun."

She unzipped the dress and was out of it before she hit the bedroom. Sitting on the bed she dialed Nathan's number. A sleepy voice answered.

"Yeah, hello."

"Nathan, its Donna."

"Yeah. Hey, how did it go?"

"She said she'd do it for us?"

"That's great. Did you two have fun?"

"Not as much as we're going too."

There was silence on the line.

"Nathan are you there?"

"Yeah, just trying to digest that last comment."

"I'll keep you posted on when the meet is."

"Great, now get some sleep. I'm going back to bed. Good night."

Donna heard the phone disconnect. Still holding the phone in her hand she felt it go off. Not recognizing the number she cautiously answered.

"Hello."

"Just making sure you got home safe and sound."

"I did, thank you and really thank you for your help."

"My pleasure."

"It will be."

"Good night."

"Good night, Toni."

THE KITTRIDGE MANUSCRIPT

Donna set the phone on the nightstand. Smiling, she removed her underwear and slipped on the oversize t-shirt she wore to bed. Climbing under the covers she rested her head on the pillow. Sleep took a while, her mind racing in all directions.

THIRTEEN

Jeff Morgan stepped out of the shower to the smell of freshly brewed coffee. Dressing quickly, he left the bedroom and walked into the kitchen. Sandy was sitting at the table, dressed in a t-shirt and sleeping shorts, her hair tied back in a bun, holding a steaming cup in her hands.

"Well, good morning. I have coffee brewed, unless you drink decaf? I could brew a cup of that for you."

"Good morning yourself. Yes, I do prefer decaf. I still need the illusion, but I can't handle the reality."

"Really?"

"Yes, I gave up caffeine some time ago. You know, just cause."

"Just give me a minute."

Jeff watched her retrieve a small coffee maker from the cabinet. She put the grounds in and pushed the button. "This just takes a minute, makes two cups."

She proceeded to pour the decaf into the cup on the counter that she then carried to the table and set down in front of him.

"There's cream and sugar on the table. I tried to catch you before you got dressed. I wanted to offer you a pair of Bob's boxers. They're clean, rather than yesterday's undies."

Jeff looked at her, holding his cup mid-rise, his mouth already open, but set the cup back down and smiled.

"I thank you kindly, but I'll be okay in these."

She shrugged her shoulders.

"Suit yourself. So, what would you like for breakfast? I've got eggs, some bacon, or sausage. I could make you French toast. I think I even have some pancake batter, if you are in the mood for those."

Again, Jeff looked at her, his cup in mid air. This time he took a sip first.

"Whatever you're having is fine with me."

"I was leaning toward the bacon and eggs, haven't had those in awhile and you give me a good excuse to cook them up."

"Sounds good to me."

Jeff noticed she didn't make a move to get up, sitting there holding her cup in her hands.

"It's not fair."

Jeff looked at her.

"You know he's gonna die. You know it's just a matter of days, hours, but you hope for another day, another hour."

Jeff saw the tears form in her eyes, then slowly run down her cheek. She made no attempt to stop them or wipe them away.

"When it's long term, you seem to ride with it, but once he entered the end-of-life facility, you know. You go there every morning hoping to see him again and you leave every night, just knowing this night you will get the call that it is over and when you don't, you put on the happy face and walk into the room the next morning, ready to do it another day, all the time knowing every minute he lays there the suffering continues. You can't even imagine the pain he is in."

She paused, the tears now a steady stream. Jeff wanted to get up to go to her, but he wasn't sure what to do. She continued.

"And when that day finally comes, you have a sense of relief, not sadness. Sure, it hurts, you know he's gone, but you also realize that he is no longer suffering and really that is a good thing. The sadness comes in the days to follow when you realize he really is gone. You can no longer visit him even in that terrible condition. Then it hits you, he's really gone."

Jeff's stomach was in knots, he knew exactly what she meant, having gone through the exact same thing with his wife. He looked away for a moment, trying to rein in his own emotions. He heard the cup hit the table. She had dropped it, putting her hands to her face, sobbing. Jeff got up, righting her cup, before pulling her out of the chair, holding her tight, letting her sobs bury deep into his shoulder. She held on just as tight, shaking as another wave racked her body. He didn't know how long he held her, but it didn't matter, she was there for him last night, he would stay with her for as long as she needed. Slowly she pulled away, placing both her hands on his shoulders.

"I guess it was my turn this morning. How do you do it?"

Jeff rubbed her back, while he spoke very softly. "I don't. I just take it a day at a time."

"Does the pain ever go away?"

"No."

"Great, now I have that to look forward to."

Although not the least bit funny, they both started to laugh. Finally she pulled away.

"Oh darn, I got makeup all over your shirt. I'm sure I have one that will fit you."

"Don't worry about it. Remember I'm still in yesterday's undies."

They laughed again.

"Well if you don't want Bob's, I can always give you a pair of mine. Nothing fancy, basic white cotton panties, I believe the kids call them granny panties."

Jeff looked at her for a moment. "Really, I'm fine."

"I must look a mess, excuse me for a minute."

Jeff watched her leave the kitchen and sat back down at the table. As he started to reach for his coffee cup, he noticed his hand shaking. Everything she had said was so very true. You do wait for the day to happen and when that day comes you are filled with a sense of relief, knowing her suffering is over, the pain is finally gone, but before you have a chance to recover, you are overwhelmed with the unbearable sadness of having lost her.

"Hopefully that's better. Not much I could do with my eyes, but the makeup is back in place. I really am sorry about your shirt."

Jeff was brought back to reality. Wiping another tear from his eyes, he perked back up.

"That's okay, really, forget about it. How about those eggs?"

"Coming right up."

Jeff continued to sip his coffee, while she went about preparing breakfast.

"I wish there was more I could tell you about Bob's project, but that's all I really know."

Jeff was thankful for the change in topics. They discussed the project some more, but both understood their thoughts were really with their lost loved ones. No more needed to be said. An awkward silence or two said it all. They finished breakfast and he helped her clean up.

"Well, I better get on the road."

"Can I call you if I think of anything?"

"Absolutely. And may I call you if I have any questions?"

"Absolutely."

Sandy walked Jeff to the door. They hugged each other one more time before he left.

———————— /// ————————

Sitting in the driver's seat, he took one last deep breath. Visiting with Sandy had been emotional on so many levels, but he also felt a sense of relief from spending time with someone that understood. He opened the carry case to put her directions in and saw the directions to Herb Miller's farm on the top of the pile.

"Why not?" He said out loud. Dialing the number, he waited for an answer.

"Hello."

"Hello Herb, I mean Mr. Miller."

"Yes, this is Herb Miller."

"Mr. Miller, this is Jeff Morgan, we spoke the other day about the bureau?"

"Yes, I remember. You still want to come see it?"

"Yes. Yes, I do. That is why I am calling. I am in downstate Illinois this morning, half way to your place. I was wondering if I could come by this afternoon? I believe I am about three hours away."

"This afternoon you say. Sure, I'll be here. What time do you think you'll be here?"

"It's just after ten, I would guess around one."

"That would be fine. Have to run an errand, should be back by then, if not just wait."

"No problem. Okay, I'll leave now, see you at one."

"Right, bye now."

The line disconnected. Jeff ran his hands across his face. Setting the carry case on the passenger's seat, he placed the directions on top. Firing up the engine, he pulled out of the parking lot.

———————— /// ————————

At five after one, he pulled into the dirt driveway leading to Herb Miller's house. He drove for a ways to reach the front of the house which was set far off the road. Off to the side he could see a big red barn. He stopped the car in front behind a well used, beat up pickup truck, cut the engine and got out. A man sitting on the front porch swaying in a rocker waved him over.

"Herb? Excuse me, Mr. Miller?"

"Herb is fine."

The man got out of the chair and made his way down the stairs. They shook hands.

"Follow me."

Jeff walked behind him to the barn. He seemed rather sprite for his age. Without hesitation, he pulled open the big doors, dodging the dust that swirled up from the door being moved. Jeff wasn't so lucky, he caught a face full.

"Sorry about that. Don't go in here very much anymore."

Jeff nodded, still waving his hands in front of his face he followed Herb inside.

"Well, there it is."

Jeff looked to where the old man was pointing, but all he saw was a pile of wood and what have you, stacked against the wall. The old man noticed Jeff staring blankly and proceeded to pull some of the items away. Slowly the outline of something big underneath all this debris stacked there, started to surface. A few more pieces later the form of what appeared to be a large piece of furniture came into view.

Herb stepped back, while Jeff stepped around him.

"Been there eighty years or more. Can't tell you how many times I thought of busting it up for firewood. Yep, many times."

Jeff looked at him, but Herb smiled and pointed.

"Too much trouble to get it out."

Jeff nodded, as he made an effort to uncover more of it.

"What are you thinking of doing with it now?"

Herb walked closer dusting off the pitted top.

"Don't rightly know. But I'll tell you what, you get it out of there you can have it."

"Really?"

Herb nodded. "I have no use for it, seems you boys have an interest, so why not?"

Jeff pointed. "I might have to have some people come in and get it."

Herb raised his hand. "Got just the feller to do that for you. Him and his son run a moving storage business locally here. I could give him a call, see what he thinks."

"That would be great."

"Com'on."

Jeff followed Herb back into the house. Herb opened a top cabinet drawer and pulled out a card. Walking over to the dial phone on the wall, he circled the digits.

"Tom, you boys working today?" Herb smiled as he spoke. "I know its Saturday, that's why I figured you might be out at the fishing hole."

Herb looked over at Jeff this time as he talked into the receiver. "What's that, yeah I'm doing good. Say listen, I got a guy here needs a piece of furniture moved out of my barn back to his house, you boys interested?" Herb nodded yes still facing Jeff. "Fine, yeah he's here now. Sure. About an hour?" Herb looked over at Jeff, who nodded yes. "Says that's fine, see you then, sure thing. Thanks, Tom."

Herb hung up the phone. He walked over and placed the card back in the drawer, but took out a pad and paper from that drawer and wrote something on it. He tore off the top page and placed that paper on the table next to where Jeff was standing.

"You got a dollar son?"

Jeff looked at Herb nodding yes. "Sure."

"Well, let me have it. That there paper is a bill-of-sale, you just bought yourself that bureau."

Jeff handed the dollar to Herb. "I don't understand?"

Herb Miller waved his hand in the air.

"I learned the hard way, you can't just give anything away anymore, without somebody wanting to know the why and wherefore. My attorney told me to always do a bill-of-sale for everything, no matter I'm selling it or buying it, there's yours."

Jeff watched Herb Miller put the dollar bill in his shirt pocket. He folded the bill-of-sale in quarters and stuck it in his shirt pocket. Herb pointed to the clock as he spoke.

"Well, we got an hour we can sit out on the porch and wait for them boys to get here. Would you care for something cold to drink?"

"Water would be fine."

Herb nodded. He retrieved a glass from the drainer on the sink, walked over to the fridge, put some ice cubes in the glass, walked back to the sink and filled it with water.

"Don't have any of that bottled stuff, get mine straight from the well."

Jeff nodded as he took the glass from him. Not sure what to do next, he watched Herb leave the kitchen and followed him out to the porch. Herb took his seat in the rocker. Jeff took a wooden chair on the other side. It wobbled a bit as he sat down, but seemed to be solid enough.

"What can you tell me about that piece?"

Herb looked his way, nodding. "I got it when the ladies passed back in '33."

"The ladies?"

Herb nodded. "Sisters. Owned the place next to this one. Spinsters, my dad called them. Died within two weeks of each other. When one went, the other one went right behind her. Younger one went first. Lived on that land nearly all their life."

Jeff took a sip of the water. It was refreshing and flavorful, for water. Herb continued.

"I used to help them out when I was a kid, easier to cross their land to get to school, started helping around the place as they got older. They insisted on paying me. Real nice ladies. We'd sit on the porch at dusk and they'd tell me stories about their life."

"Do you remember any of it, I mean anything interesting?"

"Oh sure."

Herb scratched his nose, shooing a fly away. "Told me they came from Virginia near the end of the Civil War." Herb paused, looking over at Jeff. "Can you beat that? That long ago. Just little kids then.

Herb paused and sat back in his rocker. In a moment he continued.

"Said they came by wagon, settled in town at first. They always told me with a sly smile that there was a man with their mother that wasn't their father, which was a big deal to them little girls. Hell, big deal for the town back then as well. A woman traveling with a man not her husband."

Herb let out a little laugh, scratching his stubble before he continued.

"Said the man up and left their mother about a year later, left her high and dry. The mother had a job at the local dry goods store, sewing, cleaning that sort of thing. Well, the couple that owned that store was killed in a buggy accident of some kind left the store to her. She ran it for five or ten years, I don't remember which. Well, some big outfit came along and bought the place. She used that money to fix up the piece of property she owned, even built a nice house on the land. Had a couple of cows for milk, planted a garden basically lived off the land. The mother died in the 1890s, leaving the two girls alone."

Herb paused again, thinking for a moment.

"I 'spect the girls had to be in their thirties by then, but being isolated for so long, they just stayed on the land, never socialized much."

Herb looked around the area in front of him and pointed.

"My parents built this place, helped the girls out when they needed it. Once I was old enough, they would send me over to tend to their needs."

Herb sat for a spell not saying anything. Jeff sipped his water, waiting.

"Funny thing was, I didn't understand their not having men folk around. Shows you how dumb I was."

Herb let out a hearty laugh. "Hell, I was only sixteen when they died. Lucky I knew my name at that age." Herb let out another belly laugh. "Be ninety-six, next month, still don't know shit."

The laughter continued. Even Jeff let out a smile.

"Anyway, after the ladies passed, I find out from some legal feller that I own the place, and all their belongings. My father sat me down and explained it to me. We kept that parcel separate in my name, but tended to it as if it was theirs, my parents that is."

Herb rubbed his stubble looking into the distance.

"I went over there to have a look inside the house. My mom came with me to help go through their things. It was all woman stuff, my mom kept some, the rest we donated to the church."

He rubbed his stubble again.

"My father knew a man in town that dealt with those kinds of things, so he came out and bought most of their furniture, except for a couple of pieces my mom wanted, which my father brought over in the truck. The man took everything else except that piece in the barn."

This time Herb turned to face Jeff directly.

"Said it was one of the ugliest pieces he ever saw, said he couldn't imagine anyone having it in their house. I told him, I remember the ladies used it as a sideboard, you know for dishes and linens, but they had told me the piece was their mother's bureau, you know dresser for her clothes."

Herb cast his glance back forward.

"To this day I don't know why, but I decided since nobody else wanted it, I was gonna keep it. It took everything my dad and I had to get that damn thing in the truck. In fact we left it there over night right there in the truck and wrestled it out the next morning. My dad was too tired to move it into the house let alone my room, but he needed to use the truck, so we pushed it into the barn for the time being and by God it never left there."

Herb paused wagging his finger.

"After both my parents died, I consolidated the properties into one and we moved into this house. By then that bureau was already buried and I just never had a hankering to pull it out." Herb leaned over smiling. "Don't think the misses would have wanted anything to do with that thing no how."

Herb took a moment pointing in the distance.

"I actually lived on their land, well my land with my wife when I was younger. She fixed up that little house there real nice for us."

They heard the sounds of tires crunching on the road and looked out to see a shiny new white pickup truck pulling in behind Jeff's car.

"That would be Tom and his son."

Herb got up from his rocker and Jeff followed him down the stairs.

"Tom, this here is Jeff Morgan, he's the feller I told you about. Jeff, Tom, that's his son Junior over there."

Jeff shook hands with Tom and waved to Junior.

"So Herb, what do we have needs moving?"

"Follow me."

Herb led the group back to the barn, taking them inside and stopping in front of the half exposed bureau.

"Been there over eighty years. Told Jeff here, if he could get it out, he could have it. That's where you boys come in."

"To do what exactly?"

Jeff looked at Herb, then Tom before answering. "I was hoping to get it out of there and have it delivered to my place."

"Where's you place?"

"About six hours from here in Illinois."

Tom nodded. "You really want that?"

"Actually no, but an old Army buddy of mine died recently and he thought this might be an important piece of his family history … well I just thought I would get it home and decide what to do with it after that."

Herb put his hand on Jeff's shoulder. "Like I said you get it out, you can have it to do whatever you want with it. Besides you own it now."

Tom nodded, pointing as he walked closer.

"Junior, get around that end, see if we can lift it."

Fighting to get into position, Junior worked his way to the side and tried to budge the piece, but it held fast.

"We need to get all this stuff out of the way first get a better go at it."

All four men set about moving items from on top and around the buried bureau. Finally, when they felt there was enough clearance they tried again. This time they were able to budge it and move it away from the wall.

"Boy, that's sure one ugly piece of furniture."

They all looked at Junior, but he just shrugged his shoulders. Tom nodded, pointing.

"That's not too far from the truth. You sure you want this?"

Jeff nodded yes. Tom walked around it and nodded a few times.

"I'm looking at twelve hundred to load, transport and come back dead head."

"Twelve hundred?"

"You got at least three hundred in gas, two men twelve hours on the road, load and unload, twelve hundred is the best I can do."

Jeff looked at Tom, then back at the bureau.

"That's a little out of my league, I was hoping for a lot less."

"Herb what do you think?"

"Well, Tom, I'd just be happy to get it out of here."

"Junior, get the tape measure out of the truck."

They waited while Junior fetched the tape. Tom ran the tape long ways and short, taking the measurements.

"Here's what I can do. This thing will just about fit in the back of the pickup. We'll put a tarp over it and hall it up to your place … let's say seven-fifty off the books, no insurance, no safeguard. It gets scratched or chipped it's on you. Anything happens it's on you."

"Seven hundred and fifty dollars delivered?"

"Cash, no paperwork, off the books."

"I'll take it."

Tom nodded. "One more thing, Jeff. It has to be cash, tomorrow's Sunday, can you get cash by tomorrow?"

"Tomorrow, you'll deliver it tomorrow?"

"Yes, we'll leave at four in the morning, be at your place by ten, so we can get back home by dark. Don't want to burn a workday on this for that kind of money. That work for you?"

"Yes."

"You'll have the cash?"

"Absolutely."

"Then let's get this beast on the truck."

Junior left to pull the truck as close as possible. Tom rolled out a couple of moving blankets, spreading one across the tailgate.

"The best way to load this is to turn it upside down and slide it in on its top."

The men nodded.

"Let me and Junior have a stab at it first, see what we can do."

Jeff and Herb stood back as the two men turned the bureau on its side then onto its top setting it down on the second moving blanket. They each took a side and lifted one end up to the tailgate. Walking around the other side, Junior lifted the other end in the air as his dad guided the piece into the bed of the truck. With a loud grunt, Junior had the piece in the air and the two men slid it the rest of the way in. The bureau was now sitting upside down inside the bed of the pick up. Tom tried and successfully closed the tailgate. They next placed a tarp over the piece and secured it to the sides. Checking for stability, they both nodded they were satisfied. Tom jumped down.

"Okay, we're good to go here. See you at your place tomorrow at ten."

Tom and Jeff shook hands.

"Thank you, do you need any money now?"

"Nope, we'll take the seven-fifty tomorrow and please, cash."

"I'll have it. Thanks again."

Herb and Jeff watched as the heavily loaded truck crawled down the dirt road.

"Well Herb, I'd like to thank you for an enjoyable afternoon. Thanks for the info and the update on the sisters."

"Appreciate the company, don't get many visitors anymore. Fine way to spend a Saturday afternoon."

"Well, I better get going, I've got a long drive ahead."

"You take care now. Hope you enjoy the bureau. Remember you bought it, that thing is yours now. Good luck."

Jeff climbed into his car and backed up to clear Herb's truck. Pulling away from the house he made his way down the dirt driveway. He saw Herb waving in his rear view mirror.

FOURTEEN

The sound of a telephone ringing woke her up. Realizing it was the landline, she sat up in bed and stretched to grab the receiver.

"Hello."

"Donna, it's Nathan. Are you awake?"

"No."

"Listen, I need you in the office this morning."

"What? Why? It's Saturday …"

"Listen, we have the William's hearing on Monday."

"The William's …what?"

"Donna."

"Yeah, okay." Donna sat up in bed, transferring the phone to her left ear. "Okay, okay. What's this all about?"

"I said we have the William's hearing on Monday and we need to prepare."

"So why today?"

"With all that other stuff going on, we missed this. I need you to help organize the files that were trashed, specifically the one for him."

"Can't we do that tomorrow?"

"No, the client is coming in this morning to go over his testimony. He called me early this morning from the airport in Florida, said he might be a little late for the meeting, which gives us time to get our act together."

"But I have plans for this morning."

"Sorry, darling, see if you can change them to tomorrow. I really need you on this one."

"Yeah, okay, how soon do you want me there?"

"Now."

"Yeah right, give me an hour."

"Okay, but that will only give us a couple of hours."

"We'll be fine, see you in an hour."

"Thanks. You're the best."

"Yeah, yeah. Wait, listen Nathan, I just remembered you're going to have to pick me up, I left my car … I don't have my car this morning."

"I'll be right there."

"No, give me at least a half hour to get ready."

"You're fine the way you are…"

"Nathan."

"Okay, I'll be out front in a half hour."

"Good bye, Nathan."

Donna put the receiver in the cradle, got off the bed and headed to the bathroom. A nice long morning pee gave her a moment to focus. Washing her hands off she looked in the mirror. "Ponytail today." she said out loud.

Walking back to the bed, she sat down and retrieved her cell phone off the nightstand. She hesitated a moment, then dialed the number.

"Hello."

"Toni, it's Donna."

"Donna, I've been thinking about you."

"Sorry Toni, I have some bad news."

There was silence on the line. Donna sighed and continued.

"Listen, Nathan just called, he needs me to come into the office this morning, client is coming in … I'll have to cancel our breakfast. Any chance we can do this tomorrow?"

"No, I'm afraid not. I'm leaving for New York in the morning. He's sending the jet back. Says he needs me to be there for those meetings on Monday."

Once again there was silence on the line. Finally Toni spoke. "Donna?"

"Yes. Yes, I'm here. When will you be back?"

"Hopefully, end of the week."

"Well, maybe we can get together then."

"Yes we will, I promise. I'm already thinking of things I need to discuss with Nathan that I'm sure you could take care of."

"I'll be there to give you anything you need."

"Donna, it was so good seeing you last night ... It was ... Well, I look forward to our next meeting."

"As do I. Have fun in New York, call me if you need to talk."

"I will. Until then."

"Oh Toni, I'll call you later about my car."

"No need, I'll have my driver deliver it to Nathan's office."

"That would be great. How about you drive it, stop up and your driver can take you back?"

"I'll see what I can do."

"See you then."

"Donna, I'll try."

"Good bye, Toni."

"Bye."

Donna set her cell phone on the nightstand. Noticing the clock she realized she would only have twenty minutes, before Nathan was downstairs. Pulling the t-shirt over her head, she rushed into the bathroom and turned on the shower. One more glance in the mirror confirmed her earlier thought, ponytail for sure.

———————— /// ————————

She climbed into Nathan's car and buckled up without saying a word. Nathan patted her leg. "I really am sorry, but we've been so involved with all that other shit, we missed this. If he didn't call me this morning, I wouldn't have remembered either. You know, I wouldn't ask if it wasn't important. Besides, you're the only one who can put that file together. I just hope it's all there."

Donna smiled, turning slightly in her seat facing him. She put her right hand on his chest, rubbing little circles. He looked down at her hand for a moment, but quickly back to the road in front of him. She spoke seductively.

"That's okay, you will owe me big time for this and I'm already thinking about how to collect."

"Huh? What do you mean?"

Donna turned back in the seat, facing forward and said matter-of-factly.

"I'm going to need some time off for a little vacation and you're going to say okay without any questions."

Nathan turned slightly to look at her, the smile spread wide across her face.

"That sounds a little devious."

"You have no idea."

Nathan pulled into the parking lot of the office building. Shortly they walked into the office.

Donna walked straight to his office. "You said the William's file right?"

"Yes."

"I'll start on that and you put the coffee on."

"Deal."

An hour later they were sitting on Nathan's sofa, reviewing the final thoughts.

"I think we got it." Looking at his watch, Nathan commented. "He should be here shortly."

Donna got up from the sofa, stretching. They heard a knock on the door. Sure it was too early for the client to be there, they looked at each other. A moment later the door opened and Antoinette Ri-chard stuck her head in.

"I'm sorry, am I disturbing you?"

Nathan jumped off the sofa almost standing at attention.

"No, not at all. So good to see you Mrs. Richards."

Donna and Toni both smiled. Donna corrected him.

"It's Mrs. Ri-chard now, no S."

Nathan wanted to ask, but thought better of it.

"So, what brings you here on a Saturday morning?"

"Didn't Donna tell you?"

"Damn, I completely forgot. So busy with that thing this morning."

Donna turned to Nathan. "Mrs. Ri-chard gave me a check for twenty five thousand dollars last night to put on retainer for her. She will need us from time to time to help with certain matters."

Nathan was a bit puzzled by the us part, but stayed quiet. Donna continued.

"Nathan, I apologize, the check is in my other bag, with all the confusion this morning I forgot to bring it with me."

"No problem, we can't deposit it until Monday anyway. What sort of things are you referring to, Mrs. Ri-chard."

"Toni. I think we've known each other long enough that you can call me Toni."

Nathan smiled. "Where's my manners, please have a seat."

"No thank you, I can only stay for a moment."

Toni walked over to Nathan and spoke softly, directly to him, but glanced at Donna first.

"Matters of a discreet nature and that may involve Donna's help more than yours from time to time, but I wanted to make sure I compensated you for her time."

"Yes, or course, Toni, whatever you need, we'll be at your service."

"Thank you for understanding, Nathan. Now if I may, I'd like to steal Donna away for a moment, I have her car downstairs and I dare say I'm not sure it is parked in the right spot."

Toni stopped and turned to face Nathan, a smile forming on her face.

"One more thing, I understand you may have to incur some additional expenses regarding that other matter, so I authorize you to deduct those expenses from my retainer account as well."

Nathan smiled. "Thank you, that is very generous of you."

"Thank you Nathan, for handling that, good to see you again, we'll get together another time to discuss my requirements."

"Of course."

She stuck out her hand and Nathan shook it. She smiled and turned.

"Donna, shall we?"

Donna joined her and the two of them walked out the door into the inner office. Nathan let out a big sigh. As nice and pleasant as Antoinette Ri-chard was, she still was a very wealthy and very powerful woman. He was sure happy she was on their side, even though he dare not mention it. He slumped back down on the sofa and took a moment.

———————— /// ————————

Donna walked with Toni toward the elevator.

"Let's take the stairs, it's only four floors down."

Toni smiled and followed her lead.

"Toni, I'm so glad you came."

When they reached the first floor, Donna pulled on her arm.

"One more."

Toni followed her down another flight into the parking garage. They ducked into an alcove. Donna pointed.

"No cameras here."

Toni looked up and saw the blank wall.

"It's a blind spot away from the actual parking garage."

Toni nodded and before she could ask, Donna pinned her against the wall and kissed her passionately, savoring the moment. Toni responded wrapping her arms around her and pulling her close. A moment later, Donna broke the kiss and led her back up the stairs. Back at the first floor they exited the stairway.

"I needed to do that, but if we would have stayed any longer, clothes may have been torn off and well… there are better places to become reacquainted."

Toni smiled. "Thanks, I needed that as well. It will give me something to savor on my trip to New York."

"Call me when you get back?"

"As soon as I can."

They stepped out into the sun. The driver was leaning against the black town car. Donna's car was parked in front of that. He stood up when they appeared.

"Would you give her the keys, please?"

The driver handed the car keys to Donna. Cordially she and Toni shook hands.

"Tell Nathan thank you for seeing me on such short notice. When I realized you were at the office this morning, I thought I might steal a bit of his time and return your car myself. I'm glad it worked out."

"Mrs. Ri-chard, it is our pleasure. Thank you so much for bringing my car here to me this morning."

"Not at all. Good bye."

The door to the town car was opened and she slid inside. The driver closed the door, nodded to Donna, scampered around to the driver's side and climbed in. Donna watched the town car pull away. A moment later she climbed into her car and drove it into the parking garage.

———————— /// ————————

Nathan sat at his desk, reviewing the file, making some notes, when Donna walked back in. Without looking up he spoke softly.

"Just what is it that we are supposed to do for that twenty five grand?"

Donna smiled. He sat back in his chair looking at her.

"I see. Will you tell me if and when I might need to do something?"

Nathan smiled, he wasn't sure, but Donna may have blushed just then.

As if on queue, the door opened and the client walked in.

"Sorry I'm late."

———————— /// ————————

Shortly after two, they both sat there on the sofa. The client now gone, Nathan said it first.

"Shall we get something to eat?"

Donna looked at him. "Might as well."

"I'll join you."

They both looked over to see Jason standing in the doorway.

"You have something?"

"Let's get out of here first."

"You think?"

"No. Just hungry."

The two of them got off the sofa and followed Jason into the hallway, waiting while Donna locked up.

A short time later they were seated in a back booth of a diner down the street from the office. They waited until their orders were placed before getting into it. Jason leaned in.

"Okay, I got the two guys. They run a small private security firm. One's a retired cop. He's the one whose nuts you rearranged and the other is retired FBI. The cop was a good street cop until he got shot on the job, but then rode a desk for the rest of his tenure. The FBI guy was some sort of analyst."

Jason paused and noticed Donna smiling. He punched her on the arm.

"Anyway, the equipment was cheap, a basic nanny cam."

"Nanny cam?"

"Yeah, something anyone could pick up. Used a lot lately to watch the woman watching your kids."

Nathan nodded.

"As I said, not real sophisticated. Probably do a lot of divorce work, equipment like that would work for that. I'm going to watch them for a day or two, see what else they are up to, maybe catch them meeting with someone we'd be interested in."

The food arrived and they made small talk as they ate.

"You got this?"

Jason stood up and Nathan nodded. They watched him walk out the door. Nathan pushed his plate away.

"Donna, I don't mean to be indelicate, but I need to ask."

Donna looked at him.

"What did she say when you asked her to help us?"

Donna smiled. "Basically she wanted to know some background and what this was all about, which I explained to her. She apparently knows Reggie quite well."

"Reggie?"

"Yeah, that's how she referred to him."

Nathan smiled. "Did she say when?"

"No, but she said she'd set it up and let us know. I would imagine in the next few days. Unfortunately, she's flying to New York tomorrow."

"Is that what I interrupted?"

Donna looked at him. "Something like that."

"I truly am sorry."

Donna patted his hand. "Remember what I said. You owe me."

Nathan smiled, picking up the check. "Let's get out of here, finish up at the office and maybe we can salvage some of the day."

They left the dinner, went back to the office and decided they were good to go for Monday and closed up shop. Nathan walked Donna to her car, before going to his. Together they left the parking structure, going their separate ways.

FIFTEEN

Jeff Morgan poured the second cup of decaf and glanced up at the clock. There were still at least two hours before they would arrive with the bureau. He sat down at the kitchen table, the original papers still in their neat piles. Now the additional boot box of papers from yesterday sat on one of the chairs. Setting the cup down, he reached for that.

Opening the boot box, he lifted each document up and examined the one beneath it. Deciding he would index the pile first, he then stopped and closed the box. He wasn't ready to do that just yet. He still had to go through the documents on the table, the ones Bob Kittridge thought were more important to the project than whatever was in that box.

Sipping his coffee and drumming his fingers on the table, he looked at the pile and pulled the pad toward him. Professor Hathaway. She was the only one he hadn't talked to yet. Taking the pad with him, he went to his computer and powered up the machine. When it was ready, he selected his dial-up and waited while it connected, selecting his Internet search, then maps & directions. Punching in the school's address, he hit go. He had the map and directions to the campus, driving time approximately four hours. Grabbing those pages out of the printer, he placed them on top of the pad. Satisfied, he disconnected the dial-up, but left the computer on.

Walking away from the computer and back into the kitchen, he said out loud, "Looks like another road trip." He placed the pad and directions on the kitchen table. Against his better judgment, he poured a third cup of decaf and rinsed out the coffee maker. Then, as an afterthought, he dumped the coffee and rinsed the cup, placing it in the sink.

Once again, he sat back down at the table and pulled the research documents toward him, more to kill time than anything else. Finally it was ten o'clock. He opened the garage door and waited for the truck to arrive. At ten fifteen, the white pickup pulled into his driveway, then pulled back out, turned around and backed in the driveway. Junior was driving.

"Good morning, Jeff. We made it."

Jeff walked up to Tom and shook his hand. "Any problems?"

"No, in fact I think the wind at seventy miles an hour might have helped clean some of the dust and what have you, out of that thing."

Jeff nodded. Junior was opening the tailgate.

"What you figure we do with this?"

Jeff didn't understand at first, but then realized he meant after they unloaded the piece. "I think it best for now, to just stick it inside the garage, maybe let me clean it up a bit first."

Junior nodded. "We brought a dolly with us. We'll get it off the truck and wheel in it. Set it wherever you want."

Jeff nodded, watching them slide the bureau rearward out of the truck. Slowly, Junior let the piece down, with Tom sliding the four-wheel dolly underneath it. The two of them grabbed the balanced side and lifted that off the tailgate, using the dolly to slide it away from the truck. As Tom held the dolly in place, Junior pushed the piece further onto the dolly until it was balanced.

"Just tell us where."

Jeff walked into the garage, with Tom and Junior pushing behind him. Jeff's car was parked on the right side, leaving a space on the left where the second car would park.

"How about right here?"

Junior pushed the dolly into place. "Jeff, I wonder you might give us a hand? When we lift, you pull the dolly out from under."

Jeff got into position and once they had it up, he snatched the dolly from under and stepped back. Junior and Tom turned the piece on its side, setting it on the concrete floor. Together the two men flipped the piece so that it could be set down on its legs. Once down, Junior pointed.

"This way or do you want us to turn it?"

The piece sat long ways like it was a car parked there facing into the garage towards his car.

"That should be fine right there."

Junior waved. Tom wiped his brow.

"That beast is one heavy sum bitch. You be sure that where you want it before we leave?"

Jeff nodded. "Yeah, that's good, still get around and I can get to it as needed, I can always pull the car out if I need to."

Tom nodded pointing.

"Junior, put everything back in the truck, we're good."

Jeff motioned and Tom followed him into the garage. Jeff reached into his back pocket and removed a pile of folded bills. Tom took the pile and opened it, counting seven one hundreds, two twenties and one ten.

"Very good Jeff, we thank you for the business. Good luck with that ... well, whatever it is."

The two men shook hands. Jeff watched them tie down the material in the back of the truck. With a wave, they drove off, Tom driving this time. Jeff walked around the bureau, seeing the piece for the first time out of the barn and in the light of the day. The wood was pretty beat up on the top and sides, pitted mostly, but otherwise looked intact. It was a hard piece to describe, leaving him to wonder just how he would describe it to anyone.

Basically, it looked like a bunch of two by fours had been nailed together randomly There was no design to speak of, none of the detailing you would expect from the furniture of its day. The front had three slim top drawers, one large center drawer and two smaller side drawers. Below the side drawers were two doors. Below the top large center drawer were three wider center drawers.

He opened the left hand side top drawer, nothing in it but dust and debris, same content in the center and right hand side. He opened and removed the middle center drawers, stacking them on the side to air out. Next he opened both doors, each compartment contained a shelf and he left those open as well. It took a bit of work, but he managed to remove the top center drawer and place that on top of the other three drawers. Tom was right, the wind must have cleaned out a lot of the dust and debris and whatever else might have been inside.

He tried to remove the top left drawer, but it wouldn't come out. Bending down to look underneath, he saw rope attached to the back of the drawer, run through an eye hook attached to the back that then attached to the right hand side top drawer. He reached in and felt the rope. It wasn't rope but tightly woven twine that may have once been covered in a grease or lubricant of some sort, based on the dark color. Wondering what the hell that was all about, he pulled out the top right side drawer, watching the rope or twine tightened and stopped the drawer from coming all the way out. He went over to the left hand side drawer and pulled that one out. To his amazement, the right hand drawer closed equal to the distance the left one came out.

Because the distance was longer than he could reach, he could not operate the drawers together. He pushed the left hand drawer closed, walking over to the right, and opened that as far as it would go. Looking underneath, he saw the rope was taught. He closed that drawer and saw the rope was slack. He performed the same exercise on the left side, with the same results.

An epiphany hit him. "Of course." He said out loud. Scratching his head, he repeated himself. "Of course." He went inside and retrieved his pad and pen to make notes. On a fresh page, he described the make up of the bureau, noting the same things he thought about it, but when he came to the two drawers with the rope, he noted the following passage.

The two smaller top drawers could no doubt, be opened by small hands and know-

```
ing the weight of this piece, it could
have been dangerous for a child to play
with them. Whereas the center top drawer
would have been too heavy for a child
to open, these side drawers could be. It
appears a rope of some kind was installed
to prevent these two drawers from being
pulled out, as well as being opened
together. I may have just discovered a
very early version of child proofing a
drawer.
```

He finished the notation with several exclamation points and a question mark. Setting the pad on top of his workbench, he rubbed his hand across the top to feel the depth of the pitting. Thinking there was enough wood to withstand a good sanding, he felt confident it could be restored to a finished top. The sides were not nearly as pitted as the top and could be easily sanded.

But the big question was what to do with it. Maybe with some edge work and some trim it could be made to look … well, better. Jeff leaned against his car and looked at the beast in front of him. He smiled remembering back to Tom first calling the piece a beast.

Just then, another thought entered his mind. Jeff went back into the kitchen, retrieved the copy of the diary entries and went back to the garage. Again, leaning back against his car, he read over them until he found the line: *"one ugly bureau."* Could this really be that bureau? That would mean this thing was at least one hundred and fifty years old, probably older, give or take. Was this thing really in the wagon that day the Union Soldiers stopped that man and wife fleeing the war as the diary entry infers. He looked at the document again and the other line jumped out: *"Said they were on their way to Missouri."*

Jeff took a deep breath, folding his arms across his chest, the paper still in his right hand. He shook his head from side to side before saying out loud. "Hell this may be the story right here."

He set that paper on top his pad on the work bench, but then had a second thought and brought that paper back into the kitchen and placed it back in the pile.

Sitting like that with the drawers out and the side doors open, it looked much bigger, truly like a beast. Jeff smiled at the thought. He walked over to the stack of drawers, and removing each one from the pile, carried it to the trash can in the garage, tapping and dumping whatever was left in the drawer into the trash can.

Next he got a cloth and dampened it, wiping out each drawer. He then moved to the bureau, wiping out the inside of each compartment. Finally he opened the left top drawer, cleaning it as best he could, and repeated the process on the right side.

Once more he went inside and retrieved the copy of those diary entries and stepped back into the garage. Leaning against the car he read those lines again. Could this really be that bureau? Just the thought of having a piece of furniture from so long ago thrilled him, but the added fact of the potential history behind the piece made it all the more unique, especially if this really was that very bureau mentioned in those diary entries.

Jeff Morgan spent a few more minutes staring at his find before finally closing the garage door and walking back into the kitchen. Once again he placed the sheet of paper back into its proper pile.

SIXTEEN

"Yes, this is Antoinette Ri-chard calling for Congressman Harrison."

"Will he know what this is in regards to?"

"Just tell him Mrs. Ri-chard is on the line."

She waited for him to pick up.

"Toni, how are you? To what do I owe this honor?"

"Is there somewhere you can talk in private?"

"Yes."

She heard him muffle the phone and speak to his aides. "Will you give me a moment?" She heard a door close in the distance.

"Okay. I'm alone."

"Reggie, we have a situation."

"What situation?"

"There has been some commotion regarding a certain manuscript."

"Toni, I'm sorry, I'm not following."

There was silence on the line. Finally, Toni continued.

"Just let me finish. As I said, there has been some commotion regarding a certain manuscript that has come to my attention. I have been requested to set up a meeting between you and an operative of one of my attorneys."

She paused for effect. Reggie remained silent.

"Reggie, let me just say that I like you. I fully intend to support you in your run for Senate next year, which suggests my husband will be on board as well."

"Toni, aren't we being a little premature here? I haven't announced."

"Reggie, we both know you are running, whether you've announced or not, so let's not pretend."

"Okay, but I'm still not sure I know what you are referring to?"

"Let's just say, certain facts have come to my attention that suggest that you may have knowledge of such a thing. I wouldn't want anything to get in the way of your future plans. Let's just say, I'm doing this as much for you as I am the other party. Let's just say, I want you to take that meeting."

Again, silence on the line. Finally, Toni spoke again in a softer tone.

"Listen Reggie, this isn't another one of your cocktail waitress incidents, where you can just pay somebody off. There could be some serious allegations with this that would be quite hard to make go away, certainly during a campaign.

"Toni, I think you are out of line here."

"Reggie, I'm going to say this as plain as I can. If you want my husband's and more specifically my support behind you in your run for the Senate, you will take that meeting, otherwise I can't promise anything."

"So, you're saying I do the meeting, you'll back me?"

"Reggie, you know I've always liked you and I have always supported you, even getting my husband behind you these last two elections and I'll always be there for you, but you need to do this one for me."

"That important, huh?"

"You have no idea how important. I'm sticking my neck out here. I've been put in the middle and I don't like it one bit."

"Who is it, putting you in the middle?"

"We're not going there."

There was silence once again on the line before the Congressman finally responded.

"Okay, fine, if it is that important, I'll do it. When and where?"

"It has to be alone, no one else, he wants to meet in the open, no tricks and I will assure you there will be no tricks from his side."

Silence on the line again.

"Let me think ...okay, I've got a breakfast thing at the West River Country Club on Thursday morning at eight. Have your man meet me there at seven, we can walk out on the course, should give us open privacy."

"Sounds doable, I'll pass that along. If you don't hear from me, assume it's on."

"Will you be there?"

"No, I'm in New York with my husband this week."

"Toni, I'd sure like to know more before I meet."

"Reggie, I believe you already know a lot. Remember this is a meeting to work out certain things, nothing more. Do you understand?"

"Yes."

"Good, when we are back in town, we all must have dinner, do some face time with my favorite candidate."

"That sounds more appealing."

"One last thing, Reggie, this is for your benefit as much as theirs."

"Got it. Look forward to getting together with you soon."

"Goodbye, Reggie."

Toni smiled as she disconnected the line. She had always liked messing with Reggie's head. Still smiling she then dialed Nathan Simon's number. He answered immediately.

"Nathan, it's Toni. I just spoke with our mutual friend. The meet is set for Thursday at seven am at the West River Country Club. Private but open, just like you asked. Have your man there."

"I will tell him and may I personally say, thank you?"

"Nathan, no funny business, have you man present your case and let it be. Remember, Reggie is a close friend of mine, I won't tolerate anything less."

"Yes, of course, I fully understand."

"Nathan?"

"Yes?"

"You're sure it's him. I mean, no doubt?"

Nathan relaxed, taking a breath.

"Toni, it all fits and quite frankly I believe Swifty … ah, that is what his men called him, you know Robert Swift, is in the middle of it somehow."

"Have your man tell him that. There is a chance that Reggie is in the dark."

"Toni, my man is doing some further investigation, would you like to be kept abreast, confidentially of course?"

"Such as?"

"Well, it is just a theory right now, but my guy is liking one of Reggie's aides for this. Seems he's been meeting with this Edward Samson, the lawyer that first came to me asking about the manuscript coincidently shortly after the attorney had met with Swift."

"Really? How good is this information?"

"Frankly, about two hours old."

"I see. Have your man tell Reggie all that. If he's got trouble in his house, he needs to clean it up."

"I certainly will, Toni."

"Nathan, I'm going to tell you one last thing and then you have to tell me something without hesitation."

"Of course."

There was silence on the line. He heard her take a deep breath before speaking.

"Nathan, I wouldn't have agreed to any of this under different circumstances, which I hope you understand. Reggie is a close friend of mine, in spite of his misgivings. He is not someone I would have put in this position. So please understand I don't take any of this lightly. If there is mischief underfoot, I will not under any circumstance tolerate any of that and I will act upon that party accordingly. Do I make myself clear?"

"Absolutely. Please believe me that everything that has been told to you is as we know it, nothing less, we only want this to end, a misunderstanding to be sure, nothing more, I assure you, hand to God."

"Nathan, I believe you, I just don't want your man going in there with any fool notions."

"Again, his mission is to put our cards on the table and hopefully put all this to bed for everyone's benefit."

"Fine."

The line was silent again. Nathan waited.

"Okay, Nathan, here is my question that I want an honest answer, no hesitation."

Nathan waited. He could hear her take another deep breath.

"Did they hurt her in anyway?"

Nathan breathed a sigh of relief, taking a moment before answering.

"Toni, I can tell you without hesitation, that if anybody got hurt it was the other guy."

"But she said she was stripped to her underwear."

"A scare tactic, that's all. If you know Donna, as I'm sure you do, that had absolutely no effect on her and you also know because of our history, neither did it have an effect on me. You know Donna can handle herself."

"That's good to hear. I appreciate your honesty."

Once again there was silence on the line. Nathan thought it best not to mention that one of the men slapped Donna. He waited for her to respond.

"Well, I better sign off my husband will be getting anxious about now."

"Of course, and thanks again for your help with this matter. Once again I assure you we will keep everything above board. We wouldn't be able to do this without you."

"Nathan?"

"Yes?"

"Let's keep the last part of our conversation between us."

"You need not ask."

"Thank you, Nathan. Let me know how the meeting goes, the rest I need not know."

"Will do. Have fun in New York."

Nathan heard the line disconnect. He set his phone down and

gathered himself. He once again thought how thankful he was that she was on his side. Shaking it off, he dialed Jason's number and gave him the details. After he finished, he dialed Donna's number and filled her in as well. He set the phone back down and took a deep breath.

"Well, it's on. God help us," he said out loud.

SEVENTEEN

Jeff Morgan walked across the campus to the building that had been pointed out to him. Upon entering the building he walked up to the second floor and approached a door with the markings:

Professor Delores Hathaway, Director of Historical Studies.

Nodding, he opened the door and entered. A woman sitting at a desk in an outer office immediately greeted him.

"Can I help you?"

"Yes, I am here to see Mrs. Hathaway."

"Do you have an appointment?"

"No, but ..."

"Then I'm sorry, Professor Hathaway is very busy and unless you have an appointment, I'm afraid that you'll have to make one and come back another time."

"Nope, afraid that won't work. I plan on sitting here until she meets with me."

"I beg your pardon?"

Jeff Morgan took a seat in one of the office side chairs, setting the carry case he was holding on the ground next to him. He looked up at the woman.

"Nothing to pardon. I have all the time in the world and I plan on sitting here until Mrs. Hathaway agrees to meet with me."

The woman looked at him, not quite sure what to do. "Well, you should have at least called first."

"I did, several times, left messages for Mrs. Hathaway to call me back. She never did. So, this was my only other choice."

"Professor Hathaway, or Doctor Hathaway if you please."

Jeff Morgan looked at the lady. "Of course. Would you be so kind as to let Professor Hathaway, or Doctor Hathaway know that I am waiting out here?"

The woman looked at him, not sure what to do next. "Would you excuse me, please?"

Jeff Morgan tilted his head yes. He watched the woman enter through an inner door, closing that immediately behind her. He looked around the outer office, books papers, files, just about what he expected. The inner door opened.

"Mr. Morgan, you may go in."

The secretary stepped back and allowed him to enter the office. He smiled and pushed past her into the inner sanctum of Hathaway's office. Before he had a chance to get very far into the room he was greeted by a woman's harsh voice.

"I don't do Civil War Gold."

Jeff Morgan looked around the room, then behind him as the door was closing, finally realizing she was talking to him. He looked back at her before taking a seat in front of her desk.

"I beg your pardon?"

The woman behind the desk sat back in her chair. Jeff noticed that even with the staid clothing she was wearing, for a professor that is, she was rather attractive.

"I said, I don't do Civil War Gold. Most of the people that seek me out want information on maps, letters and any number of other items that they think will lead them to some long lost treasure. I don't waste my time on any of that foolishness, so if that is your purpose you can leave now."

The woman behind the desk then leaned forward and went back to whatever had her attention before he entered. Jeff Morgan sat there in silence. Finally she looked up.

"Well?"

"Well, if you are done ranting, perhaps we can discuss why I am here."

"And just why are you here? Mr. ..."

"Morgan, Jeff Morgan, please call me Jeff."

The woman behind the desk sat back in her chair and looked at him. Jeff took that as a signal to him to start speaking.

"I was hoping to get your help in clearing up a few items for me of a historical nature. Your name was in the notes."

"What notes?"

"Excuse me. Let me start at the beginning."

"Do you think I have time for this?"

Jeff Morgan looked up at her and stared her down almost to the point of being uncomfortable.

"Looks like the notes were right, you are a real bitch."

"I beg your pardon. I have half a mind to call security and have you thrown off campus."

Jeff Morgan continued to stare her down.

"Mrs. Hathaway... sorry, I mean Professor Hathaway, or Doctor Hathaway, whichever you prefer, the lady outside didn't seem to have a preference ... anyway, I didn't come here to spar with you. I was hoping you could help clear up a few things based on your historical background described in the notes, but I'm sure there are others out there that I can contact that just might be a bit more on the friendly side and not so quick to jump to conclusions and just maybe entertain the possibility of a conversation. Good day, then."

Jeff Morgan stood up from his chair.

"Did your notes really say that about me?"

Jeff turned and looked at the lady behind the desk, her voice now much softer. He sat back down and consulted the papers.

"Actually it has your name on the page and next to that is the notation *'a real bitch'* underlined three times. However, they are not my notes."

They both sat silently looking across at each other. Finally the woman spoke.

"I'm sorry, please forgive me. I'm not usually like that, but you have to understand the number of people that seek me out with some idea that they have uncovered the final link to Civil War Gold, or more specifically, Confederate Gold that has been lost, stolen, buried, converted into … well, any number of things … and their utter lack of respect for me or my time. Unfortunately, my defenses rise immediately and I find myself shutting down, and refusing to get involved regardless of what anyone might think of me."

She paused, looking up, then down and finally back at him, speaking even softer.

"I really tried to help when I first started out, but the number of crackpots and what have you … I suppose in all fairness there were some sincere treasure hunters that came through that door, just finally became too much too deal with. I decided I would not assist anyone anymore legit or not. I just would not be the go to lady anymore."

Jeff sat there looking back at her, waiting to see if she had finished.

"Mr. Morgan, perhaps we can start over?"

"Jeff."

For the first time she smiled. "Okay, Jeff it is."

"What shall I call you? There appears to be several options. Which do you prefer?"

The woman leaned back into her chair, appearing to relax and smiled again. Jeff Morgan liked her smile.

"Which ever works for you?"

"Okay then, Mrs. Hathaway …"

"It's miss, there is no Mr. Hathaway."

This time Jeff smiled. "Okay then, Ms. Hathaway may I begin?"

She set the pen down and got up from her chair. Motioning with her hand to follow, she guided him over to a pair of chairs set across from each other with a small round table in the middle.

"We might be more comfortable here."

"Yes, of course."

They sat down and looked at each other. She motioned for

him to begin.

"Right, yes. Okay, let me see where to start."

"How about at the beginning? You have my attention and as long as it doesn't involve Civil War Gold."

They both smiled. Jeff retrieved the sheet of paper from his pile and crossed out *"a real bitch."*

"Thought I'd revise those notes, he might have been a little hasty."

She actually chuckled. Jeff watched as she drew her leg up under her and appeared to actually get comfortable.

"Please proceed, Mr. Morgan, ah Jeff."

"Okay. Right. Yes. I should tell you first off, I inherited this project, literally. An Army buddy of mine from the Vietnam War recently passed away and put my name on a list of intended candidates he hoped would complete a project he started, a manuscript, which also included a package of research documents."

Jeff took a break, clearing his throat. She sat silently waiting for him to continue.

"Basically, he had a great aunt that upon her passing, he found some letters in a shoe box dating back to the Civil War, 1864 to be specific."

Jeff noticed the woman tense up. He raised his hand in the air.

"Hold on, let me finish."

She looked hard at him, but Jeff continued.

"These letters are nothing more than letters to her husband who was presumably fighting for the Union side in Virginia in 1864. I have read each one and determined they probably have very little significance to the story. This Army buddy, sorry his name was Bob Kittridge."

Jeff paused, clearing his throat again.

"Anyway, he started researching the history of those letters and may have discovered a family link to the man and woman in those letters, as well as other potential relatives that were involved in the conflict during that time."

Jeff Morgan took a breath. "Sorry, I thought I could summarize this quicker."

She smiled again. "It's okay. So far I'm interested."

Jeff smiled. "Right. Anyway, it appears he began researching and digging into the past and put together a working manuscript that seems to tell the story of that moment in time. I have not looked at the manuscript yet, so I am not exactly sure what direction he went in, or what he may have intended the story to ultimately be."

"Are you a writer Mr. Morgan, sorry, Jeff?"

"Not really. Like everybody else I always thought I had a book in me, but, well, you know. No, I never gave it a go."

She smiled and, reaching over, patted his hand. "Don't we all?"

Jeff looked up at her, noticing more of her outer defenses loosening.

"Are you a writer, Ms. Hathaway?"

She smiled broadly, waving her hand in the air.

"Not at all. I've done the prerequisite non-fiction book and have several papers published, but beyond that I haven't found my great American novel that lurks inside all of us."

Jeff chuckled and leaned back in the chair. He grabbed the paper from his lap and wrote something down. She leaned forward.

"What was that? What did you just write down?"

Jeff looked at the paper, then turned it over to show her. Next to her name, below where a real bitch had been crossed out, he had written: *a real nice lady.*

She smiled. "Continue."

"My sole intention for coming here was to request your help in understanding what these research documents might mean. Anyway, since he had your name in the notes, he probably wanted to run some of this by you as well. Hopefully I can get a better understanding of that time and events, specifically what I can do to finish that manuscript for him. Apparently Kittridge thought I could do so as well. Quite surprised myself that I'm even considering this."

"But you haven't read that manuscript yet?"

"No."

"By any chance do you have a copy of the manuscript with you that maybe I could take a look at?"

Jeff Morgan pulled the flash drive out of a pocket in his carry case. "Sure, right here."

She looked at him for a moment, starting to ask, but then smiled broadly. "Don't tell me. You don't know what to do with that?"

"Well, I know it goes in the computer and then … no, I don't have a clue."

She laughed out loud. "Jeff, you really are precious. Don't you have a computer?"

"Sure, but short of checking emails, maybe using a simple spread sheet, some letters, like that, no I don't … you know, use it much."

Suddenly she stood up, almost startling him. "Here, let me have that." She took the flash drive from him and walked back to her computer. "Do you know what format it is in?" She looked at him still sitting there with a blank stare on his face. "Com'on, we'll figure it out."

He followed her behind her desk as she sat back down and stuck the drive into her computer. In a moment it beeped.

"Looks like a standard format, we should be able to read it at least. I don't know if it is locked."

Jeff stared at her.

"If we will be able to make changes."

Jeff nodded. He watched her scroll through the manuscript.

"Okay, it's 260 pages, not very big."

"Is that bad?"

"No, not at all. But it does look a little rough, especially toward the end, might need some polishing. A good editor can help you with that part."

Jeff nodded. They both watched as she continued to scroll through the document. Finally she paused and sat back.

"You should probably read this, get familiar with the story first, might help explain some of the documents you are referring too. Get a sense of the story and understand where he was going or at the very least what he was trying to accomplish."

Jeff nodded again, as she looked up at him, understanding.

"Right. Here let me print out a copy for you."

"You can do that? I mean, of course you can, but is that okay to use office paper to?"

"Relax, Jeff. I won't tell if you won't."

Jeff smiled as she motioned.

"Suppose we sit back down and you tell me some more while this prints out."

She struck some keys and Jeff heard the printer start. They walked back to the side chairs and got comfortable again. This time she kicked off her shoes and tucked both legs up under her. Jeff noticed her legs as she did. Just as he was about to start, the door opened.

"Professor Hathaway, if there is nothing else, I'll be leaving."

"My goodness, is it four thirty already. Yes, of course. No, I won't need anything else. Good night."

The printer sounded in the background as the door closed. They looked at each other. A beep sounded. She got up and walked over to the printer barefooted.

"Paper."

Jeff nodded. He waited for her to come back. Once again she curled up into the chair and tucked her legs under her.

"What else do you have?"

Jeff looked at the papers in his lap, but then looked back up at her, obviously wanting to ask something.

"What?"

"There is still quite a bit to go over."

"And?"

"Well, Ms. Hathaway, I was thinking we might take a break and maybe after that is finished printing, we could grab some dinner, on me of course."

"Are you asking me out?"

"No, yes. I mean no. I just thought since you have been so gracious with your time this afternoon, the least I could do is buy you dinner. After all, we did get off to a rough start and I'd like to make that up to you."

She stared at him for a long time, finally breaking into a smile, waving her hand in the air.

"It has been a long day. Sure, why not. I suppose it is the least I can do, maybe further help your opinion of me. I know this little place just off campus that might be nice, give us a chance to talk some more then. You're on Mr. Morgan ... ah Jeff. Sorry in my world, it is either Professor, Doctor, at the very least Mister. I'm just not use to first names."

Jeff nodded and smiling put his papers back into his carry case. He watched her get up, slip back into her heels and walk over to the printer.

"We're on page 196, shouldn't be much longer."

Jeff nodded and watched her as she went to her desk. She shuffled some papers and put some items in a drawer, before sitting back into her chair. The printer finished. She shut down her computer.

"That can all wait until tomorrow."

She retrieved the rest of the pages from the printer and put the whole pile into a large tie envelope, which she placed inside and stretched the ribbon around.

"Here you are."

Jeff took the package from her and realizing it was way too big to put in his carry case, placed the package on top.

"Shall we? We can walk to the restaurant from here. Where's your car?"

"In visitor's parking."

"Fine. That is close by."

Jeff stood outside the door as she turned off the lights and locked the door. Together they walked out of the building and the short distance to the restaurant. He could see his car in the parking lot, as she pointed.

"See, right there."

He nodded. For a moment he thought of dropping the documents off, but decided to keep them with him. He opened the door and followed her in. It was a small place but very well proportioned. The host directed them to a table near the back and waited while they sat, then handed them each a menu. A moment later a waiter appeared.

"May I get you started with some drinks?"

Jeff looked at her. "May I?" Before she could respond, Jeff ordered. "Two Vodka martinis up."

"Very good, sir."

The waiter was off.

"So what do you recommend?"

"Vodka martini?"

"Thought you could use one."

She smiled. "I usually do fish, but I've had the steak before and it was very good."

Jeff looked over the top of the menu to see her smiling and shaking her head. The drinks arrived and he asked the waiter for a few more minutes before ordering.

"Cheers."

They raised their glasses and clinked, each taking a sip.

"So, Ms. Hathaway…"

"Lori."

"Lori?"

"Yes, my name is Delores Hathaway, but I prefer Lori, since we're doing first names."

She took a rather large sip of her drink.

"Yes, I needed that."

Jeff raised his glass. They finished those and ordered another round before ordering dinner.

Jeff looked across the table at her. "Married?"

She looked at him, but shook her head. "No, divorced. Going on sixteen years."

"You're counting?"

"No, just one of my quirks, I keep track of things."

The drinks arrived and they took a minute to order dinner. She did get the fish, while he selected the steak. After the waiter left, Jeff restarted the conversation.

"Boyfriend?"

She shook her head no.

"Girlfriend?"

"What? No? Why would you think?"

"I'm not thinking anything, just asking. Dating anybody?"

"No. Couple of attempts, but nothing developed. Too much of a work ... well you know."

She looked at him asking.

"My wife passed a couple of years ago. Cancer."

"I'm sorry, didn't mean."

"It's okay. Children?"

"A daughter. She lives in San Francisco."

"I have two, older, from a previous marriage, a boy and a girl."

They sat silent, sipping their drinks. Jeff held his glass in the air.

"This your drink? Liquor, or are you a wine woman. Or a beer gal?"

She looked up at him, holding the glass in the air.

"I like a cocktail every now and then, but I usually prefer wine with dinner."

Jeff nodded. When the salads arrived, he looked at the waiter.

"The lady will have wine with dinner."

The waiter nodded, looking at the professor. She selected a white wine to go with her fish. Writing that down, the waiter smiled. "Very good, I'll be sure to bring that with dinner."

Jeff waited for the waiter to leave. "How often do you come here?"

She looked up from her salad. "Not very. But I've always heard good things about it. Besides it's close to campus, makes it easy and a favorite. I've only been here with other professors, usually to discuss school matters."

Dinner was brought along with her glass of wine. Jeff continued to nurse his second martini through dinner. After dinner they shared a desert and glass of port, enjoying small talk. Three and a half hours later, they finally left the restaurant. Slowly they walked to his car. Helping her inside he asked her where her car was parked, but realizing she was probably in no condition to drive, he drove back to his hotel.

He walked with her from the car to the room. Once inside, she took a seat on the bed.

"I'll put some coffee on. Maybe we can talk some more and then in a little while, you can head home."

She nodded. "That sounds like a plan."

Jeff went to the bathroom side table, to figure out the coffee maker. Finally navigating his way to brewing a cup, he returned to the outer room to see her lying on the bed, obviously asleep.

"Light weight," he said out loud, as he smiled.

He tucked the pillow under her head, lifted her legs unto the bed and removed her shoes before he pulled the bedspread over her. She looked fast asleep and didn't even stir when he shifted her into a better position.

Hearing the coffee finish, he retrieved a cup, poured the hot liquid into it, selected cream and sugar packets and turned the maker off. Carrying the cup with him he took another look at her, just to be sure, but she was out like a light. He set the cup of real coffee back on the counter. No way was he drinking that stuff. Retrieving his bottle of water from earlier, he sat in the chair by the window where the lamp was already on. Kicking off his shoes and getting comfortable, he reached for the tie envelope, removed the manuscript from the envelope and started reading.

——————— /// ———————

Jeff Morgan awoke with a start. Sheets of paper lay scattered on his lap and the floor, the reading glasses still parked on his nose. The sun was shining through the curtains and his neck had a vicious cramp. Checking his watch he saw it was just before six. As quietly as possible, he gathered papers off the floor and started to put them back in order. Before long he heard stirring from the bed and looked over. She was awake. She opened her eyes and looked over at him, then around the room, then down at her self.

"Where am I?"

Slowly she sat up, the bedspread slipping off her shoulder and into a pile beside her. During the night, one of the buttons on her blouse had come undone, exposing a glimpse of white bra. Her skirt had risen quite a ways up her legs. With some effort, she swung her legs over and sat on the side of the bed, letting her feet hit the ground. Jeff sat quietly, waiting. She turned and looked at him.

"What happened?"

Jeff got up from the chair and walked over, sitting down on the bed right next to her.

"When we left the restaurant, you seemed a bit … well, not in the best condition to drive, so I suggested we come here, have some coffee and talk a bit, give you a chance to … you know."

She looked up at him.

"And?"

"And nothing, that's it."

"That's it?"

"Yes, I left you sitting on the bed while I went to make coffee. When I came back you were asleep. I thought if you rested a bit, you might feel better and could go home then."

"That was your plan?"

"I didn't have a plan."

She looked down at her self, noticed the button open, but didn't make a move to fix it. Looking further down, she saw how high her skirt was up on her legs, but didn't do anything about that either.

"So what did we do after that?"

"Do? We didn't do anything."

She nodded. "How did?"

"When I came back in the room, you were asleep. I lifted you up onto the bed, took your shoes off and lifted your legs up. I covered you with the bedspread. That was it."

She looked up at him, asking with her eyes.

"Then I set the coffee back on the counter, in case, you know … but you didn't, so I grabbed some water and started reading the manuscript. I think I got through about a hundred pages, and then I must have fallen asleep. I woke up a few minutes before you and found pages all over the floor. That's it."

She put her head in her hands and ran her fingers through her hair.

"I must look a mess."

"Actually, you look rather cute."

She let her head go. "Cute?"

"Yeah, all kind of messy cute."

She smiled. "Glad you think so. So, how did I get in bed?"

"You were already half on the bed, just sort of fell over. I pushed you up a bit, put your legs up on the bed and removed your shoes."

She looked down again to how high her skirt was up on her legs.

"And that's all?"

"Well, I might have looked at your legs. They are very nice by the way."

She smiled, shaking her head.

"You mean to tell me, I just met you today, you got me drunk, I'm here in your hotel room and nothing happened?"

"Hey, wait a minute. I didn't get you drunk."

"Then why are we in a hotel room?"

"Because I booked the room for the night so I wouldn't have to make the long drive home late at night, that's all. I live four hours from here. Just thought I'd get a night's sleep before heading back home."

She nodded and seemed to accept that answer and put her hand on his arm.

"Thank you."

"For what?"

"For a much needed night out. For good company and for what you didn't do."

She looked up at him, her hair a bit of a tangled mess, keeping her hand on his arm. He put his hand on hers and spoke very softly.

"I'm not sure if I would have known what to do anyway."

The laugh started slow then finally went full-blown, before she grabbed her head.

"Whoa that hurt. I better freshen up a bit."

Jeff helped her stand, her skirt sliding back down her legs and watched her head towards the bathroom, staggering just a little. He went back to organizing the spilled pages and placing them back into the envelope. A short time later, she came out. Her blouse was buttoned up and her skirt was straightened back to its proper length.

"I used some of your mouthwash, hope you don't mind. I would really have liked to take a shower, but since I don't have anything to change into, I'll wait till I get home."

Jeff looked at her as she sat on the edge of the bed and put her shoes on, before standing back up.

"So nothing happened?"

"No."

"Why not?"

"What do you mean why not?"

She looked at him, still getting her bearing. "You got me drunk and took me back to your hotel room."

She paused and Jeff waited. She shook her head, speaking very softly.

"I'm sorry. What you must think of me ..."

"I think you're a very attractive lady who looked cute all messy and you have a great pair of legs, if I may be so forward, that's what I think."

She looked down at her legs now covered by her skirt and smiled.

"How much of them did you see?"

"Enough to make the call."

She nodded. "That's sweet. We should probably go, would you mind taking me to my car now?"

"Yes, of course."

They left the room and climbed into Jeff's car. She directed him to where her car was parked. He pulled up along side and turned the engine off. Turning to face her, he spoke with sincerity.

"Listen, it wasn't my intention to have the night end up like ... well, you know. I'd really like to finish our conversation, but maybe we should wait until I have a chance to read the manuscript. Hopefully I can gather my notes better and I won't take up so much of your time."

She nodded, as he continued speaking softly.

"Look I really had a good time in your company last night. It's been a while since I spent any time with a woman other than my ... you know ... well, I had a really good time last night with you."

She looked over at him and then placed her hand on his.

"It was fun. Wish I remembered more of it. Obviously, I haven't been out in awhile and forgot how much ... well what that felt like. I must have been more tired than I thought. I'd very much like to finish our conversation. Please do contact me when you are ready. I'll let my assistant know to put you through this time. I'd be very interested in hearing more, really I would."

Jeff nodded. "Will do."

She removed her hand and reached for the door handle.

"Ms. Hathaway."

"Lori."

He smiled. "I'd like to call on you again ... I mean ... I'd ... I mean ...I'm sorry, I wasn't good at this even when I was good at this."

She smiled, knowing full well what he meant. She reached over and placed her hand on his cheek.

"I'd like for you to do that as well."

Then she was out the door, closing it behind her. Smiling, he watched her get into her car. He waited until she drove off before starting his engine. A moment later he was on the way back to the hotel, to pack, check out and head back home for now.

EIGHTEEN

Jeff Morgan arrived back home late in the afternoon. As he pulled the car into the garage, he looked at the beast parked in the second spot, the drawers sitting off to the side. Deciding he was too tired to deal with the bureau just now, he closed the garage door and went inside. The papers were still in their stacks on the kitchen table.

"That can wait until tomorrow as well," he said out loud, pointing. Taking a glass from the cupboard, he added ice, retrieved the bottle of Vodka from the counter and poured a generous amount into the glass. Swirling the glass around to cool the liquid, he took the first sip. Taking two sips before leaving, he carried the glass with him into the living room.

The message light was blinking on the phone. Pressing play he listened, but when he didn't recognize the name, he hit delete. The tie file with the manuscript was in his left hand as he took another sip of the drink. The carry case had been left on the kitchen table.

Sitting in the Queen Ann chair that his late wife had bought him, he set the drink on the end table, reached up and turned on the light. Slipping the reading glasses on his nose, he pulled the manuscript out of the envelope.

Fifty or so pages later, he felt the need to eat something. For no particular reason he put the manuscript back into the envelope and carried it into the kitchen, setting it on the table. The kitchen table had become his working office. Rinsing the glass out he opened a cabinet and found a can of hearty soup.

After a quick dinner, he looked at the tie file on the table, but decided to call it a night. Undressing and crawling into bed, he switched on the television and found some news. Feeling himself start to drift, he turned off the set and rolled over.

——————— /// ———————

Up early as usual, he quickly showered and dressed. Heading out to the garage, he side stepped the drawers sitting there and got into his car. The cafe near his house served a decent breakfast and this morning he was letting them do the cooking. Breakfast consisted of two eggs, bacon crisp, hash browns and a buttered English muffin, with three cups of decaf, because their cups were smaller than his.

After parking the car back in the garage, he decided then and there to put the drawers back. The top narrower center drawer went in with no trouble, but when he tried to put the three lower center drawers in he realized they each had their own place. After fumbling a bit, he stopped and looked closer.

The center compartment was open from top to bottom, rather than having braces for each drawer, which he hadn't noticed before. Instead each drawer had a cleat fashioned on the inside to hold each drawer and each cleat was a different size. He then realized that each drawer had a groove built into the side of the drawer to line up with the corresponding cleats. As he was trying to figure out which was which, he heard the phone ringing from inside the house. Setting the drawer down, he rushed inside to pick up the kitchen phone.

"Hello."

"Yes, hello, my name is Lillian Meriweather, I'm from PUSA."

"Did you just say you're from pussy?"

"Oh, my dear Lord Sir I would never … well I never would say such a thing, why…"

"I'm terribly sorry, I just thought you said … well it sounded like … well please forgive me?"

There was a bit of silence on the line.

"I'm sorry sir, I need a moment to gather myself."

"Yes, of course. Again, I am terribly sorry. Suppose we start over?"

"By all means sir, by all means. As I was saying, my name is Lillian Meriweather and I'm from the P.U.S.A., which stands for the Preservation of Unique Southern Antiques."

"Right, I got it now. Once again, please forgive me I'm truly sorry that I misheard you."

"By all means, consider the matter forgotten."

"So, what can I do for you?"

"We, that is our curator, Allen Edward Cummings the Third, and myself understand you have recently acquired a piece of furniture that is quite old."

"Yes, but how did … how could you possibly … I've only had it two days … why?"

"My dear sir, we have many friends in the field that are always on the look out for unique items. I understand that yours is rather well… different?"

Jeff thought back to Tom's assessment of the piece as the beast, and smiled, but then realized, Tom or Junior had to be the one who probably told her about the bureau.

"Mr. Morgan, are you still there?"

"Yes, may I ask how you heard about it?"

"I'm sorry, I don't have that information directly in front of me right now, but I'm quite sure it was one of our many colleagues in the field that passed that information along to us."

Right, Jeff thought, looks like good old Tom got his price after all.

"Well, it all sounds rather strange to me that two days after I received the bureau you are calling about it."

"Actually, Mr. Morgan, I tried to reach you yesterday, I believe I even left a message."

Jeff took a deep breath shaking his head.

"So what can I do for you, miss ah?"

"Meriweather, but please feel free to call me Lillian."

"Okay Lillian, what can I do for you?"

"Our curator, Mr. Cummings has asked me to contact you regarding the piece you have. He was hoping that we may be able to come by to take a look see."

"You want to see the bureau? How?"

"Yes, we'd be happy to come by your place, unless of course you'd rather bring the piece to us."

"No, that isn't gonna work."

"Then may we come by to have a look at that item?"

"What, here? You want to come by here? Well, I'll have to think about that."

"Of course, we understand. May I give you my number in the hopes that you'll seriously consider our request and give us a ring? We'd really like to examine that piece of furniture and per-haps we just might be able to give you an honest evaluation of its worth."

"Well, I really don't care about that. It has sentimental value to me, doesn't matter at all what it may be worth."

"Of course, but never-the-less."

"I should also tell you it is not a very attractive piece."

"I understand Mr. Morgan, all the same we would appreciate the opportunity to have a look for ourselves. We are always inter-ested in viewing unique pieces of furniture. One never knows what one might find out there."

"Sure, I understand, but let me think on it. I'll get back to you in a couple of days."

"Very well. Once again, thank you for speaking with me today. Have a good day, sir."

"You do the same."

The line disconnected. Jeff put the receiver back in the cra-dle. Retrieving his cell phone from the table he dialed a familiar number.

"Professor Hathaway's office."

"Yes, can I speak with the professor please?"

"Who shall I say is calling?"

"Jeff Morgan."

"Yes of course Mr. Morgan, I'll put you right through, just a moment."

"Wow." He held the phone away from his ear. "Isn't that a nice change?"

"Jeff, so good to hear your voice. Do you miss me already?"

"Lori, good to hear yours, yes I do as a matter of fact."

"Go on, you must need something."

"Well, actually I do, but really it is good to hear your voice."

"So what do you need?"

"I just got a call from a lady that said she was with P.U.S.A., and before you ask, let me tell you I already did. I swear to God that it sounded like she said she was from pussy."

Jeff could hear laughter on the other end.

"You didn't?"

"Yes, I did."

"What did the lady say to that?"

"Well she seemed pretty put off by that, even said she needed a moment to gather herself. I apologized of course."

"So what is this … no … I'm not gonna say it."

"She said it stands for Preservation of Unique Southern Antiques."

"The what?"

"Ever hear of a group like that."

"No. Give me a minute."

Jeff waited, hearing the keyboard being struck in the background.

"Well, they do have a web site. Looks like they are legit. What name did she give you?"

"Said her name was Lillian Meriweather."

"Yeah, she's listed here. The curator is an Allen Edward Cummings the Third."

"Yeah, she told me that as well."

"So, what did she want?"

"Said they wanted to come by and see it."

"Come by and see what?"

"The bureau."

"What bureau?"

Jeff took a breath. "Well, it is a bit of a long story, but … do you have a fax number? I could fax the copy of the diary entries, which might make more sense."

"Diary entries?"

"Yes, well … well it will make more sense if you see that piece of paper."

Professor Hathaway gave him the fax number that Jeff quickly wrote down.

"Okay, I have to switch the phone line from the computer to the fax, might take me a couple of minutes, so let me give you my cell number before I go do that and call me back on the cell after you've had a chance to look at the fax."

Jeff gave her his cell number.

"Got it, will do, bye Jeff."

"Bye."

Jeff set the cell phone down on the kitchen table then went to his computer. Unplugging the phone line from the computer, he plugged the cord into his printer/fax/copier machine. Placing the document in the feeder, he dialed the number and pressed send. Once it was finished, he switched the phone line back to the computer. Before he had a chance to get back to the kitchen, his cell phone was ringing.

"Hello."

"You have that bureau?"

"I believe so."

"You have that bureau mentioned on that diary entry?"

"Yes, I think so."

"How? I mean how did you get that? I mean why do you have that? I mean …"

Jeff smiled. "Hold on Professor. I got it from a guy in Missouri. Said it was in his barn for eighty years, I had it shipped to my house and now it is sitting in my garage.

"But …?"

"It's part of the research."

"Research?"

"Yes, the research I am doing on the manuscript. The details were mentioned in the notes, so I called the gentleman listed and he said it was okay to come see for myself. I took a ride to Missouri to look at the piece and he said if I could get it out of the barn, I could have it, which I did. Actually I hired a couple of guys to do that and then have the bureau moved to my house."

"What? I don't understand?"

"As I said the piece was mentioned in Kittridge's notes so I followed up with the gentleman listed as having it and next thing I know I'm having the bureau shipped to me. I was just following up on his notes, which by the way, is pretty much how I found you."

"And you think that this is that very bureau mentioned on those diary entries?"

"Yes I truly believe so. And based on the story the gentleman told me, I feel strongly that this is that very bureau."

"I'd like to see that myself."

"Anytime, you're certainly welcome to come here, have a look."

There was a pause on the line. Jeff spoke softly.

"Lori, did I say something wrong?"

"No, no. I was trying to think when I could … How far away are you?"

"A little over four hours … say four hours."

"I could leave early in the morning and still get back."

"Lori?"

"Yes?"

"Listen, you're welcome to stay the night, I have plenty of room. You wouldn't have to make the round trip on the same day."

Once again there was silence, this time Jeff waited patiently.

"How about if I came over on Friday? I could leave early in the afternoon then head back home on Saturday. I'd be okay with that, maybe go over some of your notes while I'm there?"

"That would be great. I'll take you to dinner on Friday, we can relax and we can do study hall on Saturday."

Jeff heard a laugh in the background. "What?"

"The last time you took me to dinner, I woke up the next morning in your bed, in your hotel room. I can only imagine what will happen this time."

Jeff wasn't sure how to answer, so remained silent. Lori continued.

"I'll try to get out of here by noon on Friday, get there while it is still light, have my first look. That work for you?"

"Yes, yes it does. I'll see you on Friday."

"I look forward to it."

"Wait."

"Yes, Jeff?"

"Sorry. I almost forgot."

"What is it?"

Jeff could hear the letdown in her voice. "What about this pussy place?"

Professor Hathaway let out a loud laugh. "You know we'll never be able to mention that organization again without referring to it as that. Thanks for that visual."

Jeff smiled. "Well?"

"Well, they look legit from here. What did they want again?"

"They wanted to come by and see the piece."

"Can you stall them for a few days?"

"I told that lady, Lillian that I'd get back to her in a couple of days after I thought some more about it."

"What did she say to that?"

"She seemed okay."

"Well, she's not gonna see your thing before I do."

Jeff swallowed hard. "Say that again."

"Let's push her off until next week, let me do some more research on their organization, ask a couple of my colleagues, see if any of them might have heard of that organization. But either way, I get to see the bureau before they do."

"No problem."

"Jeff, you know what this means."

"What, what means?"

"Between now and Friday, maybe Saturday morning, at the latest, you have to do your homework."

"Homework?"

"Yes, get your notes together, form your questions. Remember I am a History Professor."

"Right, yes, of course, I'll get right on that, whatever you say professor."

"See you Friday."

"Lori, I truly am looking forward to that."

"Bye Jeff."

"Bye."

Jeff set the cell phone back down on the kitchen table, a smile stretching across his face. Taking a moment, he remembered what he was doing before all this started and headed back out to the garage.

Holding a drawer in his hands, he tried fitting it into one of the slots. This one slipped into the second slot. The top one was next. As he was putting in the last drawer, the bottom of the center three, he noticed there was a sort of a rail, or buffer of some sort, in wood on each side of the bottom of each drawer. Slowly placing it into that slot, he realized the wooden rail, was keeping that drawer tight. Pulling it back out, he noticed there was a similar rail on the drawer above, which would be the center drawer.

Now needing to know, he pulled the center drawer back out and sure enough, the rail was present on the top drawer. He watched as he slid that center drawer back in and noticed how perfectly and tightly that drawer fit in its slot, as did the bottom drawer.

Standing back, he viewed the beast with all of the drawers back in place, the two doors on each side still open. The drawers lined up perfectly and when you opened one, there was no give. It slid in and out smoothly. Scratching his head, he smiled.

"Well, it may not look like much, but it sure is well designed," he said out loud, pointing to the piece.

He retrieved his pad off the workbench and made the following notes.

```
The piece is certainly well constructed
and appears to operate without hesitation,
no hanging drawers and uneven slide, draw-
ers move in and out smoothly. There seems
to have been a lot of extra work put into
the crafting of the piece to compensate
for its extra weight. It's as if someone
wanted to build a bureau, didn't know how,
or simply constructed the piece with the
wood they had on hand, which forced the
maker to compensate for the weight by mak-
ing the working parts equal to the task. I
have a better appreciation of this thing
than I first did when we pulled it out of
Herb Miller's barn.
```

Once again he stepped back and looked at the piece before him, shaking his head in amazement. He laid the pad back on top of the workbench.

Fetching a whiskbroom from the shelf, he proceeded to dust off the top and sides, closing both of the doors. He swept the dust gathered on the floor into a pile away from the piece. Inside another cabinet, he retrieved a paint cloth, which he thought would fit. Gently, he spread the heavy linen fabric across the top. The cloth covered the whole top and fell down to about two feet below on all sides. Satisfied with the results, he scooped up the debris, depositing those into the garage trash can. Rubbing his hands together, he reached over and pushed the button, waiting while the garage door closed.

Stepping back into the kitchen, he reviewed the pile of papers on the table, but decided to continue reading the manuscript for now. Besides, he thought, he had three more days to finish his homework. He smiled at that observation.

THE KITTRIDGE MANUSCRIPT

This time forgoing the Vodka, he took the tie envelope into the living room to the same chair. His reading glasses were still on the table where he left them. Securing them on his nose, he removed the manuscript from the envelope and picked up where he had left off.

NINETEEN

At precisely six pm, Jason opened the door to Langston Securities. He already knew that neither of the men he was meeting with was named Langston. The preliminary research had shown that either Langston was retired or had sold the business. Passing through the outer office, he entered the main room. Both of the men he had come to see sat at their individual desks. He knew that the balding one on the left, the shorter of the two, was the retired cop by the name of Ed Finley and that the other man was a retired FBI agent named John Rutledge.

He had dressed as he did the previous week in the plaid jacket, but with black pants this time, the same thick glasses and the really bad comb over.

Both men stood and offered their hands, which he shook. Rutledge pointed to the chair in front of his desk, which he acknowledge and sat down. Finley came over and sat on the edge of that desk.

"So how can we help you Mr. ...?"

"Wrightwood. Oliver Wrightwood."

"Yes, Mr. Wrightwood." The FBI guy took the lead. "What can we do for you?"

Jason looked at both men through the thick lenses, nodding.

"Well you see I've gotten myself into a bit of a pickle."

Pausing, he glanced at both men again, clearing his throat

before continuing.

"I'm a clerk for the county and it wouldn't do to … well let my rather indelicate situation become known."

"I see." The FBI guy sat back in his chair. "Suppose you tell us what this is all about and we'll see if we can be of any help."

Jason removed the glasses on the pretense of rubbing his nose, as he gave the office a cursory once over. Putting the glasses back on his nose, he looked at each man.

"Well, you see, I work very hard, long hours and even some weekends. I have a very demanding job. On Friday nights, I like to … how do you say it? Blow off a little steam." He paused to clear his throat. "Well, it seems a couple of Fridays ago, I married one of the strippers."

As he paused, the FBI guy leaned forward.

"You married one of the strippers?"

Jason looked at the man speaking, the FBI agent.

"Yes, the usual place I go to, … to blow off steam … had a private party and was closed down for the night … and I knew of this other club … that I had heard about … and … so, I went there this time."

This time Jason removed his glasses and wiped his brow.

"Well, they all know me at the other place and know that I just want a drink or two, maybe watch … well, take in the show for a moment. I'm sure you understand. Well, since I wasn't known at this other place, I apparently had too much to drink and woke up in a hotel room the next morning with one of the girls in bed with me. When I finally got her to wake up … she said she had never drank that much before, but since we were celebrating, she thought what the hell."

Jason paused looking at each of the men separately, but then turned back to the FBI agent.

"You understand I don't go in for this sort of thing. My goodness, what would people say?"

Jason looked back up at the FBI guy, who motioned for him to continue.

"When I asked her what we were celebrating, she said

that we had gotten married the night before and this was our honeymoon."

The retired cop smiled into a little chuckle. "Sounds like you got hosed pal."

The FBI guy raised his hand. "Just what would you like us to do now?"

Jason looked up. The retired cop was still chuckling, but the FBI guy seemed genuinely concerned. He continued.

"Well, I've already seen an attorney to get the marriage set aside, but my real problem is her boyfriend."

"Her boyfriend?"

"Yes, Paddy. That's P-a-d-d-y. A big Eastern European guy speaks very little English. He doesn't believe we are married and won't leave us ... her ... really me alone, follows me everywhere."

The FBI guy grabbing a pencil now, looked up.

"Can you give us a description?"

"I can do better that that, he's right downstairs. Like I said, he follows me everywhere."

"He followed you here?"

"He follows me everywhere. Here look."

Jason got up from the chair and walked to the window. Both men joined him there as well.

"You see there, right there on the other side of the street, the blue sedan?"

As both men attempted to see where he was directing, Jason stepped back and in an instant, jabbed each man in the buttocks, simultaneously pressing down on each plunger. If they were aware of being injected they didn't show it and a moment later they both collapsed to the floor.

Jason took another step back, clearing the way for both bodies to finish their fall. He said out loud, "So you guys like to play with knock out drugs. Let me show you a trick or two."

Going to each man's desk, he first went through the drawers. In the retired cop's bottom drawer, he found a bra, assumed that it was Donna's and stuck it in his back pocket. In a large cabinet he found shelves of wire tapping equipment, listening devices, nanny cams and various other toys of the trade. Nodding, he left those doors wide open.

He pulled the FBI guy away from the window and propped him up in his chair. The retired cop he dragged over to a sofa that was in the office and propped him up there. Removing that man's jacket and shirt, he dug into the case he had carried in earlier.

Propping a mirror on the desk, he removed the Oliver Wrightwood get up and became the retired cop. Putting on the retired cop's shirt and jacket, he left their offices. It was just after seven.

Entering a bar down the street that he had checked out before, he sat at the end of the bar, watching the current patrons. When he saw a lady order her third drink in fifteen minutes, he knew he had found his patsy. Sliding down the bar he sat right next to her.

"Trying to drown your troubles, or your sorrows?"

As she looked up at him, he motioned for the bartender to bring her another one.

"I didn't order that."

"It's okay, I did. That one's on me. Thought you could use it. So which is it?"

"Which is what?"

"Your troubles or sorrows?"

She turned back to her current drink, damn near guzzling it, before reaching the new one.

"Troubles. I got fired today."

"Fired? What do you do?"

"I'm a teacher. Said I came to work inebriated, against policy, grounds for immediate termination, so poof, here I am."

"Were you?"

"Was I what?"

"Inebriated?"

"No, but I was quite hung over. Tied one on the night before, bad breakup."

"I see. Any other time you showed up at work drunk … ah, I mean inebriated?"

"No. Well, maybe? But this time I was just hung over, honest."

"Sure, I believe you. Sounds like you might have a case."

"A case."

The way the word *case* came out, Jason could tell that the fourth drink already was having an effect and he needed to work fast.

"Listen, I work for Langston Securities, just down the street. My boss is an attorney. Sounds like we have a wrongful termination case in front of us. Would you be interested in talking with him?"

She looked over at Jason, her eyes somewhat glassy.

"You really think so? I was wondering if I should hire an attorney, the way they fucked me over... whoops, sorry." She cupped her hand to her mouth. "Maybe, I better."

Jason smiled and helped her off the barstool, throwing a twenty on the bar. Half dragging, half carrying, he got her out of the bar and started her down the street. After quite some effort he had her upstairs and into their office.

Just about the time she saw the two men slumped over Jason stuck her in the right buttock and pushed the plunger down, catching her as she passed out. He carried the limp body over to the sofa and sat her on the other side of the retired cop. Standing back, he looked them over.

Going to her first, he flipped her on her side and unzipped her skirt, wiggling it down her legs. He unbuttoned the blouse and, pulling her forward, worked the blouse off her shoulders, down her arms and off, tossing the garment on the floor next to the skirt. Still keeping her forward, he unhooked the bra and dropped it on the floor then let her drop back into the sofa. Finally, he reached down and worked her panties off, leaving her naked, but still wearing shoes, slumped on the sofa. Taking her clothes, he tossed them haphazardly across the retired cop's desk as if she had removed them and dropped them about his desk herself. He also set her purse, open on the desk.

Moving over to the retired cop he unbuckled his pants and worked them down his legs, dropping them on the floor beside

him. Walking over to the FBI guy he removed the man's jacket.
Feeling his phone in the pocket, he removed it and put that in
his pocket. He already had the retired cop's phone. Pulling the
shirt up and over the man's head he tossed that on the ground.
Unbuckling the man's pants, he worked them off. Each man was
now dressed in boxers, t-shirt and socks. He wheeled the FBI guy
around from behind the desk and positioned the chair in front of
the sofa as if he was watching the action in front of him.

Satisfied for the moment with his handiwork, he went back to
his bag and removed the retired cop look, replacing it with Carlos
Gonzalez, one of the night janitors, complete with uniform shirt.
Grabbing his bag and the two cell phones, he left the office then
returned with a janitorial cart, parking it just outside the door to
the office and stuck his bag inside the bottom of the cart.

Going back inside for one more look, he nodded and walked
over to the sofa. Sliding the retired cop over to the woman, he
placed the man's hand on her crotch and placed the woman's
hand inside his boxers.

Using the landline phone on the retired cop's desk, he dialed
911.

"Yes, I heard a woman scream, then a big crash, then pleading.
She was yelling no, no, please don't hurt me."

Jason gave the operator the address and office number of
Langston Securities and waited. Surprisingly in a few minutes, a
police car pulled up in front of the building. He quickly walked
over to the FBI guy and stuck him in the buttock and then performed the same task on the other two. Watching them starting to
stir, he said to them in a whisper.

"First one knocks you out, second one wakes you up, but
leaves you feeling groggy and your mind quite fuzzy. Let's see
you get out of this one, ass holes."

He quickly stepped from the office and waited for the police
to arrive.

"What's going on here? Are you the one who called it in?"

"Yes, sir. I was pushing my cart past the door and I heard a
woman scream. I started to go in, but then I heard a loud crash

and the woman pleading for the man not to hurt her. Thought I'd better call you for that."

The patrol officer nodded. "You said you went in?"

"No sir. I started to go in, that's how I know the door is unlocked, but when I heard the crash, I waited out here."

The patrol officer nodded again. "You wait right here."

Jason nodded, holding back a smile, while the two officers entered. He stepped inside the outer office to hear them.

—————— /// ——————

"So what's going on in here? Hey, what the hell? Are you okay lady? Did these guys hurt you?"

Slowly the woman looked up, then down at herself. "What? What's going on? Where's my clothes? What did you guys do to me?"

"Hold on lady, that's what we're trying to find out."

"Hey, look at this."

Jason could hear the other patrol officer walk away from the door.

"What is this stuff? What is all this equipment? What do you guys do here?"

"Langston Securities. We do investigations."

Jason could tell it was the FBI guy answering.

"Hey, what about me? I might have been raped here."

"Lady, can you tell me what this envelope is doing in your purse, with five hundreds inside? Did you come up here for a party?"

"Party? That asshole picked me up in a bar, said his partner was an attorney, help me out with my problem."

"What problem?"

"None of your business. That's personal."

"Well, I've heard enough."

Jason waited. He heard one of the officer's speak into what he presumed was his two-way.

"Yeah, dispatch, we're gonna need a couple of detectives up

here. Yeah, right, got a situation that needs straightening out. Yes, it's a follow up to that woman in distress call. Yes, we'll wait here."

Jason listened while the patrolmen leveled more questions inside. Ten minutes later, he heard the elevator start up and quickly slipped back outside the office, standing by the cleaning cart. Two people, a man and a woman walked fast toward the office. He stood back pointing and let the two pass him by nodding as they did.

Once the detectives were inside, he slipped back into the outer office to listen.

"Okay, what do we have here," the male detective bellowed.

One of the officers answered. "Not real sure, that's why we called you. We found the bald guy."

"Hey, watch it."

Everyone turned to look at the retired cop."

"As I was saying, we found him on the sofa with the lady there, his hand was in her crotch and she had her hand inside his boxers. This guy..." he pointed to the FBI guy "was sitting in his chair in his boxers like he was watching them. The initial call was for a lady in distress, but it didn't look quite right when we entered so we looked around."

Walking toward the cabinet, the officer pointed.

"We found this stuff. Looks like wire tapping equipment, listening devices, some cameras, you know, stuff like that."

The detective nodded turning to face the two men sitting.

"What's up with that stuff?"

The FBI guy answered. "We own and operate Langston Securities, we use that in our business."

The other officer interrupted. "Then there's this." Holding the envelope in the air. "An envelope with their logo on it, containing five one hundred dollar bills inside. It was folded and stuffed in her purse."

"I don't know anything about that envelope."

They all turned to look at the woman still sitting on the sofa, with a suit jacket wrapped around her. She sat forward attempting to cover herself as best she could."

"Well then can you explain what you are doing here and why your clothes are scattered all over his desk?"

She looked at the detective, then the two men sitting and finally at the female detective.

"He brought me here, said his partner could help me out."

Hesitantly she pointed at the retired cop.

"Me? I've never seen you before in my life."

"You son-of-a-bitch, you bought me a drink, said your partner was an attorney and maybe I had a case."

"What kind of case?"

She looked at the detective and put her head down.

"I got fired today for being inebriated on the job."

"And what do you do?"

"I'm ... I mean, I was a teacher, but I wasn't inebriated today, just a little hung over."

The detective nodded walking closer to her.

"So, you lost your job and met this guy in a bar tonight, he offered you some money to have a party with him and his partner, you agreed, but when one or both of them got too kinky for you, you cried rape, is that about it?"

"Huh? What? No. I don't know what happened. I had a few drinks and now my head hurts something fierce. Say what did you guys give me?"

"Did these men rape you, or did you come here voluntarily?"

She looked at both men sitting there in boxers and t-shirt, herself naked except for the suit jacket and put her head down.

"I don't know."

"Fine, what's your story?" The detective turned to the two men. Neither one spoke. "How about we get some names and details? You start." He pointed to the retired cop.

"Ed Finley, I got twenty years on the job."

"John Rutledge, retired FBI."

The detective nodded, shaking his head. "You think you guys would know better. Who's Langston?"

"Who?"

"The name on the door says Langston Securities."

"Retired, we bought the business from him last year."

The detective looked at the retired cop, shaking his head.

"Look." Rutledge took charge. "Last thing I remember was meeting with a potential client and next thing I know this officer was shaking me."

"Who was this potential client?"

Rutledge looked at Finley, who shrugged his shoulders. Rutledge looked back at the detective, thinking the same thing, they really hadn't signed him up, nor had they agreed to take him on as a client, so right now he thought it didn't make any difference if they gave him up, what the hell did he care.

"Said his name was Oliver Wrightwood."

Oliver Wrightwood, Judge Hollingsworth's clerk, that Oliver Wrightwood?"

"That's what he said."

"Describe him."

Rutledge looked at Finley before answering. "Well he had on a plaid sports jacket, thick glasses and a really bad comb over."

The detective nodded. "That sure sounds like him, but I got some bad news for you. Wrightwood was with the judge tonight at the Judge's fundraiser just like he always is. We know, 'cause we were there earlier and seen him with the Judge."

Rutledge looked at the detective his face contorting. "Then we must have been set up."

"By who?"

"Somebody obviously pretending to be Wrightwood, must have drugged us and ..."

The detective raised his hand. "Hold on." Turning to the woman he asked. "What was he doing when you walked in here with him?"

The woman looked at the detective. "I don't remember."

"This is hopeless. Everybody get dressed, we're going downtown to get everybody's statements and let the DA sort this out."

"Downtown? Why?"

The detective looked at Rutledge pausing a moment before answering.

"Look, I don't know what you guys are running here, but I don't like any of it, so I'm gonna let the DA deal with this, probably pull your license for now, 'till we can sort this out. Hope you don't have anything big going on, because you're about to be out of business for a time. Any other questions?"

"Can somebody help me out here?"

The detective turned to the woman. "Help you what?"

"I'm naked here, maybe you can get everybody out while I get dressed?"

The detective looked at the female detective.

"You stay with her, while I get these guys out of here. Officers, you're with me. Go find that janitor, I want to get his statement before we leave."

The officer nodded, helping to gather clothes and pointing the two men toward the door to the outer office.

As soon as the detective said that, Jason, as Carlos the janitor slipped back outside and, grabbing up his bag, made his way to the back stairs. On his way down, he removed the moustache and wig, along with the uniform shirt. Running his hands through his hair, to fluff it back up he walked quickly to his car parked just a block away.

——————— /// ———————

At nine o'clock Wednesday morning Jason walked into Nathan Simon's office. Motioning to Donna to follow him in, they both entered Nathan's office.

"How'd it go last night?"

Jason nodded. "Went well, left them with just enough confusion they won't know who did what. And those two guys will have one nasty headache this morning. Let's just say, I disrupted their little business for a while."

Jason sat in one of the chairs in front of Nathan's desk, while Donna sat in the other.

"Oh, I have something for you." He pulled the bra out of his back pocket. "Is this yours?"

Donna looked at the bra, without touching it. "Could be? Where'd you get it?"

"From the retired cop's desk, bottom drawer."

"Who?"

"The guy whose nuts you rearranged."

"Oh, that guy. I'm not sure if I want it back now."

"Fine, I'll get rid of it. Just wanted to let you know he doesn't have it anymore. And by the way, I got their phones, no pictures."

Donna nodded she understood, Jason stuffed the bra into his back pocket. Nathan listened to their discussion and then jumped in.

"Are you all set for tomorrow?"

Jason nodded yes.

"Will we see you before then?"

Jason shook his head no. "I've got some things to take care of, get an early start in the morning." He stood up to go, before turning back around.

"Oh, FYI, you're going to see an entry for five hundred dollars cash on my next invoice. I had to stuff an envelope with my own money. Those two clowns only had eighty bucks between them, which of course I kept. Talk to you tomorrow."

Nathan and Donna watched him walk out the door. She looked at Nathan, who shrugged his shoulders, figuring it was probably best they didn't know.

TWENTY

Jeff Morgan rose early on Wednesday morning as he did most days. Yawning, he hadn't gotten as much sleep as he usually did. He had been determined to finish the manuscript the previous night and wound up staying up very late to do so.

Standing in the kitchen and pouring his first cup of decaf, he viewed the pile of papers on his kitchen table, his new makeshift office. Taking the cup with him, he sat at the table and looked at each sorted pile.

The new pile that he had added last night contained the manuscript broken down into four parts. The first part covered the early family history before the war as they settled on the ranch. The second part was the family's life on the ranch. The third part was the men marching off to war, specifically to the Wilderness Campaign and their subsequent deaths at that battle.

The last part was, well, he was uncertain. It seemed to be mostly random thoughts added to the end, not real cohesive. Maybe Sandra Nelson hadn't gotten to that yet to sort out. Or maybe it was stuff Kittridge was working on toward the end that he hadn't flushed out. Whatever the reason, Jeff felt certain they wouldn't be able to use any of that, or at the very least not in that condition. That part would require much more work to complete.

He spent some time making notes on his pad regarding the manuscript that he tore off and placed on top. Next, he reached for the research documents. The top one in his pile was the family tree, just a typed two page document stapled together that he now set it in front of him to review.

```
Albert Samuels - oldest brother - wife,
Margaret - children?
Robert Samuels - next brother in line -
wife, Annabelle
Robert Samuels Jr. - son - wife Eloise -
two daughters
Albert Samuels - son - unmarried
John Samuels - youngest brother - wife,
Elizabeth
Katherine Gordon - Daughter - one son *
Edward Samuels - son - unmarried
Peter Samuels - son - unmarried
_____

Luke Gordon - oldest brother - wife,
deceased
Samuel Gordon - son - wife, Katherine -
one son *
Harry Gordon - son
Rufus Gordon - brother - wife?
Alfred Gordon - brother - wife?

Adjoining ranches - related - could have gone
together???????
```

He flipped the first page over, folding it at the staple to see the second page attached, which contained a brief history of the family.

```
Albert and Margaret Samuels settled the
land in 1836, joined shortly thereafter by
Albert's two younger brothers, Robert and
John and their families. Through a series
```

of purchases, they consolidated the adjoin-
ing farms into the main ranch. When the
ranch between the Samuels and the Gordon
ranch became available they struck a deal
to buy it together and divide the property between them, which they did, becom-
ing attached neighbors. Their friendship
grew strong over the years so much so that
Samuel Gordon married Katherine Samuels
cementing a strong family tie. They even
had two celebrations, marking that festive
occasion, Saturday on the Samuels ranch and
Sunday on the Gordon ranch.

The next document comprised several typed or computer printed
pages, clipped together titled:

"The Wilderness Campaign"

The document gave a detailed account of the battle over the three
days that it ran. The ultimate goal of the campaign was to cause
the destruction of Lee's Army by the Union forces. Behind the
printouts of the battle were pages detailing the march to get there
and finally on the back pages were handwritten notes, presumably by Kittridge, describing how he thought the men from the
Samuels and Gordon ranch would have joined that march and
done battle at the Wilderness Campaign. The heavy casualties
that resulted would have included those men, as well. All part of
Grant's war of attrition.

Jeff made more notes on his pad. There really wasn't any evi-
dence these men were part of that march, only an assumption that
they were. A copy of a newspaper listing the dead killed at the
Wilderness Campaign somewhat supported that theory. As Jeff
scanned down the names, he found all five of the Gordon men
and all seven of the Samuels men listed alphabetically on that
newspaper copy.

Nodding at that reasonable assumption, he set that piece of paper down. Jeff sat back in his chair, contemplating all that information. Deciding that Kittridge's assumption appeared to be confirmed, he could accept Kittridge's account of the men being on the march and subsequently being killed during that Wilderness Campaign. Still, it would have been good if there were something, anything to place the men there, or something to further support that premise, but that may have been too much to expect at this juncture.

Tapping his fingers on the table he looked at that newspaper listing in front of him. Making a note on his pad he wrote—*Well, there is a historical document reporting that those men were killed during the Wilderness Campaign.*—Setting the pen down, he picked up that section of the manuscript that described the march and agreed that it was very possible those men could have been part of that march and subsequent battle.

Kittridge had done a good job of describing the march, dedicating a significant portion of the manuscript to that assumption. No doubt from the document he had and his belief that they were Union Soldiers, it wouldn't have been too much of a stretch to assume those men were part of that march, so Kittridge had weaved that premise into the story line.

Jeff turned the Wilderness Campaign packet over on top of the family tree document and did the same with the newspaper copy. Before he could pick up the next paper the phone rang. He got up to answer.

"Hello?"

"Yes, Mr. Morgan, this is Lillian Meriweather, do you have a moment?"

"Hi Lillian, sure."

"Mr. Cummings asked me to give you a ring, he wondered if you have had the chance to think over our request to visit the piece of furniture you have?"

Jeff smiled. "Actually, I have."

"You did, that's wonderful."

"To be honest, I have plans for the weekend, maybe we could

set something for Monday of the following week?"

"That would be fine, Mr. Morgan. What time would work for you?"

"Early morning would be okay."

"Shall we say ten then?"

"Sure. Ten would be fine."

"That is just wonderful, we are so looking forward to viewing that unique piece of furniture you have. We absolutely look forward to seeing you then."

"Sure. Bye."

"Good bye, Mr. Morgan."

Jeff heard the line disconnect and hung the phone back up. He couldn't help smiling. He picked up his cell from the table and scrolling down to her number, pressed send.

"Professor Hathaway's office."

"Yes, hi, it's Jeff Morgan, I wonder if I might have a word with Ms. Hathaway?"

"Sure thing, Mr. Morgan hold on."

A moment later Professor Hathaway came on the line.

"Jeff, so good to hear from you."

"Always good to hear your voice as well."

"Okay, what do you need this time?"

"Listen, I just heard from the pussy people."

"I wish you wouldn't refer to them like that, now I can't think of them without thinking ... you know."

"That's my plan."

"Your plan?"

"Anyway, I just heard from them and I said they could come by Monday at ten, give you a chance to ah ... see it first."

"Great, so sweet of you to think of me."

"So, have you heard anymore about them yet?"

"No more than I already told you, sorry."

"That's okay, maybe they are legit. I'm still surprised that they knew about the bureau the day after it was delivered."

"That is unusual."

"Oh well, no big deal, they can look at it, but it's not going anywhere."

The line was silent for a moment. Finally Jeff spoke.

"Hey, I finished the manuscript last night, broke it down into four parts, the Samuels family settling the ranch, the family living on the ranch, the march and the men's death and what I'm beginning to believe to be some unusable stuff at the end. I'll tell you all about it on Friday."

"I'm looking forward to it."

"Bye Lori."

"Bye Jeff."

The line disconnected. Jeff set the cell phone back down on the table.

The next document was some later family history that, for now, he flipped over into the finished pile.

The last document in the review pile also comprised of several pages and focused on Virginia, Richmond, General Lee and his Confederate Army of Northern Virginia. He didn't understand any of it at first, but then assumed Kittridge wanted to get information on everything that was happening around that time and maybe find some other material he could use in the story. Looking through the pages, it appeared to be no more than Internet print outs of various pieces of information covering each of those subjects. However, at the end of that group of papers, he found several pages of typewritten or computer printed notes. Curious, he started to read through those. The first page was titled "facts" and contained the following statements:

```
Virginia was a Confederate State

Pro-Union sentiment in Virginia -
Unionist delegates defeated an early
motion to secede

April 17, 1861, the Virginia convention
voted to secede
```

Confederate capital moved from Alabama to Richmond

Union Army moved into Northern Virginia

Virginia was a slave state, the Republicans in office had announced their intention of limiting slavery, however, slavery was protected by the sovereignty of the state, therefore an attack on slavery was an attack on that sovereignty on the freedom of property and political representation.

Colonel Robert E. Lee resigned his U.S. Army commission.

From May 1861 to April 1865 Richmond was the capital of the Confederacy, home of the Confederate President, Jefferson Davis.

General Ulysses S. Grant's overland campaign was fought in Virginia. The campaign included battles of attrition at the Wilderness, Spotsylvania and Cold Harbor and ended with the siege of Petersburg.

The western counties not in favor of the Confederacy formed a pro-union state government of Virginia in 1861 and formed the new state of West Virginia.

He folded that first sheet over the staple and proceeded to review the second page titled "Assumptions" which had the following statements:

The Samuels and the Gordon ranches were
located just outside of Richmond in
Virginia and must of posed a real hard-
ship on them if they were Union soldiers?
Or were they? At the very least, these men
must have been pro-union for they fought
and died for the Union Army - or did they?
Could I have been wrong and these were
actually Confederate Soldiers that died
during the Wilderness Campaign?

Impossible, there is the newspaper article
listing them as Union dead. ?????

Okay, here's what must have happened. They
owned and lived on a ranch located right
outside the city of Richmond that was the
home of the Confederate President, the
heart of the confederacy, but they were
Unionists caught up in the war. None too
happy with that situation, they left the
ranch and joined the Union Army and died
during the Wilderness Campaign.

Because of the newspaper listing them as
Union dead, killed during the Wilderness
Campaign, I have to assume they did
in fact join the Union Army to fight in
Virginia on the Union side, but then

I need more research to determine

What's going on here?????

That ended the second page of notes. He folded that over the
staple and reviewed the third page titled "Questions" with the fol-

lowing statements:

Confederate State?

```
Union Soldiers???? - Confederate
Soldiers????

Ranch outside Richmond?

Died during the Wilderness Campaign?

Why did they wait until 1864 to fight? Or
did they?

Something is not adding up here????

Why did the whole family go? And the
Gordons?

What really happened?
```

Jeff folded that page over the staple and looked at the next page, but all it had on it at the top was "Virginia?" the next page had "Richmond?" the next page had "Confederate Army of Northern Virginia" the next page had "Confederate Capital" and the last page had "Union soldiers in Virginia." Obviously Kittridge had intended to do more research into these topics, but unfortunately he didn't complete that task, or probably couldn't.

Jeff drummed his fingers on the table and, flipping the pages back to the front reread the top three pages from the facts to the questions page over again. What was Kittridge trying to say? He looked at his notes from the manuscript and again looked at the final part, the one that didn't quite make sense. Could some of that be the product of this? His best guess was, maybe. That last part being rather incoherent, it was hard to tell if any of this research had been included or maybe it was Kittridge's attempt to make sense of his questions by including that material? Either way, it was going to take a real effort to use any of that in the present condition, even if he could tie it back to Kittridge's notes. Setting the paper down on the table, he looked at the print outs from the Internet, but they appeared to be longer pieces of information that Kittridge summarized in his notes, not much help there.

Jeff rubbed his hand across his face. Looking at his coffee cup still sitting there, he knew it would be quite cold. Even the coffee maker had turned off. He realized that he had been at this for some time. He gathered those documents up and clipped them back together.

Picking up and turning the finished pile back over face up he took one more look at the diary entries and smiled at the fact that he was quite sure he had that very bureau that - one ugly bureau - in his possession.

He retrieved his pad and looked it over, making bullet points of the finished tasks, the road trips he'd been on, meeting with Magalito, meeting with Sandra Nelson, Missouri and bringing back the beast and finally meeting with Professor Hathaway, that one bringing a smile to his face.

He set the pen down on the pad, pushed it into the center of the table and leaned back in the chair. Deciding he had enough for one day, he got up from the table and walked out to the garage. The beast still sat there. He nodded as if saying hello.

A moment later Jeff climbed into his car and pulled out of the garage, closing the door. He was headed to the cafe for some lunch and a break from all this.

TWENTY-ONE

Dressed in a maintenance uniform, Jason pulled into the West
River Country Club at five-thirty, just as the sun was coming up
over the horizon. He parked his car on the far end away from
general parking. Walking the distance back to the maintenance
shed, he climbed into one of the gardener's golf carts and pulled
away from the building.

Casually making his way to the front of the course, past the
putting green and the path to the first tee, he stopped the cart and
got out. Under the pretense of working on a line of shrubs, he
kept a wary eye for any signs of unusual activity. After an hour
of watching, he left the area, figuring that if the Congressman's
people were going to do anything, they would have done it
already.

Pulling the cart behind the building, he exited the vehicle and
entered the back of the country club. Very carefully, he made his
way to an interior restroom, one of the two designed for single
usage that he already knew was located in the back.

Emerging ten minutes later, dressed in a sport jacket and
dress slacks, with an open collar white dress shirt, tucked firmly
into the slacks, he made his way over to the coffee urn. Pouring
a cup, he stepped back out onto the veranda and sat at a far table
and waited, sipping coffee.

———————— /// ————————

Congressman Reginald Harrison arrived at six-fifty, followed by his entourage. Pausing a moment, he eyed the man sitting at the far table. Jason raised his cup and the Congressman nodded.

"Would you excuse me, please?"

The entourage left and made their way inside, while Harrison walked over to the table.

"Congressman?"

"Are you Jason?"

"Sometimes."

"Would this be one of those days?"

"Yes, it would."

"Shall we take a walk?"

"As you wish."

Jason stood up, leaving his cup on the table, but he paused to pick up a small bag he had at his feet.

"What's in the bag?"

Jason held it in the air. "A present for you, but we'll discuss that later."

The Congressman nodded. Together they walked out onto the course, passing the putting green eventually approaching an open area, they stopped at a fence. The Congressman spoke first.

"So what's so important that I needed to take this meeting?"

"Perhaps I should give you some background first."

The Congressman didn't respond, so Jason continued.

"Several months ago, my boss took on a client that wanted him to hand off a project he was working on once he passed away to one of five names on a list. That client was hoping that one of those names would agree to take on the project and finish it for him. One finally agreed the fourth name on that list."

Jason paused, but the Congressman remained silent, so Jason continued.

"The interesting thing about those names is that they all served together in Vietnam. Again, no big deal, old Army buddies, totally reasonable, until you hear some of the names on that list, well, one in particular."

This time the Congressman looked at him.

"That name is Robert Swift, Swifty as he was known back in the day. He was picked because he was a wheeler-dealer sort. But, as I'm sure you know he's doing a stretch in a Federal country club. That took him out of the running. As I said the fourth name on that list accepted the project."

Jason turned to face the Congressman.

"That project is the completion and hopefully the publication of a manuscript centered on, several of the dead guy's family members wiped out in one of the many Civil War battles, on the surface, not much really."

"You've seen this manuscript?"

"I've read it. Very rough, but as I said, the man was dying of cancer, probably couldn't focus too much at the end. Not sure it will ever see the light of day, certainly not in its present condition."

The Congressman remained silent. Jason continued.

"Funny thing happened though. Right after the fourth guy accepted the project, an attorney by the name of Edward Samson came into my boss's office. By the way do you know him?"

The Congressman remained silent, nor did he wave his head either way. Jason took that as an answer.

"Anyway this attorney marches right into the office and demands to see that manuscript, which by the way, my boss was considering letting him take a look at, just as soon as he talked to the client, the current one that is."

Jason paused to see if there was a reaction, but when there wasn't he continued.

"The very next night, two goons barge into the office, assault the secretary, stripping her to her underwear, take some pictures threaten the two if they don't turn over the manuscript, drug them and trash the office, which really pissed off my boss."

Again he paused, waiting for, but not getting a reaction.

"As you can imagine that set the wheels in motion, specifically to figure out who was behind all that and why. Of course, we called this Samson guy, but surprise, surprise, he feigned ignorance, so we had to dig a little deeper, trying to put a connection together, which we, that is, I did. Turned out it was actually pretty easy to do."

Pausing, Jason faced the Congressman. "It was you."

"Me?"

Jason didn't answer, giving the Congressman the chance to state his protest of innocence.

"I can assure you that I had nothing to do with any of that, nor do I know anything about that. How can you say …?"

"Easy Congressman, let me finish."

Jason walked a little further down the fence. The Congressman followed.

"I know what happened in Vietnam. I talked to Magalito just before he died. I specifically know all about that helicopter flight, that day in Laos."

The Congressman stopped in his tracks. "Again, I can assure you I have no idea what you are referring too." Looking at Jason a few feet away from him, he pointed. "Are you wired? Is this some sort of trick to get me to?"

Jason stopped and walked back to the Congressman, stopping just short of touching him.

"Let me put this as plain as possible. My instructions were to get in, present our case, then get out, no tricks, no funny business or I would have to answer to her."

Jason stepped away, but then turned and faced him again still very close.

"And let me tell you this one time. I'd be far more concerned with what she could do to me than I ever would about someone like you. Just remember who arranged this meeting that should tell you everything you need to know, but just maybe, I'll tell you why."

Jason stepped away and continued walking for a bit. The Congressman followed and, stopping right next to him, leaned on the fence, speaking softly.

"Continue."

Jason nodded. "All right." Not expecting anyone nearby, he looked around anyway, before speaking.

"Magalito told me about the helicopter flight into Laos. It seems Swifty had a pretty good drug pedaling operation going on, but what was most interesting about the story was the box of Jade statues you carried out that day."

The Congressman remained silent.

"Magalito said he didn't know how you got those out of the country, but he did know that you did. Well, I actually do know how."

The Congressman turned to look at him this time, Jason continued.

"I have a very old friend that did … well, let's just say Air America work over there, he was tuned into most operations, and quite frankly made a buck or two for himself."

Jason paused, but turned to face the Congressman, he paused just long enough to get his attention.

"Coffins."

"Coffins?"

"Yes, seems there were far more coffins leaving Vietnam during the war then there were casualties. It was common knowledge that that was how drugs were smuggled out, so why not everything else?"

Jason turned away, looking out over the green and rested his forearms on the fence. He waited for the Congressman to get closer before speaking very softly, just above a whisper.

"Is that why you're so concerned about the manuscript, afraid that ancient history might get out? Some fairy tale that couldn't ever be proven even in the best of times?"

The Congressman shifted his stance. "Again, if I knew any of what you were talking about I might have a response, but as it is."

Jason cut him off, waving his hand in the air.

"At ease Congressman. I'm not here to make threats, or cause you any grief. Actually I'm here to assure you that there are none. No one knows about any of this. Hell, Magalito is dead. In fact that's why he told me the story then said, and I quote, 'who gives a fuck now, I'll be dead soon'. He was, two days later."

Jason turned to face the Congressman pausing a moment before continuing.

"Magalito was the fifth name on the list. That is how I got onto him in the first place. Coincidently, he was also on that helicopter that day. Thought I'd stop by see what he knew. Apparently he knew a lot and was quite willing to tell it all, death bed confession and all that as well as giving me the name of the Pilot that day, your name. He also said to forget I ever heard it."

Jason paused and smiled. The Congressman remained silent.

"Hell, if I wanted to do anything with this information, I would have done it already. I don't give a shit what you did some forty years ago, nor do I care and actually neither does anybody else."

"Then why are you telling me this ... this story?"

Jason turned to face him again looking him directly in the eyes.

"Because someone is harassing my boss for no apparent reason and if it is because of the fear of this ancient fairy tale getting out, I can assure you that that is not going to happen, certainly not from any of us, even if we think we might know something, which we don't."

Jason took a breath and a quick look around.

"Look, our client is chasing his tail pursuing some Civil War fable. He's old, retired, gives him something to do. I assure you he has no interest in this Vietnam stuff, nor is there anything to do with Vietnam anywhere in that manuscript."

The Congressman nodded. Jason continued

"So, our request is stop the harassment, let him chase his tail in peace. And more specifically, leave my boss alone."

"Again, if I had any knowledge."

Jason raised his hand. "Save it. Here's what I think. I think one of your aides went rogue, thought he could clear what ever this is, or whatever he may think it is, up on his own, without your knowledge and I may just have proof of that."

"You have proof? Proof of what?"

Jason opened the bag, showing the contents to the Congressman.

"The two goons that trashed my boss's office and assaulted the secretary, turned out to be a low level investigation firm, that's what made me suspect the job came from lower in the food chain. I can't see you turning to those two guys to help you wipe your ass. One is a retired cop, the other is retired FBI. Here's the FBI cell phone. It has been wiped clean and rendered useless, the cop's phone is at the bottom of a lake. That ass hole took pictures of the assault. I should have stuck the phone up his ass."

Jason paused, taking a breath.

"Well, let's just say those two clowns will be spending the next few months trying to explain a situation they got caught up in. I don't think they will be investigating much of anything in the very near future, hopefully never again."

Jason handed the bag to the Congressman.

"You'll find all the bugging equipment they installed in my boss's office. I'm sure I don't have to tell you the ramifications of bugging an attorney's office. Well, I assure you everything I collected is in there. We have nothing else in our possession, certainly nothing that could get back to you in any way. And my boss has no intention of pursuing the matter any further if we can agree."

The Congressman looked at the bag in his hand.

"Everything?"

"Yes, we held nothing back."

The two men stood silent. Finally Jason spoke softly.

"Look, if some low level aide thought he could make some brownie points by authorizing this, I'd burn him right now, today, cut him loose, get out in front of it. And if you had anything to do with this, even just a passing knowledge, which personally I suspect you do, I'd still burn the aide. Right now, nothing points back to you. The calls on the FBI guy's phone listed one of your aides' numbers several times. I wrote the number down for you, just in the offshoot that you really are unaware. So, we have nothing, I have given you everything we have and my assurances that none of this goes any farther, all we want is your assurance this ends now. Leave my boss alone and forget about going after our client. This has nothing to do with Vietnam or you what so ever."

The Congressman looked at the bag in his hand.

"Assuming I had any knowledge of any of this, I would certainly put a stop to any activity immediately. And if any of my people were."

"That's all we are asking."

The Congressman looked at Jason, hesitating a moment before asking.

"You said you would tell me why she went to all the trouble to set up this meeting."

Jason looked at the Congressman smiling.

"She likes you, why I don't know, but she wants you to win that Senate seat next year and I believe she fully intends to help you do that. I'm sure she would hate to have you get caught up in anything right now, anything at all, especially some fairy tale from forty years ago. She's trying to protect you, plain and simple, no doubt about that."

The Congressman nodded. Jason leaned in.

"That secretary that got assaulted, during the break in, is an extremely close personal friend of hers, left her quite upset. You might even say quite angry."

For the first time the Congressman showed emotion.

"That was her?"

Jason nodded yes, raising his hand in the air, speaking very softly.

"I will also tell you this, we had to go a long way to prove our case before she would agree to help us, which we did. But in doing so, I pushed heavy on the prospect of an aide going rogue on this, quite possibly unbeknownst to you. You'd be wise to make that your story, for your sake, as well as for her sake. Give her the benefit of the doubt, that you just might be clean on this one. But whatever you do, burn that guy today, let her see that you can clean house. I'm sure she's counting on that, more likely expecting it."

The Congressman nodded he understood. He even offered a smile.

"I suppose we both know who's in charge."

"You bet your ass we do. I certainly do. I've never gone into a meeting with these restrictions, somebody telling me what I can and can't do at least not that I've readily agreed too, but she would have it no other way."

The Congressman smiled again. As the two men walked back, Jason suddenly turned and faced the Congressman.

"Might I tell you one more thing? It's more of an observation than anything."

The Congressman nodded.

"Right now, the only other person still alive that has any knowledge of any of that fairy tale from forty years ago is Robert Swift. Did you ever stop to think, he might be the one trying to bust your balls?"

"Swift? I don't understand."

"I'm sure you know he's not your biggest fan. Wouldn't put it past him to stir up shit. Remember he was one of the names on the list … got wind of that manuscript early on, maybe he's trying to get his hands on it? The aide that I mentioned visited him up state on two occasions. Maybe he is behind some of this. Maybe he wants to get hold of the manuscript thinking there is something in there he can hold over your head."

"Really?"

"Just saying. But I'd think about looking long and hard at that possibility. He's the only one comes to mind might be a problem."

The Congressman nodded. The two men continued walking back to the clubhouse. Several aides were standing around waiting.

"Congressman we have to hurry. You need to look over the speech and we have …"

Congressman Reginald Harrison watched Jason disappear into the crowd. He clutched the bag in his left hand.

"I'll need a moment first."

———————— /// ————————

Later that night there was an item on the news regarding a

shakeup in the Congressman's staff:

"A senior aide was let go over philosophical differences. It was announced that Edgar Sweetwater, a highly regarded political consultant was brought on to get the Congressman's house in order, furthering the rumor that Congressman Harrison would indeed be running for the Senate next year."

Antoinette "Toni" Ri-chard smiled as she heard the news. A short time later her cell phone rang.

"Hello."

"Toni, hi, it's Reggie. I believe you have heard the news by now?"

"Yes, I have."

"Toni, I just want you to know that I had nothing to do with any of that. I will tell you that I sent that lawyer Samson in, but only to inquire, nothing more. I was under the belief that something in that manuscript might be damaging. But, I would never have done something like that. I hope you can believe me."

"Reggie, I will take you at your word for now."

"I swear to you, I only wanted to know what was in that manuscript."

"Fine. Consider the matter closed. You and your lovely wife must join us for dinner soon, maybe discuss some strategy now that the cat is out of the bag."

"I'd like that very much."

"Sweetwater huh? I like that move, maybe I can put together one of my fabulous fundraisers and we can convince him to stay on through the election?"

"Thank you Toni."

"Bye Reggie."

Toni Ri-chard set the cell phone down, smiling deviously.

——— TWENTY-TWO———

Professor Hathaway pulled into Jeff Morgan's driveway just after four on Friday afternoon. He stood in the garage, waiting for her to exit the car.

"I'd let you park inside, but the beast is in the way."

"The beast?"

"Yes, that's how the guy that brought it here referred to the bureau."

Professor Hathaway nodded, as she stepped into the garage. "My, but that is rather big."

Jeff nodded as he stood beside her. "You can say that again. Heavy too." Jeff walked closer to the piece, pulling the center second drawer part way out. "I discovered that there are cleats on the inside that correspond to the groves in each drawer, no two are the same. The drawers ride on these cleats as well as rails on the bottom of each drawer."

Stepping back, he closed that drawer and opened the door on the left side. "A compartment on each side." He closed that door and opened the top center drawer. "Doesn't look like much, but I have a new found respect for the way it was built."

Professor Hathaway nodded. Jeff caught himself and walked closer to her.

"I'm sorry, where are my manners? Let's get your bag and let you get inside. After that long drive I'm sure you must be thirsty, probably need a pit stop."

She smiled and watched, while he fetched her bag from the back seat.

"Shall we?"

She pressed the door lock on her key chain and followed him through the garage door into the kitchen. The first thing she noticed was the papers stacked on top of the kitchen table. "That your office?"

Jeff turned to face the table, smiling. "Sure turned out that way. It all started with me using it to kind of spread out, take a look see at what I had."

She nodded as she followed him through the kitchen further into the house. Jeff pointed.

"This here is the guest room. Has its own bathroom. My room is on the other side of the house. Hope you'll be comfortable here?"

"I'm sure I will."

Jeff set her bag on the bed. "I made reservations for six-thirty, if that's okay with you?"

She nodded, looking at him. Jeff took the hint.

"Well, I'll give you a minute."

Jeff left the guest room, closing the door behind him. Professor Hathaway sat on the bed, taking a moment. Just as quickly, she was up using the restroom, washing her hands, checking herself in the mirror and back out the door, leaving the bag for later. Jeff was standing in the kitchen.

"Would you like some water or anything?"

"A glass of water would be nice."

She sat at the table, looking over the piles of paper. "Did you do your homework?"

Jeff handed her the glass of water, the ice rattling inside as he sat in one of chairs on the side of the table facing her. "Yes and no. I have some questions, but mostly I have piles of paper that don't seem too connected."

"I can imagine. How about we leave it for now and take another look at that bureau?"

"Sure."

Jeff stood up, as did she. Together they walked back into the garage and stood in front of the bureau. She shook her head as she spoke.

"I can't believe this is the very bureau mentioned in those diary entries of 1864. I have no reason not too, but?"

"Yeah, I know what you mean, took me awhile to start to believe. When old Herb Miller first showed it to me, I still had doubts, but he eventually convinced me. If you had seen it, you would also have believed that thing was in his barn for eighty years. And when he told me the story of the two ladies that most certainly had to be the two girls mentioned on that diary and how long they had lived on their farm … well I took a leap and felt confident that this in fact is that very bureau."

Professor Hathaway walked over to the piece and ran her hand over the surface as Jeff commented. "Yeah, it's a bit pitted, but remember it has been sitting in a barn for eighty years."

She nodded, rubbing her fingers together, looking at him. "No, it isn't that. This piece of furniture is … well at least one hundred and fifty years old and most certainly was used everyday … and. Do you know what that means to a history professor?"

"I suppose I can guess."

She turned to face him and smiled, taking a moment before speaking.

"It's just that … well a realization of where this piece has been, the people who used it … the fact it was mentioned in a diary entry from 1864 by a Union soldier, why it's …it's … well, it's history." Pausing, she turned fully to look at him. "I'm sorry. I didn't mean to get, you know."

"It's okay Professor, I understand."

"Lori."

Jeff nodded, pointing at the beast. "Listen we have tomorrow to stare at this thing, what say we get freshened up, relax a bit, and then go get that dinner, before we get into any of our work?"

"That sounds fine."

As they left, she ran her hand over the top once again. Jeff waited for her to finish and followed her back into the house. He left the cover sitting on his workbench having removed it just before she arrived, turning off the light and closing the door behind him.

— /// —

At dinner, they decided not to discuss the project and instead focused on small talk revisiting their conversations about themselves that they had brushed the surface on at their first dinner.

Arriving back home, they settled into the living room. Jeff poured a glass of port for both of them and sat back on the sofa. Around ten pm, they decided it was too late to do any more work tonight and to pick things up first thing in the morning. As Jeff got up, she followed him into the kitchen and while he rinsed out the glasses, she looked at the table noticing the box sitting on the chair.

"So what's in that box?"

Jeff turned to look at where she was pointing and nodded. "Some more research stuff that I recently received but haven't had a chance to go through any of that yet."

"Would it be okay if I went through that box? You know, maybe start to get my feet wet, you know sink my teeth into some of this?"

"Sure, if you want. I'll probably be up for awhile anyway going through the manuscript again, making some more notes, fleshing out my questions for tomorrow."

She smiled. "Okay, that's a deal. We study tonight, test tomorrow."

"Test?"

She waved her hand in the air as she gathered up the box. They bid each other good night and went into their respective rooms on opposite sides of the house. Jeff turned off the living room light.

— /// —

THE KITTRIDGE MANUSCRIPT

Professor Hathaway undressed, pulling on a white camisole and leaving her panties on, her usual sleeping garb. After brushing her teeth and turning off the bathroom light, she crawled up on the bed and opened the box.

Most of the top pages looked like copies or print outs from web sites. As she made her way through the layers, she was beginning to think there was nothing of obvious value in this box, certainly nothing needing further review tonight and decided she probably should make this an early night.

With a fierce yawn she dug deeper and touched something on the bottom. Slowly removing the top layers of paper and setting them gently face down on the bed she found a well-worn leather pouch, six by twelve, with even more delicate leather tie. Carefully untying the bow and looking inside, she discovered several pieces of paper throughout the inside divided by slots.

The papers looked yellowed and brittle, which she suspected they were very old, so she very gently removed the first piece. Opening the document ever so slowly, she realized it was a letter written in a delicate lady's hand and began to read.

```
July 10, 1865


My Dearest Margaret,


I hope this letter finds you well. The
arrangement you have worked out for your
purchase of our portion of the ranch has
gone a long way to help me in my pur-
chase of a spread here in Missouri. The
bank has been most favorable to receiving
those letters of credit. I know you would
have preferred we stay, but the memories
were just too painful. Why do men have to
get caught up in war and get themselves
killed? I shall never understand such
foolishness.
```

I still don't know how you were able to
stand there so strong that day at the
train station and take receipt of our dear
departed men in those seven pine boxes,
while Annabelle, Elizabeth and myself
stood off to the side crying like school-
girls. And our dear Katherine standing by,
as the Gordon men were off loaded. How your
strength carried us that day as the men
were brought back to the ranch and laid to
rest side by side.

Well, as you may have gathered by the
length that this is not the only purpose
of this letter. As the matriarch of the
family, which I am now part of, I beg of
you to read to the end before you pass
judgment, as I am desperately seeking your
wise advice in this terrible matter.

I know you frowned upon the idea of hir-
ing that ranch hand to get me to Missouri,
but he did come with very favorable rec-
ommendations and it was always his intention to leave for the gold fields out west
once I reached my destination. I strongly
believed it would not have been in keeping
with God's good graces to travel there on
my own, with two small children in atten-
dance. As it was, we encountered Federal
Troops not more'n four hours out. I dare
say it may have been most unpleasant, had
I not had a man with me.

But, I ramble on so, please forgive me.

THE KITTRIDGE MANUSCRIPT

I must tell you everything happened so
fast, I hardly had time to digest it all,
before I found myself writing this letter.
Why, it just happened this very morning.

As you suspected, the man I hired had a
fondness for the drink and had spent most
of the money I paid him before we even
got to our destination. A situation that
being a Christian woman, left me with little choice but to keep him on for a period
in hopes that he would earn enough to be
on his way. After I purchased my mod-
est little spread, I allowed him to live
there and manage the land, while I kept up
my duties at the Mercantile. Well, month
after month seemed to pass us by and he
never seemed to have enough to light out
after his fortune. Well here we are over a
year later and things just seem to be getting worse.

As was the custom after church, I took
a ride out to the property this Sunday
morning. Fortunately, the two girls were
invited to a friend's birthday party and I
was satisfied to ride out alone. No sooner
did I pull up than he came out of the
little house on the property and I hesitate to tell you that he was sloppy with
the drink already and it was neigh eleven
in the morning. I should have turned that
buggy around right then and there, but I
was mad, foolish pride was all it was. I
was off and walking toward him, ready to

speak my mind this time, before I had a chance to think it through.

No sooner was I out of the buggy before he started ranting and raving that if he is to be the man of the house, then when was I going to provide my wifely duties to him. I informed him in no uncertain terms that I was neither his wife, nor his for his beck and call and I would have none of that. I was barely through the door when he grabbed me by the hair and started pulling and tearing at my clothes. I tried desperately to fight back, but he landed a blow to my side that took my breath away, I could feel the last of my garments falling away as I fought for a breath. Once again he had me by the hair and was dragging me to the bedroom. I will simply say he had his way with me. When he was finished, he left me sprawled on the bed and went off, for I can only imagine fetching his bottle of whiskey.

I found it hard to move and still do. I'm beginning to believe he may have cracked one or more of my ribs on that side as the pain is excruciating this much later and the skin has turned a dark shade of blue. Well, call it fate or blind luck. In his fight to drag me in there, I managed to keep my bag in my hands to the very end. It sat there on the floor inside the bedroom. Struggling to get to it, I reached inside and removed Robert's six-shooter. He gave me that for protection the day he left, previously having taught me how to use it. I staggered into the doorway in only what God gave me and confronted him.

Seeing me like that in the doorway, he must have imagined I was in for another go. That is, until he saw that six-shooter in my hand. In an instant he turned mean and threw the whiskey bottle at me smashing the bottle on the wall right next to my head. Upon seeing that he had missed, he started toward me calling me all sorts of vile names.

I put the first shot into his belly, but that only served to anger him more. The second shot hit square in the chest, which spun him around. He took two steps to the door stepped out onto the porch and immediately fell face forward into the dirt.

Keeping the pistol pointed at his prone body, I approached and with my bare foot kicked him to make sure that I had kilt him. When I got no reaction, I grabbed his arm and rolled him over. Sadly, I was right, he was sure enough dead.

Setting the six-shooter on the porch, I grabbed his arms and with some effort dragged him up behind a big old cypress tree. Fetching a shovel from the fence, I went back and dug a hole. Removing his long johns, to give the worms quicker access, I pushed him in the hole and covered him up face down.

DON MEYER

Ripping the long johns into pieces, I used
those scraps to stand by the horse trowel
and clean the sweat, dust and blood from
my naked body as best I could. In spite of
cleaning my skin off, I never felt dirtier
in my life.

I can say without hesitation, I shall
never lay with another man again and I
will instruct my girls on the evils men
have brought upon us with their insatiable
desires.

I gathered up his belongings, keeping what
I felt might be useful, took the rest into
the yard and tossing everything into a
pile, where I burned it all.

While still naked, I gathered up the tat-
tered remains of my own clothes and did
the best I could to put them in some fashion that I could wear until I got back
home. Fortunately, I was able to get back
into the house without any further interruption. When finally inside, I removed
everything I had on, tore it to shreds and
slipping into a bath, I redressed in time
to meet the girls when they arrived home.
I told them first that our ranch hand had
finally lit out for the gold fields, as he
had been promising all along, a story that
I plan to tell often to anybody who asks.
Not an unbelievable story as he was always
going on about doing just that to anybody
who would listen.

THE KITTRIDGE MANUSCRIPT

The girls have been put to bed and I have
taken the time to relate the incident in
this letter, asking for your advice moving forward. As a good Christian, I doubt
you can ever forgive me for doing such an
unchristian thing, but I hope and pray for
your guidance.

Forever yours,

Eloise

Professor Hathaway read the letter again, before setting it back inside the pouch, feeling and understanding that woman's pain. Looking back inside, she found what appeared to be a pack of papers. Again, opening them slowly, she laid each piece out on the bed in front of her.

Slowing opening the first one, it appeared to be some sort of receipt. It had a railroad marker on it and listed the contents of a delivery. Seven pine boxes, containing the bodies of seven men, along with their personal possessions and three horses. Opening the second piece of paper, it appeared to be a livery receipt for the transport, by wagon and two horses, of seven pine boxes out to a ranch for purposes of a proper family burial. That seemed to make sense.

But it was the next piece of paper that took her breath away, especially when she saw the signature at the bottom:

Gen. Robert E. Lee
Commanding.

It took her a moment to regain her composure enough to read that letter. Delicately, she picked up that piece of paper, took another deep breath and started to read.

DON MEYER

20 May 1864

Madam,

Unfortunately, the one undeniable cruelty of war is that men die, good men, all too young men, whether on the battlefield, as a civilian caught up in the fracas, or simply an innocent bystander. That such an incident happened this Tuesday last, pains me still.

First, you must understand that in times of war, an entrenched Army views any encroachment, regardless of uniform or not, in an adversarial nature, especially knowing the great Union Army is all about Virginia.

This is precisely what transpired that fateful Tuesday. Twelve men approached a forward sentry post and before proper challenge could be determined, a volley of shot was rained down on those men, regrettably killing all twelve men in a matter of moments.

Upon closer review, it was discovered that these men were merely local ranchers from outside the city traveling to Richmond for what appears to be financial reasons, as evidenced by the papers they were carrying in their document case identifying them as such, further they had a letter of credit to be presented at the bank of Richmond.

While I do not attempt to make any excuse for this tragic course of events, I must reiterate that with Federal Troops all about us, it would be reasonable to understand how and why these twelve men were engaged as they approached a forward post.

Discovering the true nature of their purpose only adds to the grief of their untimely loss, to that, I have no words. However, I have made every attempt to preserve and safeguard their bodies until they can be returned to their families. I immediately dispatched a detail to escort these men to the nearest railroad spur, to be shipped back to their respective families for proper burial. I have also insured all of their possessions, in addition to the six horses that survived the confrontation to be returned as well.

Finally, no words of mine can express my sincere regrets in having to inform you of this terrible loss, but please know, I send you my deepest sympathies and my humble apologizes for your unbearable loss.

Gen. Robert E. Lee
Commanding

Professor Hathaway read the letter again, her heart racing. Could this really be a personal letter from General Lee to the families of the fallen? What an amazing discovery that would be. Then it hit her.

"Oh my God!"

She grabbed her robe off the bed and barely got it over her

shoulders as she stepped out of the bedroom, walking down the hall to Jeff's room, the door was open and light was filtering out into the hall. She walked right in, her robe flaying open as she stepped inside the room.

"Jeff, you gotta see this."

Jeff looked up to see her standing, in the doorway holding a piece of paper in her hand, but more importantly he saw what she was wearing underneath the open robe. White panties, brief style probably and a white camisole on top that left very little to the imagination. He could see her breasts as if the material wasn't there, including the nipples protruding through the fabric.

"Jeff, did you hear me?"

He looked up at her as he placed the manuscript on his lap and pressed down on it to keep it from rising back up.

"I'm sorry?"

"So, you're a boxers man?"

Jeff looked down realizing he was dressed in t-shirt and boxers lying on the bed with the covers pulled down. The readers were still on his nose.

"Actually, I'm a briefs kind of guy."

"I don't understand. You're wearing boxers."

"That is for you."

"What?"

"Let me see if I can explain this."

Professor Hathaway stood there waiting. Jeff elaborated.

"If you were wearing a bikini bottom, nothing more would be thought about it, but standing there in your panties, which probably are covering more than a bikini bottom would anyway, is considered being in your underwear."

Suddenly aware of her appearance, she closed the robe around her.

"Whereas, if I were lying here in my briefs, you'd consider that underwear, but boxers seem to have the acceptance factor, so I thought as long as you were here, I would wear those."

She looked at him. "You actually thought about this?"

"Not really, just seemed to make sense as it was coming out."

She nodded again and walked closer to the bed, her robe falling back open. Jeff did all he could, to keep the manuscript in place. She started to sit on the bed, but got tangled in her robe. Finally in frustration, she removed it and placed the garment across the bottom of Jeff's bed, much to Jeff's delight.

"I just found this inside a leather pouch in that box I took from the table to look through."

She carefully opened it, holding it as gently as possible.

"It's a personal letter from General Robert E. Lee reporting on the untimely deaths of twelve men, your men. I mean the men in the manuscript."

Before Jeff could ask, she raised her hand stopping him.

"Do you know what this means?"

"Yes … no, I don't have a clue."

"The manuscript is wrong. Those men didn't die at the Wilderness, they died outside of Richmond."

Jeff looked at her and waited for her to continue.

"Don't you see, it's all wrong? They were in Richmond, or at the very least on their way there. How could it have been reported that they died during the Wilderness Campaign?"

Jeff started to get up, but then thought better of it.

"I have a research document on the Wilderness Campaign and a copy of a newspaper on the table that outlines the fact they died during the Wilderness Campaign. Plus that section of the manuscript."

She looked at him, then down at herself.

"Oh my God, I'm so sorry. I didn't think, here I am sitting on your bed in my underwear, what you must think of me."

"To tell you the truth, I'm thinking what a nice view …"

"Oh God. You can see right through this."

Professor Hathaway put her hands across her breasts, covering her nipples, carefully keeping that piece of paper safe. Standing up for a moment she set that paper on his dresser before sitting back down on the bed.

"Did I ever tell you how much finding a historical document turns me on? Or maybe it's really a man in boxers that does it for me ..."

Jeff sat still, not moving an inch, looking at her. She lowered her hands giving him the view of her breasts back.

"Can I be up front with you?"

Jeff nodded yes.

"I'm fifty-eight years old, I've been divorced for sixteen years. I've had a few dates during that time, even less physical encounters. I'm not sure I'd know what to do either, but I'd sure like to try with you."

She put her hand on Jeff's arm, but then reached over and removed the manuscript from his lap setting it on the dresser.

"From the looks of things, it appears you agree with me."

Jeff looked down and noticed he had actually popped out of the boxers, leaving nothing to the imagination.

"Well, obviously I'm game, if you are."

"There are two ways we can do this."

Jeff looked at her and waited, not sure what she meant.

"I can lie down next to you and we can clothes wrestle or I can take these off right now and give you the full access right now."

Jeff looked at her for a moment before answering.

"It might be easier if we just go for it."

Professor Hathaway pulled her camisole over her head and stuck her thumbs into the band of her panties. Jeff followed her lead removing his t-shirt and sliding his boxers off. She crawled onto the bed with him. Together they figured out what to do, and afterward fell asleep in each other's arms.

──TWENTY-THREE──

Slowly waking up, Jeff reached over and found that side of the bed empty. The faint smell of perfume lingered on the pillow. The events of last night brought a smile to his face. It really had been a long time since he had been with a woman, let alone spending the night with a woman.

After his wife died, he had no desire to engage again on any level, having decided he was done with all that. Just the thought of starting a relationship with someone new scared him on so many levels, which to him was as good a reason as any to hold back. But Professor Hathaway brought all those feelings back, and after last night, they had already crossed the first hurdle. The smile grew bigger.

Sliding out of bed, he put the boxers back on and walked into the bathroom, performing the morning routine. After brushing his teeth and gargling with some mouthwash, he left the bathroom. Picking up his t-shirt from the bed, he noticed that her robe was still there. Thinking, hoping she might be, he left the bedroom in his boxers and t-shirt.

Hearing a noise from the kitchen he entered that room. There she was standing at the sink, wearing only her panties and the camisole. His wish had come true. Clearing his throat as he entered, he spoke softly.

"Good morning."

She turned to face him. "Good morning yourself. I think I figured out the coffee maker and got some coffee started. I didn't look yet, but if you have the fixings for breakfast, I'd be happy to whip something up for you."

Jeff stood there in the middle of the room, taking in the view.

"I believe I do, but let's start with coffee. Actually I prefer decaf. You'll notice there are two makers for that very purpose, so we can brew both at the same time. Want me?"

She shook her head no. "I got this."

He sat down at the table as she turned back to the other coffee maker. She spoke softly, her back to him. "Any regrets."

"Regrets?"

"About last night? Are you hoping I'll leave soon?"

"Huh, what? What the hell are you talking about?"

She left the sink poured the two cups of coffee then walked over and sat at the table. She put the cup of decaf in front of him.

"You, the whole morning after thing?"

Jeff watched her take a sip of her coffee. "You lost me."

She set the cup down on the table and reached over, placing her hand on his. "Just tell me what you are thinking right now."

Jeff looked at her, taking in the sight of her breasts showing through the camisole, the nipples ... and took a much needed sip of coffee before answering, finally looking up to meet her eyes.

"I was thinking how good you looked from the back and now that you are sitting in front of me, especially dressed as you are, that breakfast probably isn't my first choice right at the moment."

She smiled, looking down at herself. "So, besides what you see, you don't want to get rid of me just yet?"

Jeff gained a little more composure. "Of all the things I am thinking about right now, getting rid of you isn't one of them."

She smiled, patting his hand. "Just checking. But since you don't want to get rid of me just yet, maybe I can push my luck and suggest that I spend the day ... and that goes without saying, the night ... and go home tomorrow."

Jeff looked at her nodding in the affirmative. "We might be able to work something out along those lines."

"I was hoping you'd consider that option."

"Yeah, I think we may have a deal here."

She smiled and patted his hand again, before sitting back in her chair, which gave Jeff a wonderful view of how little that camisole covered.

"Yeah, I definitely think we can work something out."

She took a sip of her coffee and looked down. "Jesus, I never learn."

"What?"

"This. Here I am flaunting myself again. I didn't mean too."

Jeff raised his hand. "It's okay I'm starting to like it."

She smiled and opened her arms to give him full view. He raised his cup and nodded. She closed her arms and sipped her coffee as she spoke.

"If you don't mind, I'd like to take a shower and get dressed. We still have work to do. That is unless you had something else in mind."

"Oh, I have lots in mind, but a shower sounds good and … well we do have later, even the whole night now, I'm sure we can."

She smiled and got up from the table, placing her cup in the sink.

"None of this changes anything. We still have to talk about it."

Jeff sat up startled, setting his cup on the table. "Talk about what?"

"The letter."

"What letter?"

"The letter I showed you last night?"

Jeff shook his head, still not following. Sighing, she clarified. "The letter from General Lee."

"What about it?"

"What about it? That letter changes everything. Those men didn't die at the Wilderness, they died on their way to Richmond and we have to figure out why, which also means the manuscript is flawed."

"How would you know that? We haven't talked about that yet. That is one of my questions, but how did …?"

She walked over and sat back down in the chair.

"I hope you won't think ill of me, but I read it."

"How, I have the copy here, how could?"

She placed her hand on his rubbing gently, taking a moment before speaking.

"The flash drive. When we left the office the day that you came to see me, we left it in my computer. I didn't find it until later the next day. As you may remember, I wasn't feeling too well, wasn't quite focused you might say. Anyway, I took the opportunity to read … I thought … well, I read through the manuscript, hopefully to help me understand. I hope you're not too upset?"

Jeff nodded, remembering back to her printing it out for him, smiling.

"Sure, yes of course. No, not at all. What did you think?"

She sat back in the chair, giving Jeff the full view again. Waiting for him to enjoy the view for a few moments, she crossed her arms over her chest.

"I though it was a bit disjointed, couldn't follow it all that well. I understood the basics, but … and the end stuff?"

"Yeah, that's what Sandy said."

"Who?"

Jeff hesitated for a moment noticing the pitch in her voice "Ah … Sandy, Sandra Nelson, she was Bob Kittridge's companion."

"Companion?"

"Yeah that's what she called it, said it sounded old fashioned to her as well."

"Who is she again?"

"She was Kittridge's companion."

"And who is Kittridge?"

"He wrote the manuscript."

Professor Hathaway sat in silence, digesting all this, keeping her gaze focused on Jeff. "Right, sorry, I didn't make the connection. So what did she … ah this Sandy say?"

Jeff cleared his throat. "She said that Kittridge would find things and just add them in, what Sandy did was to try to put those pieces into some kind of order, but she also said she didn't do much toward the end."

Professor Hathaway nodded, while Jeff continued.

"She's the one that gave me the box you were looking through last night."

"You met her?"

Jeff looked at the professor, taking a moment before speaking haltingly, just a tad uncomfortable again.

"Ah … yes, last week. I had to meet with the attorney at his office and when I called her to touch base, she told me she lived close by, I asked her if I could stop by afterward and she agreed."

Professor Hathaway sat quietly looking at him. Taking that as a cue, Jeff cleared his throat again and continued.

"After the meeting with the attorney, I drove to her house. She told me all about her and Bob … ah, Kittridge, filled in some of the blanks. We wound talking a bit about …"

Jeff stopped and brought his fingers to his eyes. "Sorry."

Professor Hathaway leaned over touching his arm. "Are you okay?"

Jeff nodded. "It's just that what she described about Kittridge's end sounded just like my wife's end. They both died horrible deaths from the ravages of cancer and being with someone who knew exactly what I went through reopened all those emotions. I'm sorry. I just need a moment."

Jeff paused, holding his fingers to his eyes. Professor Hathaway was up and out of her chair, holding his head to her chest.

"I'm so sorry, I didn't mean to pry."

"It's okay."

She held him that way for a few minutes longer, finally letting go and returning to her chair, waiting patiently for him to gather himself.

Jeff waved his hand in the air. "Sorry, I just have a moment every now and then."

She nodded but remained silent. Finally, Jeff looked up wiping a tear from his cheeks. He cleared his throat again before continuing.

"Anyway, she gave me that box and said that Bob would throw things in there that he didn't think were important, but thought since I agreed to take over the project maybe I'd like to have it. I opened the box when I got back home, took one quick look and hadn't gotten back to it yet."

They both sat thinking in silence. Jeff finally took a sip of his decaf.

"Would you like me to freshen that up for you?"

Jeff looked at her and shook his head no, once again clearing his throat before speaking somewhat softer.

"You were saying you thought the manuscript was disjointed."

She nodded, just a bit relived to be back on that subject for the moment.

"Yes, I could tell that it was put together in pieces and now after what you told me this Sandy said, it makes sense. He was just throwing things together."

Jeff nodded. "I thought what I should do is break it down into sections, start to fill in the blanks as best as possible and see what that version would look like."

She nodded. "Sounds right."

Jeff pointed. "But, as you say, that may all be academic now with the discovery of that letter. We may have to revisit the whole premise. Looks like we got some more research ahead of us."

"We? Us?"

Jeff looked at her. "Yeah, you're in the middle of this now."

"Yeah and why is that."

"Because it gives me an excuse to get you back here to ... you know, work on this."

"You think that will do it."

"I'll wear the boxers."

"Well, that might do it."

She stood up standing beside him. She pulled his head to her chest, holding him. "I'm truly sorry I didn't mean to stir up any unpleasant memories."

"Really, it's okay, I just ask that you understand ..."

"You need to say no more."

She bent down and kissed him on the top of the head. "I'm gonna take that shower now." In a moment she left the room.

Jeff sat there for another few minutes, taking a deep breath, before leaving for his room and the shower.

———————— /// ————————

A half hour later they were both back in the kitchen, dressed casually for the day.

"So, tell me about all this."

Jeff looked at her standing over the table and staring at the papers.

"Well, it came in two parts, actually three counting that drive thing. The first was a letter inside a plain white envelope. Oh and I also have a document assigning all rights to the manuscript and the research materials to me. But it was the letter that started everything."

Jeff reached down and picked up the letter off the table, handing it to her. She took it from him hesitating.

"It's okay, you can read it." Jeff waited while she read the letter.

Waving the letter in the air, she looked at him. "I don't understand the Vietnam part."

"Nothing to understand really, just a friendship we formed that day which appears to be the reason I was added to the list."

"The list?"

Jeff looked at her. "You remember I told you I inherited this project? Well, I was on a list of names that I thought it was because ..." Jeff saw Professor Hathaway's blank stare. "Anyway, it appears that during an incident in Vietnam." He pointed at the letter. "That was how I think he put the list together of candidates for the project to pass on too."

Professor Hathaway nodded. "I still don't see how that fits."

"It doesn't. Just a piece of information relating back to those days we were all in Vietnam. Something like that, that's all, other that that, it appears to have no bearing on the project. Just a connection we made in Vietnam."

"So you're obviously a Vietnam veteran?"

"Yes, I am one of those, an old Vietnam veteran, the operative word being old."

She waved her hand in the air. "But I still don't see what Vietnam has to do with any of this?"

Jeff nodded, thinking for a moment, trying to figure out how better to explain and decided to give it another go.

"It doesn't really other than the fact all of the names on the list Kittridge created were in Vietnam with him. Although, the attorney mentioned that Kittridge may have specifically wanted someone with a military background to take over the project, so that would make sense that he would list old Vietnam War buddies as possible candidates. Specifically the guys that he would also have been tight with back then. Basically guys he thought he could trust."

She nodded, handing the letter back. Jeff placed the paper back on the table. He could see that she was still a bit confused, so he moved on.

"By the way, I did talk to the fifth name on the list. It was Tony Mags. He was one of the other guys also there on that day that the letter mentions. Looks like those were the names he remembered, or simply that incident and those names. I didn't read anymore into that."

She nodded. Jeff continued.

"The rest of the stuff was in the big envelope. The letters, the diary entry."

"Right, can I see that again?"

"Sure."

Jeff retrieved another piece of paper from the table and handed it to her.

She examined it carefully. "This is obviously a copy. Do you know where he got this?"

Jeff shook his head no.

"That's okay, we can probably figure it out from the Internet."

Jeff nodded, took the paper from her and placed it back on

the table.

"The rest of that stuff is the research documents. I've gone through those a couple of times, but there are just pieces. The jist of it all is that he did write up some family history on the men, some more on the Wilderness Campaign and other things. I'm not sure why yet."

She nodded. Jeff motioned and they both sat at the table. Taking a breath, Jeff continued.

"I read through the manuscript the other day and thought the same thing you did. So, as I said, I broke the manuscript down into sections. I made a list of items that may require more research, certainly more facts for the back story and in many instances, further clarification." Jeff paused and looked at her. "Of course, since you found that letter, I'm not sure where we go from here?"

Professor Hathaway shook her head yes. "I think you're right. You may have to start over at some point, maybe you can still use some of what you have, but at the very least we need a new game plan."

Jeff nodded yes, while she continued.

"Do you still want to pursue this? Maybe now the manuscript won't end up how he thought it might."

"Yeah, I think so. He mentioned in the letter that he found things that will need more research and if appropriate to add that in. Maybe it will work out the way he wanted it to after all. At least we should see where it takes us, might be interesting."

"Again with the us?"

"Only thing makes the project worth pursuing."

She smiled and looked at her watch. "Damn it's after eleven we never did have that breakfast. Think maybe we can break for lunch, do our deep thinking after we have some food in us?"

Jeff nodded yes. "Sounds like a plan. What do you have a taste for?"

"Something easy, if we are going to dinner again tonight, by the way what were you thinking about that?"

"I was thinking Mexican. How are you and margaritas?"

"I've had more than a friendly relationship with a few of those."

"Then Mexican it is."

"So what should we do now?"

"There's a cafe not too far from here that I sometimes go to for breakfast. They do a lunch menu, with burgers, hot dogs and I believe they have some salad selections, if you prefer."

"That sounds like it will work."

They both stood up from the table. Jeff noticed her staring. "What?"

She looked up at him a smile forming on her face.

"We do have our work cut out for us. I'm not sure that we won't have to start over. There are still more documents in the pouch that might turn us in another direction. Looks like I'll be spending quite a few weekends here probably have to work through the night."

Jeff grabbed her up in his arms, kissing her deeply, before breaking the kiss. "I believe I have other plans for our nights."

He kissed her again. She brought her arms up around him, pulling him close, before pushing back.

"If we don't walk out that door right now, we won't be leaving and I'm really hungry."

Jeff smiled. He led her through the kitchen entrance to the garage, pushing the button to raise the door. The day light engulfed and illuminated the beast sitting there in the other spot.

Professor Hathaway stopped right next to it. "And then there's this."

Jeff nodded and pointed. "Get in the car. We need food to think straight, no more work." Jeff held the door open for her.

She smiled as she slid into the passenger's seat. He backed the car out of the garage, pushing the button to close the door.

The beast slipped back into the darkness.

TWENTY-FOUR

The cell door sprung open unexpectedly. Robert Swift looked up to see one of the guards standing in the opening.

"Let's go, Swift."

"Go where?"

"I got orders to take you to the infirmary."

"For what?"

"Look, paper says go get you, bring you to the infirmary, that's what I do. Probably another drug test, make sure you not getting over in here."

"On a Sunday?"

"Let's go."

Robert Swift stood while the manacles were placed on his hands, feet and around his waist. "When did you start doing testing on a Sunday?"

The guard looked at him, grabbing his arm. "Let's go."

Robert Swift walked as best he could, chained tightly in front of the guard. He stopped and waited as they passed through several doors that opened and closed behind him. Reaching the infirmary, he stopped and waited to be let in, turning to have the manacles removed.

"Not yet, inside." The guard pointed and waited until the door closed behind him. "Hey doc, okay I unhook him now?"

The doctor stepped into the outer office. "Who do you have?"

"Swift, I presume for a random drug test?"

Robert Swift looked at the doc, then at the guard as he started removing the chains, speaking to the doorway where the doctor had just stood.

"Didn't know you guys did testing on a Sunday?"

The doctor reappeared and motioned for him to enter the inner room.

"Didn't know that either. I was told to come in and do a couple of random tests. You piss somebody off, might want to fuck with you?"

Swift looked at the doctor. "Not that I'm aware off."

Nodding, the doctor pointed. "Remove the jump suit and get up on the table and relax."

"Really? Why?"

"Paper says full body examination, look for needle marks, track marks, anything like that, then we do blood and urine."

Robert Swift slipped out of the jump suit, placing it across the chair, while the doctor moved around the office. Not waiting for further instructions, he climbed up on the table and lay down on his back in his boxers and t-shirt. Resting his hands on his chest, he spoke in a protesting manner.

"I'm telling you doc, I don't do that shit, never did." Robert Swift watched the doctor approach carrying a needle. "What's that for?"

Without answering, the doctor stuck the needle into Swift's arm.

"Just relax, it will only take a minute."

Depositing the needle into the waste bucket, he watched Robert Swift take his last breath. Waiting a minute longer he hit the button setting off the alarm.

"Got a code here."

The only other person on duty, a nurse, rushed in pushing the cart, but it was too late. The doctor shook his head no.

"It happened so fast, we were talking and suddenly he grabbed his chest and before I could even get to him, he took one last gasp."

The nurse nodded. "Shall I make the call?"

The doctor nodded yes as he looked at the clock pointing. The nurse acknowledged, jotting down the time. He watched her pick up the phone and waited, until she indicated that the chief administrator was on the line and handed him the phone.

"What happened?"

"Robert Swift just had a massive heart attack. He died on the table."

"You sure that's what it was?"

"Sure looked like that to me. I was right here in the room with him. We were talking and next thing I know he grabs his chest and lets out one final gasp. Dead, before I even got to him."

"What about an autopsy?"

"Well, with the budget cuts, I don't think we need to cut him open to find out his heart gave out."

"Family?"

"Disowned him after he was sentenced, you know the story."

"Anybody else might be interested?"

"Not that I know of."

The line was silent for a moment, finally the administrator spoke.

"You know it's against policy, but these damn budget cuts are killing us. You make the call."

"Listen chief, I can tell you it was a heart attack, watched it myself. Remember this guy was sixty-eight years old, maybe the stress of being in here finally got to him. Hell, he might have been uptight about the surprise drug test. Hell, any number of things. I really don't think we need to go any further, let's close the book on this one."

"I agree, you back me, we get into a beef over this?"

"Absolutely."

"Fine."

"Hey chief, since the family doesn't want anything to do with him, what do we do with the body?"

"Yeah, what should we do with the body?"

The line was silent for a moment. Finally the doctor spoke.

"Listen Chief, why don't we send him to that Mortuary that the state uses for indigents? I believe we even used them once or twice."

"Yeah, I'm good with that. Go ahead let them deal with him.

"Will do. In fact, I'll do that this afternoon."

"Fine. Have his effects boxed and send them along with the body. They can figure out what to do with that. I'll do the paperwork in the morning."

The line went dead. The doctor handed the phone back to the nurse, who hung it up, speaking as she did. "You sure they will do this on a Sunday?"

The doctor looked at her, smiling. "Well, we can't keep him here, they'll just have to deal with it."

———————— /// ————————

Two hours later a hearse pulled up to the prison gate. An hour after that, they drove back out carrying the remains of Robert Swift. Within an hour of that event, Jason's phone rang.

"You're sure about that? When? How? Thanks, I got it, I owe you one. All right, yeah, yeah, I owe you several. Sure, talk to you later in the week. Again, thanks for the info."

Jason ended the call and tapped the phone in his hand for a moment. Finding Nathan Simon's number, he pressed dial.

"Nathan, hey it's Jason. I just got some interesting news. Can you talk?"

"Yes."

"Robert Swift is dead. Had a massive heart attack this morning, went quick."

"How did you hear about it so fast?"

"Do you really want to know? So, do you think maybe somebody was cleaning up loose ends?"

"I thought you said he had a heart attack?"

"Sure, we'll go with that story, but com'on."

"What are you saying?"

"I'm saying, I meet with the Congressman on Thursday, just

so happen to mention Swift might be the one busting his balls and Swift is dead on Sunday?"

"You think?"

"Him or her."

"Her?"

"Yes, probably the only other person that could get that done."

"I can't imagine."

"You're probably right, let's go with the Congressman then."

Nathan was silent for a moment, Jason waited. Finally, Nathan spoke.

"That bother us any?"

"No, I think we're good and with him gone, better. Hey, I still think he's the one stirred the pot. I gotta believe it's all over and done with, certainly for us, assuming the Congressman keeps his word and now with Swift gone."

"I hope you're right."

"You know I'm right. That Vietnam stuff is ancient history and with Morgan still chasing down that Civil War fable, he won't be a problem. Hell, he doesn't even know any of this happened. You should charge him a fee just for protecting his ass in all this."

"Hey, it was my office they trashed."

"Fair enough, but those clowns are paying dearly for that little blunder. Even the Congressman is cleaning up his house, which by the way should make her real happy."

They were silent for a moment, until finally Nathan spoke.

"But what about that stuff Morgan got from Magalito?"

"What of it? I told the Congressman that I spoke with Magalito just before he died, he won't be looking any further. Told him Morgan was chasing his tail on the Civil War thing. I also told him we had no interest in pursuing any of that fairy tale from forty years ago, or the break in at your office. That it was over as far as we were concerned. Now with Swift gone?"

"I should tell Morgan that Swift is dead."

"Wait until Monday, get it through channels, maybe the news, let it be for now."

Nathan was silent again, Jason waited. Finally, Nathan spoke. "Maybe. But I should let him know. I'll have Donna call him."

"That's your call. I'll keep on top of this anyhow, see if anything else happens next week, just to be sure, but if I had to call it, I'd say it's over, let's move on to more important stuff."

"Yeah, okay. Call me tomorrow morning in the office and I'll let you know what's next on the list for you."

"Until then." Jason hung up the phone and slipped it back into his pocket.

———— /// ————

Nathan sat for a minute before he called Donna. She answered on the third ring.

"Hello."

"Donna, it's Nathan, just wanted to let you know, Jason just called, Robert Swift is dead, heart attack earlier today."

"Really? How convenient?"

"Yeah, that's what Jason said. Let's keep this between us for now. We'll talk at the office tomorrow, act like we got that information through channels."

"Sure, no problem. See you then."

"Wait a minute. Nathan paused. "You better call Jeff Morgan. Let him know what we know. Might be better the news came from us.

"You think so?"

"Yeah, I do. Jason thought we should wait until the news is out, but … well, give him a call tell him what we know. I think it better coming from us. Tell him we'll talk more later we find out anything else."

"Will do. Whatever you say boss."

Nathan disconnected the call. He set his cell phone down on the table and leaned back into the sofa. He couldn't help but think what an interesting turn of events. He let himself smile.

——————— /// ———————

Donna Millpoint waited as long as she could, before she picked up her cell and made the call. The phone answered on the second ring.

"Hello."

"Toni, hi it's Donna, are you already in New York?"

"Yes, but it only looks like a couple of days."

"Toni, I have some news. Can you talk?"

"Give me a minute." Donna heard a door close in the background. "Okay, I'm good."

"Nathan just called me. Swift is dead."

"Swift? Dead? How?"

"Heart attack, sometime this morning. That's all I know right now. Thought you should know."

"Yes, of course. Thank you. Well, isn't that convenient?"

Donna chuckled. "That's what everybody seems to think."

There was silence on the line. Finally, Toni spoke softly. "Donna, I'll be home soon. We can talk more then. But, let me know if you hear anything else."

"Toni, I look forward to that. I will."

"Bye Donna."

"Bye Toni."

Donna set the cell phone on the table, a smile engulfing her face.

——————— /// ———————

Jeff Morgan stood in the kitchen holding Professor Hathaway's bag on Sunday afternoon. They had spent Saturday going over some of the materials he had, but the discovery of that letter, seemed to put everything in chaos. Jeff decided that in order to go any further, he should do a new reorganization and then they could get together again. He also decided that get together would have to be the following weekend, which she immediately agreed to. After dinner and those margaritas their attention Saturday night was focused on each other. Sunday morning was spent cooking breakfast and basically hanging out. In a moment she appeared in the kitchen.

"Sorry, just checking to make sure I didn't leave anything."

"No problem if you did, you'll be back here on Friday." He swept her into his arms. "Won't you?"

"Just try to keep me away."

He kissed her. "I promise I'll have more of a plan next time we get together."

She patted him on the chest. "I better go. It's a long drive."

"You could stay another night."

"I'd love too, but I have things I have to take care of on Monday, you understand?"

"I do, but it doesn't mean I have to like it."

She pushed him away. Together they entered the garage. She took another look at the beast sitting there and shook her head. "We're still not done with that."

He nodded and walked her to her car on the driveway. Placing the bag on the back seat, he closed the door as she got in. "Until next Friday."

"I'll try to get Friday off, be here early."

She backed out of the driveway. He waved as she pulled away. Crossing back through the garage he glanced at the beast. Tapping the top as he passed by, he hit the button and the garage door closed.

Standing at the kitchen table, he looked down at the new piles they had created and said out loud.

"So now what the hell do I do?"

———————— /// ————————

Donna Millpoint dialed Jeff Morgan's cell phone. He answered on the third ring.

"Hello."

"Jeff, its Donna. Nathan asked me to give you a call. We have some news."

"Some news?"

"Yes, it appears Robert Swift died this morning of a heart attack."

"Swift dead?" Jeff sat down in one of the kitchen chairs. "Wow?"

"Yes, that is what we all thought as well."

Jeff took a deep breath. Donna continued. "We just thought you should know. Hear it from us before you heard the news. Nathan said to give you a call first, you understand."

"Yes. Yes, of course. I appreciate the call. Thank you."

Just as Donna was about to end the call, Jeff spoke up.

"Listen, Donna, what about that other matter? Did everything work out okay?"

Donna was confused for a moment, but quickly caught on. "Yes it is. Everything is fine now. So, you just keep working on that manuscript. Everything has been taken care of." She flashed to the news of Swift's death, but continued. "Everybody seems to understand the situation now."

"Fine. That's good to hear. I was worried there for a minute well ... anyway good to hear everything is okay. You know, I think we are starting to make some real progress and ..."

"We?" Donna interrupted.

"Sorry. Yes, I have been working with a History Professor she has been real helpful with the project."

Donna smiled. "That's great Jeff. Well good luck with the project. Let us know if you need anything."

"Will do, thanks again for the update."

Donna didn't tell Jeff that Swift's death probably made his life and the life of the project a lot easier, probably a whole lot better. They had decided it was best Jeff need not know anymore. Let him chase that project in peace. "You're welcome Jeff."

The line disconnected. Donna set her cell phone down. But then, picked it back up and called Nathan. He answered immediately.

"Nathan, Donna, listen I called Jeff Morgan and brought him up to speed. He seemed to handle it okay. I don't think he suspects anything. Seems to be caught up in the manuscript. I'm sure he has no idea about, well, you know. He asked me about the other thing and I told him everything was fine. Right?"

"Yes. Good. Yeah, that's good. Jason thought the same thing, we should be okay and with Swift gone, even better. Thanks for making that call."

"Nathan?"

"Yes?"

"I called Toni. Thought she should know as well. In fact I called her first."

"I thought you might. Probably best she hears it from us."

"Thanks, Nathan."

"Hey, enjoy your Sunday."

"She thinks the same as the rest of us."

"Come again?"

"She said she thought that his passing away was rather convenient."

Donna could hear Nathan laugh in the background, before speaking.

"Yeah, that seems to be the consensus. Donna, enjoy your day off, we'll deal with all of this in the morning."

"Will do. Bye, Nathan."

She heard the line disconnect and set her phone back down.

———————— /// ————————

Later that night, Jeff Morgan poured two fingers of Vodka into a glass and dropped in some ice. As he slowly sipped the drink, he thought back to the call from Donna earlier. Having Professor Hathaway here and … well, the great time they had had kept him from thinking to much about it … but now the reality of it all was starting to sink in. He poured another two fingers of Vodka into the glass over the ice that was already there.

Turning and leaning back on the counter, he focused in on the kitchen table and those piles sitting there. The reality had been sinking in all afternoon, but now he felt it start to take hold.

The glass was empty again and while he hesitated a moment, he did refill the glass. Walking back to the table he sat down heavily into the chair. Setting the glass down on the table, he finally said what he had been thinking, out loud.

"I'm the only one left."

The stark realization of that fact overtook him for a moment. He raised the glass and slowly sipped the cooling liquid. Talking out loud to the papers in front of him he recapped the situation.

"The Lieutenant was already gone, Tony Mags is gone, Magic is basically gone. And now, Swifty is gone. What the fuck?"

He took another long sip, holding the glass in his hand.

"I'm the only one left. If I don't do this, no one will. But, why should I care? I mean really? What does it matter to me, to anyone, to complete this project? And now with the discovery of that letter...?"

He took another sip, setting the glass back on the table, looking at the piles of paper pointing.

"Well, maybe we are on to something. I don't know what the hell that is, but something?"

Picking up the glass and finishing the liquid inside, he nodded in the affirmative.

"For whatever God Damn reason I was selected to do this, by God, I'm going to finish it."

He thought of Professor Hathaway and how she became involved in the project in more ways than one and smiled.

"Sure makes the project a lot more fun."

He looked at the piles one more time and lifted the glass in a mock toast.

"Alright Kittridge, we'll figure this out and complete the project however it falls, and whatever it takes to do that. I still don't know why you picked me, but you did and fate has left me the last man standing, so I'll take this wherever it goes, for you buddy."

He downed the last of the liquid in the glass, which was mostly melted ice and sat there for a few more minutes. Finally, he got up from the kitchen table and made his way to the bedroom.

Lying down on the bed fully clothed, he looked up at the ceiling and said out loud, "So, I'm the only one left and I was fourth on the list."

TWENTY-FIVE

Professor Hathaway sat in her office on Monday morning concentrating on how she could make her week shorter, with the goal of getting Friday off. She heard a voice before he entered her office.

"Lori, you have a minute?"

"Doctor Hammond?"

"Please call me Justin, we've been at this too long for formalities."

"Of course. So what brings you to my office on a Monday morning?"

Doctor Hammond sat in one of the chairs in front of her desk, while she sat back in her chair. "I understand you have been asking around about an outfit called the Preservation of Unique Southern Antiques?"

Professor Hathaway smiled and let out a small chuckle.

"Something funny about that?"

Professor Hathaway raised her hand in the air and waved it back and forth taking a moment before answering.

"No, no. It's just that a friend of mine who asked me about that had a very unusual way of pronouncing those initials and I'm afraid every time I hear that name I can't help but think about that."

"I believe I know what you are referring too and if you ever heard Lillian Meriweather, with her southern accent say it, you'd think the same thing."

"So you have heard of her?"

Doctor Hammond shook his head yes, holding up three fingers. "Why yes, and Allen Edward Cummings the Third as well. I believe he calls himself the curator?"

Professor Hathaway nodded, pointing to her computer screen. "So says the web site. So tell me what you know about them? Are they legit?"

Hammond smiled. "Well, let's just say they skirt the boundaries."

Professor Hathaway leaned back in her chair. "How do you mean?"

Hammond waved his hand in the air taking a moment before speaking.

"Well, the way I understand it is that they have several 'scouts' out there, their word, that let them know when a piece of furniture appears that may be of value, regardless of if it is antique or even southern in nature. This Lillian then calls the person on behalf of Cummings and asks to see the piece."

Doctor Hammond paused, clearing his throat.

"Excuse me. Anyway, their MO is to low ball the value of the piece hoping to convince the owner that the piece is basically worthless, but since they are a museum they will take the piece as a donation and give the owner the proper documents to take a generous tax write off for having donated the piece."

"I see. At least, I think I understand."

Hammond pointed. "But here is the best part. Once they have the piece, they then loan that piece to one of several private collectors for a handsome cash donation to the museum and as far as anybody knows those pieces never come back. I've been told they only have five or six actual pieces in their so called museum."

Professor Hathaway nodded her head. Hammond continued.

"So basically, they get the pieces for next to nothing, if not actually nothing and then in effect sell them off to private parties. While technically not illegal, they probably wouldn't hold up under any sort of scrutiny."

Professor Hathaway nodded her head once again, leaning forward.

"Have you ever had contact with them?"

"Not specifically, but I did run into Lillian Meriweather at a conference one time and I thought it interesting that if you listen to her for any length of time, you'll notice her southern accent fades in and out."

Professor Hathaway smiled. "How would you describe her?"

Hammond thought for a moment. "Very pleasant, easy on the eyes, but not too forward, fashionably dressed, that sort of thing. She appears to be sincere and probably is, but knowing what she does, puts an edge on that persona."

"Again, I think I understand."

"Well, that's about all I know. I'd tell your friend to tread lightly and at the end of the day, he should probably avoid their clutches. I understand they are quite convincing as a team."

"Thanks, Justin, I'll pass that information along. How can I ever thank you?"

Doctor Hammond was up and out of the chair standing in front of her desk, hands on his hips, smiling. "Well there is one thing, I've been meaning to ask you and if this gives me a little leverage, I just might use it."

Professor Hathaway sat back in her chair looking up at him.

"You might have heard that I am hosting a round table discussion on nineteenth century politics post war, which I understand is one of your areas, so if you are free Saturday morning, I'd sure like to have you at the discussion. Right now there's only myself and Professor Caruthers and you know how closed minded he is these days ... well having you there might actually help my students get a better picture."

Doctor Hammond looked at her with sad eyes and a tilt of the head.

"Saturday morning?"

"Yes, from nine 'till noon."

"Justin, I'd love too, but I already have plans for this weekend and ..."

DON MEYER

"It's just a few hours. I could really use your support."

Professor Hathaway looked at him, saw the pleading look in his eyes and finally nodded yes. "I'll see what I can do. Maybe I can rearrange some of my plans."

"That would be great. I'm sure Caruthers will enjoy having you there."

"Nothing I'd like more than to put some holes into Caruthers' thinking. If I can work it out what time should I be there?"

"Well, the discussion is set to start right at nine, how about you get there around eight thirty? I might even arrange for you to present a brief overview of the … well something to the effect of the turmoil of the times and how that played a role."

Professor Hathaway nodded. "I'll do my best to be there. I'll call you tomorrow and let you know either way. And thanks again for the update on … no, no, I'm not going to say it either."

"Smart choice. See you then."

"I'll try."

Professor Hathaway watched Doctor Hammond leave her office and close the door behind him. She waited another moment for the outer door to close before picking up her phone, quickly dialing Jeff Morgan's number.

After four rings the answering machine picked up.

"Hey, it's Jeff, you know what to do."

"Jeff, hi, it's Lori, listen I have that information on you know who, and no I'm not going to say it. Please call me back as soon as you get this."

——————— /// ———————

"Mr. Morgan, do you need to get that?"

Jeff Morgan looked at Lillian Meriweather. They had arrived just moments ago, pulling into the driveway in a nondescript sedan. He was thankful he had said ten o'clock. His head was a bit tight this morning.

Lillian Meriweather was wearing a nice form fitting dress, but not to tight, just enough to let you know she had curves and where they were, without giving away the whole picture. The dress stopped just short of her knees, with plain but effective pumps.

Allen Edward Cummings the Third was dressed in a two-piece business suit, with tie and highly polished shoes.

"No, Ms. Meriweather, the machine will get that."

They were all standing in the garage just a few steps away from the beast.

"My but that is an extraordinary piece you have there, not much on the eyes, but one solid example of wood construction."

Jeff looked at Allen Edward Cummings the Third.

"I dare say, suh."

Jeff honed in on his pronunciation of sir.

"What ever would you do with a piece like that? I imagine it would be just too large to fit properly in any room."

"Hadn't."

"Hadn't, suh?"

"No, I hadn't thought about what, if anything, to do with it yet."

Allen Edward Cummings the Third walked back and forth in front of the piece. "Ms. Meriweather, might you fetch the tape measure from the bag."

Jeff raised his hand. "I can tell you that it is just over seven feet wide, two and change deep and stands three and a half feet high, if that is what you need."

"Why, I thank you suh that is precisely what I was requesting."

Allen Edward Cummings the Third paced back and forth a couple of more times before finally stopping and setting his right elbow over his left hand. Completing the pose, he framed his chin with his right hand.

"Well suh, my honest opinion would be no more than a couple of hundred dollars, at best, mind you, if you can find just the right buyer."

"Buyer?"

"I'm sorry, didn't Ms. Meriweather tell you that we would give you our best appraisal for the piece for your most gracious offer to let us see it?"

"Yes, she did mention that, but ..."

"Then might I make another suggestion?"

Jeff remained quiet, watching Allen Edward Cummings the Third pace back and forth. Finally, turning to face Jeff he pointed as he spoke.

"We run a museum that showcases fine works from time forgotten. As I'm sure you know, many items were destroyed in the South's lost cause to become their own nation and whenever a piece becomes available, it is always our first choice to try and recover that piece for our museum."

Allen Edward Cummings the Third paused, but Jeff remained silent. Pointing, he continued.

"Here then is my suggestion. When you feel that it is the time to part with this piece, as I'm sure you have already thought about given its size and weight, then I would suggest donating it to our museum. In so doing I can arrange to present you with the proper documentation for a most generous dollar value to present to your accountant when the time comes to prepare your taxes. Would that be of any interest to you?"

Jeff thought he would play along for now. "And what might that amount be?"

"I would say, and this may very well be increased upward, but on first blush I would say in the neighborhood of fifteen hundred dollars."

"But you said it is only worth a couple of hundred."

"Indeed I did. However, when we are talking donations, there is an intrinsic value to an antique piece of southern ancestry that transcends a merely cash purchase price."

"I see and you think as much as fifteen hundred."

"I dare say it just might be higher."

Jeff nodded. "And how would this happen?"

Allen Edward Cummings the Third paced back and forth a couple of times before finally stopping and again resting his right elbow in his left palm framing his chin.

"May I ask you a few questions in regards to the piece? Ms. Meriweather would you be so kind as to jot down a few notes?"

Jeff nodded. Lillian Meriweather removed a device from her

bag and stood at the ready.

"Now these questions may be of a delicate nature and if I am over stepping my bounds, please feel free to stop me at any time."

Jeff nodded okay.

"May I ask what you paid for this piece of furniture?"

"Nothing. The deal was, if I could get it out of the barn, I could have it."

"Really? That is most extraordinary?"

"Said the piece had been there for eighty years. It was quite buried."

"I see. And how did you get it here?"

Jeff started to answer but then caught himself, remembering the deal was off the books. "Actually that's a private matter. I'd rather not say. Let's just say I worked out an arrangement."

"I see. Can you give me some general idea of the cost to move the piece here? Something I may be able to work with?"

"Sure, let's say seven-fifty."

"Dollars?"

"Yes."

Allen Edward Cummings the Third massaged his chin with his right hand, still folded into his left palm.

"I see. May I then say that at the very least you have seven hundred and fifty dollars tied up in the piece?"

"Sure you can say that."

"So then, Mr. Morgan, would it be correct to say that at the very least you'd like to get your money back or some equivalent there of?"

Jeff remained silent. Allen Edward Cummings the Third continued.

"What I'm trying to ask is, if we were to say, split the cost of the shipping charges to our museum, basically to remove the piece from here, we would still give you that tax document, perhaps with a slightly greater dollar value, to offset the additional expense would you consider donating that piece to our museum?"

"Well, let's cut to the chase. If that's okay with you?"

Allen Edward Cummings the Third raised his eyebrows, but

kept his composure. "By all means, Mr. Morgan, by all means."

"Right now, it's more of a sentimental thing. I'm not sure what I want to do with this, but until I finish the project I'm working on, I feel that the best solution is to let it sit right there."

Allen Edward Cummings the Third nodded his head. "Of course. But are you then saying there is a possibility you would consider our offer in the future?"

"Anything is possible."

"Of course. May I ask you one final question?"

Jeff nodded. "Sure."

"Why would you want this piece in the first place? Something this big and I presume very heavy, to then pay for the shipping to get the piece here and now be faced with what to do with that very piece. Why on earth would you want to take that on?"

Jeff looked at Allen Edward Cummings the Third and then glanced at Lillian Meriweather standing off to the side, she almost looked doll like with the sun framing her outline, standing at the ready with her device. Jeff took a breath before turning back.

"Mr. Cummings, have you ever been in the service, Army, Navy, anything like that?"

"No suh, I have not."

"Then you might not be able to understand this, but an old Army buddy of mine sort of asked me to do just that. Let's just say I did it for him."

"I'm not sure I follow, Mr. Morgan."

"Most times in war, when the bullets are flying, you form a bond with a group of guys that you may not have otherwise and when one of them asks you to do something, you just do it. You don't ask why, you don't hesitate you just do it. That's simply what I did. What I'm trying to say is that right now, I'm not sure why I did it and quite possibly in the near future I might just ask myself that very question."

Allen Edward Cummings the Third nodded. Lillian Meriweather blinked her eyes.

"Well, I'm not sure I completely understand, but I do thank you for your candor. Here is my card. I pray that when you make your decision, we may be the ones you call. I'd certainly feel privileged to have this piece in my museum."

Jeff took the card from him. "Mr. Morgan?" Jeff shook Allen Edward Cummings the Third's hand. "It truly has been a pleasure meeting you. Again, I pray that it is our number you remember when the time comes. Have a good day, suh."

Lillian Meriweather walked over, offering her hand. "Mr. Morgan, it has been a most delightful morning. I can't thank you enough for letting us stop by to have the opportunity to view such an unusual piece."

Jeff shook her hand, getting a whiff of her perfume. "Don't mention it. Glad I could help."

Jeff watched Lillian slide back into the passenger's seat waving as the sedan backed out of the driveway only imagining the conversation inside. The whole ordeal left him a bit tired. If not for the connection he had to the piece, he most certainly would be helping them load the beast unto a truck by now. Allen Edward Cummings the Third's pitch was something else and actually made perfect sense. What else could he possibly do with the piece? And Allen Edward Cummings the Third's question of why would he decide to take on something like that and furthermore to pay for the privilege to do just that? He smiled taking one last look at the beast sitting there. "Why indeed?" He said out loud.

Stepping back into the kitchen, he saw the message light blinking and listened to the voice mail. He was truly sorry that he missed her and immediately tried to call the Professor back, but her assistant informed him that Professor Hathaway left the office for a meeting and wouldn't be back until later, but she would surely give her the message. He thanked the assistant and hung up.

Checking his watch, he realized he had another hour before the next appointment, which was time enough to grab a bite to eat. Putting together a quick sandwich and a cold beverage, he took a break.

DON MEYER

Standing inside the garage, he watched the pickup truck pull into
the driveway. He waited as the man inside gathered up something
before exiting which he then saw, was a clipboard.

"Mr. Morgan."

"Yes, but please call me Jeff."

"Sure thing. Stan Williams. You called about a piece of furniture you'd like appraised?"

"Yes, it's right here."

Jeff turned and swung his arm around. Stan Williams entered
the garage, stopping right in front of the beast.

"Wow, that's some piece."

"Ever seen one like that?"

"Not one that big, usually only much smaller versions about
half that size, maybe three-quarters at the most."

Stan raised his clipboard and was about to pull his measuring
tape off his belt when Jeff gave him the measurements. Stan nodded and jotted those down.

"Where you'd get something like this?"

"It was in a barn for eighty years, buried under a whole bunch
of stuff."

"Why?"

"Long story."

Stan Williams nodded. "What are you planning on doing
with it?"

"Don't know yet."

Stan Williams nodded again. "Okay, I examine it a bit?"

"Sure, have at it."

Jeff watched Williams open the drawers and the doors carefully, making notes as he went. When he was finished, he wrote
some more down and set the clipboard on top the bureau.

"You mind me asking what you were looking to do with it?"

"Sure, but like I said, I haven't decided yet."

"Well, I can tell you this right out of the gate. Not much."

———— 278 ————

Jeff nodded. Stan continued pointing.

"And I say that for a couple of reasons. One is the size and the second is the weight. Must have cost a few bucks to get that piece here. Anybody who would consider buying it would expect to have it shipped to that location, which brings me to the second reason. The looks. Sure not much to look at."

Jeff nodded. Stan continued.

"But I can tell you this. It is a rather unique piece and there is certainly someone out there that would want it for any number of reasons. I've seen smaller versions used as all sorts of furniture pieces, mostly as sideboards, but it will hold just about anything, even saw one used as a wine storage. They cut the middle out, put one of them wine fridges in there."

"You don't say?"

"What else do you want me to tell you?"

"What kind of value would you put on it?"

"Five hundred, might go as high as seven fifty, but if you found that perfect buyer, could go as high as twenty five hundred, maybe even as high as five thousand, all depends on how badly the buyer wants it."

"Really?"

"Like I said the buyers are out there. But you got to dig and search. If you put it with a house that could broker it for you, they may take as much as forty percent and stick you with the shipping charges, only leave you with the couple of hundred I mentioned."

Jeff nodded. Stan folded his arms across his chest before continuing.

"I was you I'd turn it into a workbench. The strength alone would support all your tools and then some fit right nicely right here in your garage."

"Turn a one hundred and fifty year old piece of furniture into a workbench?"

"As I said, I have seen it all."

"So Stan, can you tell me a little bit about the piece?"

"Well, standard furniture, functional for sure, probably made on a farm or a ranch where they were going for functionality rather than looks. Wasn't made by a cabinetmaker that's for sure, wasn't bought in a store, or ordered custom made, but whoever did this had carpentry skills, that's for sure. That's why a lot of these pieces got busted up for fire wood, lot of wood, not so much looks."

"That's what the guy I got it from said, he considered doing just that, but didn't want to go through the work of getting it out of the barn."

"I heard that."

"So Stan, why would somebody want this piece, is there something else that would give it value of some kind?"

"How do you mean?"

"Well, I had some folks here earlier that seemed mighty interested in having me donate this piece to their museum."

Stan Williams smiled pointing to the bureau, taking a moment.

"There'd be two reasons for that. One is that they are genuinely interested in putting a piece like this on display, truly appreciating that it is a one hundred and fifty year old unique piece of furniture."

"And the other."

"They already have that buyer."

Jeff shook his head smiling. "Now that makes sense."

"Any other questions I can answer."

Jeff looked at him for a moment. "Yes, for sake of discussion. Say you were interested in buying this piece, or brokering it, how would you get it out of here?"

Stan nodded and took a long look over at the bureau, before answering.

"I have a company I use for bulk moves. I'd guess off the top of my head, I'd allocate one fifty to pick it up and move it to my location, but something this size, I'd take pictures and post those, leave it right here and move it once to the buyer."

"I see. How about say three hundred miles?"

"Five hundred easy. At least a two-man crew, truck, gas and hope the place they are dropping it off poses no problems. You wouldn't be able to get that into most homes."

Jeff nodded. "Thanks, I really appreciate your coming out. Gives me some much needed information going forward."

"Guess you didn't think about that when you had it brought here?"

"Seemed like the thing to do at the time. At least I know my options going forward. Again, thanks for coming out."

"No problem. Here's my card, in case you have any more questions or are looking for options in the future. Be glad to help you out"

"Thanks."

Jeff watched Stan Williams get back into his truck and back out of the driveway. Once he was gone, he stepped back into the garage and pushed the button lowering the door. Walking back into the kitchen, he took a quick check at the message machine and saw he had no messages waiting.

———————— /// ————————

It was almost seven o'clock before Professor Hathaway called him back.

"So sorry Jeff, I've had quite the busy day, in one meeting after the other."

"No problem, I understand, had a rather interesting day myself."

"Yes, how did that go? Did you get my message before you met them?"

"No, but I'm here to tell you that they pretty much followed that script. That Cummings guy damn near had me loading the beast unto a truck. He sure talks a good game."

"Really? What about Lillian?"

"She stayed in the background, he ran the show."

"So what did they propose?"

"Said if I donated the bureau to their museum that he would give me a fifteen hundred dollar donation credit to present to my accountant and then he offered to pay half the shipping cost to his place. In other words not only do I get to donate the piece, I also get to share the expense of getting it there. I gotta tell ya he talked a good game."

"That's exactly how Doctor Hammond explained it, a game they would work to get a piece of furniture."

"Well the bureau is still here and it ain't going anywhere."

"You said you had another meeting today?"

"Yeah, with an antique furniture dealer. I'll tell you all about it on Friday."

There was silence on the line. Finally, Jeff spoke softly.

"Lori, is everything all right?"

"Yes Jeff, everything is fine … it's just that?"

"What? You can tell me."

"I'm so sorry Jeff, I got roped into attending a seminar this Saturday morning, so I won't be able to come out Friday as we had planned. I could come afterwards on Saturday, at least we'd have one night together."

Jeff remained silent and Lori quickly continued.

"But, I do have another suggestion if you'd like to hear it."

"Sure."

"Why don't you come here on Friday? You can stay at my place and except for Saturday morning, we'd have the whole weekend together."

"I think I could arrange that."

Jeff could hear Lori take a deep breath before continuing.

"That would be great. I promise we'll do the next weekend at your place. I want to spend some more time with the beast."

"The one in the garage or …?"

Jeff heard her laugh.

"I'm so excited you agreed to come, I was just fretting over telling you."

"You didn't have to. I understand you're still a working stiff, I get it, duty calls and all that."

"Speaking of work, I fully expect you to bring your stuff so we can review it. Besides I have high-speed Internet, in case we need to look something up."

"What are you trying to say? You don't like my dial-up?"

"You're funny. I'm just saying why don't you arrange your questions toward things that can be researched while you're here with me. I'm just saying it might be easier that's all."

"Problem is, when I'm with you I'm too easily distracted."

"Yeah, and what so easily distracts you?"

"You standing there in your panties and that camisole."

"If that's all it takes, how soon can you be here on Friday?"

"I'll be on the road by six, probably around ten thirty."

"I look forward to it."

"Good night Lori."

"Good night Jeff, call me if you have any questions."

"How about I just call you?"

"That works too, good night."

Jeff heard the line disconnect. He set the cell phone down on the table, the piles still before him. He rose from the chair and retrieved a glass from the cupboard. Dropping some ice into the glass, he reached for the Vodka bottle and poured two fingers worth into the glass. Sitting back down at the table, he took a sip as he eyed the piles before him.

However, his thoughts went back to the first time he saw Professor Hathaway standing in front of him in that camisole and her panties and the piles seemed to disappear. He finished the drink, got up from the table dumped the ice in the sink and rinsing out the glass set it back into the sink.

He left the kitchen and turned off the light. Nodding his head in the affirmative, yes there were much better things to think about than those papers, at least for tonight.

TWENTY-SIX

A few minutes before six on Friday morning, Jeff Morgan backed out of the garage. Pushing the button to close the door, he took one last look at the beast sitting there. After waiting for the door to lower, he backed into the street and drove away.

Just after ten he drove into Professor Hathaway's condo driveway, pulling into visitors' parking. He fetched his overnight bag from the back seat and set that on top of the box containing all the materials. Setting those down for a moment he locked the car. Picking up the box with the bag on top, he walked toward her building.

She buzzed him in and he climbed the flight of stairs to the second floor, continuing to the back as she had instructed. Approaching her door, he noticed it was open and walked in, pushing it closed behind him. Setting the box on the floor he called out.

"Lori?"

"Be right there."

Jeff waited, not wanting to venture in any further until she directed him. In a moment she appeared from the hallway, dressed in panties and that camisole. She walked right up to him and kissed him, he put his arms around her and pulled her in closer. Finally she pushed away but still kept her arms around him.

"I believe you said this was the outfit you preferred?"

Jeff smiled, running his hand down her back and resting it on her butt. "I have a vague remembrance of you wearing this once before and you know what happened that time?"

"I believe I do." She took his hand and guided him to the bedroom.

—————— /// ——————

Two hours later they were both sitting on her sofa, the box still in the corner where he had set it down. Jeff was giving her the update on his meetings with the P.U.S.A. people and his subsequent meeting with the antique dealer.

"You know what's funny?"

She shook her head no.

"That bureau sat in a barn for eighty years, almost became firewood without anyone much caring about that piece of furniture, or any regard to the historical significance for that matter and now that I've got it, there seams to be a sudden interest in that bureau. You know, I'm still not sure why I had that thing moved to my house, but actually, right about now I feel very glad that I did."

She looked at him questioning.

"Well, Herb Miller said he would be ninety-six and didn't know what would happen to the bureau after he was gone."

Jeff paused and waved his hands in the air.

"I know this probably doesn't make sense, but the fact that Kittridge thought it was important and realizing that it may be the very bureau mentioned in those diary entries ... well I just reacted and decided I would go ahead and get it home, think about it later."

Jeff paused again and looked at her a smile forming.

"Do you know how cute you look sitting there like that?"

She smiled. "I'm sure glad you think so."

Jeff sat for a minute before continuing. "Well it just seemed like the thing to do at the time."

She nodded. "We'll deal with that next weekend when I'm at

your place."

Jeff looked at her and smiled. "I like the sound of that."

"Are you hungry? I can fix you something. We're not going to dinner until later."

"Where are we going?"

"Same place where you got me drunk."

"I didn't get you drunk."

She slid over and sat next to him, putting her arms around his neck.

"Would you like too?"

Jeff pointed to the box on the floor. "Think maybe we ought to at least give it a go?"

She turned and looked at the box on the floor. "Sure, we got a few hours before dinner."

She slipped away from him and stood up. Dressed in a loose fitting blouse, with no bra and shorts that were very form fitting, he knew she had panties on underneath having watched her get dressed, he smiled at her movements. He had simply redressed in what he originally had on. She pointed to the box as she spoke.

"By the way, I researched that diary page and found out where he got it. A library has the whole diary, actually they list the diary as a log book kept by that unit of Union soldiers and will do copies for research projects, so I'm fairly confident it is real, which means."

She turned to look at him, looking at her.

"What?"

"I was just admiring the way you look in those shorts."

She pulled her blouse up a bit to completely expose the shorts and wiggled her butt.

"Shall we get to work or do you have other ideas?"

"Oh, I have plenty of ideas, but maybe we should do some work."

"Okay then, set the box on the table there and I'll put your bag in my room."

Jeff watched her grab up his bag and disappear down the hallway. He picked up the box from the floor and placed it on the table. Shortly she came back in carrying some clear see through folders.

"I want to go through the leather pouch again and if you don't mind put those letters in these so they are better protected."

"Yeah, we probably should. No doubt, that paper is pretty old."

Jeff watched her delicately remove the letter to Margaret from Eloise and insert the pages into several clear folders then she removed the letter from General Lee and did the same as he noticed the smile grow wider on her face.

"I still can't believe I'm holding a letter personally written by General Robert E. Lee. I thought I should put these other documents in these folders as well."

Jeff nodded, smiling and pointing. "You know, it was because of that letter ... that ... well, maybe we ought to thank General Lee for our ... for us getting together ... you know, in that way."

She smiled. "I told you what happens to history professors when they find original historical documents."

"I thought it was the boxers."

"Yeah, those too, but the letter, my goodness."

"Glad I was there at the time either way."

She looked at him with a smile growing on her face. "It wouldn't have worked with anybody else."

Jeff smiled and patted her on the fanny. "So what else is in that thing?"

Gently she peered inside. Having removed the letter to Margaret, the letter from Lee and the receipts, she looked in the last slot.

"Here's something else." She removed the documents from that slot and opened them up. "Can't quite tell yet ... yes I see ... could this be?"

Jeff leaned over to take a look. "Is that?"

"I think it is."

Once unfolded there was a letter of credit on top, to the bank of Richmond and the next piece appeared to be an identity document, for safe passage, indicating the man carrying this paper was a Virginia rancher who would be traveling to and from Richmond for purposes of visiting the bank regarding some financial matters for his ranch. The name on that document was Albert Samuels.

Jeff pointed. "Albert was the oldest brother. I remember that from the family tree Kittridge did."

She gently pulled the papers apart.

"Here's another one. This one has Robert Samuels. This one has John Samuels. All three also say The Samuels Ranching Combine."

Jeff nodded, raising his hand, looking in the box.

"Here, let me get that out. Yes, here it is. According to Kittridge the family consisted of three brothers, Albert the oldest, a younger brother Robert and the youngest brother, John. Robert had two sons, Robert junior and Albert. John also had two sons, Edward and Peter."

He watched as she gently put those papers into additional clear folders. She had brought home some of those ribbon tie envelopes and proceeded to put everything in one of those, including the well-worn leather pouch.

"Well, that holds with Lee's letter. Who was Eloise?"

Jeff looked at her, but she pointed to the paper in his hand.

"Oh? Yes. Let me see? Yes, here it is. She was Robert junior's wife."

"How about Margaret?"

"She was Albert's wife."

"The matriarch of the family."

"Who?"

"The letter Eloise wrote was addressed to Margaret, who she referred to as the matriarch of the family."

Jeff pondered the results of the latest find and nodded as he spoke.

"Okay so we know who some of the players are. This leather pouch must have been in Margaret's possession at some point and eventually passed down from her somehow. We know it didn't come from Eloise, so it must have passed through her side of the family. In any event the leather pouch made it to that great aunt, probably just simply passed down through the generations. I wonder if anyone ever looked in there."

Professor Hathaway looked at him, but Jeff continued.

"I mean that pouch has been in the family all those years. I can't imagine nobody ever thought to look inside."

Lori nodded. "Maybe they did, but already knowing the story they wouldn't give much thought to the papers inside. And you know how the years pass by. Stuck in a box and put in a closet somewhere. Well, at least until your guy got his hands on that, but even then it doesn't appear he paid much attention to the contents. I mean how could he not see?"

Jeff nodded pointing. "Maybe finding the letters was all he needed to get into the project without regard to anything else."

Lori looked at Jeff. "I wonder how the pouch got here."

Jeff pointed to the pouch. "I guess we can still assume the pouch passed down from Margaret. It seems logical that the leather pouch was in her possession, at the very least, certainly right after those men died."

She removed the folder with the receipts in them and nodded her head yes, pointing.

"Yes, see here, Margaret Samuels signed for those pine boxes, all seven of them and this other receipt shows transport, so we must also assume it appears the men would have been buried on the ranch."

Jeff nodded. She set everything down and looked at him.

"How could he have missed this?"

"Who?"

"Your guy, Kittridge, the manuscript, this pouch contains so much crucial information. How could he?"

"Yeah, I thought that myself, but I believe he was so focused on the original letters and when he started researching he focused on the family members being killed during the Wilderness Campaign."

"But they weren't killed during the Wilderness Campaign."

"Yeah, we know that now, but I don't think he ever went in that direction. Besides, I have this paper that appears to be a list of men killed at Wilderness and the seven names are listed, as are the Gordon men."

She took the paper from him and looked it over.

"Looks like a copy, or print out of a newspaper clipping. The newspapers of the time would list the war dead, which usually they would then post outside their offices."

Jeff nodded, tapping his finger on the paper. "That says all those men, the seven Samuels and the five Gordon men were killed during the Wilderness Campaign right along with all those other names. How do you explain that?"

She looked at the paper some more, finally nodding and pointing.

"I think I might know what happened."

Jeff waited, looking at her. She thought for a moment longer, before answering.

"Remember the bodies were returned by rail? Well, I would imagine some railroad clerk probably thought the pine boxes he turned over to Margaret Samuels were men killed in battle and since the Wilderness Campaign was the current confrontation, the clerk probably assumed that was where the men were killed and simply reported it that way. No doubt, he passed that information to the newspaper who just posted those names with the rest of the war dead without further inquiry. You have to understand the times. There would be no reason to think otherwise."

Jeff nodded. "Makes sense. He surely wouldn't have known about the letter from Lee, or any other details of how the men died. Assuming they were more war dead would have been logical, I suppose."

She nodded, handing the paper back to Jeff. They sat there in silence for a few minutes, each digesting those facts. Finally Jeff sighed and spoke softly.

"Too bad Kittridge had it all wrong, except maybe for the first part where he delved into the family history. I'm beginning to think there might not be much of a story here. Those men don't appear to have even been soldiers, let alone killed during the Wilderness Campaign. That would be too bad after all this to discover we really don't have a story here … well, that Kittridge didn't have a story to begin with."

She nodded. "Let's wait and see what shakes out once we incorporate these new developments. Who knows, there might still be something to be told. I mean the letter from Lee, could still give it some interest. Maybe we can retell the story the way it is starting to line up, you know, just follow the facts, but maybe still incorporate Kittridge's theories somehow, you know, why he may have thought that. That might prove interesting on some level."

Jeff nodded. "Well, I'm ready to call it a day."

"It's only been a couple of hours. We still have a couple more before we have to get ready for dinner."

Jeff smiled. "Well maybe there is one thing you can look up on your fancy computer."

"Yeah, what's that?"

"This document here."

"What is it?"

Jeff showed it to her. "One that has me baffled."

"How so?"

Jeff sat back in his chair taking a deep breath before continuing.

"Well, Virginia was a Confederate state, hell Lee had his home there. So, if that was the case and the Samuels, you know the whole family were ranchers in Virginia, wouldn't that make them Confederates on some level? I saw in Kittridge's notes that he was having those very thoughts. Could these men have been Confederate soldiers? I mean otherwise, how could they operate in a Confederate state?"

She smiled. "Actually that is a good question. The simple answer is that many a town, farm or ranch operated right in the middle of the war, regardless of who was controlling the state at the time."

Jeff nodded and started to ask, but she held up her hand.

"Hold on. I was going to say, but it was obviously more complicated than that. Often times, one side one week and then the other side would control towns the next week. It would have been wise to not take a side."

She paused and cleared her throat.

"I would imagine based on the family tree Kittridge did this family were Virginia ranchers long before the war started. Probably didn't want to pack up and leave, probably couldn't. It appears they just tended to their business during the war. Unfortunately at that time in 1864, the Confederate Army of Northern Virginia led by General Lee was entrenched in Richmond and they were preparing to do battle with the advancing Union Army led by General Grant and those men would have been right in the middle of all that with a lot of uncertainty of what would ultimately happen."

Suddenly she stopped and raised her hand in the air pointing her finger.

"I got it. I think I got it. I mean, I have an idea."

Jeff raised his hands in a "what do you mean" position. She continued waving her finger in the air.

"The letter. The return of the bodies. Lee might have thought they were southerners, being Virginia ranchers, their identity papers said as much. Remember their ranch was right outside Richmond, so they were by all accounts Virginians first and foremost. Lee might have even known them or known of their ranch, you know fellow Virginians. That would go a long way to explain why he was so sympathetic to the loss of these men. I mean why else would he get personally involved in such an everyday incident?"

Jeff nodded. "Makes sense, when you put it that way."

"Then there's our story."

"What's our story?"

"A family of ranchers caught up in the Civil War all wiped out while simply tending to the family business. Don't you see? If we can frame the story around those events, a little family history, their every day life in the middle of the greatest conflict the country has known and being innocent victims simply going about their normal business. Yes, I think if you frame the story around those events, you might be able to put something new together, something more tangible."

Jeff looked at her, noticing she was smiling broadly, obviously enjoying being in her element. She continued, another smile forming.

"Don't you see the historical side to all this? Boy, you sure have your work cut out for you now."

Jeff raised his hand. "I'll be sure to make notes later, but let's get back to the original question."

She looked at him still smiling. He continued.

"Being ranchers in Virginia, fellow Virginians as you said, the inclination would have been to be aligned with the Confederacy, rather than the Union, which appears to be a big part of the Kittridge manuscript that these men were in fact Union soldiers ultimately listed as Union war dead. How do we clarify any of that? How do we reconcile any of that?"

She nodded waving her hand in the air. "I see your point. If they were a ranching family, or even if they had Confederate leanings, certainly being in Virginia and actually just outside of Richmond, they would have had to walk a fine line regardless. The story then becomes quite interesting knowing that they wound up being listed as Union war dead, killed at the Wilderness. Yeah, we may have to spend more time on those facts, weave that concept into the story somehow. That will certainly give the story more of a twist."

Jeff nodded and pointed, pulling out the clipped papers with the notes on the back regarding Virginia. "Then there is this." He handed the notes to her, which she read. Putting the papers down, she looked at Jeff as he pointed to the papers and spoke matter-of-factly.

"I think Kittridge was having some doubts of his own. Based on his facts sheet he really delved into Virginia history. The assumption sheet starts to open a window and the question sheet asks the same questions we are. Too bad he didn't finish the research on any of this. We may just have to do that."

Jeff paused, Lori looked at the notes again, while Jeff

continued.

"I was beginning to wonder if some of the last part of the manuscript that appears to be somewhat incoherent might not be his attempt to answer some of those very questions."

Lori looked at Jeff, handing those notes back to him, nodding in agreement. "You're right we may just have to finish all that research to make sense of this."

"Sure something to ponder. Who were these men, if not actually Union Soldiers as Kittridge built his story around?"

"Well Jeff Morgan that will have to wait until another time. I need to start to get ready for dinner and based on our past history, I dare say no work will get done tonight."

"Oh, I still have a lot more research to do tonight."

"You do?"

"Yes, I want to learn everything about you, right down to the birth mark just above … well near your right hip, but lower."

"After dinner you can investigate every part of me."

Jeff smiled putting his head down, speaking very softly. "You know I feel like a damn teenager, on a first date, well except for. Hell, I'm sixty-three years old for God's sake."

"Jeff, we are on a first date basis, still getting to know each other. Besides we're old, not dead. Why shouldn't we act like a couple of teenagers fooling around on … well I guess a second date now?"

"I suppose, but?"

"But what?"

Jeff smiled, taking a deep breath, while Lori pointed at him.

"You know we just uncovered some more historical documents and you know what they do to me, maybe we won't make it to dinner? Or would you rather we go out to the car and climb into the back seat?"

Jeff watched her get up from the couch walking toward her bedroom, but she turned around and showing him her blouse was unbuttoned said softly.

"Of course there is always the anticipation of what is to come, over a good meal, a couple of drinks. Think there is anything else in that pouch might be of historical interest?"

Jeff watched her disappear down the hallway, but heard her in the distance.

"Give me a half hour, then the bathroom is all yours, I'll save you some hot water, but then again, you might be wanting a cold shower right about now."

Jeff smiled and adjusted the position he was sitting in. Good thing she wasn't here at the moment or it would be quite obvious what he was thinking.

———————— /// ————————

Later that night as they both sat on the sofa enjoying a glass of port, Jeff turned to face her. He spoke just above a whisper.

"Do you really think we have a story here? I mean something we can put together that makes sense, or even be interesting for that matter?'

Lori looked at him. "Yes, why, what do you mean?"

Jeff looked up. "I have to tell you something that might not make sense, but … well, I believe it is important and since …"

Lori turned fully facing him, tucking her legs up under her, leaning just a bit toward him she spoke softly. "What? You can tell me anything. What is it?"

Jeff took a sip of his drink and a deep breath. He set the glass on the table and clasped his hands together. Taking a breath, he began.

"You may remember I told you I was on a list as one of the potential candidates to inherit this project, actually I was fourth on that list, but that is not important right now."

Jeff took a moment before continuing.

"The list was apparently made up of guys that were in Vietnam with Kittridge, guys he trusted and respected, at least I think so. Anyway, the first name on the list was our platoon leader, a Lieutenant Roberts, but he had passed away. The second name on the list was Robert Swift, our platoon sergeant, but he is currently doing a stretch in a Federal facility for running an investment scam. The third name on the list was a guy we called Magic that was tight with Kittridge even after the war, but he has dementia and couldn't possibly … well he couldn't."

Jeff paused a moment, taking a breath.

"The fourth name was me and as you well know, I accepted the project and agreed to complete the manuscript and well here we are."

Jeff paused again, looking over at Lori. She was intently focused on him. He continued.

"The fifth name on that list was Tony Mags. I visited Mags two days before he died. He helped me clear up that Vietnam stuff in the letter I showed you. As a matter of fact, he was there that day in Vietnam, specifically on that helicopter flight as well."

Jeff paused. Lori remained silent not sure where he was going with this. Jeff picked his glass up from the table and finished the rest of the port.

Lori reached for the glass. "Would you like another?"

Jeff shook his head no. He looked back up at her before continuing.

"As you can see two of the five candidates are no longer with us and one is not mentally here, which means there are only two of us left, me and Robert Swift."

Jeff paused and looked directly at her.

"I found out last week that Robert Swift had died in prison, apparently of a massive heart attack."

Lori nodded, starting to get the picture. "That means?"

"Yes, that means I am the only one left. That means I now have to complete the project, whatever that entails. Simply put, I have to finish that manuscript somehow."

Lori slid over and took his hand in hers. "Then we will, together."

Jeff looked at her nodding. "I was thinking the same thing last week when I heard the news about Swift passing. But?"

"But what?"

"But do we have a manuscript to finish? Is there a manuscript here to be completed? We seemed to have dug so many holes in this story and quite frankly, right now it sure doesn't look like we have any filler for those."

Lori slid closer, putting her arms around his neck pulling him toward her and kissing him. Leaning back, she smiled and whispered softly.

"To be honest, I don't know yet, but we seem to have new pieces that we can work with. Maybe it won't be the story Kittridge thought it would be, or the story he was working on, but it will be a story. That much is sure. At least we've uncovered some pieces that might make it more comprehensive. Right now all I can say is we have something, what that will become is still to be determined."

Jeff smiled. "Maybe you're right. Maybe we can put something together that might make sense. We now have the historical stuff. Maybe that will bear fruit."

"And you know what that historical stuff does to me?"

Jeff smiled again, but lowered his head down and said very softly. "I just don't want this to be nothing. After all that has happened, I feel obligated to make this something, to finish this manuscript somehow."

Jeff paused and sat up holding her. "Wow look at me getting all melancholy. I'm sorry I didn't mean too ... maybe it was those two Vodka martinis ... I mean ..."

"It's okay. I understand what you are saying, really I do and as your History Professor I'm saying we can do this. The details are there, we just need to put it all together somehow. It may not be easy, but let's see what we have when we make sense of all this."

"You really think so?"

"Yes Jeff, I really do. I promise next week at your house we'll dig into everything, lay it all out and build from there. How does that sound?"

Jeff smiled. "Sounds like a plan."

Lori stood up and took his hands pulling him up off the sofa.

"How about tonight we let it rest and tomorrow we'll make some notes and next week we will put a game plan together, at least something that you can work with?"

Jeff smiled. "That sounds like a plan and thank you." Jeff paused and ran his hands down her back resting on her butt. "I think I know just the cure for tonight."

Lori smiled and moved in closer to him. "Does it involve the removal on my clothes?"

"Most certainly."

"Then I'm in."

Jeff kissed her and reached behind her unzipping her dress. Pulling the garment from her shoulders he pushed it down until it dropped at her feet. Unclasping her bra she let the material slide from her shoulders to the floor. Working his fingers into the band of her panties he worked them down her legs. She stepped back working them the rest of the way off.

Lori looked at him with a sly smile. "This what you had in mind?"

Jeff nodded. "Yeah, something like that."

Lori reached out and grabbed his hand. "Then you're really gonna like the finish."

Hand in hand they walked to her bedroom. A short time later they figured out what to do once again.

——TWENTY-SEVEN——

Shortly before eleven on Friday morning, Jeff Morgan leaned against the beast in his garage, waiting for Professor Hathaway to arrive. The wait was short. He watched her pull into the driveway and smiled as she got out of her car.

"I made pretty good time."

Looking at his watch, he smiled. "I'd say you did. What time did you leave?"

"Just after seven."

Jeff walked to her car and grabbed her overnight bag, waiting while she locked the car. Together they walked through the garage and entered the house through the kitchen.

"Those piles look the same as I remember them."

"You have no idea. Working through the manuscript, I was only able to salvage the first one hundred and twenty-five pages. The rest all centers around them being Union soldiers, basically now unusable."

"Were you able to incorporate any of the new stuff yet?"

"No, still trying to put it together. Quite frankly, I'm still hung up on the fact they were ranchers in Virginia, a Confederate state. I can't seem to reconcile that with the original story."

She started to answer, but he stopped her.

"I know what you said. This is now a new story, but going back over those research documents, somehow Kittridge was on to something, that I can't quite put my finger on. If you look at those pages I have eliminated, you will see that for over one hundred pages he has those men involved with the Union, specifically as Union soldiers that were eventually killed at Wilderness. It's more than a posting in a newspaper, it's something else, I can feel it, but just can't put my hands on anything to support that."

They reached his bedroom and he set her bag down. She stopped and turned to face him.

"Jeff, I have a personal question to ask you?"

He looked at her. "Sure."

"I know we've shared a bed and all, so that's all good, but how do you feel about sharing a bathroom?"

"I don't follow?"

"At my place it kind of just happened. My stuff was already there, but here? Well are you okay with my stuff being in your bathroom? If not, I can use the other bathroom, I mean?"

Jeff smiled. "Have at it. I don't mind. Really, I don't, obviously I didn't notice."

She smiled and kissed him. "Aren't you the trooper?"

Jeff watched while she entered the bathroom, waiting a moment before speaking. "One more thing that keeps bothering me."

"What's that?" She emerged from the bathroom. "I'm sorry what did you say?"

Jeff watched her remove items from her bag, setting them on the bed.

"I cleaned out a drawer in that dresser if you need it?"

She smiled, gathering some of the items. "Thanks."

He watched her put things in the drawer and then carried other items into the bathroom. Deciding to wait until she was unpacked he sat silently on the bed. She sat on the bed next to him and patted him on the leg.

"Everything okay?"

Smiling, he put his hand on hers. "Great, now that you are here."

She patted his leg once more and got up from the bed. He

watched a while longer before getting up.

"I'll meet you in the kitchen when you're done."

"What's that?"

"I'll be in the kitchen."

"Okay."

Standing in the doorway, of the kitchen he eyed the bottle of Vodka on the counter and just for good measure, he checked his watch. "A little early for that." he said out loud. Instead, he leaned against the counter, looking at the piles of paper on the table. Before he knew it, she entered the room. She had removed her jeans and put on a pair of shorts.

"Thought I'd be more comfortable in these while we worked."

Jeff nodded, while she sat down at the table, waving her hand across the piles.

"So tell me what you have so far?"

Jeff joined her at the table, sitting next to her. He clasped his hands together setting them in his lap. He took a breath. "Well, not as much as you probably think I should."

She remained silent and waited for him to continue.

"I spent a lot of time breaking down the manuscript again and I gotta tell you the more I got into it the more I had a problem with this whole Union Confederate thing. I just can't wrap my arms around the fact those men lived in a Confederate state and some-how stayed neutral. Add that to the fact Kittridge believed these men to be Union soldiers killed during the Wilderness Campaign."

She remained quiet, her chin in her hand. Finally, he continued.

"I mean what if the story is as Kittridge wrote it? What if the letter you found pertained to someone else, or was fabricated to explain something else?"

"What do you mean?"

"Well I got to thinking about what you said. How could Kittridge be so far off the mark? I mean the manuscript is basi-cally about those men being Union soldiers, killed at Wilderness. And his research documents all seem to favor that belief."

Jeff paused and reached for her hand. He lowered his head,

looked up at her and continued. "I mean everything flows until you introduce that letter. Do you understand what I am saying?"

She nodded. "I do, Jeff, I do and maybe you're right on some level? But remember it's not just the letter, the receipt from the railroad and those transit documents with the names on them, names you verified as being those men."

She squeezed his hand, as he looked up and smiled at her.

"There's something else, isn't there?"

He nodded. "I don't know, maybe."

"What?"

Jeff reached for one of the piles and handed her a document. She took it from him and read it.

"Is this for real?"

Jeff shook his head yes.

"Where did you get this?"

"It was clipped to the back of the document regarding the Wilderness Campaign. I decided to look at each piece of paper clipped together to make sure it belonged in that group, in case something got stuck together and sure enough, I found that."

She looked at it again. "It looks like the real thing, not a copy."

"That's what I thought too, so I looked it up, took a while. Wish I found it when we were at your place and we could have used your super computer."

She smiled. "And what did you find?"

"It appears to be real. There was a certificate given to Margaret Samuels in 1877 by President Grant, near the end of his term in office."

She nodded as she looked at the paper in her hands and read it again.

```
The country is in debt to the Samuels
Family for their gallant service to the
Union in time of war and cannot express
how deeply their sorrow must be upon los-
ing so many of their family members to our
just cause. The Union, your fellow country-
```

```
men and certainly I, am forever grateful
for their heroic actions in our time of
need.

President Ulysses S. Grant
October 1877
```

"I don't understand."

"I don't either. Therein lies the rub."

She held the piece of paper a moment longer. "Something else must have happened on that road that day."

"Maybe, but what? Which brings me back to my original question."

She nodded. "Well, I could go through the box again, maybe there is something else in there that we missed?"

Jeff nodded. "I hope so, because I am thoroughly confused right about now."

She sat up and smiled. "Instead of trying to figure it out, let's be happy that there is a letter from General Lee regarding these men and an award from General, then President Grant. You can't imagine that happening too often?"

Jeff finally smiled pointing at her. "Well, you may have something there. Surely something happened, to get the attention of both Civil War Generals, even if one was actually President of the Untied States at the time."

She smiled again. "You know what this means?"

"What?"

"You found another historical document."

He smiled and sat back, finally relaxed. The whole ordeal had been digging at him ever since he found that document. "That I did, that I did."

"I tell you what, how about we leave the paper stuff alone for a bit and go play with the beast?"

"You mean the one in the garage?"

"Which ever one will keep you smiling?"

Jeff stood up. "Let's try the one in the garage for now. I forgot to show you something last time."

"You still mean the one in the garage?"

Jeff smiled. "Yes, get up, let's go."

She stood up and took his arm. "Whatever you say boss."

Together they walked toward the door, separating to enter the garage.

"You might find this interesting?"

She stood off to the side while he removed the center drawers, stacking them off to the side.

"Here look at this."

She bent down and looked inside the middle section to where he was pointing.

"See there, looks like an early version of child proofing."

"I'm not seeing … oh now I see what you mean. What is that for?"

He motioned for her to back out and helped her stand back up.

"When you open the small top drawer the rope tightens and prevents you from opening the small top drawer on the other side. Since they had two little girls in the house I surmised that it was installed to prevent either of them little girls from opening the drawers at the same time, or at the very least from pulling the drawer all the way out. Look, one person can't do it, the distance is too great."

She watched him try to reach the other top drawer.

"But if both girls were playing, they could pull these drawers out and possibly get hurt. I believe the others were far too heavy to open by themselves, but these two smaller ones they probably could."

He stepped back, smiling. "Isn't that neat?"

"Yeah, modern technology, at least for its time."

"Now watch, if one drawer is open and you try to open the other side, watch what happens."

Jeff went to the other side, leaving the left side drawer open, but when he went to pull that drawer open it wouldn't budge.

"That's strange, it worked the other day. Maybe the rope is stuck?"

He crawled inside and rubbed his hand against the rope. "It does feel pretty dry. I suppose after all these years whatever lubricant they used would be gone. Might be why the rope isn't moving, probably too dry to slide, or maybe I hit a worn piece. Here let me move the rope a bit and see if that works."

Jeff stood up and closed the left side just a bit. "Maybe if I adjust it a little?" Again he walked over to the right hand side and pulled on the drawer, but still no action. "Okay, let's do this. I'll wiggle this side and you do the same on that side."

Lori stood in front of the right hand side top drawer, while Jeff stood on the left, pointing.

"Okay, I'll try pushing this one in a bit, while you pull that gently."

Still no action on the right side.

"Okay, let's do this, you come over here and I'll go over there. You push and I'll try to pull."

They switched sides and Jeff gripped the drawer, but instead of pushing, Lori pulled at the same time. They both heard a loud pop.

"Oh, oh, that can't be good." Lori said afraid to move.

Jeff bent down to see what happened and as he looked into the middle section he saw a piece of wood standing up but open from the back side so Jeff couldn't see around the raised board.

"Looks like we snapped something."

Lori bent down next to him. "Did we break it?"

"I don't think so, looks like a piece of the bottom may have split, probably dry rot and our wiggling the bureau broke it loose. I don't think we did much damage."

Jeff crawled further in to see if he could put the piece back in place, but once he was able to see around the raised board, he found the surprise.

"Oh my God." Jeff sat back on his legs. "You're not gonna believe this?"

"What? What is it? Did we break something?"

Jeff shook his head no. "Look for yourself."

Lori looked at him, then bent down to crawl inside and took a look around the piece of wood standing up. Her reaction was the same.

"What is that?"

"Looks like we found a secret compartment built into the bottom."

"Is there anything in there?"

"Don't know yet."

Jeff crawled back inside, reaching around the extended piece of wood and as best he could he looked down inside the opening.

"Looks like another leather pouch."

Very slowly he removed the pouch from the compartment and handed it to Lori. Pushing the piece of wood back down he heard it click back in place. He tried pulling on the eyehook, but it wouldn't move. Crawling back out he motioned to her.

"Let's try that again. Obviously something we did made that open."

She nodded and set the well-worn leather pouch on top of the beast.

Jeff pointed. "Okay, we'll pull at the same time. Easy though."

It took a bit of work, but they finally heard the pop again. Looking inside immediately, the board was back up.

"Well I'll be damned. Child proofing my ass. Those boys were mighty clever. You can't tell that it is even there, even though now that I know it is there. It blends naturally into the bottom."

Jeff stopped talking and saw the look in Lori's eyes. "You want to see what is inside don't you?"

She nodded yes.

"Wait until I close this up."

Jeff crawled back inside pushing the wood plank back down hearing a click as it locked back in place. Standing back up Jeff looked at the open middle section.

"Moving those two top side drawers at the same time must release the mechanism somehow. That's probably why one person can't reach both drawers at the same time, a fail safe, so the trigger can't be opened accidentally. How ingenious? It takes two people with just the right movement to open the compartment."

Jeff crawled back inside the middle section and looked, but

THE KITTRIDGE MANUSCRIPT

he couldn't find the trigger and the fact the eye hook wouldn't move confirmed the two drawers were somehow the trigger. Crawling back out, he wanted to do the release again, but saw the look in Lori's eye and knew she was anxious to look inside that leather pouch.

"Okay, let's go."

She followed him back into the house stepping around the stacked drawers and waited while he pushed the button lowering the garage door asking softly.

"What do you think maybe more documents?"

They sat at the kitchen table and Jeff combined some piles to give them room. Very carefully Lori set the pouch on the table and undid the leather tie. Opening the pouch slightly she smiled. Inside were more papers.

"I can't believe I'm shaking."

Jeff saw her hands doing just that. "Want me to do it?"

"No ... I mean if you don't mind, I'd like to open these?"

"Of course, you're the History Professor in this bunch."

She smiled nervously. Slowly she opened the pouch further, but this one didn't have slots just an open center, containing a small assortment of papers. Gently she removed the stack from the pouch. The first piece of paper was on note style paper folded in half, she opened it and laid the paper on the table trying not to touch it too much. They both read the writing contained inside.

```
CiC will disavow all knowledge, but
personally he wishes you God speed. The
mission is a go.

US Grant, Commanding
```

She looked at Jeff. "CiC?"

"Commander-in-Chief."

"Grant?"

"No, that would have been Lincoln."

"Lincoln?"

"Yeah, the President is the Commander-in-Chief of the army."

Lori looked at the paper. "What mission?"

Jeff shrugged his shoulders and pointed to the contents. "Keep looking. Maybe something in there will tell us."

She nodded, gently placing the note to the side. Next was a bundle wrapped in what appeared to be a heavy outer paper cover. Slowly opening it she saw what looked like money, large pieces with the number 100 in gray circles. Jeff took the bills.

"Those look like one hundred dollar bills. Look there is a treasury band on them, with *$6,000 - Gold* written on it and the initials *AL* across the band."

She looked at him holding the pack of bills.

He smiled back. "Sure a lot of them."

"I think I know how many." She showed him the piece of paper.

Jeff looked at the paper in her hand. It was a receipt for $12,000, $6,000 in Gold and $6,000 in One hundred dollar notes, redeemable on demand by the bearer in gold from the United States Treasury. The receipt had twelve names on the face, seven named Samuels and five named Gordon. The twelve men.

Jeff whistled. "Twelve thousand Dollars for what?"

Lori shook her head. "I don't know yet, but I would think it safe to assume one thousand dollars for each man who is named on the receipt."

"Again for what?"

She shrugged her shoulders, but turned over the next piece of paper.

"It looks like a map. Yes, it is. It's a map of the city of Richmond Virginia. Look there is a house circled on the map and something written next to it. Can't quite make it out. Brock … Brockburg … Brockenbrough, Brockenbrough, the Brockenbrough house."

She sat back in her chair, catching her breath, looking at Jeff. "Do you know what the Brockenbrough house is?"

Jeff shook his head no. "I have no idea."

She took another breath before speaking.

"That house was used as the Confederate White House."

"Really?"

She looked at him wanting to ask, but he just shrugged his shoulders.

The next piece of paper was a hand drawn map of all the entrances to the Brockenbrough house.

The next piece of paper was a hand drawn map of the second floor offices.

The next piece of paper was a hand drawn map showing a marked escape route out of the city.

"Jeff, I don't like where this is going."

"Where what is going? What do you mean?"

"Let's look at the next piece of paper first."

Upon opening that piece of paper, she gasped and leaving the paper on the table she sat back in her chair breathing heavily. Jeff leaned over her shoulder to read.

```
You men will enter the city as Virginia
ranchers with your regular identity papers
to gain safe passage into and through the
city. A letter of credit for the bank of
Richmond has been established for your
purpose.

You will make every effort to insure the
prisoner is captured for transport back to
Union lines, but falling that he is not to
be left alive.

Capture or death of any members of the
raiding party will be disavowed and no
recourse will be provided. You men are
completely on your own. God speed.
```

The middle notation was circled several times and "not to be left alive" was heavily underlined.

Jeff sat back in his chair and looked at Lori. "Is that what I think it means?"

She nodded yes. "They were going after the president."

"Lincoln?"

"No, the other President."

"The other President?"

"The Confederate President, Jefferson Davis."

"No shit?"

She nodded, while he pointed back at her.

"Sure, makes military sense, take out their Commander-in-Chief?"

She looked at him waving her hand, thinking a moment before speaking.

"You could be right. You have to understand that in early 1864 the war wasn't going well for the Union. Grant was still chasing Lee and Lee was getting the better of him. Sherman hadn't started his march to the sea and Sheridan hadn't entered the Shenandoah Valley yet. No, it wasn't looking too good for the Union at all in early 1864."

"So, go get the big guy on the other side?"

She nodded and read that last page again. Breathing deeply, she pointed at the paper in front of her.

"Apparently the plan was to capture Jefferson Davis, but barring that he was not to be left alive, pretty final and specific instructions. Somebody sure meant business."

Looking over the other documents she nodded several more times. "Looks like these men were paid a thousand dollars each to go on this mission, five hundred in gold and five hundred in notes, those notes." She pointed to the pack of bills sitting on the table by Jeff. "And we certainly now know what happened to them."

Jeff nodded and smiled. "A pretty ambitious plan foiled by a trigger happy forward post."

She looked at him. "Can you imagine?"

Jeff nodded. "Would have been something, they made it."

She pointed at the papers spread out on the table. "I think

we're starting to get an idea why these men were favored by both sides now."

"Well, I think we also just cleared up the conflict."

She looked at him in a questioning gesture. He continued.

"Well look, these men were Virginia ranchers, lived right outside of Richmond, surely knew the city and no doubt were known in the city. It would have been easy for them to go in unabated. Begins to make some sense of Kittridge's notes I showed you, his own questions of something else going on."

Lori nodded. "Of course, so the only question is? Were they recruited or did they volunteer?"

"Volunteer for sure."

Lori looked at Jeff. "How can you be sure of that?"

"Back to my question. Confederate state. Maybe they just got tired of having the Confederate soldiers in their back yard, especially if they may have been Unionists and figuring, if they could help end the war before the two great Armies took on each other, they could get on with their life as ranchers. Had to believe any drawn out battle between the two sides would be more detrimental to their livelihood than it already was. My bet is that they volunteered. Hell, they might have even come up with the plan themselves."

Lori nodded, accepting Jeff's theory for the moment. "I would tend to agree with you, although they did volunteer as you say for a price, a mighty big price for those times."

"They were ranchers, money was a factor sure."

Lori nodded. "You're probably right."

Jeff looked at her. "But?"

"No but. I don't see the Union taking a chance on recruiting Virginia ranchers for the simple reason of what you have been saying all along, were they Confederates, or at the very least, Confederate sympathizers? After all they were in a Confederate state, probably *the* Confederate state. Recruiting someone like that would be just too risky."

Jeff got up from the table with the packet of bills in his hand.

"Where are you going?"

"Thought I'd look these up on the computer, see what I can find out about them."

She nodded and got up and followed him. Together they waited as each screen painstakingly filled in. Finally they found the information. The bills were series 1862, the very first series of one hundred dollar bills issued. They were described as United States Notes and in what appear to be uncirculated condition, and as such they have a value of $17,500 to $20,000 per bill. Simple math put their value at between one million fifty thousand dollars to one point two million. Jeff took a deep breath, while she put her arms around his neck, gasping.

"Oh my God?"

"You can say that again."

A moment later she reached around him and keyed in a few instructions, finally a screen appeared. She filled in the blanks and the answer appeared, she smiled.

"That thousand per man would be somewhere in the neighborhood of $45,000 for each man in today's dollars, quite a bit of money no matter how you slice it. Maybe you're right, maybe they did volunteer for that kind of money."

Jeff whistled, before grabbing her. "We need to get this stuff someplace safe." He checked his watch. "It's only two thirty, banks are still open. Let's go, I have a box, we can put everything inside for now."

She nodded. "Can we make copies of the documents first?"

"Yeah, good idea."

Using Jeff's printer/fax/copier she very carefully made a copy of each document. Before they got in the car, she put the original documents back inside the leather pouch and put that into a large manila envelope, the very same one Kittridge put his research documents in. It was all they had on short notice. She waited at the bank while Jeff put the contents of the manila envelope into his safe deposit box. Back at the house, she went over the copies of the documents again.

"Jeff, I don't know where to begin, but we have one hell of a story here. Kittridge was on to something, if only he knew what it would become."

Jeff nodded. "How about you put those away and we go get some dinner and something to drink. The reality of what we found is starting to sink in."

"Yes, but do you know what this means?"

"Historically, probably not."

"This is the first new discovery from the Civil War in over a hundred years, maybe longer. I mean the discovery of written documents regarding the capture or execution of the Confederate President why that's beyond description and throw in the fact that Grant and it appears even Lincoln knew about the plot, it's … it's."

"I know, historical."

She looked at him. "It's so much more that that."

Jeff waved his hand in the air. "Don't you think there were other plots, on both sides even? We certainly know of one against Lincoln."

"I'm sure there were, probably all kinds of ideas bandied about, but to have documented proof of the existence of one, not to mention the two biggest names on the Union side attached to that. Well … well, you can imagine."

"Lori, I understand and on Monday you can shout it to the world. I'll get that attorney, Nathan Simon involved and we can get every thing buttoned up, legal issues and all that."

She nodded. "Jeff what do you think you'll do with the documents?"

"Hell, that's your department. You're the History Professor. We'll do what you think is best for them."

She nodded. "So much to do."

"Monday. Tonight you're mine."

She watched as Jeff delicately removed the papers from her hands.

"Shower, dressed, dinner."

She smiled, stood up and kissed him. "What a day? What a find?"

He swatted her on the butt. "Now."

——————— /// ———————

Several hours later while they lay in bed having once again figured out what to do, she had her head on his shoulder, while his
left arm was wrapped around her, cupping her left breast, gently
massaging it, he whispered in her ear.

"So, how'd you like handling those documents today?"

She shifted and whispered back.

"Remember what I said about historical documents?"

Jeff felt her move on top of him, looking down at him smiling.

"So many documents, we may have to do this all night."

With very little effort they figured out what else they could do
together.

——TWENTY-EIGHT——

On Saturday morning, they both sat at the kitchen table, she in her camisole and panties, he in his boxers and t-shirt, sipping the first cup of their respective coffee.

Lori spoke softly. "I've been thinking."

Still sipping the hot liquid, Jeff looked at her. She set her cup down on the table and leaned in closer.

"Maybe we should sit on this for a few days, give it time to sink in."

"How do you mean?"

Lori picked up her cup and took a sip of coffee. Holding the cup in both hands, she continued.

"Well, we got three things going here."

Jeff set his cup down. "Which are?"

Lori set her cup back down and rested her arms on the table, looking up, smiling. "Well, first of all we have the manuscript."

"The manuscript?"

Lori looked at Jeff. She got up from the table and retrieving the two pots, freshened each of their coffee.

"Hear me out. Right now I'm thinking out loud."

Jeff nodded and picked up his cup, adding cream and sugar before slowly sipping the fresh hot liquid.

"As I said, first we have the manuscript. I think now we can complete the story, actually we can tell the whole story. I think we should do that first, you know, complete the manuscript."

Lori paused and took a sip of her coffee, while Jeff waited for her to continue.

"Then we have the documents. Once those are released or even just known about, they will overshadow everything, the manuscript will get lost in the wake. We will be just too involved to focus on that completely."

Lori took another sip of her coffee. Jeff sat quietly waiting for her to finish.

"Then of course we have those hundred dollar notes. That discovery will also create its own frenzy. I don't know what specifically that will mean, but I suspect those notes in that condition will certainly create some kind of demand. Most certainly further distracting us from our focus. Do you see what I mean?"

Jeff nodded. "I think so. You're saying we tell the world what we found and the manuscript gets lost in all that hoopla."

Lori pointed. "Not only that, but with all the attention the other stuff would get, not to mention the attention we would get, we wouldn't have time to concentrate, let alone work on the manuscript, at lest not properly further pushing it aside."

Jeff nodded. "So, what are you saying? We finish the manuscript first?"

Lori nodded yes. "Yeah, that's what I'm thinking."

"How do you propose we do that?"

Lori reached across and put her hand on his arm. "What are you doing the next couple of weeks?

Jeff looked her. "You're kidding right?"

Lori shook her head no.

"You want me to write the story in two weeks, that story?"

Lori shook her head yes. Jeff sat back in the chair and looked over the papers piled on the kitchen table. She patted his arm, speaking softly.

"We can do it. You write chapters during the day, email them to me and I'll review at night, email you any changes back. What do you think?"

"You're serious about this?"

THE KITTRIDGE MANUSCRIPT

"Yes."

Jeff sat for a moment, finally looking up at her. "Hell, I'm game if you are. We already have about forty percent done I think. The front part stays you know, all the family stuff, but we just have to focus on the middle, whatever that may entail and of course, now an ending."

"That's the spirit. Let's start right now."

"Now?"

"Sure why not. I brought the flash drive with me, we'll load it up on your computer and select out the sections we need into a new document you know, to get a starting point."

Jeff pointed to the doorway and she got up from the table. He followed her loving the view of her dressed like that. She sat in front of the computer and inserted the flash drive, bringing up the manuscript. With Jeff's help they selected the part that was okay and created a new document.

"So what is this part?"

"Family history, you know, starting to build the ranch in Virginia about thirty years before the war, Albert and eventually his two brothers, Robert and John. Basically follows Albert actually building the ranch with the help of his two brothers. Stuff like that."

Lori nodded. Still sitting at the computer, she selected the save option and looked at Jeff.

"For now we'll call it, THE KITTRIDGE MANUSCRIPT."

Jeff nodded. "Works for me."

"Next we'll create some notes."

Jeff watched her open a new document.

"Here's what we need to concentrate on."

Jeff watched her type.

```
The family at the start of the war, the
effect.

During the war, the effect to their busi-
ness, their ranch.
```

Virginia being a Confederate state.

Were they Confederate or Union? I think still open for discussion.

How did the plan come together?

Meet with Grant or somebody to discuss plan?

The attempted execution of the mission.

The unfortunate killing of the men.

The effect of the letter from Lee, believing they were Southern Gentleman, or more specifically Virginia Ranchers.

   The certificate from President Grant several years later.

The discovery of the documents verifying all this, or shall we say revealing all this

"There, that is a start. We have to tell that story from the point of what we have, basically what we now know. Now, of course we don't know some of those details, specifically who initiated the meetings or who actually devised the plan, but we know the when and the how and of course, the aftermath, so we will just have to make some assumptions as to those particular facts."

Lori paused, while Jeff waited, watching. She noticed him looking at her.

"See something you like?"

"Yes, you dressed like that always gives me ideas."

She smiled. "And?"

"Well, it sure makes this a lot more interesting."

"Shall we continue?"

"Yes, but one question."

"Let me finish first, it may answer your question."

He motioned for her to continue. She spoke as she typed.

"I think we can present multiple theories, you know like … did the Samuels family or one of them bring the plan to the Union side, volunteer like you said. Or, maybe someone from the Union side came to them with the plan. The Samuels men could very well have been Unionists and someone on the Union side may have known that fact and brought the plan to them because of their ability to get around Richmond. I think for sake of discussion, we need to present both scenarios in the manuscript."

Lori paused again, while Jeff stood silent. She leaned forward and began typing that last thought onto the list, once again sitting back in her chair when she was finished. Smiling, she looked at Jeff.

"Better yet, let's do a sequence of events."

Jeff watched her open a new page and start typing again talking out loud as she pounded away on the keyboard.

"Okay we know Kittridge was pursuing a belief that these men were Union soldiers and according to his research paper, he had them on the march to and subsequently being killed during the Wilderness Campaign. We now know that that is factually untrue. What he failed to see, or conveniently ignored, was the fact that these men were ranchers in the State of Virginia, a Confederate state and no way would they decide to abandon their ranch to join the Union army, certainly not so late in the war. I think we can reference that document, or rather those notes you found on Virginia that seem to say a lot of what we are suspecting."

Jeff nodded, holding the papers she was talking about. Nodding, she continued.

"So given that fact, and even though we know that to be false, I think it still should be part of the story, because something led him down that path and we should recognize that. There appears to be enough information to suggest that may have happened and Kittridge had enough to pursue that theory, so I think we need to keep both scenarios in, just flavor it accordingly and preface it as Kittridge's original theory based on his assumptions and what documents he had to use. "

She stopped and looked up at Jeff, standing by her side.

"Do you agree with that idea keeping some of that story line in for now? We can certainly clean it up later, makes for a good twist, don't you think?"

Jeff smiled, setting the paper back into the yes pile. Lori patted his leg.

"Okay, so let's get back to what we do know. We know this much. At some point a plan was hatched as evidenced by those hand drawn maps, but we still need to flush that out some more. Specifically, were they drawn as part of the plan, or rather to present the plan? Pretty interesting either way, of course we may need to develop that theory more."

She stopped and looked at Jeff for a moment before turning back to the keyboard.

"You know it could have even been by one of the Samuels men. They were most likely in and out of Richmond on a regular basis, and certainly had access to the city during the war. Yeah, I like that idea, let's work that concept in for now."

Jeff went into the kitchen to retrieve one of those chairs and set it down right next to her. She smiled and patted his leg rubbing along his thigh.

"Okay, next we have the meeting. I still like your idea that they volunteered, but I don't think we can rule out the fact they may have been recruited. And I base that on the money, that was a lot of money in those days, I mean $45,000 for each man in today's dollars. That would convince a lot of men to do most anything. But, for sake of discussion, we should offer it both ways, because in either event the plan was formulated, discussed, accepted and almost executed."

She stopped and sat back for a moment stretching. Jeff

watched the camisole tighten across her breasts. In a moment she leaned forward and continued.

"Okay and this is where it gets exciting, now we have the note from Grant, telling them it is a go. Now we don't know how long they waited between receiving the note and leaving the ranch, but I would suspect that it wasn't very long, maybe only a day, but it could have been a few days to put it all together. So they leave the ranch on their way to Richmond and encounter a forward post that may not have been there before, at least one they may not have known about. I think we can put that theory together without too much effort."

She stopped and looked at Jeff. Smiling mischievously, she spoke excitedly.

"Imagine if that didn't happen? Imagine if they got through that day and actually captured Jefferson Davis, how that might have changed things. How that may have affected the outcome of the war, even history? Hell, we might have another manuscript here, a novel of course, but what a story we could fabricate from that concept?"

"You're serious?"

"Could be?"

Jeff smiled and patted her on the shoulder. "Let's write this one first."

Lori smiled, turning back to the keyboard.

"Okay. Remember Lee was preparing for a probable attack by Grant, no doubt he set up additional forward sentry posts, in fact he sort of alluded to that in his letter that the men probably wouldn't expect that post to be there. Which brings us to that letter. So the men are killed on their way to Virginia, which Lee believes was a terrible mistake, that those men were no more than Virginia ranchers on their way to Richmond, totally unawares of the men's true purpose. How ironic is that? He takes great steps to send the bodies and possessions home, which I now believe included that leather pouch I found in the box with the identity papers and the letter of credit still inside."

She stopped and sat back again. Jeff sat silent, listening and watching.

"We have the receipts or whatever they are, that the bodies arrived at the train depot, then were transported back to the ranch for burial, so we now know that was the unexpected end of the mission."

She stopped and sat back, obviously thinking. A moment later she reached forward and started typing outlining her thoughts as she spoke.

"Now we have the log book entries showing who we now know must have been Eloise leaving Virginia, with the bureau —*one ugly bureau*—which means the bureau must have been in her and Robert junior's house. Maybe he is the one who built the thing and maybe he was the one who brought the plan to the family. That's worth thinking about. We know the documents and money were put in the bureau's secret compartment for safekeeping. So who built the bureau? And how did the bureau come to be in Robert's possession? Could he have been the one? Eloise may not have known about any of that? But maybe she did know something because she took that big heavy thing with her when she left town. Why? What did she know? Could it have been simply sentimental reasons? If she knew about the hidden compartment, I would imagine she would have at least removed the money? We may need to address that in some regard, because without that bureau, that one ugly bureau, none of this ever comes to light. Anyway, we do know she left the ranch with the bureau and then her letter a year later suggests that there was some kind of buyout agreement for her piece of land, keeping the original ranch in tact. But, I bet she still had some of Robert junior's gold. I mean five hundred dollars in gold, there had to be some left. You could go a long way in those days with that kind of money."

She stopped typing and turned to Jeff. "Is this making sense?"

Jeff nodded. "So far, it sounds right. Might have some work ahead of us filling in all the variables you're creating."

"Okay, last thing we have is that certificate from President Grant, obviously acknowledging the men's actions presented to Margaret, as Eloise said, the matriarch of the family without specifically saying what those actions were. However, we now know the men weren't killed on the battlefield, but it could have been one more indication these men were Union soldiers to support Kittridge's theories. Without knowing the details, certainly a certificate presented by President Grant would indicate that these men must have died in battle. That would go a long way to support Kittridge's concept and certainly convince him they were Union soldiers killed in battle. I think we can concede that premise."

Lori paused, shaking her head. "Okay I think that puts a cap on everything and closed the chapter."

"All that in one chapter?"

"No, I mean the whole event as we now know it."

Jeff nodded and patted her leg. She smiled, but continued.

"One last thing we should consider at least from a historical perspective and I guess from a personal perspective for the family. This event produced a personal letter from General Robert E. Lee, a personal note written by General Ulysses S. Grant and a Certificate from then President Grant, all to one family, just think about that, a letter from both sides in the war. I don't think you could find any other example of that from, during or after the war. That in itself is a pretty amazing turn of events and I think that aspect should be incorporated into the story somehow. I also think we need an appendix with a copy of all the documents we found and how they relate to the story, maybe they should be in the story ... well, we'll figure that out later, maybe both."

She sat back again, but then leaned forward.

"I think you actually have two stories here, the one Kittridge was trying to put together from what he believed to have happened and the documents he found to support that theory, and the one that actually happened, which we are able to chronicle from the documents we found. I'm beginning to think we need both stories represented, we just need to frame it all together somehow."

She sat back again, looking at Jeff right next to her. "What do you think?"

"I think, I agree with all of that. Looks like I have my work cut out for me. Two weeks huh?"

She patted his leg. "I'll do the research from my super computer and help fill in the blanks, as historically possible as we can."

Jeff nodded, turning in his chair, taking a breath before speaking.

"So let me get this straight, these men operated a ranch in the middle of a Confederate stronghold, I mean the actual Confederate capital, defended by Lee's entrenched Army of Northern Virginia. Somehow they decide to help the Union out by trying to capture the other sides Commander-in-Chief? Southerners agreeing to help the North? Even with everything we found out about Virginia being a Confederate State and the very real possibility these men were Unionists, caught up in a really bad situation, I still say why?"

She turned in her chair to face him full on, which gave Jeff a great view of the see through camisole, bringing a smile to his face, only looking up as she started to speak.

"Frankly I don't think they decided to do anything, I think the circumstances decided for them. Look, as you said you had Lee's Confederate Army entrenched in and around Richmond. By 1864, you knew Grant was coming to try and take Richmond. Here is your ranch right in the middle of that potential conflict. I think this was strictly business for these men, save the ranch and these men were willing to do whatever was necessary to do that. Capturing one side's leader, gives the other side bargaining power, you know like in business. Remember there was an awful lot of money on the table for them to do just that. I'm sure the last thing they wanted was a full-scale battle between these two great armies happening quite possibly right on their land more likely right through their land. You know, that's good, I better add that concept to the list."

Jeff watched her type that last part into the notes. He waited until they were printed out and she handed the pages to him. He took the sheets of paper, tapping them down into a neat pile.

Lori sat back in the chair. Jeff still sat beside her. She reached over.

"Think you can do that?"

Jeff smiled. "No problem, I'll pound it out tomorrow."

Lori smiled and patted his leg. "I knew you could."

Jeff smiled again, putting his arm around her and pulling her closer, kissing her on the head, whispering into her hair.

"How about you lay out a plan for me and I'll try to work from that?"

"I'll do better than that. Let me create an outline of the flow and you can build story chapters off that outline."

Jeff watched her open a new document and starting from the piece they salvaged from the original manuscript, she created working chapter titles, writing a paragraph or two on each step.

"There now all you have to do is, flush out each chapter. Just tell the story as if you were telling someone what you found out, but put it on paper. Don't get hung up on being complete or perfect, let's just get a working draft and we can revise as we go."

Jeff nodded. "Yeah, let me have a go at it. Promise me you'll be tough, I can handle it. You don't like something, say so, we'll fix it."

"Deal."

———————— /// ————————

They spent the rest of the day and most of Sunday creating chapters, putting pieces of clipped paper into the order of the outline for Jeff to use as material to build from before Lori had to leave for home.

On Monday, Jeff dug in and created the first two new chapters, which he emailed to Lori for review. They did that for the next five days, back and forth. By the end of the week, Jeff had what he thought was a working middle section to the manuscript, but still incorporating Kittridge's theory of these men being Union soldiers killed during the Wilderness Campaign. He left what had been salvaged from the original manuscript, mostly about the family and considered that to be the beginning, the Union theory part of the middle and the new chapters he worked on to be the second part of the middle, roughly about two thirds there.

On Friday afternoon when Lori arrived, they worked together flushing out what Jeff called the end of the story section. Lori worked on strengthening the new finished chapters, while Jeff created his own working chapters for the end.

At six o'clock Friday night, Lori got up from the computer and sat down beside Jeff, placing her head on his shoulder.

"Shall we go out, or do you want to order in?"

"Let's go out, I need a break and at least a drink, maybe two."

"Just let me freshen up a little."

Jeff watched her leave the room and went back to making a few more notes. He had never fancied himself a writer and at best what he was doing now was creating pages of words, but with Lori's editing, those words became chapters and he was actually starting to get into the flow of this writing thing. Lori came back into the room.

"You ready?"

Jeff nodded, setting the pad and paper he was working with, on the sofa.

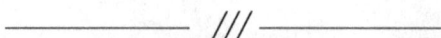

——————— /// ———————

At the restaurant they couldn't help but talk about the project, but after the second Vodka martini, the conversation drifted back to each other.

"Jeff, I really like spending time with you and when this is over, I'd like to take a vacation some place where we can just concentrate on each other." Lori caught herself. "I'm sorry, was that too forward of me? I didn't mean."

Jeff raised his hand in the air. "I was kind a thinking the same thing myself. We've been a bit consumed in this project. I'll be glad when it's over."

Lori looked down at her drink. Jeff sat up.

"I'm sorry, did I say something wrong?"

"No, Jeff. It's just that once it's out there, it will never be over. We've made a significant find and should the manuscript get published … well we're going to be in the spotlight from that point on, at least for some time, I'd say."

"Well as long as we do it together. I couldn't imagine doing any of that pomp and circumstance without you by my side, it's all over my head."

Lori reached over and placed her hand on his. "Do you mean that?"

"Damn right, I mean that. We're in this together. I'm sorry if I dragged you into this, but you're here now and you ain't leaving."

"What about when I have to present to the Historical Society. Will you be able to sit through that?"

"Sure, I'll just picture you standing there in your panties and camisole."

Lori broke out laughing. "Now so will I. Thanks for that image."

Jeff laughed with her.

——————— /// ———————

Later that night as they lay in bed after having figured out what to do once again, she spoke softly.

"Have you thought about what you're going to do with the money?"

"You mean the money we might make off the book?"

"Well, that too, but I meant those bills we found. You said they could be worth a million?"

"Really haven't thought about that, since we put them away. Of course, they may not be worth that much and who knows if anyone wants them at those prices. Maybe we'll sell a couple to collectors, but probably the rest will sit in the box, sell one every now and then. So, I'm not too concerned about those. We won't see any of that money for awhile."

"You're probably right. Would be nice they were kept intact, especially with that band around them."

Jeff reached around and cupped her breast as he usually did when they lay together.

"What about you and those documents. They seem a lot more important than the money."

"They are significant that's for sure. I'd like to present them to the University where I work, let them decide what to do next. While I would suspect there probably is a monetary value in there somewhere, I'd rather they were available for public display and to me that would be invaluable."

"Well you got my okay on that. You're the professor, so whatever you think is best, works for me."

Lori hugged him.

"And to think you tried to throw me out of your office that first day."

Her hand slid over his abdomen. "Anyway, I can make that up to you?"

———————— /// ————————

Jeff worked day and night over the next week finishing what he called the end section and by that next Friday, when Lori arrived at his house, they had a draft manuscript in place.

By Sunday morning after two more passes through, some changes here and there, they both agreed - THE KITTRIDGE MANUSCRIPT - was finished.

The story was told covering all the known facts and what they could only surmise was the missing facts. Included was how the project got started, the discovery and logistics of the documents and how those documents affected the story, working the Kittridge theories of Union soldiers and explaining the logic and facts behind that conclusion. They were able to keep the original manuscript intact, removing only that incoherent ending and eventually created what Jeff called the second middle and finally an ending that took into account both scenarios and using the documents as their guide, they incorporated the flow of the story into a factual conclusion.

THE KITTRIDGE MANUSCRIPT

When the dust settled, they had a five hundred plus page manuscript encompassing over one hundred twenty-five thousand words. The work opened with a dedication page to Robert Kittridge and his incredible journey to get the party started and went on to include a forward, an appendix listing all the documents with a full picture of each one, including a picture of that "one ugly bureau" and a final thought about the historical discovery.

Lori had taken Monday and Tuesday off. They had scheduled a meeting with Nathan Simon on Monday and would be leaving early in the morning to get there. They decided to take Sunday afternoon off and just spend time together figuring out what else they could do together.

TWENTY-NINE

Jeff Morgan pulled into the now familiar parking lot outside Nathan Simon's office. Lori walked into the office ahead of Jeff who was immediately greeted by Donna.

"Why Jeff, so good to see you. Who is this lovely lady with you?"

"This is Professor Hathaway."

"Nice to meet you, please go right in."

Lori stepped through the door, with Jeff right behind her and Donna following.

"Jeff."

"Nathan. I'd like you to meet Lori Hathaway, ah Professor Hathaway."

"Lori is fine."

Everyone shook hands and took seats around Nathan's desk.

"So what brings you to my office that is so important I have to drop everything? You're starting to act like a real client."

Lori looked at Jeff and let him take the lead.

"We found something that well … I'll let Lori explain."

Lori looked at Jeff, but he motioned for her to go.

"We discovered several historical documents pertaining to an event that happened during the Civil War that will most certainly add to the war's storied history. These are documents of a significant nature and I dare say once they come to light … well they will certainly create a buzz in the historical world."

Nathan nodded. "And you need me because?"

Jeff raised his hand. "Hold on, there is a lot more to the story."

Nathan sat back in his chair Donna leaned forward ready to take it all in, with her note pad at the ready. Jeff took the lead back.

"Nathan, as you know, you handed me a project started by Bob Kittridge, an old Army buddy, I wouldn't … well, someone from my Vietnam days, for me … well, hopefully for me to finish that research and complete the project, but really to compete the manuscript. Well, I have done just that and boy let me tell you, have I opened a Pandora's Box in doing so."

Nathan and Donna both flashed to the recent activities they had been through regarding this project all of which were unbeknownst to Jeff, but remained quiet letting Jeff continue. However they couldn't help stealing a glance at each other and smiling, if Jeff only knew? They both looked back at Jeff as he continued.

"Although, I must tell you when you first called, I was quite skeptical, thought you were trying to run a scam on me." Jeff paused, but everyone remained silent waiting for him to continue. "Not to mention the excitement this adventure has created."

Again, Nathan and Donna glanced at each other, letting a smile cross their faces. Jeff continued oblivious to their actions.

"You know, hearing Kittridge died of cancer brought back all those feelings of losing my wife to cancer. That alone almost made me walk away." Jeff paused, taking a deep breath before continuing. "Anyway, little did I know the magnitude of what we would encounter just trying to sort this all out … well, let me tell you. I couldn't begin to guess what Kittridge did or didn't know and it certainly would have been interesting to see how he would have reacted to what we ultimately found."

Jeff paused and looked over at Lori, taking a deep breath. He faced her as he spoke. "Never could have I imagined meeting someone again, especially someone as special as you."

Nathan cleared his throat. "Can we continue?"

"Yes, of course." Jeff turned back to face Nathan. He took

a deep breath before he continued. "It's funny ... maybe sad I suppose, but there were five names on that list and it all came down to me. Frankly, I had serious doubts about that manuscript ever happening. I mean it was so rough. But I'm getting ahead of myself."

Nathan shifted in his chair. Donna leaned back in hers. Lori held Jeff's hand. Jeff looked at each of them before continuing.

"I mean ... well, let me back up a bit. Suffice it to say, I sure had my doubts, still did especially after I was the last man standing. But I had no choice then."

Jeff paused. Lori squeezed his hand. Jeff nodded and continued.

"Okay, well, after I got the package, I contacted a few people from the notes Kittridge left, including his companion, who gave me another box of papers. Lori then found some interesting pieces of information including an old worn leather pouch with some pretty interesting documents inside."

Jeff cleared his throat, there was so much to tell, his enthusiasm bubbling over. "But the biggest find, figuratively and literally was the bureau."

"Bureau?"

They all looked at Nathan, who shrugged his shoulders. Jeff continued.

"Anyway, I went to Missouri ... but that's not important. I got the bureau back to my garage and while Lori and I were fiddling with it, we discovered a secret compartment and that's where we found another old worn leather pouch containing some incredible documents and the money."

"Money?"

Jeff stopped and looked at Nathan, before continuing.

"Yes, sixty one hundred dollar bills from 1862, still wrapped in the original treasury band."

Nathan sat forward. "You're kidding?"

Jeff and Lori both shook their head no. Lori pulled her cell phone out and brought up the picture to show Nathan.

"Any idea what they are worth?"

Jeff nodded yes. "$17,500 to $20,000 each."

Nathan sat back in his chair. "And you found these in that, what did you call it, a bureau?"

"That's correct."

Nathan sat forward and made a note on a sheet of paper. "Those documents you're talking about as well?"

Lori nodded yes. Nathan wrote another note, before looking up. "Tell me about that bureau again."

"I got the bureau from a guy in Missouri, one Herb Miller, it had been in his barn for eighty years, but we're pretty sure the bureau dates back to 1864, at least based on that diary entry, actually the log book entry from that Union soldier. The bureau was mentioned in Kittridge's notes. Miller said if I could get the bureau out of his barn I could have it."

Nathan stopped writing and sat back. "He just gave it to you?"

Jeff paused smiling, looking at Nathan, but continued.

"Yes. Said if I could get it out of the barn I could have it, which I did and then had that bureau shipped to my house where it still sits in my garage. But truth be told, Miller sold the piece to me for a buck."

Jeff pulled the bill-of-sale out of his carry case and handed it to Nathan, who took the paper from him smiling.

"Well that sure helps. I'll need a copy of this."

Jeff raised his hands. "What do you mean?"

"It means you had the legal ownership of that bureau at the time you found the documents and the money. That little fact will go a long way to avoid any problems later. Donna would you make a copy of this please?"

Nathan sat back in his chair. "So what do you need now?"

Jeff looked at Lori and motioned for her to speak. Slowly she started.

"Well I'm planning on turning those documents over to the University this week and we just wanted to make sure we have legal representation before we do, for what ever reason we might need, so we wanted you to know all the details and be prepared in case we needed to call on you for anything. In addition, as Jeff said, we have finished that manuscript, which will coincide with the release of those documents and tells the story which is now completed thanks to the finding of those documents. We'd like you to represent us in that matter as well. We haven't submitted the manuscript to anyone yet, but we fully believe, once those documents are made public and the word gets out that the manuscript exists, we fully expect that there will be interest. We'd like you to handle those inquiries."

Lori took a breath while everyone waited. Donna returned and handed the copy to Nathan and the original bill-of-sale back to Jeff.

"Well, I believe that's it. I can assure you Mr. Simon those are significant documents and will create a bit of a stir once they are made public."

Nathan shook his head, looking first at Jeff, then Lori and finally, Donna.

"Donna, we have any problems with any of that?"

"Looks okay to me."

"Then I believe we have a deal. I'm not exactly sure what you need me to do, but I trust you'll let me know."

Nathan stood up and shook Jeff's hand, then Lori's. Donna walked them out of Nathan's office and jotted down Lori's phone number as well.

A few minutes later Jeff and Lori were standing on the street outside Nathan's office.

"Well tomorrow, we go to my place and Wednesday we make the presentation."

Jeff hugged Lori. "It will be just fine. You'll be the belle of the ball."

Lori hugged him back. "I hope it goes well. I've never done anything like this before. Hell, I've never seen anything like this before."

———————— /// ————————

On Wednesday morning they stood inside the auditorium at Professor Hathaway's University. Jeff had packed a suit for the occasion, but at the last minute had decided against the tie. Lori was dressed like a professor, but for good luck, she had worn just the panties and camisole underneath. A bit nervous about not wearing a bra, Jeff had assured her that with the blouse and jacket she had on, only he would know.

The documents were all in separate clear folders inside a large tie envelope, tucked into her left arm. She had presented copies and pictures of the find to the various heads of the history department and the dean had arranged the unveiling and press conference. Several Professors from other Universities and quite a few members from the historical field were in the audience as well. The dean motioned. She turned and kissed Jeff on the cheek. He whispered good luck in her ear.

Taking the podium, she began her dissertation by showing the documents on an overhead screen, explaining how they were found and their meaning. At the very end, she mentioned that the find grew out of an attempt to grant a dying man's wish to finish a manuscript he had started, which they had now done. She described how the manuscript had been reconstructed to incorporate these new finds, but kept the focus of the original manuscript offering both sides of the story as it were and again reassured that the manuscript had been completed.

When she was finished, she got a standing ovation and handed the documents over to a caretaker, never again to be touched by human hands. They would be stored in one of the air controlled vaults and could only be viewed by appointment and from now on gloves would have to be worn, the usual treatment for very old historical pieces of paper. Lori would be the last person to have ever touched the documents.

Jeff stood off to the side while she did the meet and greet, occasionally getting in on the conversation. After an hour and a half of that, she begged off and assured everyone that a subsequent paper on the subject would be forthcoming.

She grabbed Jeff's arm and pulled him toward the door.

"Let's get out of here."

Jeff nodded and helped her get through the crowd.

A screen overheard still had the documents displayed for everyone to review.

They left the campus and headed back to her place for the night, Jeff would be going home in the morning, because Professor Hathaway had a full schedule for the next two days, but they had plans to get together for the weekend no matter what, preferably at his place where nobody could find her. In any event, they wanted the rest of the night for themselves.

Stepping into her condo, she closed the door and leaned back against it.

"Well, it's on."

Jeff stopped and looked at her, removing his jacket and placing it over the back of a chair. "Just like you said it would be."

"Oh Jeff, are you sure you want to be a part of this? I mean I'm not sure I want to be."

Jeff walked over and kissed her. "I want to be a part of you, the rest we'll figure out."

As Jeff walked away, she stood up and removed her jacket dropping it to the floor. Jeff turned in time to see her removing her blouse and dropping that to the floor. A moment later the skirt unzipped also dropped to the floor. She stepped out of it, standing there in her panties and camisole and her shoes.

"This is what I want. Do you know how nervous I was standing at that podium imaging myself standing there like this, realizing that you knew this was underneath and standing off to the side?"

Jeff was there in a flash, scooping her up in his arms, kissing her hard but passionately.

"I'll always be there, Lori. I'll always be there."

Letting her go, he bent down to pick up her clothes placing them on the sofa. She sat down next to the garments and he sat down next to her. Just then his cell phone rang. He didn't recognize the number so he casually answered.

"Hello."

"Mr. Morgan, Lillian Meriweather here? Mr. Morgan, I hope

you don't mind my calling you on your cell. I do apologize if that is a bother, but you did give us the number."

Jeff held the phone away from his ear, so Lori could hear.

"No, that's quite alright. What can I do for you Lillian?"

"Mr. Morgan, I wonder if you would have a minute to speak with Mr. Cummings?"

Jeff turned to look at Lori, but she shrugged her shoulders.

"Sure, I have a minute."

In a moment, Allen Edward Cummings the Third was on the line.

"Mr. Morgan, so good to hear your voice again. May I add my name to the list of those congratulating you and the esteemed Professor Hathaway on your tremendous find. Why it has set the historical world on fire, I dare say."

Jeff elbowed Lori, while she stifled a laugh.

"What can I do for you, Mr. Cummings?"

"Well, Mr. Morgan, you might find this a bit strange, but I have a client, forgive me, a private collector that just has to have that bureau, I was hoping you might entertain an offer?"

Jeff was about to answer, but Allen Edward Cummings the Third kept right on talking.

"Now mind you, this is only an offer that certainly leaves room for negotiation, so if you will bear with me, I will present his thoughts."

Cummings took a breath and Jeff waited.

"He has authorized me to offer you five thousand dollars cash for the bureau and he will pay for all shipping and handling charges. What would you say to that Mr. Morgan?"

"Well, that is a mighty generous offer, far greater than you and I discussed."

"Mr. Morgan, you are so right, had either of us known of the treasure inside, or the true uniqueness of that bureau, I dare say we would have done business a bit differently. But that is water under the bridge now, don't you agree? What would you say to that offer?"

"Mr. Cummings, meaning no disrespect, but I would have to

say no at this time. I truly haven't decided what to do with that bureau."

"Mr. Morgan, if I may, I have been authorized to raise that offer to ten thousand dollars, of course my client will still pay for the shipping and handling charges."

"Mr. Cummings, once again that is a most generous offer, but regretfully I will have to decline at this time. Should the situation change, I promise you, you will be the first person I call, but for now the bureau stays with me."

"Mr. Morgan, I do understand and I would certainly appreciate your contacting me in the very near future. I would only ask that if there is a price that would be more satisfactory to you, you need only name it and I will present that to my client. Good day, Mr. Morgan, it has been a pleasure. Again, my congratulations to you and Professor Hathaway for a most extraordinary find. Good day, suh."

The line disconnected. Lori let out a huge laugh.

"Oh my God, if I wasn't already in my underwear, that man would have me there. Gracious, can he talk?"

Jeff nodded. "Esteemed all right, too bad he couldn't see you sitting here like that, takes all the steam out of that esteemed."

Lori punched him on the arm.

"What's wrong with the way I'm sitting here?"

"Nothing in my eyes."

Jeff reached over kissing her cupping her breast through the camisole, before sitting back up.

"I would bet he already has a buyer for twenty five thousand. I wonder if I told him that amount what he would have said? How'd you like Lillian?"

"She's something all right."

Jeff nodded, slipping his arm around her cupping her breast. She placed her hand on his chest.

"Can I ask you something?"

Jeff looked at her. "Sure anything."

"Have you thought about the bureau? What you might do with it?"

"Sure have. Already done it."

Lori pulled away causing his hand to pull up on her camisole before it slipped free.

"Can I ask what?"

Jeff nodded. "You sure can. I donated it."

"Donated it? To whom? I mean where? I mean?"

Jeff raised his hand in the air. "Slow down. Same place you donated the documents."

"To the University?"

Jeff nodded yes. "While you were off meeting with the dean, I talked to the woman that took the documents away, nice lady. I asked her about it and she said they would love to have the bureau, especially to showcase with the documents that it would complete the find and add to the experience. I tried to explain the size and weight, but she said that absolutely didn't matter, that they had many big pieces all that was important was having the find all together. So I said okay. I told her you would work out the details with her."

"Me?"

"Yeah, your place, your people, I thought who better to coordinate that?"

"Really, you're going to give them the bureau, but Cummings said he'd give you ten thousand, maybe more."

"It's okay, I get a nice tax write off this way."

They both broke into a hysterical laugh, beating Cummings at his own game. They ended up in each other's arms.

"You know you're really overdressed at this moment."

Jeff nodded and stood up. He removed his pants showing he had boxers underneath. "For good luck." She watched him remove his shirt, but he didn't have a t-shirt underneath. "Too hot with the jacket." She nodded waiting for him to sit back down.

"This might be one of our last nights away from it all, let's make the best of it."

Lori pulled the camisole over her head and leaned into him, kissing him deeply. Once again they figured out what to do, but this time right there on the sofa.

THIRTY

Two weeks later Jason walked into Nathan's office carrying a box. He promptly set the box down on a table in the office.

"What's that?"

Jason reached into the box and removed a little black book, handing that to Donna. He spoke with a smile. "Here, this is a present for your friend, tell her it's a thank you from us for her help, I'm sure she'll appreciate it."

Donna held it in her hands. "What is it?"

"Robert Swift's black book. There are a lot of interesting things in there, especially the page on Congressman Reginald Harrison. Makes for fascinating reading, rather enlightening information on a few other people she might be interested in as well."

Donna nodded, setting the book down. "How did you get Swift's black book?"

Jason looked at Donna, then Nathan, taking a moment before answering.

"It's kind of a long story. I found the Mortuary that got Swift's body. Paid the kid two C-notes…"

"C-notes?"

Jason and Donna looked at Nathan. Donna spoke first. "Yeah, that means two one hundred dollar bills."

"I know what a C-note is just surprised to hear it called that anymore."

Jason nodded. "I guess old habits die hard. Know a crowd still uses that term. Anyway, after I talked to the kid ... let's just say the place didn't know what to do with his stuff and called me to ask if I could find the rightful owner."

"Come again?"

"After Swifty passed, his personal belongings, including what he had on him when he entered prison was put into a box that was picked up when the body was released to the Mortuary. I started to say, I paid the kid two bills to let me make a copy of that black book because he wouldn't let me take anything. But, the box sat around, nobody claimed it and after thirty days, the kid called me and asked if I wanted the rest of the stuff. Of course I said yes. Picked it up this morning."

Nathan raised his hand in the air and shook his head. "I don't think I want to know anymore."

Jason nodded as he looked at Donna. "Just wanted to stop by and give you that for your friend. No need to return it, like I said I already made copies of anything I might need. She can do whatever she wants with it."

Jason started to leave then stopped, resting the box on the arm of a chair.

"You know, she's been cleaning up Reggie's messes for awhile, I got to wondering why, but hearing that she will support his run for the Senate next year got me to thinking, in spite of everything ... well I gotta believe she's doing this as much for her benefit as she is for him."

Donna spoke up first. "What do you mean?"

"Think about it? She's the one could make or break Congressman Reginald Harrison, but she chooses to make him. Makes you wonder don't it. Then I realized how nice it would be to have a Senator in your pocket and with that book, if she doesn't already, she will certainly have one now. Anyway, give her my regards. Tell her thanks again for her help."

Donna and Nathan watched Jason leave the office.

——————— /// ———————

Jeff and Lori entered Nathan's office just as Jason was leaving. Jeff held the door for him and nodded hello, as he exited the outer office. Stepping into Nathan's office, Jeff knocked on the door.

"This a bad time?"

Nathan and Donna both looked in his direction. Nathan motioned.

"No, not at all, please come in."

"Will you excuse me a minute?"

They all watched Donna leave the office, but she was back in a minute. She had left to put Swift's little black book directly into her purse. She patted Jeff's shoulder as she passed by.

"Well, good to see you two again. It's been quite a whirlwind hasn't it?"

Jeff looked over at Donna, smiling. "Donna, you can certainly say that again. Lori's presentation hadn't even finished when it exploded on the Internet. The calls and messages haven't stopped yet. But, that's not why we are here. Nathan, you have something?"

"I have several something's."

They all sat around his desk and waited for Nathan to organize his notes.

"I understand you've reframed the manuscript to tell the story of the story? What the hell does that mean?"

Jeff and Lori smiled, but Lori answered.

"Well, we decided to tell Bob Kittridge's story within the actual story and how this all came about. A professor, a colleague of mine suggested that to give the documents their proper due, they should be showcased in the nature of their findings, but the only way to do that was to reframe the story."

Nathan raised his hand. "Yeah, whatever the hell that means. I'm here to tell you that whatever you did appears to have worked. There is interest in the manuscript with relation to the finding of those documents as the centerpiece, or some crap like that.

Sorry, I don't mean to sound cynical but, the calls I've been getting asking me that very question has been exhausting, especially considering I don't know what the hell any of that means."

Nathan paused, while Jeff and Lori sat silent smiling.

"Anyway bottom line. I've had three legitimate offers so far, one of which is for a one hundred thousand advance."

"A hundred thousand?"

Nathan looked at Jeff. "That got your attention huh? I turned it down. I told all three I wouldn't entertain anything less than two fifty."

"Two fifty?"

Nathan looked at Jeff again, this time smiling. "Look this stuff is red hot. Your professor there has set the historical world on fire, everybody wants in and they're lining up for the story. Two hundred and fifty thousand is the lowest I'll consider."

Lori held Jeff's hand and squeezed tightly. Nathan continued speaking looking directly at Lori.

"I've also received a call from a major Hollywood name, not one of his people, but him personally. He wants to secure the rights to the novel."

"What novel?"

Nathan looked at Lori. "The one you mentioned."

"I never said anything about a novel."

Jeff was about to remind her, but Nathan spoke first still looking directly at her.

"I'm sure you were aware there were any number of reporters present the day you made your big splash. Well, it just so happens one of them quoted you."

Nathan paused and picked up a newspaper clipping proceeding to read from that story, keeping his focus on Lori.

"Imagine if those men weren't killed at that forward post? Imagine if those men had made it through that day and imagine if they were successful in their mission? Imagine how that might have changed the war, how that might have changed history? Now there's a story. Certainly that story would make for a great novel."

Nathan set the newspaper clipping down on his desk. Lori dropped her head speaking very softly.

"I guess I did say that."

"So do you have this novel?"

Lori looked up, first at Nathan and then at Jeff. Panic crept into her face. She tightened her grip on Jeff's hand and spoke very softly. "No. There isn't any novel."

Nathan smiled, picking up another sheet of paper. "That's even better. He said if you haven't finished the novel, he would be willing to significantly increase his offer for the exclusive rights to the story forgoing the novel. In addition, he would pay you a consulting fee to work with his screenwriter to flush out that story for the big screen. Lastly, he would pay you an additional fee to consult on set during the filming of the movie. So what do you want me to tell him?"

"Oh my God! Sure. I mean, I guess so. I mean, I don't know. I don't have a story."

Nathan sat back in his chair. "What's to know? It's your story, you just tell them how to write it and what to do and they will pay you a whole bunch of money to do just that."

Lori looked at Nathan first, then turned to Jeff. He squeezed her hand as he spoke.

"Why not? Let's do this. You can put together the facts and I'll write the story. They are gonna do whatever they want with the story anyway, so let's give them a story. Besides it is all supposition anyway, we can say whatever we want. How hard can that be?"

Lori nodded, turning back to Nathan. "Okay, I guess we'll do it."

"That's the spirit, but I still have one more." Nathan looked at Jeff. "A cable station wants to do your story, how you got involved, The Civil War angle, what you did to pursue the story, how you found the documents and what you two did with those findings and of course, how you put the manuscript together. Basically, they want to put together a documentary telling the story of this wonderful find - their words."

Jeff spoke first. "My story?"

"Yeah, you and her about how you found these docs and like that. I'm still waiting to hear a serious offer from them, but they sure sound interested. What can I tell you, the professor was right, she lit a fire."

She squeezed his hand tighter. Jeff cleared his throat before speaking.

"Nathan, there's something else we need to get settled."

"Such as?"

"How we divide this up."

"Divide what up?"

"The money, the proceeds, whatever it is."

"The royalties."

"Yeah, how does that work?"

"It's pretty straight forward. They pay me and I take my commission, which by the way is fifteen percent, then I cut you a check for the rest."

"I want to change that and I want to you to put that in writing, you know, create the legal documents to do that."

"Change it how. The fifteen percent is industry standard. I ..."

Jeff raised his hand. "I'm fine with that. I mean the rest as you call it."

Nathan sat back in his chair. "Tell me what you were thinking."

Jeff sat forward in his chair, still holding onto Lori's hand. He took a moment to gather his thoughts before speaking.

"He's what I want to do. After your commission or whatever, the remaining money is to be divided like this, twenty percent goes to Sandra Nelson and the remaining eighty percent is split between us, Lori and I forty percent each."

"Jeff you can't be serious?"

Jeff turned to Lori, still holding her hand. "I told you that you were in this to the end and I meant it. Without your help we wouldn't be sitting here and none of this would have happened."

Lori squeezed his hand tighter and used her other hand to wipe away a tear. Nathan leaned forward, this time with pen in hand.

"No problem, I can set that up, but I must ask who is Sandra Nelson?"

"You damn well know who Sandra Nelson is."

They all looked over at Donna. She continued.

"Nathan was afraid she would muddy the waters with Kittridge. He saw her that day at the facility, had me look into who she was. He wanted to make sure she wouldn't file a claim, be a nuisance you know screw things up. It was his idea not to give you her name, but it appears you found her anyway, good for you, Jeff."

"That's not quite true Donna and you know it. I just thought we should cover all our bases, protect our client, that's all, why …"

Donna raised her hand in the air. "You could have at least called her."

"You're right. I'm sorry. That was my mistake. Can we get on with this now?"

Donna turned to Jeff and Lori. "Jeff that's a fine thing you're doing for her, may I ask why?"

Jeff looked at Donna, bowing his head for a minute. He used his free hand to wipe away a tear, taking a moment before speaking.

"She was Kittridge's companion, with him to the end. I know what that is like, went through that with my late wife. You can't understand unless you were there. She went through the cancer with Kittridge, she understood, she shouldn't be forgotten now when it counts. She's as much a part of this as we are. Besides Kittridge came to Nathan to protect her, wanted her kept out of anything."

Jeff paused, Lori squeezed his hand tighter, placing her other hand on his.

"Just thought it was the right thing to do, that's all."

Donna put her hand on Lori's shoulder. "Lori, you got yourself one hell of a good man there, don't ever let him get away."

"I won't."

"Can we get on with this?"

They all looked at Nathan. He sat there with his hands in the air. "Sorry, but we have work to do here. How do you want me to set this up anonymous or do you want her to know?"

Jeff thought about it for a moment. "I had an idea that I thought might work."

Nathan waved his hand in a go ahead motion.

"His estate goes to me right?"

"Yes, but?"

"I need you to fix it so that a clause says … what did you call them, royalties from the manuscript that a percentage payable to the estate would go to her, something like that, do your legal thing to make that happen, let her think Kittridge did that for her, she'll appreciate it more that way. Tell her that Kittridge set up a twenty percent clause for any monies received regarding the project, for her in case the manuscript did get published. I'll sign whatever and we'll make the twenty percent payable to her through the Estate of Robert Kittridge. I don know if I'm saying that right, but you can figure out how to make that happen and then explain all that to her. That work for you, Donna?"

"Yes, I like that, let him talk to her this time, yeah, I like that a lot."

"Good, then it's done. The other two parts will be paid forty to me and forty to Lori. That should be straightforward. Do up the paperwork and I'll sign it before the first dollar comes in."

Nathan nodded. He looked over at his secretary.

"We'll get those papers drawn up for you right now. Donna?"

"Sure thing." She took the notes from Nathan. "Give me about fifteen, maybe twenty minutes."

Donna left the office and they sat silent for a moment. Nathan leaned forward and spoke softly.

"There is another matter we need to discuss."

Jeff and Lori leaned in closer, she still held onto his hand.

"Those bills, I've had an offer for them."

"The bills?"

Nathan looked at his notes. "Yes those sixty 1862 One Hundred Dollar first series United States Notes. Yes I've looked into them as well."

Jeff nodded, while Lori smiled. Nathan continued.

"So I understand those bills as you call them are extremely rare and in that condition, pristine I believe the collector called it, have quite a demand. I've had several offers for five or ten or one or two, but remembering what the Professor here requested, I've avoided those offers."

Nathan looked at Lori before continuing. "So here's the offer, are you ready?"

Jeff and Lori both nodded.

"A cool million for the whole pack, all sixty bills."

"A million?"

"This offer came from a man that is an avid collector. He said the value was in keeping them together and he could not imagine selling them separately. He also said, and this part is for you my dear Lori, he would agree to let them be reviewed, made public, not hide them away especially based on their relationship to the other documents. He said he has the resources to do that. I looked him up and he has put other items on public display, loaned them to museums and like that and by the way he said to have the University contact him in that regard should we close the deal. Will that meet with all your expectations my dear Lori?"

Lori was smiling from ear to ear. "I think that will do quite nicely. What do you think Jeff?"

"Sounds like it will work for me."

Nathan raised his hand in the air. "There's more."

"More?"

"Yes, when he saw the picture he noticed the band still wrapped on the bundle, he asked if the band was still there, I told him it was, right?"

Jeff and Lori both nodded yes.

"Good. Why didn't you tell me what was on the band?"

Jeff shook his head not understanding.

"Instead he told me what was on it from the picture I sent him that you two gave me."

Jeff and Lori sat there not remembering.

"The hand writing? Remember now, the *$6,000 - Gold* and the initials *AL* that could only be one person, the only person who could have made that mark. You have a pack of rare bills with Abraham Lincoln's initials on it as well. How could you not remember that? The collector said he thinks that Lincoln was personally guaranteeing the bills could be redeemed for gold later. Jesus, how could you miss that?"

Jeff smiled and Lori giggled, laughing as he spoke. "Sorry we forgot. Been so focused on the other documents. I only looked at the packet once, before putting them in the safe deposit box."

Nathan sat back in his chair. "Well, that little piece of information got you another hundred thousand dollars. He's willing to pay one point one million for the pack if it is in tact."

Jeff sat up. "Really?"

"Yes, really."

Jeff and Lori snuggled together and kissed.

"Will you two cut that out?"

"Sure, sorry."

Nathan waved his hand in the air, taking a moment.

"There is one other thing to discuss. We didn't … well we didn't discuss my fee for finding a buyer for the money and I was wondering how you felt about that? What your thoughts were on the subject?"

Jeff looked at Lori and she nodded yes. Nathan watched them both, until finally Jeff spoke. "Tell you what, you keep the hundred and we'll take the cool million. That work for you?"

Nathan smiled. "I think that sounds fair." Nathan made a note on his pad, before looking back up. "One more thing, he'd like to physically see the packet before he transfers the funds. Can we work something out in that regard?"

"Sure, the bills are in my safe deposit box at the bank, we can meet there and he can take a look and if he is ready, he can have them right then and there."

"Fine, I'll tell him we need the first one hundred thousand as good faith, fully refundable and the million upon acceptance of the bills. I'll draw up the papers today for the purchase of those bills."

Jeff nodded, squeezing Lori's hand as he spoke. "Remember Nathan all proceeds go into the split, no exceptions."

Nathan looked at Jeff. "I thought you would want this to be negotiated separately?"

Jeff shook his head no. "It all goes in. Everything from this point on, the book, the movie, the documentary any monies we earn from this project goes in from now on. No deal until I sign the papers instructing as much."

"Fine, I'll take care of it."

Donna returned with a stack of papers that Jeff signed and she notarized.

Nathan stood up. "Well, I believe that does it. Pleasure doing business with your two." Nathan stuck out his hand. Jeff shook it, then Lori. They each shook Donna's hand and walked out of the office, hand in hand.

"Aren't they cute?"

"Donna, will you stop?"

"Ah, you're no fun."

Nathan sat back in his chair. He looked at the ceiling then back to Donna.

"Wow, who would have thunk, Kittridge walking into the office that day with his manuscript would lead to all this? The last couple of months have certainly been entertaining."

Donna nodded. "Sure gave us a run and Jeff will never know the half of it. Well, I better be going."

"Going? Going where?"

"Remember that ten days I said I would need off, well that starts tomorrow."

"What about the office?"

"I arranged for a temp to be here on Monday."

"A temp?"

"Relax, you'll be fine, you always are."

Nathan sat back in his chair. "So where are you going?"

Donna just smiled. "Better you didn't know."

Nathan actually smiled back and waved his hand. "Go. Go on get out of here, tell her I said hi."

"Will do."

"And remember I never saw that book."

Donna smiled. "What book?"

Nathan watched her leave, returning to the pile of papers on his desk, finding the number he was looking for and dialing it.

"Hi, yes, Nathan Simon here. Yes, I believe we have a deal. Yes, it is all there, the band is intact, yes, thank you as well."

———————————— /// ————————————

Jeff and Lori sat in his car. He hadn't started the engine yet.

"Well, I guess it's happening, we have our first million, well forty percent each any way."

Lori smiled and leaned into him kissing him. "I apologize now."

"For what?"

"We'll be on the circuit for the next couple of months, lectures and what have you, I'm sure a few rubber chicken dinners. You sure you don't mind?"

Jeff shook his head no. "Just promise me one thing."

"Sure, anything."

"When you come back to the hotel room at night you have to change into the panties and camisole that will make everything all better."

"That's a deal, but only if you wear the boxers."

Jeff turned in his seat to face her, as did Lori to face him, waiting for him to speak.

"Remember what you said to me that first day in the office?"

Lori tilted her head asking. Jeff pointed at her.

"You said and I quote: 'I don't do Civil War Gold'."

Lori dropped her head smiling.

"And then you said and I might be paraphrasing here, but you said: 'I don't want to be the go to lady anymore'. Would you like to revise those two statements now?"

Before Lori could answer, Jeff continued.

"Because I believe you will be the go to lady for quite some time to come. And once the book comes out, just think of the book tours and discussions we will be on?"

Lori raised her hand in the air. "I'm not sure I want to be."

"Hey, why not, give it a ride for a couple of years, or however long it lasts, then just cut and run. We'll get away somewhere and no one will find us."

"What about my job?"

"Your job is already over. The University will want to parade you around to tell the world what you found and more importantly that they have it. Hell sitting behind the desk five days a week is history, sorry, no pun intended, but you really are done with all that."

Lori nodded. "I hadn't thought about that."

"Well I have, but here's the deal, all they get is two years, then you're mine."

Lori looked at him, smiling. "Really, you mean that?"

Jeff nodded. "I'm not letting you go."

"Where would we go?"

"Doesn't matter, anywhere."

Jeff paused, Lori held his hand. Jeff spoke very softly.

"Look, none of this stuff matters to me, not the documents, not that one ugly bureau, certainly not the money, because I found my gold when I found you."

———————— ### ————————

www.ingramcontent.com/pod-product-compliance
Lightning Source LLC
Chambersburg PA
CBHW030153290725
30233CB00079B/400